A
heart
stolen...
An
heiress
returned?

"I have been having trouble sleeping, Alexandra," Sebastian confessed.

"I hardly see how that is my concern," Alexandra replied, although warmth was already stirring in her at the implication of his words.

"It is because of you. I used to be quite content with being by myself. I find that I am not any longer. I want you in my bed again."

"If this is another ploy to try to convince me to marry you..."

"No, just the plea of a desperate man. I keep thinking about that night in the highwayman's lair...."

He raised her arm and kissed the tender inside of her wrist. "Come to my room tonight."

"Are you mad?"

"Then marry me."

"Stop." Alexandra went on tiptoe to brush her lips lightly against his cheek. "Good night, Sebastian."

"You call that a good-night kiss?" His arm swooped around Alexandra and he claimed a lengthy kiss. "Dream of me tonight."

CANDACE CAMP

A STOLEN HEART

MIRA

ISBN 1-55166-552-2

A STOLEN HEART

Copyright © 2000 by Candace Camp.

All rights reserved. Except for use in any review, the reproduction or
utilization of this work in whole or in part in any form by any electronic,
mechanical or other means, now known or hereafter invented, including
xerography, photocopying and recording, or in any information storage or
retrieval system, is forbidden without the written permission of the publisher,
MIRA Books, 225 Duncan Mill Road, Don Mills, Ontario, Canada M3B 3K9.

All characters in this book have no existence outside the imagination of the
author and have no relation whatsoever to anyone bearing the same name
or names. They are not even distantly inspired by any individual known or
unknown to the author, and all incidents are pure invention.

MIRA and the Star Colophon are trademarks used under license and registered
in Australia, New Zealand, Philippines, United States Patent and Trademark
Office and in other countries.

Visit us at www.mirabooks.com

Printed in U.S.A.

Prologue

Paris, 1789

Lady Chilton pushed back the draperies of her bedroom window and peered out into the night. In the distance she could see fire leaping up, and she shivered. *It was the Mob.* She was sure of it; she had heard their howls the day before, seen them pushing through the streets like some great amorphous beast, hungry for blood.

She stepped back from the window, her hands twining together nervously. Emerson was certain that the Mob would not turn on them. Her husband had that careless, casual confidence of the English that no harm would dare come to them. Simone was not so sure. She was, after all, French, and a member of that aristocracy whom the Mob was so eager to destroy. The fact that she was married to an Englishman might not be enough to save her if the Mob came here—indeed, she feared that her French identity might destroy her husband, as well.

And the children.

It was that thought that made her sick with fear. What

would happen to her little ones if the *sans-culottes* came to their house?

She stood for a moment indecisively, a beautiful woman with liquid brown eyes and clouds of dark hair, dressed in the finest clothes that Paris had to offer, her neck circled with precious gems, yet paper-white with fear, her huge eyes haunted.

Finally, with a little sob, she went over to her dressing table and pulled out her jewelry case. Quickly she took out her jewelry, glittering gold studded with diamonds, rubies and emeralds, satiny pearls strung together or dangling from ear studs. Some were family heirlooms, others gifts from an adoring and wealthy husband. Simone was a woman who loved decoration, and her vivid dark coloring and white skin were perfect foils for the richly colored jewels.

She stuffed the pieces into a velvet bag, paying little attention to the sparkling gems. Last, she reached up and removed the emerald drops that hung from her ears, then the matching emerald pendant that had been a wedding present from Lord Chilton eight and a half years before. Her hand closed around it for a moment; it was still warm from the heat of her skin. Then, with a little sigh, she slipped it, too, into the bag.

Her friend could be trusted; after all, she was trusting her with her children, far more important than any jewelry. If she survived, she would be reunited with them all.

She opened the false bottom of the jewelry case and took out three small items. Though relatively inexpensive, they were the most precious, for they belonged to her children. There were two lockets that opened up to reveal miniature portraits of herself and Emerson. The Countess had given them to the girls last year at Christmas. The third object was a plain, bulky ring, far too large for her son's finger. She strung it on a piece of string so that he could wear it around his neck. The ring was ordinary looking, flat-topped with an odd design. But it was hundreds of years old, the family ring of the Earls of Exmoor. Only heirs to the title were allowed to wear it. Emerson owned it now, though he did not wear it. One day it would be his son's.

Simone went to her desk and took the quill from the inkwell and began to scratch out a note. She was never the best of letter writers, and this note was disjointed and almost illegible. But it would at least let the Earl and the Countess know what had happened. She stuffed it into the bag with the jewels.

Clutching the velvet bag and the three small pieces of jewelry, Simone left her bedroom and started up the stairs to the nursery. Downstairs, she could hear Emerson's voice, growing impatient as he tried to explain to her parents why they had to leave Paris as soon as possible. Simone shook her head. Her parents were frozen by fear, so much in shock from the upheaval of their world that all they seemed capable of doing was staying still and saying no. Simone and Emerson could hardly leave them behind; it was why they had not left already. But she refused to let her children die because her parents were too stubborn or too silly to do what they ought to.

That was why she was sending the children away. She would entrust their lives to her dearest friend here, who was leaving for England and its safety tomorrow. She had not asked yet, but she was sure that her friend would do it. Childless herself, she had always doted on Simone's children, especially the youngest. Simone would get them away to England, and the jewels would help pay their expenses, if necessary. Once they were safe, if Simone did not make it, they would be her last present to her children.

Simone reached up to dash the tears from her eyes. She could not let the children see her crying; that would frighten them even further. So she pasted a smile on her face before she opened the door to the nursery and went inside. The French nurse was already putting them to bed. Simone dismissed her, saying that she would tuck the children in herself.

Once the maid had left, she turned to the three children. For a long moment she let herself look at them, the lump in her throat swelling as she faced the thought that perhaps she would never see them again. There was John, with the thick, dark hair he had inherited from her and her own dark brown, almost black eyes. A sturdy boy of seven, he had his father's long bones and mischievous smile, and Simone had not met a woman yet, of any age, who did not succumb to his charms. She bent to kiss his forehead, then moved on to kiss Marie Anne's cheek. Marie Anne had her father's eyes—deep blue, guileless orbs—and the bright red curls that had surprised them both, coming as she did from his blondness and Simone's black hair. But the Countess had nodded wisely and said that red hair cropped up periodically among the Montfords.

She had to swallow hard as she moved on to Alexandra, the baby. Only two, she was a delight; chubby and sunny of spirit, it seemed she was always laughing or babbling. She was, Simone's mama said, the very image of Simone when she was a toddler, with black curls and merry dark brown eyes and a laugh that made everyone who heard it smile. Simone picked Alexandra up and hugged her, then sat on the floor with the children and put Alexandra in her lap.

"I've come to tell you that you are going on a trip,"

she said lightly, hoping that her voice displayed none of her anxiety. "You're going home to England to see your grandmama and grandpapa."

She told them about her friend, whom they knew and liked, and how they must go with her by themselves, but that Mama and Papa would be joining them later. Though she usually spoke French with her children, who were as fluent in it as in English, she used English with them now.

"You must only speak English," she cautioned them. "Not French, because you are going to pretend to be her children, not mine. Won't that be a fun game?"

John regarded her solemnly. "It's because of the Mob, isn't it?"

"Yes," Simone admitted. "That is why I am sending you this way. It will be less danger to you. So watch out for the girls, John, and make sure that they don't get into trouble. Don't let them speak French, even when you are alone. Can I rely on you?"

He nodded. "I'll take care of them."

"Good. That's my little man. Now, here are some things you must wear. Don't take them off—even Alexandra. John, you make sure of it."

She hung the ring on its rough string around his neck and tucked it under his shirt so it did not show. She did the same with each of the girls, stuffing the lockets down the necks of their dresses.

The children were dressed fairly plainly, in the clothes they wore to play in. That was the best that she could do, Simone thought, to hide their aristocratic backgrounds. Quickly she placed a few more changes of play clothes, nothing with lace or velvet, in their little cloaks and tied them up into bundles.

"Now we must go very quietly down the stairs," she told them.

"Can't we say goodbye to Papa?" Marie Anne asked, bewildered and looking about ready to cry.

"No, he is talking to Grandmère and Grandpère. We must not disturb them."

She knew that Emerson would be furious with her for sneaking the children away without telling him. But she could not risk letting them say goodbye to him. His confidence in his indestructibility was too great. She was afraid he would forbid her to send them away, sure that they would be safest with him.

Simone gave them all a shaky smile and stood, picking up Alexandra to hold her in one arm and carrying Alexandra's little bundle in the other. "Now, children, pick up your bundles of clothes. Stay close. Hold on to my skirts and don't let go, no matter what happens. And be very quiet—like little mice."

John and Marie Anne nodded, though she could see the uncertainty in their faces. They walked quietly out of the room and tiptoed down the stairs. Simone did not go out the tall front door, but led them to the side door. She paused, her hand on the knob, taking a deep breath. John and Marie Anne clutched her skirt.

Simone opened the door, and they scurried into the night.

1

London, 1811

Alexandra Ward glanced at her companion in the carriage. He looked as if he were about to fall into a swoon. His face was a pasty white, and sweat dotted his upper lip. Alexandra suppressed a sigh. Englishmen, she was discovering, seemed to be a curiously poor-spirited lot, always gaping and staring and sputtering about how something could not be done. It was a wonder that the country had ever achieved its place in the world, either politically or financially.

"Don't worry, Mr. Jones," she said in a pleasant tone, trying to ease the man's fears. "I am sure that your employer will be quite amenable to seeing us."

Lyman Jones closed his eyes as he let out a small moan. "You don't know Lord Thorpe. He is a…a very private sort of man."

"So are many men, but that doesn't make them poor businessmen. I cannot imagine why a man would not be interested in meeting someone who had just signed a quite lucrative contract to ship his company's tea to America."

Frankly, Alexandra had been amazed that Thorpe had not been at the office to meet her and sign the contract this morning. He had not even attended any of her meetings with his agent, Lyman Jones. It seemed foolish in the extreme to turn over so much of one's business to another without supervising him. She herself had many employees on whom she depended, but she would never think of not joining them in an important meeting with a client. However, she refrained from pointing this fact out to Mr. Jones, who seemed too upset as it was.

"I—I don't know how it is in America, Miss Ward," Mr. Jones said carefully, "but here, well, gentlemen don't generally engage actively in business affairs."

"How do they get any business done, then?" Alexandra asked in amazement. "Someone must be engaging in business affairs. How else can England be so prosperous?"

"Well, of course, men engage in business affairs. It is *gentlemen,* men like Lord Thorpe, that I'm talking about."

"Oh. You're talking about the nobility?" She appeared to consider the idea.

"Yes." Mr. Jones looked relieved. He had had a rather difficult time talking to Miss Ward through the negotiations. It had seemed most bizarre to even be discussing business dealings with a woman, much less bargaining with one—especially one who looked like Alexandra Ward. Lyman Jones would never have imagined a woman running a business, as Miss Ward seemed to, so he would have been hard put to say exactly what he thought such a woman would look like. But he knew that she would not have been a tall, statuesque woman with a cloud of thick black hair. Nor would she have had Alexandra's strawberries-and-cream complexion and large, expressive brown eyes, eyes so dark that they were almost black.

But then, Alexandra Ward was unlike any other woman Lyman Jones had ever met. Perhaps it came from her being American; he wasn't sure. But she spoke in a blunt, decisive manner and left no room for disagreement, sweeping everyone before her in a way that was almost impossible to resist. After a session with her, he usually found himself exhausted and unsure exactly how he had been talked into something. He was feeling that way now. He wondered sinkingly if Lord Thorpe would end his employment for this.

"I am afraid I'm not used to such distinctions," Alexandra admitted. "In the United States, a gentleman is determined more on the basis of his actions, I believe, than on his birth." She paused, then asked curiously, "This Thorpe is a feckless sort? I suppose he must have inherited his wealth. Still, one wonders how he has managed to hang on to it."

"Oh, no, miss," Jones protested hastily. "I didn't mean that. It's not that his lordship doesn't know or care about the business. He does. What I meant was that a gentleman wouldn't be, well, *seen* in the day-to-day running of it."

"I see. It is a matter of appearance, then." Alexandra thought that Thorpe sounded more and more foolish.

"I suppose." Jones frowned. He didn't like the way that sounded. "I mean, well, it just isn't done." He hastened to add, "Lord Thorpe is an excellent businessman. He made most of his money himself, actually, in India."

"Ah." Alexandra's dark eyes sparkled with interest, all thoughts about Lord Thorpe's business acumen fleeing. "That is precisely why I am so eager to meet the man. His collection of Indian treasures is well-known, and I am rather a devotee of the subject myself. I have even corresponded with Mr. Thorpe, I mean, Lord Thorpe, on the subject.''

Alexandra thought it prudent not to mention that she had asked Lord Thorpe about seeing his collection when she was in England this year and had been turned down flat. That was, actually, why she had settled on the Burchings Tea Company with which to negotiate a contract. The company had an excellent reputation, of course; Alexandra would never have made a bad business decision just to satisfy a personal whim. However, the fact that the Burchings Tea Company was owned by the same Lord Thorpe whose collection she so wished to see was a very pleasant bonus. She had been sure that she would meet the man—who, she presumed from the tone of his letter, was a crotchety old fellow—during her business dealings with his company.

"I understand that his collection is quite impressive," Mr. Jones replied. "I, of course, have never seen it."

"Never? None of it?" Alexandra looked at him in surprise.

Jones gazed at her with a slightly puzzled expression. "No. I mean, I have, of course, sometimes brought something to his lordship at his home, and I have seen some objects in his foyer, but generally, Lord Thorpe comes to the office to discuss his business."

It seemed odd to Alexandra, whose family had always held open house every year at Christmas for their employees, that one's highest-ranking employee would not have spent time inside one's house. She felt a close, almost familial bond with many of her employees. Indeed, some of them were related to her. But, she supposed, it was simply another example of how the British—or perhaps it was just the nobility—were different.

The carriage pulled up in front of an impressive white

stone edifice and stopped. Lyman Jones looked out the window and said in a stifled voice, "We're here."

He turned to Alexandra with an almost pleading look on his face. "Are you sure you wish to do this, Miss Ward? Lord Thorpe is—he's a bit of a recluse. He truly does not appreciate visitors. I—it's quite likely that he will refuse even to see us."

"Then we shall have to leave, won't we?" Alexandra returned lightly.

"On the other hand, he might very well agree to see us just to tell us what he thinks of such impertinence." Jones felt slightly sick at the thought.

"Buck up, Mr. Jones," Alexandra said, trying to instill some spirit in the poor man. "I promise you I have dealt with many an old grump, and I generally handle them rather well."

"But he's not an—"

"Whatever he is, I feel sure that I shall be able to deal with him."

Mr. Jones subsided, reflecting that perhaps she *would* be able to sweep Lord Thorpe before her, just as she had him.

"Don't worry," Alexandra went on. "If he rings a peal over your head, I shall tell him that it was all my fault."

Jones doubted that such a statement would change his employer's opinion about his intruding on him this way, but he said nothing. He was almost resigned to the berating he would doubtless receive. He opened the door and stepped from the carriage, turning and reaching to help Alexandra.

Alexandra politely took his hand and stepped down, turning to look at the graceful white stone house in the Georgian style. It was built close to the street, as so many houses in London were, with a black wrought-iron fence stretching the length of it to separate it from the traffic. A set of six steps led from the street to the imposing front door, centered by a rather fierce-looking door knocker in the shape of a lion's head. Her companion, gazing in the same direction, faltered, and Alexandra took his arm, gently pushing him in the direction of the door. She felt a little guilty at using the poor fellow so. However, she was determined to see Lord Thorpe's collection of Indian treasures. She had read much about it in her correspondence with other aficionados of the style. Lord Thorpe's collection was generally considered to be the finest in the world, and it had been one of the things she had been most looking forward to on her first trip to England. She was not about to let this man's faint heart keep her from seeing it. Lord Thorpe himself would have to bar her from the door.

"Don't worry, Mr. Jones," she said, to soothe the prickings of her conscience, "if Lord Thorpe lets you go for bringing me here, I shall employ you myself."

Jones gave her a small smile. Miss Ward, for all her odd ways and bossy nature, was a kindhearted person. "Thank you, miss. I am sure that won't be necessary."

He wished he felt as confident as his words sounded. Though Lord Thorpe was a fair employer, there was a hard, implacable quality to him that made one leery about crossing him. He had made the bulk of his fortune in India, and there were many rumors, some of them unsavory, about how he had gone about doing so. Mr. Jones discounted most of them, but there were times, when Lord Thorpe's face hardened and his eyes turned that flat, almost silvery color, that Jones wondered if at least some of the rumors were true.

Drawing a steadying breath, he took the ring of the knocker and brought it down heavily, sending a resounding thud through the house. A moment later, a liveried footman opened the door. He looked from Jones to Alexandra, then reluctantly stepped back and let them into the house.

"I am here to see Lord Thorpe," Lyman said.

"Wait here," the footman said shortly and left them standing in the foyer.

It was, Alexandra thought, rather rude behavior for a footman, but she did not dwell on it. She was too busy looking around her. At her feet the parquet floor was overlaid with a plush woven carpet of wine red depicting a hunting scene, with a turbanned man spearing a tiger. On one wall hung an elephant mask of beaten silver, and below it stood a wooden trunk, the top of which was intricately carved into a garden scene of two Indian maidens standing amidst drooping trees.

She was bent over, examining the trunk more closely, when there was a soft shuffle of footsteps and a man entered the foyer, followed by the footman. Alexandra raised her head and barely suppressed a gasp of pleasure. The man whom the footman had brought in was swarthy-skinned, with large, liquid dark eyes, and he was dressed all in white from the top of his turbanned head to the bottom of his soft-shoed feet. As Alexandra stared in fascination, he placed his hands together at chest level and bowed to them politely.

"Mr. Jones?" he said in a soft, accented voice. "Was Lord Thorpe expecting you today? I am most sorry. I have no knowledge of your visit."

"No, uh…" Lyman Jones had spoken to Lord Thorpe's butler many times, but he always found the event unnerving. He invariably stumbled over the man's name, and his unswerving dark gaze made Jones uncomfortable. "Lord Thorpe does not know about it. I—it was quite unexpected. I had hoped to introduce Miss Ward to his lordship, although of course if this is an inopportune moment, we can—''

The butler's eyes moved consideringly to Alexandra. She, seeing that Jones was making a mess of things, took over in her usual way. ''I am Alexandra Ward, Mr....''

''Punwati is my name, miss.''

''Mr. Punwati. I have business dealings with the Burchings Tea Company, and I had hoped to meet Lord Thorpe while I was in London. I think it is very important to know exactly with whom one is dealing. Don't you agree?''

There was a flicker of something—humor, perhaps—in Punwati's dark eyes as he said, ''Oh, yes, miss.''

''So Mr. Jones kindly agreed to introduce me to Lord Thorpe. I do hope it is not too much of an inconvenience.''

''I am sure that Lord Thorpe will be most interested to hear of your visit, Miss Ward,'' the servant said, bowing slightly. ''I shall tell him that you are here and see if he is receiving guests this afternoon.''

''Thank you.'' Alexandra rewarded the man with a smile that had dazzled more than one man into doing what she wanted.

After Punwati had left the foyer in the same quiet way in which he had entered, Mr. Jones smiled a little awkwardly. ''As I told you, Lord Thorpe is a...trifle different. His servants are somewhat odd. The butler, as you saw, is foreign, and some of the servants look, frankly, as if they would be more at home among the criminal class. I am sorry if you were, um, taken aback.''

Alexandra cast him a puzzled glance. ''What do you mean? There's nothing to apologize for. This is wonderful! I have never before met a person from India. I have a thousand questions I would love to ask him, but I am sure it would be much too impolite. And did you see this exquisite elephant mask? And the rug...the chest!"

Alexandra's eyes glowed with excitement, and her cheeks were delicately flushed. Jones, looking at her, realized that she was even more lovely than he had originally thought. He wondered if her beauty would soften Lord Thorpe, one of the most dedicated bachelors in London. But then, he doubted that Thorpe would ever even see Miss Ward. No doubt his Indian servant would reappear in a few moments with the news that his lordship was unable to receive them, and that would be that—except, of course, for whatever Thorpe decided to do because of Jones's presumption in coming to his door unannounced, a visitor in tow.

So sunk was he in his gloomy thoughts that Jones did not notice someone had quietly entered the foyer from the opposite end until the man spoke. "Ah. Mr. Jones. Punwati tells me you have brought a guest with you."

Mr. Jones jumped. "Lord Thorpe!"

Alexandra, who had been squatting beside the chest, tracing the intricate carvings, stood and turned toward the voice. It was all she could do to keep her jaw from dropping. From the moment she had received the letter from Lord Thorpe, she had envisioned him as a crotchety old man, averse to company and probably quite eccentric. She had been sure that once she met him, she could talk her way around his oddities and convince him to let her see his collection. But now, seeing him, she realized that she had been completely wrong.

The man standing at the other end of the foyer was in the prime of his life, no more than in his thirties. He was tall and broad-shouldered, with long, muscular legs, accentuated by close-fitting buff-colored pantaloons and rich, butter-soft brown boots. He was dressed well, but simply. He started toward them, and Alexandra realized with a funny jump of her stomach that Lord Thorpe was not only young, but also quite handsome. His hair was a thick, dark brown, cropped close to his head. He had a sculpted face, with high, jutting cheekbones, an aquiline nose and a squared jaw, the rather stern features softened by a wide, sensual mouth. His eyes were large and intelligent, gray in color and ringed by thick, black lashes that gave them a smoky look. His expression gave little away, but Alexandra thought she detected the faintest bit of humor in his eyes. When his gaze fell on her, the oddest feeling started up deep inside Alexandra, a strange, effervescent, tumultuous sensation she had never experienced before. All thoughts seemed to scatter.

"I'm sorry, my lord," Jones began awkwardly. "I should not have come here unasked, I know, but I—I was sure you would wish to meet Miss Ward."

"One wonders why," Lord Thorpe drawled, his words dipped in sarcasm.

Alexandra, seeing Jones pale at his employer's words, shook off the peculiar feeling in her midsection and stepped forward, assuming a pleasant, confident smile. "Pray, do not blame Mr. Jones, Lord Thorpe. It is all my fault. He did not wish to bring me at all. It was I who insisted."

"Indeed?" Thorpe arched one black brow in an expression of polite disdain that had intimidated more than a few people.

Alexandra scarcely noticed. She was far more aware of the fact that his eyes were so light a gray they were almost silver, and that her knees had begun to tremble in a most unaccustomed manner.

"Yes. You see, I believe in meeting the people with whom I do business."

"Business?" Thorpe looked genuinely puzzled, and he turned inquiringly toward his employee. "I don't understand."

"It is Miss Ward with whom I have been negotiating a contract this week—I believe I mentioned it. With Ward Shipping, to transport Burchings Tea to the United States."

Thorpe looked at Alexandra blankly. "*You* work for Ward Shipping?"

"Mm. My family owns it, actually. Unlike you, I prefer to keep an active hand in my businesses. While I have found Mr. Jones to be both agreeable and acute, still, I feel that I get a better impression of a company from meeting the owner. Ultimately, all decisions come back to you. Or do I have that wrong?"

"No. I am in charge of my company," he answered a little wryly. "You, I take it, do not approve of the way I run my business."

"Well, it is your business, and you may do as you choose," Alexandra began.

"How kind of you." Thorpe sketched a satiric bow in her direction.

Alexandra cast him a quelling look and continued. "However, I have always felt, as have my managers, that a business runs more smoothly if the owner takes an active role in it—unless, of course," she added smoothly, "the owner is not competent to run it." She ended on a slightly questioning note, casting Thorpe a sideways glance that contained more than a little challenge. She was not sure exactly why—whether it was Thorpe's arrogant air or a dislike of the unaccustomed response he had

aroused in her—but she felt a certain need to set Lord
Thorpe in his place.

To her surprise, he let out a short bark of laughter.
"And that, I presume, is what you are suggesting about
me? That I am incapable of running a business?"

Lyman Jones let out a small groan and closed his eyes.

"Ah," Thorpe went on, a faint smile hovering about
his mouth. "Mr. Jones brought you here so that you could
see that at least I am not drooling or locked in a cage in
the attic?"

"My lord!" Mr. Jones exclaimed, shocked. "No, nothing like that was ever suggested. I swear to you, it was—"

"Stop teasing Mr. Jones," Alexandra retorted bluntly.
"You know as well as I that Mr. Jones had no wish to
bring me here. I was the one who insisted on it. I was not
worried that you were completely incompetent. But I do
think one can tell a lot about a company by the owner's
personality."

"And what can you tell about Burchings Tea, Miss
Ward?" he asked, the faint smile lingering on his lips.
"Now that you have met me?"

"For one thing," Alexandra said tartly, "I have a better
understanding of why your employees are scared of you."

"Scared of me!" The smile disappeared at her words,
and he looked nonplussed.

Lyman Jones covered his face with his hands, certain
that all was lost, so he did not see the short, considering
glance Lord Thorpe shot at him.

"Yes. Oh, they do not tremble at your name, but Mr.
Jones's reluctance to bring me over here was quite obvious. Why? I wondered."

"I think I can answer that," Thorpe replied coldly.

Sebastian, Lord Thorpe, had been amazed when Punwati had told him that his business agent was at the door

with a young woman in tow, and he had been sufficiently intrigued that he had decided to see them. He had not known what to expect, but it had certainly not been to find this tall, black-haired beauty in his entryway examining his property. Even more unexpected had been the sudden, hard jolt of desire that had shot through him at the sight of her. She was dressed in a demure sprig muslin day dress, but its high waist emphasized the voluptuous curve of her breasts, and its soft folds could not conceal the long, slender legs beneath it. Her skin was touchably soft and smooth, and her full lower lip fairly cried out to be kissed. Thorpe was not a man who was immune to feminine charms, but he had learned his lessons early and hard, and his passions were usually kept under strict control. It had been some time since he had felt such a swift and deep response to a woman.

As he listened to her speak, he had been by turns amused, bemused and irritated, and underneath it all had lain the hot, heavy thrum of arousal. Miss Ward was unlike any woman he had ever met, and Thorpe was a man who appreciated the unusual. But now, with her last statement, she had decisively pushed him over the line into the realm of anger. How dare this upstart American question his running of his business or imply that he terrorized his employees?

"Mr. Jones is well aware that I value my privacy," he said, his jaw set and his eyes flashing silver. "I am not accustomed to every person who does business with my company showing up at my home."

"Mm. Yes, I can see that you believe yourself superior to the rest of us humans."

"I beg your pardon." Thorpe stared. Each statement this woman made was more outrageous than the last.

"That quality generally does not make one a pleasant

companion," Alexandra said blithely, ignoring the thunder beginning to grow in his face. "However, as you know, that is not my primary concern. My concern, of course, is how does this attitude affect Burchings Tea?"

"Ah, yes, Burchings. For a moment there I thought we had wandered far afield."

"I am inclined to think that your belief in your superiority would carry over into your company, that you would not allow an inferior product or any sort of base dealing that would reflect badly upon you," Alexandra decided.

"Thank you," he responded sardonically. "I think."

"Also, the awe and even fear in which your employees regard you would ensure that they pay careful attention to the details so as not to incur your displeasure. Sometimes such fear can be so extreme that it has the opposite effect—people are so worried that they make more mistakes than they would normally. However, having seen that you are more sarcastic and biting than in a rage over Mr. Jones having invaded your privacy, along with the fact that Mr. Jones was willing to try what I asked even though he thought you would not like it, leads me to think that your wrath is not such that it renders your employees terrified and therefore useless."

"Then you approve of my business?" he asked, tight-lipped. "I am indeed honored at the encomium."

"I am sure you are being sarcastic," Alexandra replied. "However, the truth is that you should be pleased. There are those who value my opinion in business."

"The United States must be quite different."

"Yes, it is. I believe we are more inclined to value honesty."

"Bluntness, I would say. A lack of tact, even."

"I find that tact is generally not a valuable commodity

in doing business. I would much rather know where I stand. You, I take it, prefer to remain in the dark?''

For a moment Lord Thorpe simply stared at her. Then he chuckled, shaking his head. ''My dear Miss Ward, you almost leave me speechless. Do you conduct all of your business in this fashion? I am surprised that you have any customers.''

Alexandra smiled back at him, finding it difficult not to respond to the softening of his face. ''No,'' she replied frankly. ''You seem to raise my hackles more than most. However, I do find that, being a woman in business, I have to spend an inordinate amount of time arguing with men before they will accept me on equal terms.''

''Equal?'' His lips curved up. ''I would think that would be too paltry for you. I would imagine utter subjugation would be your goal.''

''Oh, no,'' Alexandra retorted blithely. ''I, you see, have no inclination toward arrogance.''

''A direct hit,'' Thorpe murmured. It occurred to him that the purpose of this odd American's visit had been accomplished, and that the interview should be at an end. But he found himself curiously reluctant to send her on her way. He wasn't sure whether she more annoyed or aroused him, but he realized that he wanted her to stay.

He hesitated for an instant, then said, ''Now that we have met, Miss Ward, perhaps you would care to have a cup of tea with me.'' He turned a bland gaze toward Lyman Jones's astonished face. ''You, too, of course, Jones—unless you have pressing matters at the office?''

''Oh, no, sir,'' Jones replied, blushing with pleasure at the honor of taking tea with his lordship. ''That is,'' he added hastily, realizing that his words might sound wrong, ''of course I have things to do. There are always things to do at the office. What I meant was that today I think everything will run quite well without me for an hour or so. I'm ever so grateful—it is such an honor—if you're sure, of course." His voice trailed off uncertainly.

"Of course he is sure," Alexandra said firmly, coming to the floundering man's rescue. "I doubt that Lord Thorpe is ever anything but sure." She turned to Thorpe. "Thank you, my lord. Tea would be most welcome."

Thorpe rang for his butler and ordered tea in the blue saloon, then led his visitors down the hall and into a gracious room, the walls of which were decorated in a delicate blue-and-white wallpaper above the wainscoting. It was an airy room, the heavy drapes pushed aside to let in the afternoon sun, and it was furnished not in the heavy, dark woods that Alexandra had found common in London, but in a wickerwork that gave the room a look both informal and exotic. The foreign air was heightened by the lush carpet in a design of stylized flowers and vines, and the rich, jewel-tone patterns of the chair cushions. A trumpeting elephant carved out of ivory stood on a small table, and on the wall hung a series of small, colorful paintings.

Alexandra drew in her breath and went to the paintings. "Are these Rajput?" she asked, referring to a kind of manuscript illustration of Hindu epics that had flourished in India in earlier times.

Mr. Jones looked blank, and Lord Thorpe's eyebrows shot up in astonishment. "Why, yes, I started collecting them when I lived in India. Do you know Indian art?"

"I have seen very little of it," Alexandra confessed, "but I am quite interested in it. I have read descriptions, of course, of the bright colors and the patterns, and I have seen some drawings made from them, but never the actual thing."

At first she studied the paintings intently, unaware of Thorpe's gaze lingering on her. Then she turned and caught him watching her, and she flushed. There was something about the look in his eyes that made her feel suddenly warm all over. She glanced away quickly, casting about for something to say to cover her reaction. "I, ah, have purchased a few things—a small jade Buddha and, um, a Paisley shawl, of course, and a few ivory carvings, but Indian things are somewhat rare in the United States."

"Perhaps, after tea, you would like to see some of my collection?"

Alexandra's face lit up, causing Thorpe to draw in his breath sharply. "Oh, yes, I would like that more than anything else." She sat as the butler entered with the tea tray and set it on a low table, but she continued to talk excitedly. "I have a confession to make. That was one of the reasons I bullied Mr. Jones into bringing me here today. I was hoping to catch a glimpse of some of your Indian treasures. I have heard so much about your collection...."

"Indeed?" Thorpe studied Alexandra, wondering what bizarre thing would come out of her mouth next. He had never met a woman who enthused over his Indian objects, except perhaps for a luxurious Paisley shawl or a spectacular piece of jewelry.

"Oh, yes, I wrote you, in fact, a few months ago, when I knew I was going to be in London, asking you if I could see your collection, but you turned me down flat."

"I did? How rude of me." He frowned. "But I don't remember.... No, wait, there was a letter from some fellow in the United States, but I thought—wasn't it Alexander Ward?"

"Alexandra. People often make the mistake. They don't expect an enthusiast of art objects to be a woman."

"At least not to be writing letters to strange men and trying to set up appointments."

"And what would you have me do?" Alexandra asked, her dark eyes firing up. "Ask my uncle or cousin to write a letter for me, as if I were incapable of writing a coherent letter myself?"

"It is not a question of your competence, Miss Ward, but a matter of taking care of, of protecting, a woman."

"From what? The rudeness of a letter such as yours, denying me admittance?" She chuckled. "I was not pleased, of course, but it did not send me to my bed in a state of despair and shame. I have been told no before, I assure you."

"I find that hard to believe," Thorpe retorted, grinning. "Well, please allow me to make up for my rudeness by showing you as much as you would like to see."

"That would be the entirety, I'm sure."

They talked a little while they drank their tea and ate the small cakes and biscuits that accompanied it. It was general talk, about the weather and London and the state of Massachusetts, where Alexandra lived. He inquired how she was enjoying her visit, hoping that it was not all business, and she dutifully related the sights she had seen and the things she had done. They spoke of Burchings Tea and of her own company, though Alexandra could see in Thorpe's face that he found it odd to speak of such things with a woman. She wondered if he usually talked to women only about the weather and such and concluded that he must find it dull, indeed.

Mr. Jones returned to his office soon after tea was finished, assured by Lord Thorpe that he would see Miss Ward home in his own carriage. Thorpe offered his arm to Alexandra, a faint, almost challenging smile on his lips. Alexandra slipped her hand into the crook of his elbow and tilted up her chin, tossing back the challenge, although she was not entirely sure what it was.

"You know," Thorpe said in a low, conversational tone, "your staying and walking through these rooms with me by yourself is not recommended behavior for a young lady."

"Oh?" Alexandra rounded her eyes into a look of great innocence. "Are you in the habit, then, of attacking defenseless young women in your home?"

"Of course not. Although I would hardly call you defenseless."

"Then I have nothing to fear, have I?" Alexandra went on coolly, "You, being a gentleman and so concerned about protecting women, will doubtless see that no harm comes to me."

"You've the tongue of an adder, my dear Miss Ward."

"Why, what have I said, my lord?"

He cast her a look heavy with irony and abruptly turned into a room, pulling her in with him. Gripping her upper arms, he looked into her eyes, so close to her that his face filled her startled vision. His bright silvery eyes bored into hers, and she could feel the heat of his body, the power of his hands on her arms. She was intensely aware of his mobile mouth hovering only inches above hers. She could not move.

"You know, sometimes even a gentleman can be pushed beyond his control by a beautiful young woman."

Alexandra had the wild thought that he was going to kiss her right there, and she realized with a start of amazement that the thought was more exciting than scary. "But I am sure that you never lose control," she replied, annoyed at the shakiness of her voice.

"It would be foolish to count on that. If you had talked to the good ladies of London, you would know that I am

considered capable of almost anything. I am, my dear naïve Miss Ward, the black sheep of my family. Not one to
be trusted alone around young ladies.''

''Then it is a good thing that I am not a young English
lady, but an American woman who learned early on how
to discourage unwelcome attentions, is it not?''

''Indeed.'' He leaned a little closer. ''And would my
attentions be unwelcome?''

Alexandra drew in her breath sharply, her heart ham-
mering within her chest. She found it difficult to think,
with his eyes staring into hers.

''No.'' The word came out breathily as she swayed
toward him.

2

"No!" Alexandra repeated, horrified at what she had been about to do. She jerked away from Lord Thorpe, moving farther into the room as she tried to bring her rapid breathing back to normal. "What—what nonsense you talk!"

Thorpe followed her into the room, but he did not touch her again, as she had feared. She felt curiously let down. Sternly, she tried to focus on the room. It was large and furnished entirely in teak. From the desk and the shelves of books behind it, Alexandra identified it as Lord Thorpe's study. An ornately engraved rifle hung on one wall, and below it hung a sword with a wide hilt made of ebony and steel, also engraved. In one corner stood an unusual shirt of chain mail armor with metal plates across the chest and a long mail neck guard hanging down around the helmet on three sides. The edge of the neck guard was bordered in red velvet, and gold inlay was worked across the chest plates.

"Indian armor?" Alexandra asked with real interest, going over to study it. She tried not to think about how his hands had felt on her arms or the way she had yearned to press herself against him.

"Yes. It belonged to a Mogul officer from the last century." Lord Thorpe's voice was as calm as if the moment in the doorway had never happened. "The rifle was a present to me from a rajah."

"Really?"

He nodded. "I happened to be with him on a hunt and shot a tiger that had him targeted for lunch. He gave me the rifle and several trinkets in gratitude. The trinkets turned out to be sapphires and rubies."

"You're joking."

"No. I sold them and bought my first piece of land."

"A tea plantation?"

Thorpe nodded, somewhat surprised to find himself telling Alexandra the story of his early years in India. He had told very few people anything about what happened to him there. But, somehow, looking into Alexandra's huge brown eyes, alive with interest, he felt little hesitation. She might know as little about the place or people as any of the other young ladies he knew, but one thing he was certain of was that her interest was genuine. It occurred to him that perhaps there was something to be said for Miss Ward's policy of frankness. "I spent every bit of profit I made investing in land. Eventually I bought a piece that connected the rest of my plantation to the sea. It had a lovely white beach. I was walking along it one day and stepped on this dull round stone, but when I lifted it up, I saw that it wasn't like other stones. It was an unpolished ruby."

"On the sand?" Alexandra asked in astonishment.

He nodded. "Yes. About the size of a gold sovereign. I've never been so shocked in my life." He smiled faintly, remembering the heat of the sun on his shoulders, the sound of the surf crashing nearby, the pounding excitement in his heart as he had stared at the stone. "A stream ran through there, joining the sea, and it had washed the ruby and several other stones down, depositing them on the beach. I found some other small rubies and a number of sapphires. So I started mining the stream and the area around it. And that is how the tea plantation became my secondary business.''

"So you own a ruby mine?''

"Mostly sapphires. But I sold it before I moved back to England. I kept the plantation because I had a very good manager, but the mine—well, I find, like you, that things don't run very well without one's personal effort.'' He shot her an amused glance.

"You have lived a very exciting life.'' It was no wonder, she thought, that a dangerous air clung to him.

Thorpe shrugged. "I have done what I had to do.''

Alexandra raised a brow. "You have to admit that you have done things few of the rest of us have—lived in exotic lands, shot tigers, found gemstones littering the sands....''

He chuckled. "It sounds more exciting than it seemed at the time. Then it mostly seemed like heat and sweat and trying to escape death.''

"That is what my uncle says about the War. He says everyone always wants to think of it as romantic and brave and daring, but mostly it was dirt and sweat and fear.''

"The War?''

"Yes. You know. That small war thirty-odd years ago in America...''

"Ah, yes.'' He quirked a smile. "The conflict in the colonies. Fortunately, I wasn't in the tea business at the time.''

Alexandra chuckled. "You take, I see, a large view of world affairs.''

Thorpe went to his safe, unlocked it and took out two packets of soft cloth. He laid them on his desk and unwrapped the first one. On the velvet lay an old necklace. Seven separate pieces of enameled gold dangled from the circlet by separate strings of emerald beads.

"It's beautiful. It looks quite old." Alexandra leaned closer.

"It is. It's called a *satratana*. Each of these sections represents a planet in the Indian astrological system."

"Fascinating," Alexandra murmured. "It is such beautiful workmanship."

He unrolled the other cloth, revealing a necklace of startling beauty made of sapphires and diamonds, with a large sapphire pendant hanging from the center.

"Are these from your mine?" Alexandra asked.

Thorpe suppressed a smile. Every other woman who had seen the necklace had practically salivated over it, caressing the jewels and holding it up to her throat. He supposed it should not surprise him that Miss Ward seemed more interested in the background of the jewels.

"Yes." Perversely, he found himself wanting to see the jewels around her neck, though she had not asked.

"Was this a gift to your wife?"

"I have no wife. I intended this piece for no one," he answered harshly, pushing aside the memory of the woman whose neck he had envisioned it on, knowing even as he did so that he would never see it.

He began to roll the necklace up in its velvet, then paused and looked at her consideringly. "Did you think I had a wife and yet was—" He glanced toward the doorway.

"Making advances to me?"

"Yes, making advances to you in my own wife's home. You must think me a very low creature."

Alexandra shrugged. "I know nothing about you, sir. I mean, my lord. You were, after all, intimating that I was putting myself in danger by being alone with you. If you are the sort to take advantage of a woman alone, I would suppose the fact of a wife would not stop you."

He winced. "You don't pull your punches, do you?"

"I try not to." Alexandra softened her words with a smile, a dimple peeking in one cheek. "Actually, I did not think you were the sort. But I have always found it best not to assume too much."

"Mm." He wrapped the other necklace and returned them to the safe.

"Where is the original ruby?" Alexandra asked. "Did you keep it?"

He smiled at her intuition. "Yes. Would you like to see it?"

"Very much—if you don't mind showing it to me."

He reached into the safe again and pulled out a small pouch. Bringing it to where Alexandra stood, he opened the pouch and turned it upside down. The uncut ruby rolled into his hand. "I'm afraid it's not as impressive as the necklace. It's not polished or cut. I left it as it was."

Alexandra smiled with something like approval. "That is exactly what I would have done."

He held it out to her, and she took it, holding it in her palm and looking at it from this angle, then that, and finally handed it back to him. He replaced the ruby in its bag and closed it up in the safe. He turned to her. Normally he would have shown a visitor no more than what he already had, if that much. But he found himself wanting to show her more. He took her arm.

"Come upstairs. I will show you the India room."

They climbed the wide, curving staircase to the next floor. Alexandra knew that this must be the floor on which the family bedrooms and more private sitting rooms lay, and it made her feel a little odd to be here alone with him. But she put the thought aside; she was not going to allow proprieties to spoil her enjoyment of this day. She had waited for years, it seemed, for a chance to view the kind of things Lord Thorpe was showing her.

Thorpe ushered her into a room, and Alexandra let out an exclamation of pleasure. The entire room had been given over to India. Huge jewel-toned cushions were scattered around the floor, which was softened by a wine-colored rug in the stylized Mogul fashion. Precisely realistic portraits of men in Indian dress hung on the walls, along with two more ornate swords. A chest of beaten brass, a low, round table of intricately carved wood and several pedestals and shelves held more treasures. There was a large head of Buddha made from gold and decorated with jewels. A vase of obvious antiquity filled with long, lovely peacock feathers stood on the floor, and several other pieces of pottery, some painted or gilded, others glazed, sat atop pedestals. There were ivory and jade statues of various animals, from elephants to tigers to coiling cobras, as well as figures of Hindu gods and goddesses and legendary heroes. Alexandra could not resist picking up first this one, then that, running her finger over the delicate carving.

"They're beautiful," she breathed. "Look at this knife." She picked up a small, curved knife with an ivory hilt carved into the figure of a tiger, smoothing her finger over the hilt. "It seems odd that there would be such beauty expended on a thing of destruction."

Thorpe watched her as she examined the things in the cabinet. Her face glowed as if lit from within, making her even more beautiful. He wondered if she would glow like that, her eyes soft and lambent, when she was making love. He knew, with a heat low in his abdomen, that it was something he would like to discover. Her fingers moved over the objects sensually, as though she gained as much enjoyment from touching them as from looking at them. Thorpe imagined the cool, smooth feel of the jade and ivory beneath her skin. He imagined, too, the warmth of Alexandra's skin as she touched them, the softness and the faint texture, and the fire deep in his loins grew. This was a woman who used and enjoyed her senses, a woman who could dwell in the physical plane as easily as the intellectual. Nor did she try to hide her pleasure behind a cool mask of sophistication. She would be a passionate lover, he thought, as uninhibited in bed as she was in her speech, as eager to taste all the pleasures of lovemaking as she was to enjoy the beauty of his works of art.

Was she experienced? She was a woman of some wealth and position, at least in her country, and she was not married. Normally he would assume that she was, indeed, a virgin. But there was little that was normal about Miss Ward, he knew, and therefore he wondered if in this regard she flouted convention, also. It would be an interesting topic to pursue.

Alexandra laid the knife down with a sigh and looked around her one more time. "They are all exquisite. Thank you so much, Lord Thorpe, for allowing me to see them." She smiled. "I realize that I pushed myself on you quite rudely. I have no excuse except my intense desire to see your treasures for myself. You have acted in a most generous manner."

"It was a pleasure," he responded truthfully.

"Thank you. I should be leaving now. My aunt and mother will be expecting me."

"You are visiting London with them?" he asked, strolling with her out of the room and down the stairs.

"Yes. Mama was somewhat reluctant to come, but I could not leave her behind. And Aunt Hortense would never have forgiven me if I had come here without bringing her, too. Besides, even in America, we have rules about what a young lady may or may not do, and generally I find it easier to obey them. Traveling by oneself is not one of the things one may do."

"Miss Ward..." They were approaching his front door, and Thorpe found himself filling up with an odd feeling of loneliness. "Would you—that is, I would be most honored if you would accompany me to a ball this evening."

"What?" Alexandra stared at him. The last thing she would have expected from him was this. He had been quite forward, of course, in the doorway of his study, but once she had made it clear that she was not a loose sort, she had assumed he would have no interest in seeing her again.

"I am asking you to a dance." He had not planned on going to one, but he felt sure that he could pull an invitation to one ball or another out of the pile of invitations on his desk.

"But I—" She realized that she wanted very much to go. She had little interest in London society, but the thought of dancing with Lord Thorpe set up a jittery, excited feeling in the pit of her stomach. "But surely your hostess would not wish you to bring a stranger to her party. Someone uninvited."

A cynical smile touched his mouth. "My dear Miss Ward, no hostess would object to my bringing whomever or whatever I wanted to a ball, provided it meant she was able to score the coup of having me there."

"My," Alexandra said mockingly, "it must be marvelous to be so important."

He let out a short laugh. "You think me arrogant again. Let me assure you it is not self-importance, only an acquaintance with London Society. I am a hostess's prize for two reasons only." He held up his hand, ticking off the points. "One, I never go to parties, therefore it is considered an accomplishment of the hostess to get me to come. Two, I am a prime candidate on the marriage mart, being both titled and wealthy. It matters not at all that very few of these same hostesses have any liking for or knowledge of me. In fact, I am considered something of a bad apple, but that is overlooked for the sake of my fortune."

"Goodness. I don't know which is worse, your arrogance or your cynical view of the world."

"No doubt that is why I am not a well-liked guest."

Alexandra had to laugh. "No doubt." She hesitated, then gave a little nod. "Yes. Yes, I would like to go."

Alexandra leaned back against the cushioned seat of Lord Thorpe's carriage, a small smile playing about her lips. She could imagine the look on her aunt's face when she told her she was going with a lord to a London ball. Aunt Hortense, who had grown up during the war with England and the incendiary time period before that, had a deep-seated suspicion of Britain and all things British. Her dislike had only been strengthened during the last few years, when the British, in the midst of their war with Napoléon Bonaparte, had been stopping and impressing American sailors and impounding ships that were bound for France. Ward Shipping had lost a number of men and two ships that way. Aunt Hortense had been insistent upon accompanying Alexandra to London, stating flatly that she had to protect and help Alexandra, who would, in her words, be "like a lamb among the wolves."

Of course, her dislike of the British was not as unswerving as that of Alexandra's mother, who had argued steadfastly against her making the trip. Alexandra sighed. She didn't want to think about her mother right now. She turned her mind to what gown she would wear tonight.

When she stepped inside the front door, however, all such pleasant thoughts fled. One of the maids was standing on the stairs, crying, with another maid trying vainly to soothe her, while her mother's companion Nancy Turner stood apart from them, looking disgusted, her hands on her hips. From upstairs came the sound of pounding, punctuated by her aunt's voice, calling, "Rhea? Rhea? Let me in!"

"Mercy's sake, child, stop all that blubbering!" Nancy Turner exclaimed, her voice filled with exasperation. "You'd think nobody'd ever gotten mad at you before."

The girl's only response was to cry harder, and her companion said sharply to Nancy, "None of her employers has thrown a teapot at her head before! It's not her fault. It's you and your heathen American ways, all of you."

"Exactly what heathen American ways are those, Doris?" Alexandra inquired icily.

Doris gasped and whirled around. When she saw Alexandra, she blushed to the roots of her hair and bobbed a curtsey. "Oh, miss, begging your pardon. I was—that is, I wasn't thinking clearly. I'm that distracted. I didn't mean—well…" She wound down lamely in the face of Alexandra's coolly inquiring expression. "It ain't what we're used to, and that's a fact!" she declared defiantly.

"Presumably not, if it involves flying teapots. That's not exactly accepted behavior in the United States, either.'' Alexandra turned toward her mother's companion, a sturdy American servant they had brought with them and who had worked for their family for years. ''Nancy?''

''Mrs. Ward didn't want her tea, miss, and she, well, flung it, but I'm sure she wasn't aiming at the girl. You know Mrs. Ward couldn't aim that well.'' Nancy sent the snuffling maid a hard look. ''It wasn't even hot—and I must say, I don't know what she expects when she brings a pot of barely warm tea to the missus.''

''Probably not to have it thrown at her,'' Alexandra said with a sigh. ''I take it that Mother is in one of her moods?''

Upstairs, the pounding, which had been going on throughout their conversation, grew more fierce, and Aunt Hortense's voice was sharp as she shouted, ''Rhea! Unlock this door this instant! Do you hear me?''

Nancy nodded, sighing. ''Yes. Miz Rhea's locked her door now and won't let anyone in.''

''All right. I'll go up and see about her. Doris—you take Amanda down to the kitchen and get her a cup of tea. See if you can calm her. I am sure that my mother meant her no harm. Perhaps she should take off the rest of the afternoon and go up to her bed and rest.''

The maid nodded, put her arm around the other girl and led her toward the kitchen. Alexandra started up the stairs toward Nancy.

''What happened?''

''It was my fault, miss,'' Nancy admitted with the air of a martyr. ''I shouldn't have left her alone. But she's been right agitated all day, and I thought a cup of hot cocoa might calm her down. So I went down to make it myself because she likes it just the way I fix it, you know, and I can't get that foreign cook to make it right.''

Alexandra nodded sympathetically, resisting the urge to

point out to Nancy that she was the foreigner here, not the English cook.

"But then, when I get down there, they tell me they already sent up a cup of tea—and after all the times I've told them that Mrs. Rhea doesn't like tea in the middle of the afternoon! Not only that, that silly twit Amanda took it, and she's enough to make anyone throw something at her, I say. Always blathering on in that little voice of hers, and you can't even understand half of what she says. By the time I got back up the stairs, I hear a crash, and Amanda comes flying out of your mother's room, crying up a storm, a big wet spot all down the side of her dress—where that tea was, I'll warrant the pot didn't come anywhere near her head—and then Miz Rhea slams the door and locks it. She's been in there for twenty minutes, refusing to come out, and Miss Hortense can't make any headway with her, it seems like."

"Oh, dear."

"She'll open it for you," Nancy went on confidently.

Alexandra wasn't so sure. There had been one or two times since they'd been in England that her mother hadn't even seemed to know who she was.

However, she continued up the stairs and strode with more confidence than she felt toward the door where her aunt stood, red-faced, her hand poised to knock again. When Aunt Hortense saw Alexandra, she let out a sigh of relief and started toward her.

"There you are. Thank heavens. Maybe you can get through to her. Rhea's locked herself in and won't come out. It's bad enough when she acts like this at home—I don't know what she's thinking, behaving this way in front of a bunch of Englishmen." Her tone invested the term with scorn. Alexandra's aunt was a sturdy, middle-aged woman in a sensible brown dress with a plain cap covering her hair, and her features, now frowning, were usually pleasant.

"I'm afraid she doesn't think about such things, Aunt Hortense—or care, either. Why don't you go down to the sitting room, and I will see what I can do. Oh, and, Nancy, get her some of that cocoa now. It might just do the trick."

Alexandra waited while her aunt and the other woman walked away, giving her mother a moment of silence. Then she tapped lightly on the door. "Mother? It is I. Alexandra. Would you let me in?"

There was a moment's silence, then her mother's voice said faintly, "Alexandra? Is that really you?"

"Yes, of course it is, Mother," Alexandra replied pleasantly. "Why don't you unlock the door so we can talk?"

After a moment there was the sound of the lock being turned, and then the door opened wide enough for Alexandra's mother to peer out. Her face was drawn and worried, her eyes suspicious. Her expression lightened a little when she saw Alexandra. "Where have you been?" she asked as she opened the door wide enough to allow Alexandra in.

"I had business to conduct. I told you that this morning. Remember?"

Rhea Ward nodded vaguely, and Alexandra was not sure that she remembered at all. "Why do you have on your hat?" Rhea asked in a puzzled voice.

"I haven't had time to remove it, I'm afraid." Alexandra reached up, untied the ribbon and pulled the hat off, continuing to talk in the soothing voice she used with her mother. "I just walked in, you see, and I came right up. Aunt Hortense was rather concerned about you."

She studied her mother unobtrusively as she spoke, taking in her untidy hair and messy appearance. Several buttons were unfastened or done up wrong, and stray hairs straggled around her face. Remembering her mother's once neat, trim appearance, Alexandra felt her throat close with tears. What had happened to the gentle, sweet woman she had known in her early years? Though she was still a pretty woman, even in middle age, her face was becoming lined beyond her years, with an unhealthy puffiness that was echoed in her once petite figure. The degeneration was due, Alexandra was sure, to Rhea's obsessive worries and her unfortunate, secretive dependence on bottles of liquor.

"Mother, what's the matter?" Alexandra asked, her worry showing through her assumed calm. "Why did you lock the door against Aunt Hortense?"

Rhea Ward made a face. "Hortense was always a bossy soul. You'd think the world couldn't run without her."

Certainly their household had been unable to run without her, at least in Alexandra's youth, she thought wryly, but she kept the opinion to herself. One of the things that her mother frequently despaired about was her own lack of ability.

"But why did you lock the door? I don't understand. Was Amanda rude to you?"

"Amanda? Who is that?"

"The maid who brought your tea."

"Her!" Rhea scowled. "Always sneaking in here. Spying on me."

"I'm sure Amanda wasn't spying on you, Mother. She was just bringing you your tea."

"I don't want tea! I told her that, and she acted like I'd grown horns. Nancy had gone to fetch my cocoa. That was what I wanted." Tears were in the woman's soft brown eyes, and her face started to crumple.

"Yes, dear, I know." Alexandra put her arm supportively around her mother's shoulders and led her to a chair. "She's getting you some right now."

"I don't know what's taking her so long." Rhea's mouth turned down in a pout.

"She heard the commotion and came running upstairs. You know how loyal to you Nancy is. She was afraid you needed help."

"She was right. I did. They're always watching me, and I know they laugh at me behind my back."

Alexandra thought with an internal sigh that her mother was probably right about both the laughter and the curiosity, after the odd things she had been doing since they got here. Was it possible that her mother had been drinking this early in the day? It had proved more difficult to keep liquor out of her mother's hands since they had been in London, where it was always easy for Rhea to find a street urchin or some peddler who would fetch her a bottle for a few extra shillings.

"Don't worry about them," Alexandra told her mother firmly. "Why, we don't even live here. You won't see them again after a few more weeks."

Rhea did not look much encouraged by Alexandra's words. She sat for a moment, frowning, then jumped up, went to her dresser and opened a drawer. She took out a small cherry-wood box that lay within and caressed it, then carried it to her chair and resumed her seat, holding the box firmly in both her hands. Alexandra suppressed a sigh. Her mother's fascination with this box had grown worse the past few weeks, too. She had had the box for as long as Alexandra could remember, and she kept it locked, the key on a delicate chain around her neck. No one, not even Aunt Hortense, knew what was inside it, for she adamantly refused to discuss it. When Alexandra was young, her mother had kept the box hidden away on a shelf in her wardrobe. The mystery of it had so intrigued Alexandra that she had on one occasion stacked books on a chair and climbed up them in order to reach the box on its high shelf. She had been discovered trying to pry the thing open, and it had been one of the few times her mother had ever spanked her. Alexandra had never tried to open it again, and it had remained inviolate on its shelf. But in recent years her mother had taken the box down and kept it in a drawer beside her bed, locking the drawer, as well. She had brought it with her on the trip, and nowadays she seemed to have it in her hand most of the time.

"Mother, what is distressing you so?" Alexandra asked softly, reaching out to take her mother's hand.

"I don't like it here!" Rhea pulled her hand out of Alexandra's grasp, replacing it around the small wooden box. "It's always cold, and the people are odd. They don't like me. None of the servants like me."

"They don't dislike you," Alexandra assured her, not adding that they were more scared of Rhea than anything else. "They just have a different way about them. There are so many wonderful things yet to see. Why, we haven't even left London yet! There's still Stonehenge and Stratford-on-Avon, and Scotland. It's supposed to be beautiful there."

"Here we go, Miz Rhea." Nancy entered the room briskly, a small tray in her hand. "I've got your chocolate all ready."

Rhea brightened, turning toward the servant and reaching for the cup of steaming liquid.

"Now, I reckon that will hit the spot," Nancy went on cheerfully. "And then, if you like, I can loosen your hair and rub lavender on your temples, and you can have a nice little nap before teatime. How does that sound?"

"Just the thing," Rhea murmured, a smile beginning to touch her lips.

Alexandra decided to leave her mother in Nancy's capable hands and made her way downstairs to the sitting room, where her aunt was installed, working away at a piece of embroidery.

"Hello, dear." Aunt Hortense looked at her. "It sounds as if you succeeded."

"I got her to open her door, if that's success." Alexandra sank into a chair near her aunt. "Oh, Auntie, I'm afraid I made a terrible mistake in bringing Mother here. Perhaps I should have left her at home."

"Oh, no, dear, she would have been so lonely."

"I don't know. She didn't want to come. She didn't even want me to. But I wouldn't listen. I was so sure that she would be better with me, that she would enjoy it once we got here—that she was just afraid to travel, you know."

"I am sure she is better with you. It's better that we can...well, keep an eye on her. You would have worried yourself silly if we had been over here and your mother back home, and you had no idea what she was doing or if anything had happened to her."

"Yes, but she's so much worse!" Alexandra shot to her feet and began to pace. "I've been selfish. I wanted to see England, to visit all the places I've always heard and read about. I was so sure it would help our business."

"And it has, hasn't it?"

"Yes, I think so. And I have enjoyed myself. There is no denying it. I would have hated to give it up. But Mother has been acting so strangely—locking herself up in her room, saying odd, wild things. Why, do you know last night that she looked at me as if she didn't even know who I was! And today, throwing a pot of tea at that poor girl. I don't care how cold it was or how little she wanted tea. It is decidedly bizarre behavior for a grown woman."

Aunt Hortense sighed. "Yes, it is."

"I mean, it isn't as if she were some ignorant person who had grown up in the wilds somewhere. Why, she used to be a diplomat's wife!"

"I know. And she was excellent at it. Rhea was always so good at giving parties, so skilled in getting people to talk and enjoy themselves. She always had odd turns, of course, when she was rather melancholy, but most of the time she was quite vivacious and happy—sparkling, really. I used to envy Rhea her ability to make friends, to draw people to her."

"What happened to her?" Alexandra asked bleakly.

Her aunt shook her head. "I don't know, dear. She has been getting worse for years. It was better when you were young. But even then, it seemed to me that she had very melancholy moments. I often wonder—well, she was never the same after she came home from Paris. Hiram's death affected her greatly, you see. They were most devoted. I've often suspected that she saw things during that Revolution, horrible things that affected her long afterward. She had a great deal of trouble sleeping at first. I could hear her up, pacing the floor long after everyone had gone to bed. Sometimes she would cry—oh, fit to break your heart. I felt so sorry for her. But what could I do? All I could think of was to take care of you and the house as best I could, to help her with all the business things that she disliked so. Even with Mr. Perkins managing the shipping business and her cousin running the store, she hated to have to listen to their reports and try to sort out their advice. I don't know, perhaps it was a mistake. Perhaps I took away too much responsibility from her. But she seemed so helpless, so needy..."

"I know. I'm sure you did what was best. Mother could not have handled raising me or managing the house by herself, much less running a business, too. You must not blame yourself."

"And you must not, either," her aunt retorted decisively, bobbing her head. "Your mother is the way she is, and who's to say she wouldn't have been worse if you had left her back in Massachusetts with only servants and distant relatives to take care of her? She is used to having the two of us with her. She probably would have taken it into her head that we had abandoned her or some such notion."

"That's true."

"And don't tell me that you shouldn't have come to England at all, for I won't hold with that. You can't live your whole life around your mother's...oddities."

"I suppose you're right. It's just so distressing to see her this way. Sometimes I——" She stopped abruptly.

"Sometimes you what?" Aunt Hortense turned to look at her niece when she did not continue.

"Nothing."

"It sounded like something to me. Out with it. Is something else troubling you?"

"No. Only——" Alexandra's voice dropped to little more than a whisper. "Do you ever wonder if Mother is—well..." She twisted her hands, frowning, reluctant to voice the fear that had been nagging at her for some time now. "What if she's not just odd? What if she's mad?"

"Wherever did you come up with such nonsense?" Aunt Hortense demanded indignantly. "Your mother is not mad! How can you say that?"

"I don't want to think it!" Alexandra cried, her voice tinged with desperation. "But you've seen how she acts. Most of the time I tell myself that she isn't insane—ob-

viously she's not insane. After all, she doesn't run screaming naked through the house or tear her clothes and try to
do herself harm like Mr. Culpepper's sister did.''

"I should say not!'' Aunt Hortense crossed her arms
pugnaciously.

"But sometimes I can't help but think these things she
says and does are not simply genteel eccentricities. Aren't
they something worse? More peculiar? In a person without wealth or standing in the community, mightn't they
be called evidences of madness?''

"It doesn't matter what they'd call it if she were poor,
because she isn't and never has been. She's *not* mad.
She's just...more fragile than the rest of us.''

"I hope you're right.'' Alexandra summoned up a small
smile for her aunt, but she could not completely rid herself
of doubt. Nor could she admit, even to Aunt Hortense,
the other cold fear that lay beneath her worry. If her
mother did indeed lean toward madness, would the taint
of it lie in her own blood, as well? Might she, someday,
disintegrate into insanity?

3

Alexandra took a last look at herself in the long mirror of the hallway; then, satisfied that she would look her best among the titled crowd this evening, she turned toward the staircase. Her deep rose satin gown would doubtless be outshone by many of the gowns on the ladies present at the ball. Her clothes, while of good cut and material, were not in the first stare of fashion in London, and she had not brought her very best ball gown with her, not thinking that she would attend anything dressier than the opera. Still, she knew that the dress was fashionable enough to cause no comment, and she had the satisfaction of knowing that its rose color was excellent on her, bringing out the rose in her cheeks and contrasting stunningly with her black hair. Her hair was done up in a mass of curls, thick and shining, with a pale pink rose nestled on one side as adornment. In her hand she carried, besides her fan, a small corsage of rosebuds delivered an hour earlier and sent, she was sure, by Lord Thorpe, though the card had contained no message.

Her eyes sparkled with anticipation as she walked into the formal drawing room. Much to her chagrin, she saw that Thorpe was already seated there with her aunt. Alexandra had made it a point to come downstairs as soon as the maid had brought her word of Thorpe's arrival precisely because she did not want Lord Thorpe to be subjected to her aunt's inquisition. From the frozen look on Thorpe's face, she guessed that he had already been here for several minutes, and Alexandra was struck with the suspicion that her aunt had deliberately bade the servants to delay taking Alexandra the message that his lordship had arrived.

As she started into the room, Lord Thorpe was saying tightly, "I assure you, madam, it is a most respectable party, given by one of the leading peers of the realm."

Alexandra had to stifle a smile at the man's barely concealed look of affront.

Her aunt continued blithely. "Be that as it may, Lord Thorpe, I don't know any of your peers of the realm, so their respectability is unknown to me. I've heard stories of some of the doings of so-called noblemen, and it's not what would be called suitable in America. The Hellfire Club, gaming hells, houses of—"

"Miss Ward!" Lord Thorpe looked shocked. "You can't believe that I would take your niece to such places!"

Alexandra wasn't sure whether his dismay came from the idea that her aunt thought him capable of such ungentlemanly actions or because she so bluntly brought up the subject.

"Too bad," Alexandra interjected lightly. "They sound terribly fascinating, I must say."

"Miss Ward." Thorpe jumped to his feet, relief spreading across his face.

"Good evening."

"You look—"

Alexandra raised an eyebrow as he paused. "I hope you are not going to say 'like a country bumpkin.'"

"No, indeed. It is simply that you render me speechless." His gray eyes shone in the candlelight as they drifted involuntarily down the front of her body, taking in the curves to which the rose satin clung. "You look stunning. I fear you will cast our London beauties into the shade."

Alexandra chuckled. "Very pretty words, my lord, but I am not so naïve as to believe that." She turned toward Hortense. "Good night, Aunt. I am going to take your victim away from you."

"Victim!" Aunt Hortense assumed a look of great offense. "I was merely looking out for my niece's best interests."

"Your aunt is a very careful woman," Thorpe remarked politely. "You are quite rightly cherished."

Alexandra grinned. "You see, Aunt Hortense, how polite he is."

A servant brought her Paisley shawl, which Thorpe took and draped across her shoulders with a courtly air. The brush of his fingertips against her bare arms sent a tingle through Alexandra, intensified when he leaned in to murmur, "It seems a shame to cover up such beauty."

Alexandra ignored the little thrum that started along her nerves and smiled at him. "It is a lovely dress."

"It was not the dress of which I spoke." His gaze dropped significantly, if fleetingly, to the expanse of bosom that swelled above the square-cut neckline.

Alexandra wrapped the shawl more tightly around her, covering the swell of her breasts. "I think it's time to leave," she said repressively. "Good night, Aunt."

She smiled across the room at her aunt, who was glowering suspiciously at their whispered conversation. Lord Thorpe sent the other woman a polite bow, and they left the room.

Outside, he helped her into the same elegant carriage that had taken her home this afternoon, and they settled across from each other on the plush seats.

"I was beginning to fear that your aunt was about to question me about my intentions toward you," Thorpe said dryly.

"I am sure she would have, given enough time. Her first concern, of course, was the wickedness of the place you were taking me. Aunt Hortense has a collection of stories of what has happened to innocent girls in the Babylon of London."

"I don't doubt that. What intrigued me was why she presumed I was going to introduce you to these evils."

"That is easy," Alexandra replied with an impish grin. "The English are given to wicked pursuits, but those who are most given to them are English noblemen, who, apparently, spend most of their time abducting or seducing innocent maidens."

"Indeed? I suspect that abducting you would prove to be a tiresome experience, so I must stick to seduction." His sensual mouth curved up in a way that made Alexandra's heart pound.

"Indeed?" Alexandra smiled, striving to keep her voice light. "I'm afraid you might find that experience equally tiresome."

"Oh, no." His eyes glittered in the dim light. "Lengthy, perhaps, but never tiresome, I assure you."

Alexandra's mouth went dry, and she had to glance away from his gaze. She looked out from beneath the rolled-up curtain of the carriage window, watching the houses go by as she tried to collect her scattered thoughts. Why did this man have such a strange effect on her?

After two blocks, the carriage turned and joined a long

line of carriages stretching down the block. At the front of the line stood a house ablaze with lights.

"Is that where we are going?" Alexandra asked in some astonishment.

"Yes. Why?"

"But it—it can't be more than four blocks from my house."

"Probably." He looked at her, faintly puzzled.

"Wouldn't it have been easier to walk?" She looked at the stalled line of carriages again. "Faster, too?"

"Undoubtedly."

"Then why did we take the carriage?"

He smiled. "It wouldn't do to be seen arriving on foot, my dear Miss Ward—as if one didn't own a carriage."

Alexandra gazed at him for a moment, unsure whether he was joking. "That is the silliest thing I've ever heard. It's a balmy night, the distance is short, and in a carriage we will have to wait substantially longer. Yet we don't walk because it would look wrong?"

His eyes danced. "I think that about sums it up."

"I presume it would be too gauche for words to get out of the carriage now and walk the rest of the way instead of sitting inside it for twenty minutes."

He nodded. "Decidedly déclassé."

She shook her head. "Sometimes I think my aunt is right."

"What? That we English are all debauched?"

"No. That the nobility are rather absurd."

"Absurd? I have never heard that one. Arrogant, yes, prodigal, yes, impractical and even decadent. But absurd?"

"Of course. It's too silly a concept to be taken seriously. What else would you call a system where the wealthiest and most highly regarded people have done nothing to earn their position but are there simply because they are descendants of other people?''

"Family is often considered a good indication of character, I believe. Do you have no regard for bloodlines? For what is passed from one generation to the next? Do you not believe that families instill their values in their offspring, and so on and so on, for generations?''

Alexandra felt a slight chill run down her spine at his mention of bloodlines. She wondered what he would think if he knew what sort of mother she had and what she might have passed on to her daughter.

"Family is an indication of character, yes, and certainly there are families who instill courage and honesty and all sorts of commendable traits in their children. My point, however, is that in England it doesn't matter whether one's family is good or bad, but simply what one's family name is.''

"Are there no leading families in America?''

"Of course there are, but at least they have done something to earn it. They have worked hard, built up wealth, been educated or simply been honest, decent people.''

"But let us say one's grandfather did that. His descendant today is regarded highly because of who his grandfather is. Isn't that right?''

"Sometimes.''

"It is the same principle. It is just that with us the ancestors were farther in the past.''

"What did they do to deserve their titles to begin with?'' Alexandra asked tartly. "Wage war? Take lands from others who were not as strong?''

"Service to King and country,'' he countered.

"Ha! Catering to the whims of another man who is revered solely because of *his* ancestors!''

Thorpe let out a short bark of laughter. "I am looking

forward to this evening! I can just imagine what furors your conversation will stir up."

Alexandra raised an eyebrow. "Is that why you invited me? To stir up a social tempest?"

"No. That is simply an added benefit."

Alexandra studied him for a moment. "Why *did* you ask me?"

"I'm not entirely sure," Thorpe admitted. "I think because you intrigue me." He paused, then asked, "Why did you agree to come with me?"

A smile curved Alexandra's lips as she said, "Perhaps for the same reason."

They inched their way along the line until their carriage was at last in front of the door. They climbed down and followed the family in front of them across the red runner laid over the front steps and through the imposing double front doors, held open by two liveried footmen.

They stepped into an entry hall that was, by any standards, grandiose. Black and white marble tiles checkerboarded the floor, and the walls rose to the second floor. It was large enough to fight a pitched battle in, Alexandra thought. At the far end a double staircase curved upward, the mahogany balustrades twined with masses of white flowers. Candles burned in a multitude of wall sconces and struck sparks off the glass drops of two enormous chandeliers, casting soft prisms of light over the people. Huge portraits of people in various styles of dress hung around the walls of the entry room. In the place of honor hung an enormous portrait of a bay horse.

"Where are we?" Alexandra asked, glancing around the room, aware of an unaccustomed feeling of awe.

"This is Carrington House, the town house of the Duke of Moncourt. That is the second Duke's favorite mount," he added, noticing the direction of her gaze. "It's said that he ordered the painter to make sure that its portrait was twice as large as that of his wife.''

''What an odd man.'' Alexandra's gaze went from the surroundings to the people going in a line up the graceful staircase, to where a couple waited at the top to greet them. The woman was dressed all in black, with diamonds around her neck and arms and a diamond spray in her hair. ''Obviously this Duke must value his wife more.''

She nodded toward the bejeweled woman.

''Ah, yes. The Carrington diamonds. Been in the family for centuries. This Duchess had the temerity to have the earrings reset. The Dowager Duchess hasn't stopped talking about it yet.''

Alexandra could see that she had been right when she had assumed that most of the women here would be dressed more elegantly than she. Lace, satin and velvet were everywhere, sewn in the latest styles by London's most fashionable modistes. Jewels winked at ears and throats. Hair was curled and upswept, decorated with roses, feathers, jewels, combs. It was, Alexandra thought, the most breathtaking display of extravagant beauty that she had ever seen.

She was therefore rather surprised to realize, after they had passed through the receiving line and gone into the ballroom, that she was the woman who was the most at the center of stares. She was too busy for a few minutes looking around at the mirrored and gilt walls and the crush of people to notice the whispers and the sidelong looks. Finally, however, she did. Alexandra shifted uneasily and glanced at Thorpe. He was gazing coolly across the room, seemingly oblivious to the small ripples they created wherever they went.

''Lord Thorpe,'' she whispered. ''What is going on?''

"What do you mean?" He glanced at her with polite inquiry.

"Don't tell me you don't see it. People keep looking at us. They're whispering." She heard with a little chill the eerie echo of her mother's words, but she shoved the thought aside. This was entirely different.

"I would think you would be accustomed to that. It is often the fate of beautiful young women."

"Don't be obtuse. I look the same as I always do, and I am not usually talked about."

He cast her a wry look. "With your tongue? You must give me leave to doubt that."

"Rudeness is not called for."

He smiled. "Whatever you may think, Miss Ward, you are unusually attractive." He cast a look at her smooth, sculptured face, the dark glowing eyes, the thick mass of dark hair that made her head look too heavy for the fragile support of her slender white neck.

"There are many women in this room just as pretty as I and doubtless others who are prettier."

"But none as...arresting." She was tall and statuesque among a ballroom of dainty women, vibrantly black-haired among a plethora of sweet-faced blondes. Alexandra Ward was different. Thorpe felt sure that there were as many biting comments being made about her as there were admiring. But whatever the words, they came because it was impossible not to notice her.

"Bosh," Alexandra retorted rudely. "Actually, I think they are looking at you."

"I am not a usual guest at such events," Thorpe admitted. "The London social world is such a stagnant pond that even so small an event as my appearing at a party will cause a ripple. When I appear with a stunning beauty on my arm, and no one has the least idea who she is, the ripple turns into a wave."

"Ah. I see."

"Sebastian!" As if to prove his point, a man's deep voice rang out, and they turned to see a large, broad-shouldered man shoving his way through the crowd toward them, a fragile-looking beauty walking with him, her hand tucked into his arm. "What the devil are you doing here? Beg pardon, ma'am, Nicola." He nodded toward Alexandra, then glanced at his companion, who smiled with easy grace, obviously used to the man's unbridled speech.

"Hello, Bucky," Thorpe answered. "I had an invitation, actually, so I came."

"Not like you, old fellow," the man whom Thorpe had called Bucky responded cheerfully. He had an open, pleasant sort of face, with wide-set blue eyes that looked out on the world with an expression of vague bonhomie. "Everyone's wondering what brought you out." He smiled at Alexandra. "And who your lovely companion is."

"It always astonishes me how interested everyone is in my comings and goings, considering that I scarcely know half the people at this gathering."

"That's what happens when you're marriageable." Bucky shrugged. "They've been after me for years, and I'm nothing but a Baron."

"Ah," the willowy blonde with him said, smiling and casting a significant look at Lord Thorpe. "But you are a man of charm, Buckminster, which gives you a certain advantage over others."

"Nicola, you wound me," Thorpe said, looking anything but hurt. "I'm sorry. Allow me to introduce you to Miss Alexandra Ward. Miss Ward is visiting from the

United States. Miss Ward, this is Lord Buckminster and his cousin, Miss Nicola Falcourt.''

"How do you do?" Nicola said, smiling at Alexandra, and Alexandra decided that her initial impression of the woman as fragile was wrong. It was her slenderness and pale beauty that made her look deceptively frail, but in her eyes and warm smile, Alexandra sensed a definite strength.

"An American, eh?" Lord Buckminster repeated with affable astonishment, as if he had never expected to meet such a person. "Pleased to meet you. However do you know Thorpe?"

"She is a friend of the family," Thorpe said smoothly before Alexandra could open her mouth to explain the relationship. She shot him an odd look, but said nothing.

When, after a few more pleasantries, the couple moved on, Alexandra turned to him, eyebrows soaring. "A friend of the family? Afraid everyone will shun you for associating with someone in trade?"

"Since I rarely seek out anyone's company, the prospect of being shunned scarcely frightens me," Thorpe retorted. "I was trying to shield *you* a bit from the gossip."

"Oh. I'm sorry."

"An apology? I am shocked." He held out his arm toward her, crooked at the elbow. "Shall we stroll around and let everyone look their fill at us?"

Alexandra smiled. "All right."

She tucked her hand in his arm. They had taken only a few steps when a man turned away from a knot of people, almost running into them. He stopped abruptly and stared at Alexandra. It seemed to her as if for an instant he turned deathly pale. He looked at her for a full beat, then drew in a breath, the color returning to his face.

"Lord Thorpe," the man said stiffly. "I'm sorry. I was—a trifle startled to see you."

"Lord Exmoor." Thorpe nodded briefly at the man, his face carefully devoid of expression. Alexandra, feeling the tensing of his muscle beneath her hand, glanced at him. He did not like this man, Alexandra thought, though she was not sure how she knew.

Intrigued by the change in attitude that she felt in Lord Thorpe, Alexandra looked with interest at the stranger. He was tall and slender, with light brown hair and eyes a hazel color. Wings of silver ran from his temples. Everything about him was long and angular, from his hands to his narrow nose to the careful eyes beneath his straight eyebrows.

Lord Exmoor returned her gaze inquiringly, and Thorpe, with a sigh, went on. "Miss Ward, allow me to introduce you to the Earl of Exmoor. Lord Exmoor, Alexandra Ward."

"How do you do?" Alexandra nodded politely toward him.

"Are you an American?" Exmoor asked.

"Yes."

"How interesting. I thought I detected it in your speech. You are here visiting relatives?"

"No. I have no relatives in England," Alexandra replied, finding that she had little desire to tell the man anything about herself. "I am traveling with my mother and my aunt."

"Ah. I see. I hope you are enjoying your visit."

"Very much, thank you."

"I had no idea you knew anyone from the United States, Thorpe," Exmoor went on.

"I am sure that I have many acquaintances about which you know nothing, Lord Exmoor."

"Yes. No doubt." He sketched a bow toward them. "Good evening. It was nice to meet you, Miss Ward. I look forward to running into you again."

He turned and walked away. Alexandra glanced at her companion. "Why don't you like him?"

Thorpe looked at her coolly. "Exmoor? What makes you say that?"

Alexandra raised a sardonic brow. "I was standing right here. Even one as ignorant as I of the behavior of the English nobility could tell that you were nothing more than polite to him."

Thorpe shrugged. "We are not friends," he said carefully. "We are not enemies, either. Merely two people who are not interested in extending our acquaintanceship. Now...would you care to dance?"

It was hardly a subtle change of subject. Alexandra felt that there must be more to the story, but she let him lead her onto the dance floor without protest. The waltz began, and they swept around the ballroom with the other dancers in time to the music. Alexandra's hand rested lightly in Thorpe's; his other hand was at her waist. It was quite proper, yet a little titillating, too, to be standing so close to him, gazing into his eyes only inches from hers, feeling the heat of his hand at her waist, as if at any moment he might pull her tightly against him.

Alexandra wondered how he felt about her. It was not a question that normally concerned her. She was sure of her own worth, and while men usually were attracted by her beauty, it did not worry her if they were equally dismayed by her brains or bluntness. But this time, it did matter, just as this time she found his nearness, his touch, his smile, all disconcerting.

After the waltz, Alexandra danced with several other men, but she found them dull compared to Thorpe. She was relieved when Thorpe reclaimed her after the cotillion and escorted her to the informal supper on the floor below. Alexandra sat in a chair against the wall while Thorpe went to get plates of food for them. She started to protest that she was quite capable of getting her own food, but she saw that most of the other couples were doing the same thing, and she decided to say nothing. It seemed remarkably silly to her, but the English were attached to their customs.

As she sat, idly watching the other people in the large room, she noticed that a woman across the room was watching her. She was a small woman, even delicate, and that image was amplified by the gauzy, floating dress she wore. She was quite beautiful, with fair skin and golden hair. Alexandra wondered who she was and what she found so interesting about her.

The woman cast a quick look at the buffet tables, where Thorpe stood, then floated—there was no other word for the graceful, dainty way she walked—over to where Alexandra sat. Alexandra watched her approach with interest. As she drew nearer, Alexandra could see that the woman was older than she had initially thought, with fine lines around her eyes and mouth and a certain brassiness to the gold in her hair that Alexandra thought betokened the touch of something other than Nature. Still, she was lovely in a cool, elegant way.

"I see Thorpe has taken you up," she said without preamble.

"I beg your pardon?" Alexandra looked at her in surprise. Did the woman not realize how rude she sounded?

"They say you are an American," the woman went on, ignoring Alexandra's comment.

"Yes, I am. What does—"

"Then you obviously don't know about his reputation."

"Lord Thorpe's?"

"Of course," the woman answered impatiently. "Mamas keep close watch on their daughters when Sebastian is around."

This woman must know him well to refer to him casually by his given name, Alexandra reasoned. She had discovered that the British were amazingly formal about such things.

"They do so with good reason," the woman went on, her blue eyes frosty.

"And what is that reason?" Alexandra asked, matching the freezing tone of the other woman's voice.

The woman gave a small, twisted smile. "Ah, I can see that he has already worked his spell on you. Just take my word for it—he is well-known for his seductions."

"I am surprised that he is received in polite society, then."

"Money and a title have an amazing power to make up for all sins."

"Lady Pencross." Both women, engrossed in their conversation, started and glanced up at the sound of a masculine voice a few feet from them.

It was Lord Thorpe, and his eyes were fixed on Alexandra's visitor. His face held no emotion, but the tone of his voice was as unyielding as iron. A little shiver ran down Alexandra's spine. She would not relish having Thorpe look at her in that way.

"Sebastian." Lady Pencross opened her eyes a little wider, her mouth turning down in a hurt way. "You don't sound pleased to see me."

"I doubt you are surprised," Thorpe replied dryly. "I am sure you have business somewhere else, don't you?"

Alexandra drew in a sharp breath at his blatant rudeness. The blond woman's eyes flashed, and for an instant Alexandra thought she was going to lash back with something venomous, but then she merely smiled and moved away.

"Another person with whom you are not interested in extending your acquaintanceship?" Alexandra asked lightly.

Thorpe, who had turned to watch the woman walk away, swiveled to Alexandra. His eyes were dark, his face etched in bitter lines. He looked at Alexandra for a moment, then relaxed, letting out a little laugh. "Yes. Lady Pencross and I have had far too much acquaintanceship as it is."

Alexandra was filled with curiosity about the incident, particularly what had caused the ill will between the lady and Thorpe, but, infuriatingly, Thorpe did not elaborate on the matter. He seemed to shrug it off, handing Alexandra her plate and sitting beside her.

"I hope I did not keep you waiting too long," he said. "The tables were rather busy."

"No. I was well entertained."

He glanced at her sharply. "Did Lady Pencross disturb you?"

"No. Not disturb, precisely. She was, ah, concerned about my virtue in your company."

He let out a short, humorless laugh. "Trust me, she is not disturbed about anyone's virtue, especially her own. I would not refine too much on what Lady Pencross says."

"I won't. I am well able to make up my own mind."

Thorpe looked at her, a smile beginning in his eyes. "Of course. How could I have forgotten that?"

They ate their food, a delicious repast that had Alexandra regretting the supper she had eaten earlier, and occupied their time with discussing the various people around them. Thorpe knew most of them and their foibles, and painted them with an acid wit that kept Alexandra chuckling.

"How hard you are on your peers," she told him.

He shrugged. "I am a mere novice compared to many of them. Malice and vitriol are the oils that keep the *ton* running." He set aside their plates. "Are you ready to return to the dancing?"

"Of course. It will be much more enjoyable watching everyone now that I know all their secrets."

"You have barely scratched the surface, my dear girl."

They left the room and made their way to the stairs, but Alexandra paused to look at some of the paintings that hung on the walls of the huge entry hall.

"That is the present Duke's mother," Thorpe told her, pointing to a picture of a woman with her arms around a young girl and two toy spaniels at their feet. "Painted by Gainsborough."

"It's beautiful."

"He has some fine art, nearly all portraits, of course— that is what the former Duke valued in art."

"His favorite, doubtless, was the horse." Alexandra nodded toward the massive portrait of the animal that she had noticed when they first walked in.

"Definitely. Would you like to see some of the other things?"

"Why, yes, if you think it would be all right."

"I'm sure of it." He guided her up the stairs and away from the ballroom, heading down the long gallery. Just past the stand of armor began a row of portraits, many dark with age.

"Why, this looks like—"

Thorpe nodded. "A Holbein. It is of Isabella Moncourt,

the lovely young wife of the then Marquess of Moncourt. The young woman met an untimely end."

Alexandra eyes widened. "Really? She was murdered?"

Thorpe shrugged. "Who knows? She died young—a fall down the stairs one night. Murder was definitely rumored—a charge the Moncourts vehemently deny to this day. But it is said that she had caught the eye of one of the Howards. And her husband was known to be a jealous man."

"Caught his eye? That was all? Why didn't the husband kill the Howard, then? It sounds to me as if he were more at fault."

Thorpe chuckled. "No one even knows if it is true. But if it is, I would guess that the lady was not entirely blameless."

They continued along the hallway, peering to see the portraits in the light of the wall sconces. "I would love to see them by day," Alexandra commented.

"I can show you an even better collection another day, if you'd like."

"Your family's ancestors?"

"No. My family's art, such as it is, is primarily at the estate in the country. I spend little time there. And my house, as you know, is given over to 'heathen art,' as Lady Ursula has told me."

"Who?"

"The daughter of a very good friend of mine. I hope you will be able to meet her tonight."

"Lady Ursula?"

"No, although I dare swear we will be unable to avoid that if the Countess is here. But it is the Countess I want you to meet."

"She is someone special to you?"

Thorpe nodded. "Yes. Her grandson and I were friends at school, and I often visited with them. The Countess was— Well, let's just say I found more understanding and love there than was ever at my home. Sometimes I feel that she is almost my mother—or grandmother."

"I look forward to meeting her, then."

They reached the end of the gallery and turned to look back down the empty hallway. There was a pool of darkness at the end of the long corridor, the golden circles of light cast by the wall sconces ending several steps before them.

Alexandra turned, her eyes going to Thorpe's. His face was shadowed, but the gleam in his eyes was unmistakable. Her breath caught in her throat. Was he going to kiss her? He took a step toward her. She knew that if she turned away, it would break the moment, and he would not touch her. But she found that she had no interest in turning away. She waited, her eyes locked on his.

He smiled faintly as he reached out and brushed his knuckles down her cheek. "You intrigue me, Miss Ward."

"Indeed?" Alexandra struggled to keep her voice light, even though the whisper-light touch of his skin upon hers made her blood race. "Is this your common practice with women who intrigue you, my lord? To lure them down dark, deserted corridors on the pretext of showing them art?"

His eyes danced. "'Twas no pretext. We have been looking at art. And you are free to go any time you wish. I am not holding you here."

Alexandra could feel the pulse pounding in her throat, the heat rising in her face. She did not move.

A smile touched his lips, and his hand moved to cup the back of her neck. She watched him, her breath coming faster in her throat as he leaned in. She had no thought of scandal or propriety, only of the fact that she wanted to feel his kiss. She turned her face to him.

His lips were soft and hot on hers, and she shivered a little at the new sensation. Only one man had ever tried to kiss her on the mouth, and his wet, inebriated kiss had felt nothing like this. She had given that man a good, hard shove, and he had ended up sitting on his backside in the snow. This time, however, she had no desire to push Thorpe away.

Little tendrils of sensation darted through her, raising tingles and heat throughout her body and a sudden strange weakness in her knees. She leaned in, her hands going up to grasp his lapels for support, for she felt as if her legs might give way beneath her. She heard Thorpe's breath draw in sharply at her movement, and his arms slid around her, pulling her tightly into him. His body was deliciously hard against her softness, pressing into her all up and down. Their mouths blended; their arms sought to pull each other closer and closer still; their skin surged with heat.

Alexandra was lost in the experience, dazzled and dazed. Her flesh quivered, and blood pooled in her loins, throbbing and heated. There was an ache between her legs, and her breasts felt swollen and tender, her nipples hardening.

His tongue swept her mouth, exploring and arousing her. Alexandra moaned, clinging to him, as she tentatively answered with her own tongue. Thorpe made a noise deep in his throat, and his hands moved down her back and onto the rounded flesh of her buttocks. His fingers dug into the firm mounds, lifting her up and into him. She could feel the ridge of his desire against her, hard and insistent, and somehow the knowledge of his hunger for her aroused her even more.

Finally Thorpe raised his head and looked at her, his face flushed, his eyes glittering in the dim light. "Good God! I had not meant—"

Alexandra gazed at him, stunned momentarily into speechlessness. Her thoughts tumbled crazily, scattered by the tumult of sensations coursing through her.

"This is far too public a place," he said finally. He drew a deep breath and stepped back, his arms falling away from her. He glanced over his shoulder, relieved to see that the corridor was still empty. "I do not want either of us to be fodder for the rumor mill."

"What *do* you want?" Alexandra asked, the first words that came into her mind.

The sensual curve of his mouth as he smiled was answer enough. "You must know what I want."

"Indeed. I think I have some idea." Alexandra struggled to pull herself together. She was well aware of what he wanted; the same desire was pounding through her veins. Keeping her virtue had never been a difficult decision before; indeed, it had not required any thought at all. She had never felt tempted to give it up. Now, for the first time, she had to struggle to make the right decision. "You, I take it, do not have honorable intentions."

Thorpe smiled sardonically. "My dear Miss Ward, my intentions are rarely honorable. Surely someone must have told you that by now."

"It has been mentioned to me that you have... something of a reputation."

"You put it delicately." He crossed his arms. "The truth is, I am scandalous, Miss Ward. I am considered a roué. While I am welcome husband material, having a fortune, I must be watched at all times by any young girl's chaperone.''

"You are in the habit of seducing young girls?" Alexandra asked, her back stiffening. Could it really be true that he vilely preyed on innocent maidens? That he sought out and seduced vulnerable girls whose heads were easily turned by a man of looks and fortune?

"No. I am not. I find simpering young debutantes deadly dull. There are many mamas who would love to think that I covet their darlings' virtue, but I rarely find virtue interesting. Nor am I interested in tricking a woman of any age or amount of innocence into my bed."

"Then what do you seek, if I may ask?"

"A night of pleasure with a woman who knows what she wants."

"I see. Love, I take it, plays no part in your plan."

His lip curled slightly. "Love, Miss Ward, is a notion for young fools, neither of which I am any longer."

Any longer. "I see," Alexandra said again, thinking that indeed she did. Thorpe's words were bitter, not indifferent, the words not of a man who had no use for love but of one who had been disappointed in it. "So you are offering me a brief, loveless moment of mating? I must say, it seems hard to turn down."

Her words surprised a grin from him. "You have a way with words. I would hope it is not exactly that." He reached out and looped a single finger through hers—the briefest of touches, yet it sent heat shimmering through her. "I would say a time of passion, hopefully not brief, a mutual sharing of pleasure between adults without any efforts to control or gain an advantage."

Alexandra looked down, smoothing her skirt. "I fear you must think I am someone other than who I am."

"Are you going to tell me that you are a conventional

shrinking maiden?'' he asked, humor lacing his voice. ''My dear woman, I just kissed you. I would have to differ.''

She raised her eyes, looking at him in her usual honest way. ''I would be a fool to deny what I felt. And I realize that I am rather unconventional in many of the things I do. Nor am I a young girl. I am twenty-four years old and used to making decisions.''

''I am quite aware of that.''

''However, I think you seek a woman of experience.''

His eyes seemed suddenly to burn hotter. ''And you are not?''

''Not of the sort I believe you require.''

''Excuse me. I had thought—when I kissed you—''

Alexandra blushed. ''I am sorry to disappoint you.''

He smiled slowly. ''Oh, no, you did not disappoint me. But I can see now that I rushed my fences. I am not usually so foolish.'' He took her hand and raised it formally to his lips. ''My dear Miss Ward, please forgive my importunities. I can see that we need to take our time.''

''Then you are setting out to seduce me?'' Alexandra asked curiously.

''If you mean to trick you into my bed, no,'' he replied. He kissed each of her fingers lightly on the tip as he went on. ''But to supply you with the information you need to make a decision, yes. As a businesswoman, I am sure that you would appreciate the distinction.''

A laugh burst from Alexandra. ''You are clever, my lord. But I think we are miles apart. I, you see, believe in love. Without it, passion is a hollow pleasure.''

''This, I believe, is an argument we shall have ample time to discuss,'' he said, a sensual smile playing on his lips. "In the meantime, perhaps we should return to the party. Otherwise tongues will indeed be wagging."

He offered her his arm, and Alexandra slipped her hand through the crook of his elbow. They strolled down the hallway to the ballroom.

They had just stepped into the room when Thorpe's gaze lit on a group of people, and he smiled with satisfaction. "Ah. There she is."

"Who?" Alexandra turned and looked in the direction of his gaze, her curiosity aroused.

He was looking at a group of four people who were chatting with Nicola Falcourt. There was a balding, plump man, rather ordinary-looking, and beside him a formidable middle-aged woman in deep royal blue. She was squarely built with a jutting bosom like the prow of a ship. A young slip of girl was with them, colorless in a maidenly white dress. Her hair was a nondescript brown, and Alexandra could not tell the color of her eyes, for they were hidden behind spectacles. The last member of the party, who was bending to kiss Nicola's cheek, was, in Alexandra's view, the most interesting. She was older than the formidable woman, but infinitely more attractive and intriguing. There was the air about her of a woman who had always been attractive to men, a certain confidence of carriage, a poise and even a hint of flirtatiousness as she smiled. She was tall and slender, with a mass of white hair, and her blue eyes, hooded by age, were still keen and twinkling with amusement.

"The elegant lady in gray and silver crepe?" Alexandra asked Thorpe. "Is she your Countess?"

Thorpe smiled fondly. "Yes. She is indeed my Countess."

They started across the room toward the group. Thorpe said as they walked, "Her granddaughter, Penelope, is a pleasant girl, but don't expect much from Lady Ursula. She was never fond of me—always thought I was a bad influence on her son, Artie.''

''And were you?''

''Doubtless,'' he responded, smiling. ''But, then, Artie desperately needed a bad influence. Poor lad, he grew quite dull after I left.''

They drew close to the group. Lady Ursula turned and saw them, and her mouth drew up like a prune. ''Thorpe,'' she said without enthusiasm.

The Countess turned at her daughter's words, smiling brilliantly. ''Thorpe! How wonderful to see you.'' She held out her hands to him. ''I didn't expect to find you here.''

Thorpe stepped forward, between Alexandra and the older woman. He took the Countess's hands and raised them to his lips. ''My lady. I, on the other hand, had hoped that I would find you here. There is someone I would like you to meet.''

He stepped aside at his words, holding out a hand toward Alexandra. She moved toward them. ''Countess, allow me to intro—''

The Countess looked beyond him to Alexandra, and the blood drained from her face. ''Simone!''

She crumpled to the floor.

4

For an instant the group was frozen in horror, staring at the Countess in a heap of silver gauze upon the floor.

"Countess!" Thorpe moved first, going down on one knee and gently lifting her upper torso from the floor, his arm around her shoulders.

"Mother!" Lady Ursula declared in startled accents. "Good God, why did she—" She bent over her mother. "Is she all right?"

Thorpe felt the older woman's pulse. "I think she just fainted. Let's get her out of here."

"Yes, of course." Ursula glanced uneasily around at the room, where faces were turning curiously toward them.

Thorpe put his other arm under the Countess's knees and stood up, lifting her easily.

"What made her say that name? It's so bizarre." She turned to look accusingly at Alexandra, as if somehow the incident were her fault. She stopped in midsentence, staring at Alexandra. "Good God!"

Alexandra gazed at her wonderingly. The other woman whirled abruptly and hurried after Thorpe.

"Wait here." Thorpe tossed the words over his shoulder toward Alexandra, and then he was gone, striding out the door with Lady Ursula, her husband and her daughter scurrying after him like a flock of agitated chickens.

Nicola and Alexandra turned toward each other in astonishment.

"How extraordinary," Nicola commented. "I've known the Countess all my life, and I've never seen her faint. She's a very strong woman."

"She seemed to, ah, find the sight of me disturbing."

"I am sure it wasn't that," Nicola reassured her.

Alexandra, however, was not so sure. Lady Ursula had reacted strongly to the sight of her, as well, even though she had not fainted. "Why do you think she said that name? Was she calling me Simone?"

"I don't know. Why would she call you that?"

Alexandra shook her head. "Perhaps I reminded her of someone?"

Nicola shrugged gracefully. "I don't know of anyone named Simone among our acquaintances. It sounds French, doesn't it?"

"Yes, it does."

Alexandra glanced to the side and saw a man making his way purposefully toward them. It was the Earl of Exmoor, to whom Thorpe had introduced her earlier in the evening. Nicola let out what sounded very much like a curse beneath her breath.

"I hope there was nothing wrong with the Countess," the man said smoothly as he joined them.

"I am sure she will be all right," Nicola said coolly. "No doubt it was the heat of the room."

"Mm. I am sure you are right. The Countess is getting a trifle advanced in years, perhaps, to be attending such a crush."

"You make her sound as if she were feeble, Richard. She's a strong, vibrant woman."

"My dear sister, I meant no insult to the woman. She is a remarkable woman, and I admire her tremendously."

"I am not your sister."

Alexandra glanced at Nicola, recognizing the iron in her voice. Thorpe's earlier coolness toward this man was as nothing compared to Nicola's obvious dislike.

"Come, come, Nicola, you will give our visitor here the wrong impression."

"If I have given her the impression that I do not like you, then it is a very accurate one."

Alexandra was impressed. Nicola might look as fragile as a flower, but her backbone was obviously made of steel. She stood facing the man, her body stiff, her arms rigid at her sides, her eyes flashing.

Exmoor made a wry face, looking at Alexandra. "I am sorry, Miss Ward. Miss Falcourt and I have the problem of perhaps being *too* close."

His words seemed deliberately suggestive, and the look he shot Nicola was challenging.

Nicola answered by curling her lip into a sneer. "Don't make a fool of yourself, Exmoor." She turned toward Alexandra. "Please excuse me, Miss Ward."

"Of course." She watched the other woman walk away. Then she turned toward the Earl. He certainly did not seem to be a popular man.

He shrugged and smiled. "Nicola and I have always had our little disagreements. Still, we are family."

"Oh?"

"Yes. Her sister is my wife."

"Oh." Alexandra was taken aback. There was certainly no love lost between these in-laws.

"Perhaps that explains her antipathy toward me. She

and Deborah were quite close growing up. It can often cause jealousy in a younger sister when the older one marries.''

"I suppose it can," Alexandra replied noncommittally.

"What happened to the Countess?" he asked, abruptly reverting to his earlier subject. "It looked as if she fell."

"I believe she fainted."

He frowned. "I trust she was not ill." He glanced toward the door. "Perhaps I should go see about her."

"Lord Thorpe and her daughter are with her. I am sure that they will see that she is taken care of."

"Do you, uh, know the Countess?" he asked.

"No. That is, I just met her."

"I see. Remarkable woman. Quite a beauty in her day, I understand."

"I'm sure she was."

He continued making polite chitchat. Alexandra supposed that the Earl felt he must keep her company since Nicola had left. However, she soon grew tired of the insipid conversation about her life in America and her visit to England. As soon as she could politely take her leave of him, she did so. She strolled around the room for a while, but she soon grew bored with that. She knew no one there except Nicola, and while she liked her, Alexandra felt that she could not hang upon Nicola's skirts all evening like a lost child. Quite frankly, without Thorpe's presence, the gathering had lost most of its appeal. She wondered when he would be returning and whether the Countess was all right. Finally she went in search of the group.

She could not find them outside the doors of the ballroom or in the entry hall. When she asked one of the numerous footmen if he had seen Lord Thorpe, he informed her that he had left with the Countess of Exmoor and her group.

Alexandra's first thought was that he had abandoned her, and she felt a flash of hurt. But she reminded herself that he had told her to wait as he was leaving, and that must have meant that he intended to return. She sighed. She had little interest in hanging about here being bored until Thorpe came back for her. Surely she could leave by herself and go home. After all, it had been only a short distance from her house to this one, a matter of mere blocks, and she was certain that she could find her way. She could walk it easily.

The idea of going home and indulging in a cup of hot cocoa and going to bed grew more and more appealing. Her feet hurt; she was bored; she felt like a fool standing around in the front hall. She made up her mind, then sent one of the footmen for her Paisley shawl. She wrapped it around her shoulders and walked out of the front door, ignoring the rather shocked expression of the footman. Doubtless properly brought up Englishwomen did not walk home from a party, she thought, but Alexandra had little patience for such foolish rules.

It was a pleasant walk. The May breeze still held a hint of coolness, but her shawl combated that. The evening was quiet, as it never was in the daytime. She was used to walking quite a bit back home, and she realized that she had missed it.

She crossed the street and started up the block toward her house. There was the sound of footsteps behind her, walking rapidly. They were gaining on her, and for the first time, she felt a bit of unease. She reassured herself that this part of town was quite safe, but nevertheless, she picked up her pace. Suddenly the sound of the steps stopped. She turned around, surprised, and suddenly a figure burst out from the shrubbery behind her and launched himself at her. They tumbled to the pavement.

Alexandra let out a shriek before he covered her mouth with one hand. They rolled across the ground, grappling, until finally he succeeded in wrapping his arms around her, pinning her arms to her sides. He stood up, jerking her to her feet.

"Dammit! You virago!" he whispered, holding her immobilized from behind. "Go back where you came from. You understand?" He shook her a little.

Alexandra kicked back, the heel of her slipper connecting hard with his shin. The man let out a grunt of surprise and pain, and his arm slackened around her. Alexandra pulled away from him, and he grabbed her, catching her sleeve. It ripped, tearing her dress loose at the shoulder and leaving him with only a sleeve in his hand as she raced away.

Alexandra ran toward her house, screaming, as the front door opened and two footmen stuck curious heads out. They goggled at the sight of Alexandra running toward them. Aunt Hortense pushed them out of her way as she ran onto the front stoop.

"Alexandra!" She hurried toward her niece, holding up her lamp to see, and the two footmen, embarrassed, came running out, too.

Behind her, Alexandra heard her attacker take off in the opposite direction. She swung around to see the dark figure receding down the street. The two footmen gave chase but gave up by the end of the block.

"Alexandra! Child! What happened?" Aunt Hortense wrapped an arm around her shoulders. "Did that Englishman attack you?"

Alexandra smiled a little at her aunt's warlike expression. "No, Auntie. That is, I suspect it must have been an Englishman, but not the Englishman you mean."

"What happened? You're all a mess." Aunt Hortense led her into the house. "Your cheek is scratched."

"I'm not surprised. Someone jumped out at me." Alexandra shivered a little, suddenly cold in the aftermath of the excitement. Her nerves were jangled, and she felt stunned and rather fuzzy. Her cheek was beginning to sting, and she felt sore all up and down the front of her body where she had landed so hard on the pavement. Her dress was torn and dirty. She drew in a straggly breath and blinked away the tears that were threatening to pour out.

"Jumped out at you! Exactly where was that man who took you away from here?"

"You make it sound as if he abducted me."

"I assumed, when he escorted you from your home, that he would return you safe and sound, not abandon you to be set upon by thieves."

Aunt Hortense steered her into the nearest room, the formal drawing room, leading her toward the blue couch.

"He didn't abandon me," Alexandra retorted with irritation. "He had to leave, and I was bored, so I came home by myself. It was only a few blocks. I could easily walk it."

"Ha! You obviously couldn't," her aunt pointed out. "I'd like to know what kind of man would just walk off and leave you at a party! Well, never mind that now," she went on as Alexandra drew breath to argue. "Sit down here on the sofa. What you need is a stiff shot of brandy."

Aunt Hortense looked around and caught sight of the clot of servants standing just outside the drawing room door. "You, there, what do you think you're doing, standing about like a gapeseed? Go fetch your mistress a glass of brandy. The rest of you, take some lanterns and go check the street—make sure that scoundrel isn't still out there.''

The servants scattered at her words. Aunt Hortense sighed. ''No sense, the lot of them.''

There was a gasp at the door, and they turned toward it. Alexandra's mother stood in the doorway, staring in horror at Alexandra.

''My baby!'' she wailed. ''What happened? Did they get you, too? Are they attacking us?''

She rushed into the room and dropped on her knees beside Alexandra. Tears gushed down her face as she patted ineffectually at Alexandra's hair and arm and tried to wipe some of the dirt from her skirts. ''Oh, my dear, oh, my dear,'' she repeated over and over.

''Mother, it's all right. No one is attacking us,'' Alexandra said, trying to keep her voice soothing. Her mother's light, frantic touch and words jarred her already frazzled nerves. ''Really. It's all right. It was just an accident. I fell.''

''No. No. They're coming here. I know it. We have to flee. Get the carriage.''

Alexandra's breath caught in her throat. The light in her mother's eyes was alarming. She looked almost mad. ''Mother, it's all right. No one is coming to get us. We are fine. There are plenty of servants, and we are inside the house.''

''You don't know! You don't know!'' Rhea's voice rose in panic. ''The servants will turn against us! We'll be helpless!''

''Mama!'' Alexandra gripped her mother's arms. ''It's all right!''

Nancy, her mother's companion, came hurrying into the room, her feet bare and her voluminous white cotton nightgown billowing around her. "Miz Rhea! There you are! I'm sorry." Nancy cast an apologetic glance at Alexandra and Aunt Hortense. "I didn't know she was up."

She bent over Rhea Ward and pulled the hysterical woman to her feet, wrapping her arms around her in a hug that was both comforting and restraining. "There, there. Nothing's going to happen to you or to any of us."

"It's not?" Rhea turned toward the other woman, hope dispelling some of the panic in her voice. "Truly?"

"I promise you. You know I wouldn't let anybody hurt you."

"But the mob—" She cast an eye agitatedly toward the front window.

"There's no mob out there, ma'am. Listen. Do you hear a mob?"

Rhea paused, her head cocked, listening. "No." A tremulous smile broke across her face. "You are right. They must have turned and gone somewhere else."

"That's it," Nancy agreed soothingly. "Now, let's you and I go back to bed."

Rhea nodded and went along with her docilely.

"Nancy," Aunt Hortense said as the two of them reached the door, "perhaps it would be best if you slept in Mrs. Ward's room tonight."

"Just what I was thinking, Miss Hortense. I'll have someone set up a cot for me."

Alexandra watched her mother leave with the servant, and tears welled in her eyes. "Oh, Mother," she breathed. She looked at her aunt. "What is the matter with her? What should we do?"

"She'll be all right in the morning," Aunt Hortense told her matter-of-factly. "You'll see. The noise woke her up, and she got scared. Probably heard all the servants jabbering and running around."

"But what was she talking about? Why did she think there was a mob?"

"Oh, that. She used to do that a lot when you were little. You just don't remember. She would wake up from nightmares, terrified and talking about the mob coming to get her and you. It was that thing she went through in France, I think. That revolution, with all those people rioting and running around with torches pulling people out of their houses. Rhea never wanted to talk about it, but I think it scared her to death. She was afraid they were going to try to kill her and you, too—mistake you for aristocrats or something, I guess."

"But why now?"

"Oh, I doubt it was anything but being jerked out of her sleep and seeing the servants acting scared. She probably heard you screaming. It scared me, I'll tell you. She was confused. Ah, there's that brandy." Her aunt turned as the butler entered the room, wearing a dressing gown over his nightshirt, a nightcap on his head, and carrying a silver tray with a bottle of brandy and two snifters on it.

Alexandra subsided, a troubled expression on her face, as her aunt bustled to the small table where the butler set the tray and began to pour her a healthy dose of brandy.

"Here, you'll feel much better after this."

Alexandra took the snifter from her with both hands, surprised to find that she was trembling too much to hold it with one, and took a gulp. The liquor burned like fire all the way down to her stomach, making her eyes water. She coughed and tried to hand the glass to her aunt, but Hortense crossed her arms and told her to finish the liquor.

"Brandy was always Father's cure for a case of the nerves—and anything else that ailed you, actually. And he lived to be eighty-six, so he must have gotten something right.''

"All right." Alexandra tried not to breathe and took another gulp. A shiver ran through her, and her stomach felt as if it had burst into flames, but she could feel relaxation stealing through her.

"Good God, you fool, let go of me!" A man's angry voice came ringing down the hall. "What the devil is going on?"

"Thorpe!" Alexandra surged to her feet just as Thorpe stalked into the room, shaking off the restraining hand of one of the footmen. The sudden movement made her feel dizzy, and she swayed.

"Alexandra!" he exclaimed, taking in her disheveled condition in a glance, as well as her wobbliness, and he crossed the room in two quick strides, then caught her in his arms. "My God, what happened to you? And why is your front door open and all the servants prowling about with lanterns?"

Alexandra sagged against his chest, warmth flooding her. "Oh, Thorpe. There was a man and he—he jumped out—"

"What!" Thorpe looked stunned, then thunderous.

"I—I—" Suddenly, surprising everyone, including herself, Alexandra burst into tears.

"Alexandra! My dear girl." Lord Thorpe's arms went around her, and he cuddled her close to him, bending his head over hers. "It's all right. I'm here. I won't let anyone get you. It's all right."

Gently he stroked her hair and back, murmuring softly. Aunt Hortense, who had watched in wonder the joy that spread over her niece's face when she saw this man, as well as the way she collapsed against him, stood for a moment looking thoughtful, then tiptoed out of the room, closing the door softly behind her.

Alexandra snuggled into Thorpe's arms, luxuriating in the feeling of warmth and security, and gradually her tears abated. She stood for a moment with her head against his chest, listening to the soothing beat of his heart. It felt so nice here that she didn't want to leave.

She lifted her tear-streaked face to Thorpe. "I'm sorry."

Thorpe looked at her, her cheeks soft and damp, the big, dark eyes luminous. He smiled. "No need to apologize."

He took out his handkerchief and began to blot the tears on her cheeks. She was beautiful, and so soft in his arms. Her hair was in charming disarray, curls escaping from their pinnings and tumbling over her shoulders. His gaze slid farther, to where her dress had been torn in the struggle. It had come completely off one shoulder, the little puff of a sleeve torn away, and the front of the bodice had fallen on that side, exposing the creamy top of her breast, swelling above the lacy camisole.

Thorpe's mouth went dry. He was unable to look away from that delectable mound of flesh. He could see the dark circle of her nipple through the sheer material of the camisole. He thought about putting his lips to the soft, quivering orb; he thought of taking the pink-brown nipple into his mouth and teasing it into diamond hardness. Desire swelled in him.

He dragged his eyes to her face, but he found that her beauty did not decrease his desire in the slightest. Her lips were full and deep red, moist and soft from her bout of tears. As she looked at him, they parted slightly.

Thorpe pulled her tightly against him, and his lips came down on hers. He kissed her fully and deeply, drinking in the sweetness of her mouth, his desire as suddenly full and tumultuous as it had been in the gallery. Alexandra pressed into him eagerly, her arms going around his neck and holding on. He let out a soft moan, his lips pressing harder against hers. Passion thrummed in him. She was soft and pliant against him, and the little sounds that rose from her throat stoked his desire.

His hand slipped to her breast, covering it and stroking the quivering flesh, bare above her camisole. He could feel her nipple hardening beneath his palm, and he wanted to feel it without any cloth between them. He pushed down the camisole, sliding it across the budding nipple, and took her nipple between his thumb and finger. Gently he rolled and pressed, caressing it, delighting in the way it thrust out even more, firm and proud.

He had to taste it. Pulling his mouth from Alexandra's, he kissed a trail down the slender column of her throat and across her chest. His mouth moved tenderly over the slope of her breast until he found the prize he sought. Softly his tongue traced the button of engorged flesh.

A groan escaped Alexandra's lips. She sagged against Thorpe's arm, her eyes closed, lost in the sensations he was creating in her. With every movement of his tongue, her loins quivered and grew hotter. She felt like wax melting in his arms. When he took her nipple into his mouth and began to suckle, she cried out softly, her body jerking in a paroxysm of delight. She had never felt anything like this, had never even known that such sensations existed. Her body was consumed by heat; each rhythmic pull of his mouth sent another shock of desire through her. There was a deep ache growing between her legs, a yearning that she didn't know how to satisfy.

Alexandra moved her hips against him instinctively, searching for satisfaction, and Sebastian shuddered. His hands went to her buttocks, digging into them and shoving her even more tightly against him. His desire throbbed against her, hot and rigid. Slowly he moved her hips over him, and Alexandra gasped at the new sensation, her passion spiraling.

In the hall there was the sound of footsteps and a man's voice saying, "Nothing, Miss Ward."

"No trace of him?" Aunt Hortense bellowed, sounding irritated.

Alexandra gasped and stepped back, jolted from her haze of passion by the sounds. She put her hand to her mouth, her eyes huge, looking at Thorpe.

Fury stabbed through Thorpe, and he wished the servants and Aunt Hortense to hell for interrupting them. He wanted to reach out and pull Alexandra into his arms, ignoring the world outside the room, but then reason returned to him. This was hardly the time or place for lovemaking. Anyone could walk in at any moment, and the scandal would be all over London within a day. He realized, too, with something of a jolt, that he was acting like a cad. Alexandra had just gone through a frightening experience; she was unusually vulnerable—and he was taking advantage of that vulnerability. He certainly had no qualms about having a mutually satisfying affair with a woman, but he knew that it would be unfair and dishonest to lure her into lovemaking when she was so shaken and frightened by an attack.

Irritated at himself, he turned away, saying gruffly, "Forgive me. I should not—"

Alexandra wrapped her arms around herself, feeling very empty and alone. She cleared her throat, telling herself not to be a fool. "There's no need. I was not myself. The circumstances were—"

"What happened?" He turned, seizing on the topic. It

was doubly irritating, he found, that he was still throbbing with desire, even if his good sense had taken over enough to stop him before they tumbled together on the floor.

"I'm not sure." Alexandra frowned. "He jumped out at me from behind some shrubs. He followed me—at least, I think he did. I started hearing footsteps, and then they were gone, and the next thing I knew, he was rushing out of the shrubs down the street. He grabbed me from behind and he said—this is what is so very strange—he said, 'Go home!'"

"'Go home?'" Thorpe repeated in disbelief.

"Yes. Or go back where you came from. Something like that."

"Are you sure?"

"Of course I am!" Alexandra snapped. "I could scarcely mistake something like that. He distinctly told me to leave. Why would anyone care? Why would someone attack me just to tell me to go back to the United States?"

Thorpe stared at her dumbfounded. "I cannot imagine. You must have heard him wrong."

"I did not hear him wrong. That is what he said."

Thorpe looked at her for a moment. He felt quite sure that the man had not grabbed her to tell her to leave the country. It was absurd. No doubt his intent had been to rape her; Alexandra was probably just too naïve to realize that. The thought made his blood boil. He thought with great satisfaction of what he would do to the man if he had him in his hands.

Frustrated, he snapped, "What the devil were you doing out there in the first place? Haven't you any sense?"

Stung, Alexandra retorted, "I was walking home. If you will remember, *you* left me at the ball."

"I told you to wait."

"I didn't feel like it. I was tired, and I didn't know anyone. The footman told me you had gone away in the carriage with the Countess, and I had no idea when you would be coming back—or even if you would."

"You think that I would simply abandon you there?"

"Well, you did."

"I was coming back. I wanted to see the Countess home, to make sure she was all right. I specifically told you to wait. If you had listened to me instead of charging off on your own, it wouldn't have happened."

"Oh!" Alexandra glared at him. "Now you are blaming *me* because some man decided to attack me?"

"I'm not blaming you. I am simply saying that it was foolish of you to walk home without an escort."

"May I remind you that I am perfectly able to take care of myself. I don't have to sit around kicking my heels, waiting for my escort to reappear and trundle me home like some piece of baggage."

"Able to take care of yourself?" He raised a scornful brow. "It hardly appears that way."

"What do you mean?" Alexandra clenched her hands, jutting her chin forward pugnaciously. "I did take care of myself. I kicked him and tore away from him and ran to the house. No one helped me but myself!"

"The point is that you wouldn't even have been attacked if you had not been walking alone. He probably thought you were—"

"Were what?" Alexandra's eyes flashed fire, and she set her hands on her hips.

"Easy prey," Thorpe said, tight-lipped. "And, blast it, you were."

"I think it's time for you to leave," Alexandra said coldly.

Thorpe started to speak, then stopped. "Yes. No doubt

you are right. I will take my leave of you." He turned and strode toward the door. He stopped as he reached it and turned. "I'll pick you up tomorrow afternoon," he said peremptorily. "I promised the Countess that I would bring you over then. She wants very much to meet you." He gave her a nod and added, "Good night. Make sure all your doors are locked."

Alexandra's jaw dropped. How dare he tell her where she was going and what she was doing tomorrow afternoon? She whirled and took out some of her frustration by kicking a stool across the room.

"Ow!" She hurt her toe and hopped over to the sofa, holding it. "Blast that man!"

Lord Thorpe, she decided, was the most arrogant, aggravating, high-handed man she had ever had the misfortune to meet. First he left her at the party, telling her to wait there, as if she were a dog or a servant. Then he had the nerve to tell her that she should not have left the party without him, that she had not heard what she had, and that it was her fault someone had attacked her because she had walked home alone. And he had finished it all off by telling her that he was taking her to the Countess's the next afternoon, as if she had nothing to say in the matter!

The awful thing, she had to admit to herself, was that despite all that, no matter his arrogance or his ordering her about, she was still all aquiver from those moments when they had kissed. His kisses had stirred her in ways she had never known before, and even now she felt hot and jittery—and if he walked in the door this instant, she would have to struggle to keep from running to him to kiss him again! How could a man infuriate her so much and at the same time make her want him so? Alexandra would not have thought it possible.

Her aunt bustled in. "Has he left?" Her eyes searched Alexandra's face carefully.

"Yes. Why are you looking at me like that?"

"Like what?"

"I don't know—as if you are searching for something."

"No. It's only...I've never seen you look at someone that way."

"What way?"

"The way you looked at Mr. Thorpe."

"Lord Thorpe."

"Of course. *Lord* Thorpe." Her aunt rolled her eyes. "These Englishmen and their infernal love of titles. As if that makes any difference to what the man is." She paused. "Alexandra, do you...have feelings for this man?"

"Feelings?" Alexandra could feel heat rising in her face, and she hoped the light was dim enough that her aunt could not see. "Don't be absurd. He's an egotistical, overbearing—" She made a noise of frustration, then said, "If I have any feeling for him, it is one of dislike."

"Oh."

"And don't give me that look. I am going to bed now," Alexandra went on grumpily.

"I think that's an excellent idea for all of us," her aunt agreed.

Alexandra stalked upstairs and got ready for bed, finally dismissing her maid, who kept chattering about the attack and asking Alexandra excited questions until she was ready to scream. She finished brushing her hair herself, which she preferred, anyway.

She didn't know when she had ever felt this strange, this jangled and puzzled and uncertain, even scared. Why had that man attacked her tonight? No matter what Thorpe said, she was certain he had told her to leave. Why would anyone threaten her like that? Why would anyone care whether she stayed or went home? It made the whole thing seem somehow much more frightening than if the man had been a common thief.

Adding to her mental turmoil were thoughts of Thorpe. She didn't understand her feelings for him, and she also didn't know how she could possibly get to sleep with this yearning still bubbling through her. And, finally, she could not get out of her head this evening's meeting with the Countess. She had thought about it ever since, her mind returning like a tongue to a sore tooth, and she was still no closer to an answer than she had been in the beginning. The Countess, whom she had never seen before in her life, had looked at her almost with horror. What had she thought? What had she felt? Alexandra could not see how the Countess's reaction could have anything to do with *her*.

And most unnerving of all, why had the Countess called her Simone?

A shiver ran through Alexandra. For the first time since she had been in London, she got up and turned the key in the lock of her door.

5

Alexandra woke the next morning feeling vastly better than she had when she went to bed. She got up, unlocked her door and retrieved the tray of tea and rolls that the maid had left there upon finding her door locked. Alexandra wondered what the girl had thought—no doubt that she was shivering in fear after her attack. Alexandra grimaced. She hated anyone to think that she was hiding in her room like a coward.

Last night, she told herself, had been an aberration. She was not going to live in fear just because some madman wanted her to leave England. It was absurd, and that was exactly the way she was going to treat the incident. She rang for her maid and got dressed, putting on her most attractive day dress. She had considered not going with Lord Thorpe to the Countess's, just to show him that he could not order her about. However, her curiosity had finally won out over her righteous indignation. Even if it meant that Thorpe would assume she was obeying him, Alexandra knew that she had to meet the Countess and find out what the woman had meant the night before when she called her by a strange name. She would have to teach

Lord Thorpe that she was an independent woman in some other manner.

As for the way she had felt about him last night, Alexandra resolved that the most easily. She had acted the way she had because she was in turmoil. She had been frightened and confused, as was only natural when one was attacked, and so she had clung to him. Her feelings had been all stirred up, and she had thought that it was because of him. But it was simply an aftermath of her scare. She could see that now, in the clear light of day.

So Alexandra was ready and waiting for Thorpe when he drove up to the house the next afternoon in a sporty curricle. Her aunt, of course, deplored the vehicle, saying it was ridiculous, but Alexandra was thrilled. She had seen several of them since she had been here, and she had wanted very much to ride in one. Shushing her aunt, she tied on her chip straw hat and sallied forth with Thorpe.

The Countess's house was smaller than the one she had visited the evening before, but very graceful in its lines and much warmer and more intimate. The butler showed them into a drawing room, an elegant room done in tones of blue, and said that he would inform her ladyship that they were here.

Alexandra looked around the room. When she walked in, she had thought it was empty, but as she turned toward the sofa, a middle-aged woman popped up from behind it. Her hair was brown, streaked with gray, and she was a trifle plump. She wore an unremarkable brown merino gown, and in her hand she held a skein of yarn.

"Excuse me, I was just—" She stopped in midsentence, staring at Alexandra, her mouth forming an *O*. "My goodness." One hand went to her heart. "Her ladyship said you were a likeness, but I never imagined—"

"I beg your pardon?" Alexandra said politely. Whatever was the matter with everyone? Obviously she must resemble someone, but why did the fact strike them all dumb?

"I'm sorry. You must forgive me. I'm so silly—I shouldn't really be here. I mean, be the first to talk to you. That is the Countess's place, of course. I am, well, I am only living here because the Countess is such a good, kind woman. Certainly I should not be taking her place in greeting you. You see, I remembered that I had dropped my yarn in here yesterday, and I thought I would simply slip in and retrieve it, but I hadn't expected anyone to come in. I mean, I knew you were expected, but—"

"It's perfectly all right, Miss Everhart," Thorpe broke in, stopping the woman's flow of words. "I am sure no one will think badly of you for fetching your yarn from the drawing room, least of all the Countess."

"Oh, yes." The woman beamed. "She's such a dear, good woman."

"Miss Everhart, allow me to introduce you to Alexandra Ward. Miss Ward, this is Willa Everhart, the Countess's cousin."

"Only second cousin," Miss Everhart added, ever deprecatory. From her words and manner, Alexandra deduced that she must be a poor relation, living with the Countess on her charity and acting as a companion to her. Alexandra thought that the Countess must be charitable indeed. Ten minutes of this woman's undiluted company would, she thought, drive her straight out of the room.

There was the sound of footsteps in the hallway, and an older woman's voice saying, "Really, Ursula, I do not need to lean on your arm. For pity's sake, I do not have one foot in the grave yet."

"No, Mother, of course not. But you shouldn't tax yourself so. After last night..."

The Countess came into the room. Slender and tall, with a regal carriage, she looked every inch a Countess— or even a Queen, Alexandra thought. Snow-white hair was coiled elegantly on her head. A strand of pearls glimmered at her throat, a lovely contrast to the tobacco-brown silk gown she wore. A huge diamond ring and a smaller ruby one winked on her fingers. Behind her came the squarely built Lady Ursula, accompanied by the plain girl who had been with them the night before. The plain girl, once again dressed in an unbecoming white gown, looked at Alexandra with interest from behind her spectacles. Lady Ursula frowned fiercely.

"Miss Ward. How kind of you to come." The Countess went to Alexandra, her hand outstretched. Alexandra took her hand, and the Countess held it for a moment, looking into Alexandra's face. The older woman's expression was sad, almost longing, and Alexandra thought she saw a shimmer of tears in her eyes. The Countess managed a tremulous smile and let go of Alexandra's hand with a squeeze.

"I am the Countess of Exmoor, Miss Ward."

"Exmoor?" *Wasn't that the name of the man she had met last night, the one whom both Nicola and Thorpe disliked?* "I'm sorry. I find these titles somewhat confusing. Are you related to the Earl of Exmoor?"

"He is a distant cousin," the Countess said coolly. "He inherited the title from my late husband."

"I see," Alexandra replied, although she did not really understand—except that this woman seemed to dislike the Earl as much as everyone else did.

"I see you have met my cousin, Miss Everhart," the Countess continued.

"Yes. She made me feel quite comfortable." Alexandra smiled at the woman, as did the Countess.

Miss Everhart launched into an apologetic ramble, which Lady Ursula soon brutally cut off. "Oh, for mercy's sake, Willa, do be quiet. No one begrudges you for being here, and you know it. Of course you're interested in seeing Miss Ward. We all are."

The Countess raised an eyebrow at her daughter. "My daughter, Lady Ursula," she told Alexandra. She turned toward the plain girl, smiling, "And this is her daughter, Miss Penelope Castlereigh."

Everyone made their polite hellos as they sat down. The butler brought in a tea tray, and some time was spent in the ritual of dispensing tea. The Countess, stirring her tea, smiled at Alexandra.

"Sebastian tells me you are visiting here from the United States, Miss Ward."

"Yes, we've been here for two weeks now."

"Ah, you are traveling with your family?"

"My mother and aunt."

"I wish you had brought them with you," the Countess said. "Sebastian, you should have told me. I would like to meet them."

"My mother doesn't get out much. She—England doesn't seem to agree with her."

"The damp, no doubt. Still, I should love to meet her. Perhaps some time when she is feeling well..."

"Of course," Alexandra answered politely.

The Countess smiled. "I am sure you must be wondering why I asked you to call on me today. I wanted to apologize for my behavior last night."

"There's no need for apology," Alexandra assured her quickly.

"You must have thought me very strange," the Countess went on wryly. "No, don't deny it. *I* would have thought my behavior very strange if I had witnessed it. I wanted to explain to you. And I—frankly I wanted to see you again. To make sure that my eyes had not deceived me."

"Mother, there is no need to go into all—"

"Ursula, please." The Countess's modulated voice hardened, and she shot her daughter a glance that shut up even that formidable woman. "I wish to explain it to Miss Ward." She turned to Alexandra. "You see, as you must have guessed, I thought you were someone else when I saw you last night. In the candlelight, you looked almost exactly like her. Even now, the resemblance is startling. Of course, it is impossible that you could be she. She would be Ursula's age now, not a young woman. But you looked so much as she did when I last saw her, over twenty years ago."

The Countess paused for a moment, then went on. "You resemble my daughter-in-law, my son's wife, Simone. She died twenty-two years ago. She and my son and their three children."

Alexandra drew in a quick breath. "Oh, my lady! I am so sorry."

"Thank you." The Countess sighed. "It was a terrible time. My son, Emerson, and his family had gone to visit Simone's parents. My husband grew ill and died while they were gone, and we sent for them, but then all that rioting broke out. I don't even know if they ever got the message. The mob killed them. It didn't matter to them that Emerson was English. They were staying with Simone's parents, obviously aristocrats."

A chill ran through Alexandra. "The mob, ma'am? Where were they?"

"They were in Paris when the revolution broke out. The mob stormed their home and dragged them all out and killed them. Even the children."

"Paris?" Alexandra repeated in a stifled voice. "But that's—"

"That's what, dear?"

"That is where I was born."

The Countess stiffened, one hand going to her throat. "You—you lived in Paris?"

Alexandra nodded. "Yes. My father was an American diplomat at the Court."

"When was that?" the Countess asked intently. "When were your parents in Paris?"

"At the time of the Revolution. I was born about a year and a half earlier. They left during the rioting and returned to the United States. That is, my mother did. Unfortunately, my father caught a fever and died on the passage over."

"I'm sorry." The Countess paused. She was paler than she had been, her eyes brighter. "Were you—could you be related to Simone's family? The de Viponts?"

"No. Both my parents were Americans. Rhea and Hiram Ward."

"This is so peculiar," the Countess murmured.

Thorpe frowned in concern and went to the Countess. He knelt beside her chair and took her hand in his. "Please, you mustn't get upset over this. I understand that the resemblance must be quite striking. But it's merely a strange coincidence. The fact that Alexandra was born in the same city where your son, Lord Chilton, and his family died doesn't mean that—"

Lady Ursula gasped.

"What!" The Countess went paper-white, and she stared at Thorpe. "What did you call her?" She swung on Alexandra. "What is your given name?"

"Alexandra." She looked at the older woman worriedly. "Please, my lady, don't upset yourself."

"But that is one of my grandchildren's names! John, Marie Anne and Alexandra. She was the baby."

There was a long moment of silence while all the occupants of the room stared at Alexandra and the Countess. Finally Lady Ursula broke the silence, saying in a crisp voice, "This is nonsense, Mother. It's utterly impossible. She could not be Chilton's child."

The Countess swung on her fiercely. "Don't you remember how Allie looked—those rosy cheeks and big brown eyes! That curly black hair! Her coloring was exactly like her mother's."

"My lady!" Alexandra exclaimed. Her stomach felt as if it had dropped to her feet. "Are you suggesting that *I* am your granddaughter?"

"You are the right age. You look like Simone. You were in Paris when they were."

"It's impossible," Lady Ursula said flatly, shooting Alexandra a dark look. "Thorpe, tell her. It's absolutely absurd."

"I don't see how she could be your granddaughter, my lady," Thorpe agreed, gazing worriedly at the older woman, whose cheeks were aflame with color. "They were all killed by the mob, weren't they? That's what I have always heard."

"They were," Lady Ursula agreed heartily.

"How do you know?" the Countess demanded. "We never received their remains—any of them!"

"Of course not. They burned the whole place down," Lady Ursula said with brutal frankness. "There weren't any remains. But several witnesses saw them killed. Bertram Chesterfield testified to it in court. Don't you remember?"

"Of course I remember. I'm not senile yet," her mother

snapped. "But I also know that Bertie Chesterfield is a fool."

"He may be a fool, but he's a gentleman. He wouldn't lie about such a thing."

"Perhaps not, but he could exaggerate. Or be mistaken. Or make a false assumption."

"Wait," Alexandra interjected. "I couldn't be your granddaughter, my lady. I don't see how it's possible. I am Hiram and Rhea Ward's daughter, their only child."

"That's right," Thorpe agreed. "How could Chilton's baby have wound up in America, the daughter of some other couple?"

"I don't know. But how could a young woman named Alexandra, like my grandchild, bear such an uncanny resemblance to my grandchild's mother *and* have been in the same place at the same time and it be mere coincidence?" the older woman countered. "I'm not in my dotage, Sebastian. I realize that it is exceptionally strange, and I do not understand it. But look at her!"

"I never saw Lady Chilton. I was only ten when it happened."

"Then come here." The Countess rose lithely to her feet. "You, too, Miss Ward. I want you to see this."

"Mother, don't excite yourself," Ursula pleaded.

Her mother ignored her and strode out of the room with a wave for them to follow her. Thorpe glanced at Alexandra with a shrug, and the two of them went after the Countess, with Ursula and her daughter and Miss Everhart trailing after them. The Countess led them up the stairs and down the hall, then opened the door to one of the bedrooms and stepped inside.

"There is a portrait of Chilton and his wife. It was done not long after their wedding. Look at her."

Obediently, Thorpe and Alexandra moved closer to the

portrait and looked at it. A strong-jawed young man wearing an old-fashioned white wig gazed solemnly at them. He was much taller than his wife, a petite woman who looked as if she knew an amusing secret. Her large dark eyes fairly sparkled, and her rosy mouth was curved up deliciously. Her hair was upswept into an intricate hairdo, all liberally powdered. Except for the powdered hair, she bore an uncanny resemblance to Alexandra.

"Good Lord!" Thorpe exclaimed.

A shiver ran down Alexandra's spine. It was unnerving to stare into a face that looked so much like her own reflection in the mirror. There were differences, of course. This woman was obviously shorter, and her cheeks were fuller, her mouth not quite the same shape, but the differences were slight and the likeness remarkable.

"You see?" the Countess said triumphantly. "And the hair beneath the powder is both black and curling."

"Yes, she looks like her," Lady Ursula snapped. "I saw it immediately myself. But such things happen."

"Do they?" the Countess asked quietly. "I have never seen such a likeness except within family." On that note, she turned and walked from the room, leaving the others to look at each other, then follow her.

Alexandra took one last long look at the portrait, then tore her eyes away and went after the others. By the time she and Thorpe, who had waited for her, caught up with the others, they were in the drawing room and Lady Ursula was arguing furiously with her mother, who was serenely ignoring her.

"Tell her, Thorpe," Lady Ursula commanded, swinging around when he entered the room. "Tell her that it's ridiculous."

"It is not ridiculous," the Countess replied coolly. "Alexandra could have gotten away. She was a mere toddler. She could have run away without anyone ever noticing. Or perhaps one of the rioters took pity on such a little girl and let her go, even took her with them. Bertie Chesterfield never said he *saw* the children killed.''

''I suppose it is possible,'' Thorpe agreed, watching the Countess's flushed face with some concern. ''But don't you think that you would have heard something by now if that had happened?''

''Not if she just ran away—who would have known who she was or where she belonged?''

''But how did she get to America?'' Lady Ursula asked triumphantly.

''I don't know. It isn't as if I have all the answers,'' her mother answered somewhat testily. She turned toward Alexandra eagerly. ''Perhaps your mother knows.''

Alexandra shifted uneasily. She couldn't tell these people that she had trouble getting straight answers about anything from her mother. ''I can ask. But, my lady, it doesn't seem possible. I mean, I know who my parents are, and they aren't your son and daughter-in-law.''

''Sometimes,'' the Countess began carefully, ''families keep secrets.''

''I think I know an easy way to clear this up,'' Thorpe suggested. ''Alexandra, when is your birthday? How old were you when the revolution took place?''

''I was born January twentieth, 1787. So I must have been about a year and a half old during that summer.''

''There! You see?'' Lady Ursula exclaimed triumphantly. ''Very clever, Thorpe. Chilton's daughter would have been two years old at the time. She was born in the summer of eighty-six.''

''June eighteenth,'' the Countess murmured a little sadly. She looked at Alexandra. ''I'm sorry. I suppose there is no way it could be you, could it?'' However, the look on the Countess's face told Alexandra that she still wasn't entirely convinced.

Alexandra still felt uneasy. It *was* odd that she looked so much like this Simone and that she had been in Paris at the same time and was close to the age of the Countess's granddaughter.

"I'm afraid there isn't," Alexandra said. She went to the Countess and took the woman's hand in hers. "I'm very sorry. I think it would be lovely to be your granddaughter, but I don't see how it is possible. I—I hope you will allow me to be your friend, though."

The Countess smiled and patted her hand. "Very prettily said, child. Yes, we will indeed be friends."

"Mother, I think it's time you rested, don't you?" Lady Ursula said, giving Alexandra a glare. "Thorpe will take Miss Ward home."

"Yes, I do believe I would like to take a little nap." The Countess, who had been so full of energy a few minutes before, sounded weary. She gave Alexandra a small smile. "Please excuse me. I find that age makes boring companions of us." She held out her hand. "Thank you, my dear, for indulging an old woman's fantasy and coming to see me. I do hope you will call on me again soon. We will talk about America or something else that is more normal."

"Of course, my lady. I was very happy to meet you."

The Countess started toward the door, and her companion, the self-effacing Miss Everhart, jumped up and hurried over to give the older woman the support of her arm as she walked out the door. Lady Ursula turned toward Alexandra.

"Thank you for coming, Miss Ward," she said in the tone of one dismissing a servant or tradesman. "My mother sometimes takes odd fancies, but, as you see, she realizes how unlikely they are soon enough. One cannot fool her long, and she has family to make sure that no one takes advantage of her."

Her words sounded vaguely like a threat, Alexandra thought, though she wasn't sure what the woman could be threatening her about. Lady Ursula explained herself no further, just swung around and marched out the door, leaving Alexandra looking after her in surprise.

"Ah, Lady Ursula—ever the diplomat," Thorpe commented dryly.

"Oh, Miss Ward, I'm so sorry." Lady Ursula's daughter rose from her seat and came over to Alexandra. Alexandra had completely forgotten about the girl's presence until then, so much did she girl fade into the background. "My mother can be quite rude sometimes. She doesn't even realize it, I'm afraid. Please forgive her. It is just that she worries about Grandmother."

"Of course." Alexandra did not think it was worry over the Countess that made the woman rude and brusque, but she would not add to this obviously domineered girl's burden by criticizing her mother. "It is only natural that she should be concerned about her mother." She smiled at the girl, who answered with a shy smile. "I do hope that you and I may be friends, too."

"I would like that very much!" Penelope answered, her face lighting up. "I didn't get to meet you last night, but Nicola told me you were ever so nice. If it's all right with you, Nicola and I would like to call on you while you're in London."

"That sounds lovely." They discussed where her leased house was and chatted politely for a few more minutes before Thorpe and Alexandra took their leave.

"Nice girl," Thorpe commented as they went down the steps. "Penelope, I mean. Her mother's a tyrant. I don't know how the poor girl survives. At least Artie was a boy and could set up his own establishment. Penelope's stuck with her—for life, I fear. Lady Ursula isn't bad in her intentions. She simply cannot keep from running everyone's lives for them.''

"Poor girl." Alexandra took his hand and climbed onto the high seat of the curricle.

Thorpe went around and climbed up on the other side. He took the reins from the servant who had been walking the horses, tossed the lad a coin and slapped the reins. "I hope you weren't upset by all that."

"What the Countess said? No... Well, I must admit it was eerie looking into that woman's face in the painting. She did look a great deal like me, didn't she?"

"It *was* rather uncanny," Thorpe admitted. "I could understand why the Countess fainted when she saw you last night. She's never really gotten over the loss of her son and his family, you know. It's been twenty some-odd years, and she never talks about them, but there's always been something a little sad in her eyes."

"I feel sorry for her. It must have been awful. I wish I could have said something to help her. I can see how she would want to believe that one of her grandchildren was still alive. But it couldn't be me!" she added almost defiantly.

"No doubt there is some explanation. Why, you could be a distant relative of the de Viponts. That would be possible—that some member of the family moved to the United States."

"I suppose," Alexandra agreed a little doubtfully. "I've never heard any mention of them—or, indeed, of any Frenchmen, in our family tree."

"More likely, though, than that you're the Countess's dead granddaughter."

"Yes, that's true." Alexandra was consumed with a desire to get home and talk to her mother. Rhea was the only one who could shed any light on this. She could tell her the details of her birth, where and when and what the midwife said and—oh, all the things that made something reality. Her mother could convince her there was no possibility Alexandra could be anything but her very own beloved daughter—for that was the thing that set up the awful, cold feeling in her stomach. If by some wild happenstance the Countess was right and Alexandra was somehow her granddaughter, escaped from the ruin of the rest of her family, then that meant her mother was not really her mother. That her whole existence was based on a lie!

"It couldn't be true," she said, more to herself than to her companion. "It just couldn't."

"Of course not," Thorpe agreed soothingly.

He pulled the curricle up in front of her house and helped her down. The lad at the end of the street, who earned his pennies sweeping the crossing for the fine ladies and gentlemen to walk on, abandoned his job and came running, eager to hold Thorpe's horses' heads as he had earlier this afternoon. Thorpe waited for him to hand over the reins, but Alexandra started up the steps without him.

She could see that something brown lay on the stoop at the top of the steps, but she could not make out what it was. Curious, she moved closer. Then she saw it clearly, and a little shriek escaped her before she clapped her gloved hand over her mouth.

A very large, very dead rat lay across her doorstep!

6

"Alexandra!" Thorpe was beside her on the porch in an instant. His eyes, at first on her, went to the doorstep, and he saw the animal. "Good God! What the devil is that doing here?"

Alexandra shook her head. "I have no idea. Ugh." She gave a shudder.

"Your dog or cat brought you a present?" he guessed.

"We have no dog or cat. Not with us."

"The housekeeper might have one—nearly any kitchen has a cat for mousing."

"Perhaps. I'm not sure. But it would take a monstrously big cat to bring this thing here."

"True." His hopes of fobbing her off with a pleasant lie died.

"A person brought it."

"It would seem so," Thorpe agreed reluctantly. He reached across and hammered on the door.

A moment later a footman opened the door. He looked surprised to see Alexandra knocking at her own door, but then his gaze flickered to the animal on the steps, and he gave a sharp gasp.

"Blimey! Oh, 'scuse me, miss. I mean, uh..." He looked in fascinated horror at the corpse.

"I assume that you have not seen this before?" Thorpe asked.

"Cor! No, sir, not likely!" He struggled to regain his usual dignified demeanor. "I beg your pardon, my lord. I cannot imagine how this came to be here."

"Get the butler; I want to ask him a few questions. And get rid of that carcass right away."

"Let's go in by the servants' entrance," Alexandra suggested. "It'll be quicker than waiting for them to clean this. And I am *not* stepping over that thing. We can question the servants there."

"Of course." Thorpe wondered why it had even occurred to him that Alexandra would hand over the task of investigating this incident to him, as any other woman would. He followed her around the corner of the house and along the narrow passageway to the servants' entrance.

He did manage to get there before Alexandra and open the door for her. She nodded her thanks and swept inside. Everyone in the kitchen stopped and turned to look at them in astonishment. Thorpe wondered if any of the former occupants of the house had ever casually walked in the servants' entrance.

"I need to speak to all of you," Alexandra began crisply. Thorpe knew that if he had not heard her shriek with his own ears a few minutes earlier, he would not have thought she had been at all discomposed.

The servants lined up before her, rather like troops about to be inspected. Thorpe watched them for any flicker of expression that might show that one of them already knew about the dead rat on the doorstep. After all, the person who would have easiest and most unnoticed access to the stoop would be someone who worked here.

"There is a dead rat on the front doorstep," Alexandra began without preamble.

Everyone stared at her in astonishment.

"What, miss?" the butler asked, unsure he had heard correctly.

"I found a dead rat on the stoop when Lord Thorpe and I returned home just now." All eyes swung to Thorpe, as if for confirmation. He nodded, and the group turned to Alexandra.

"What I want to know is whether one of you put it there," Alexandra went on.

So she had already figured that out, too, Thorpe thought admiringly. Of course, it would be just like Alexandra to look at a problem head-on, with no attempt to make anything seem better or nicer.

"Miss Ward!" The butler appeared genuinely shocked, as did most of the servants. None of them looked in the slightest guilty or as if the news was not new to them. "None of us would think of such a thing!" He swung around to look at each and every member of the staff with his piercing gaze. They immediately fell into a chorus of noes, accompanied by a multitude of accounts of their whereabouts the entire afternoon.

"Did any of you see or hear anything suspicious?" Alexandra asked, cutting into their babble.

The answer, once again, appeared to be a universal, emphatic no.

"You needn't have seen someone putting the rat there," Thorpe added, glancing from one to another. "It could have been something like seeing someone on the street this afternoon who looked as if he didn't belong or someone in a hurry."

They appeared to take a second to think, but once again, they shook their heads in the negative.

Alexandra and Thorpe gave up and left the kitchen. Behind them, a buzz of noise broke out among the servants.

Alexandra sighed as they walked along the hall and into the formal drawing room. "Adding another bit of gossip to their lore about the mad American."

Thorpe smiled. "I doubt they think you're mad."

No, it was her mother they thought mad. But she could not say that to him.

"Near enough," was all she replied. "They think I am decidedly unusual to begin with. Then last night I came running home screaming, and today I find a dead rat on the doorsill."

"Probably not the typical events of this household," he agreed.

Alexandra cast him a look. "You probably think I am equally strange. Worse than strange—Countesses faint at the sight of me."

Thorpe chuckled. "Being with you is never dull, I must admit."

He looked at her, admiring the way she did not break down, did not cry, but straightforwardly faced the problem and sought to find out what had happened. There were some, he knew, who would find her coolheadedness quite unfeminine, but Thorpe found the contrast of her no-nonsense demeanor with her lush figure and beautiful face appealing—indeed, downright erotic. It made a man long to find out exactly what it would take to shake her composure.

"I can assure you that my life is usually much duller than this," Alexandra told him. "I've never had such things happen to me before. It is only since I came to England. Indeed, it is only since I met you.''

His eyebrows rose lazily. "Are you saying that I am to blame?''

Alexandra laughed. "No. All I am saying is that it is the last two days. Since I've mingled in London Society.''

Thorpe stared at her. "Are you suggesting that someone from the Duchess's party is doing these things to you?''

Alexandra hesitated. "I'm not sure what I'm saying. It sounds absurd. It *is* absurd, I'm sure. It is just—well, they seem to have fallen one upon another. Someone wants me to leave England. But I cannot think why—other than Lady Ursula, of course," she added dryly.

Thorpe let out a bark of laughter. "Somehow I think we can acquit Ursula of sneaking around leaving dead rats at your door. Or attacking you. After all, I was with her last night when that happened. And we were with her this afternoon, as well. Of course, I guess she could have spurred on the Honorable Augustus to do it, like Lady Macbeth."

Alexandra had to giggle at the idea of the Lady Ursula's portly, blank-faced husband committing either crime. "No, you're right. I think we have to acquit them both. I suppose it could be one of the servants. Some of them resent me. On the other hand, if I were to leave, they would lose their jobs—and they could simply quit, after all, if they dislike me enough to be willing to lose their income."

"We don't know that the attack last night and this afternoon's present are related."

Alexandra cast him a disbelieving look. "More coincidence? I think it highly unlikely. My attacker told me to leave last night, and now he is giving me a reminder."

She set her jaw. "He obviously doesn't know me if he thinks a rat on my doorstep will make me turn tail and run. I confess, I'm growing more and more curious by the moment. I may stay here even longer now."

"No doubt you would."

Alexandra cocked one eyebrow at him. "You would prefer that I left?"

"No." He smiled. "I would not prefer that at all." Heat flooded him as he thought of exactly how much he wanted her to stay. Any other woman he knew would have been in tears, leaning on him and asking him to solve her problem. The fact that she was not somehow made her all the more desirable to him. It also, perversely, made him want to help her. "But I do want you to take precautions."

"I will. All the doors and windows are locked at night. And I think that, after today, I may just keep a footman posted outside."

"I'll send you my valet."

"Why? What would I do with your valet?"

"He's not your ordinary sort of valet," Thorpe assured her. "He was an officer's batman earlier in his life. That's the only reason he has any qualifications as a valet. I hired him in India after he had been cashiered out."

"Cashiered! That hardly sounds like a recommendation."

"He was insubordinate to an officer, which does not lower him in my opinion. Many of the officers I met in India were idiots. He's completely loyal to me and a very good fighter. He and Punwati helped me in some tight situations in India. Perhaps you would rather have Punwati. He is a trifle smoother than Murdock."

"I need neither of them," Alexandra said firmly. "My aunt and I are quite capable of handling the situation.

Once they see that I cannot be frightened off, whoever they are, I imagine that they will cease this nonsense. In the meantime, nothing serious has occurred. Just a few annoying things.''

"I would say that your being attacked goes beyond annoying."

"I wasn't hurt—not really."

"Who knows what might have happened if you had not been able to escape him."

"But I was. That's what I mean—I can take care of myself. I don't need your valet trailing about after me and frightening all the servants."

"You've heard about Murdock?"

"Well, Mr. Jones did tell me that he was a trifle unusual."

He let out a short bark of laughter. "He looks as if he's been in a few fights. Not a bad sort of way to look when someone is after you."

"Still, it's quite unnecessary. I wouldn't dream of taking your valet from you."

Thorpe grimaced. "You are an exasperating female. I presume you've been told that."

"A few times." Alexandra smiled.

"Why are you so stubborn?"

"I'm not stubborn. I simply don't want or need your valet to protect me."

"It's a very little thing. Why are you so set against him?"

"Because I am an independent woman. I like to take care of things myself instead of depending on someone else. I am in charge of this household, and I don't want someone working in it who is working for someone else, not me," Alexandra told him lightly.

He looked at her in offended astonishment. "You think that I would have him do anything against you?"

"I certainly hope not. However, I do not think it is a good policy to have employees who are loyal to someone else."

She wasn't about to tell him that she had another reason—she did not want one of his servants in the house, listening to all the stories of her servants and reporting to Thorpe that Alexandra's mother was mad. Rhea wasn't mad, only a trifle...odd. She chose not to examine why it seemed so important that Thorpe not think badly of Rhea.

Thorpe glowered at her, and Alexandra gazed back imperturbably. He was surprised at the little stab of pain her words had brought. She didn't trust him! He thought that it would give him a distinct sense of pleasure to grab her by the shoulders and shake her until she agreed to his plan. Another part of him wanted equally to grab her and kiss that faintly smug look off her face.

Finally he gave in to the latter emotion, grasping her shoulders and jerking her to him for a quick, hard kiss. He was gratified to see that, when he released her, her eyes were darker and faintly dazed.

"If one more suspicious thing happens, I am going to put Murdock here to guard your house, even if he has to loiter about in the street to do it. Is that clear?"

"Abundantly." Alexandra's tongue stole out to touch her upper lip. "Is that always the way you make your point?"

His eyes went to her mouth, and heat rippled through him. "Only if I have to."

He leaned down and kissed her again, this time more slowly and thoroughly. Memories of the night before flooded his brain, and his skin flamed. He wanted to go on kissing her until neither of them could stop, but finally, reluctantly, he pulled away. "I must leave now."

Much as he wanted to stay, there were things Thorpe had to do. His valet, Murdock, had quite a few connections with certain criminal elements here in London—Thorpe had always found it wiser not to enquire too closely into the hows and whys of those connections—and Thorpe was going to set him to nosing out whatever he could about anyone attacking a beautiful American woman. Alexandra might refuse to let him provide a guard for her, but that didn't mean he wasn't going to protect her some other way. Alexandra would find out that he could be every bit as stubborn as she was.

After Thorpe left, Alexandra made her way upstairs to her mother's room. She had not wanted Thorpe to leave—However much she might insist on handling things herself, she could not deny that the events of the past two days had left her shaken, and that Thorpe's presence had made it all seem not quite so bad. However, she certainly could not ask him to stay when she had just been telling him how capable she was of taking care of things.

Besides, whenever she was around the man, she felt confused and uncertain, emotions she was not accustomed to experiencing. She had made up her mind that the passion she had felt for him last night had been a fluke, something caused by her state of nerves. But when he had kissed her this afternoon, she had felt the same welling of desire, the same rush of fire through her veins and pulsing heat in her loins. Alexandra was not used to such feelings, and they unsettled her. Even more confusing was the fact that she had such conflicting emotions about the man, irritated one moment and pulsing with desire the next. It was better that she have some time alone to collect herself and decide how she felt and what she wanted.

Right now, she knew, she had to talk to her mother. Her visit with the Countess had left her troubled and uncertain, and her mother was the only person who could help her. She sighed, thinking that her mother was rather a weak reed upon which to rely, but she pushed such thoughts away and, summoning a cheerful smile, she knocked on Rhea's door and went in.

"Ah, Miss Alexandra." Nancy looked up from the sewing in her lap and smiled. "I was just about to go down and fetch your mother a cup of cocoa."

There had been an unspoken conspiracy among the three of them, Aunt Hortense, Alexandra and Nancy, not to leave Rhea alone since the incident with the teapot. Nancy got up, put her sewing aside, and left the room.

Rhea leaned toward her daughter and whispered, "Thank heavens, she's gone. I can't think what is the matter with Nancy. She has scarcely left this room all day. I practically had to kick her out of the room when I wanted to take a nap. I think the servants frighten her."

"They do?"

Rhea nodded. "They are different, you know. Sometimes I find myself quite exasperated with them. I can hardly blame Nan for disliking them. Well, it was only a few years ago that we were at war with them, wasn't it?"

Alexandra would not have considered the almost thirty years that had elapsed since the Revolutionary War only a few years, but she wasn't going to quibble about a thing like that.

"That's true," she agreed. "Still, I suppose they are more like us than any other country. I mean, the same language and all. The same stock." She paused, then added, "Not like the French, say."

Her mother looked up sharply. "The French? What are you talking about?"

"I was just saying that the French are more foreign. Don't you think? Different language, different customs."

"Yes." Rhea regarded her a trifle warily, Alexandra thought.

"You have never talked much about the time you and Father spent in France. When he was working with the Ambassador."

Rhea blinked. "I...well, there was little to talk about."

"What was it like? Paris, I mean. Everyone says it is beautiful."

"I—I suppose so." Rhea looked away, rubbing her forehead. "I don't like to talk about it."

"Talk about what?"

"That time. Paris."

"But it interests me. After all, I was born there." Her mother glanced at her, then away. She said nothing, and Alexandra prodded. "Wasn't I?"

"What? Yes, of course. Why are you asking such silly questions?" Rhea reached into the capacious pocket of her skirt, and Alexandra could see her hand through the material, rubbing something in a circular motion.

That silly box, Alexandra thought in irritation. What was in there that her mother was so attached to?

"Mother..." Alexandra leaned forward, looking into her mother's face earnestly. "Would you tell me about when I was born?"

"What?" Rhea's agitation increased. She glanced all around the room, everywhere but at Alexandra's face. "What an odd question."

"It was in Paris, wasn't it?"

"Yes, of course."

"Where?"

"Where? Well, at our house."

"Did you have a midwife?"

"Yes. This is a very peculiar conversation."

"Not so odd. I would think most people would want to know something about their origins. What was the midwife's name?"

"Name? I don't know. How can I remember something that long ago?"

"What was she like?"

"Why are you questioning me like this!" Rhea bounded to her feet and walked away from Alexandra, going to the window and looking out. Despite the warmth of the summer day, she huddled into her arms as if she were cold.

"I just want to know, Mother, it's important." She paused, then asked in a quiet voice, "How old was I when the rioting started?"

Rhea whirled and looked at her sharply. "How old were you! What does that matter?"

"It just does. Surely you must know."

"Of course I do. You were a toddler. You were always running everywhere—I had the worst time keeping up with you. I was so afraid when that gang of hoodlums stopped our carriage on the road to Calais. I was afraid you would slip out and go exploring, like you had that morning at the inn. That big, rough man that opened the door and peered inside—" Rhea shuddered, her face scrunching with remembered fear. "And Hiram was already ill. And the—"

She stopped suddenly and turned her face toward the window.

"And the what, Mother?"

"Nothing," Rhea said brusquely. "It was terrible. Your poor father was so sick, I was afraid you would catch it, too, and then I would lose everything." Tears welled in her mother's eyes. "But you were so good in the inn in Southhampton, when I was half out of my mind with worry over Hiram. You would sit beside me, good as gold. You didn't run about a bit. And you would pat my hand—just as though you knew how sad and scared I was."

Tears flowed from her mother's eyes, and she put up a shaky hand to her face. "Please, Alexandra, don't ask me any more. I don't want to talk about it."

"I'm sorry, Mother." Alexandra rose and went to her, her chest contracting in sympathy at her mother's pain. She felt like a selfish monster for having disturbed her. "I shouldn't have asked. I didn't mean to upset you."

She put her arms around the older woman, and Rhea leaned against her for a moment, murmuring, "My baby. It'll be all right."

"Of course. It will be all right."

Rhea pulled away and went to her bed. "I believe I'll lie down now. Tell Nan I don't want the cocoa. I'll just lie here until supper."

"All right. Mother, I'm sorry...."

Rhea nodded, curling up on the bed and wrapping her shawl around her. She closed her eyes. With a sigh, Alexandra sat and waited for Nancy to return. Her mother had not soothed away any of her uneasiness. Indeed, her evasive answers only troubled Alexandra more. It wasn't surprising, she supposed, that memories of the revolution bothered Rhea; she had been afraid for their lives, and her beloved husband had succumbed to a fever on the frantic trip from Paris. But that did not explain why she was so reluctant to talk about Alexandra's birth a year and a half before that. Surely that would have been a joyous occasion, one she would have remembered with love. After all, she had been a doting mother when Alexandra was little. Alexandra could remember Rhea telling her how much she loved her, how perfect she was, how long she and her father had waited before they had a child, hoping for a beautiful daughter like Alexandra. How could Rhea have forgotten the name of the midwife or what she had looked like? Why would she dismiss the event as if it had been unimportant?

Alexandra wandered into her room and went to her dresser, where a small double frame stood. In it were two pen-and-ink sketches of her parents, done during the time when they were in Paris. The small folding frame had been one of the few things her mother had grabbed and stuffed into their suitcases when they fled the riots. Her father looked sternly from one side, his head covered by a formal white wig. He had a long, thin, ascetic face, nothing like hers. She could not tell his eye color nor his hair color from the drawing, but Aunt Hortense had told her that Hiram's coloring was much like Aunt Hortense's—light brown hair and hazel eyes. His stature, too, had been much like Aunt Hortense's, short and square. Her mother was short, as well, though softly rounded rather than square. Her hair in the picture was powdered, and it was now quite gray. What color had it been when she was young? Had it been dark like Alexandra's?

It was odd, surely, that she resembled neither of her parents. Alexandra searched the portraits, looking for some similarity in chin or mouth or nose. Of course, she reminded herself, some people did not look like their parents. There was Elizabeth Harmon, for example, whose plain face was an anomaly among her attractive parents and siblings. But it was said Elizabeth was the spitting image of her father's sister Abigail. Perhaps, Alexandra reasoned, she looked like some other member of her family, though she could think of no one on either side who was tall and dark-haired. But she had no idea what her grandparents had looked like when they were young. And her mother had had a brother who had died when he was a child and a sister who had died in childbirth before Alexandra was born. Perhaps they had been cut from the same cloth as she.

She whirled and hurried out of her room, going first to her aunt's bedroom, then to the informal sitting room on the second floor. There she found Aunt Hortense sitting, working on the needlepoint she was sewing for seat cushions back home. Aunt Hortense looked up and smiled.

"Hello, dear, did you have a nice outing?"

"I met a nice woman, but she is troubled."

"That's too bad. What—"

"Aunt Hortense," Alexandra interrupted, not even aware that she was rude, so wrapped up was she in her worry. "What was my mother's hair color when she was young?"

Aunt Hortense stared at her. "Your mother's hair? What an odd question. It was brown."

"What sort of brown? Very dark like mine?"

"Oh, no, dear. Much lighter."

"So was Father's, wasn't it?"

"Yes." Aunt Hortense stuck her needle into the piece of cloth stretched across her frame and set it aside. "Something's troubling you. What is it?"

"Is there anyone in my family who looks like me?" Alexandra asked almost desperately.

Her aunt's brows rose, but she considered the question thoughtfully. "My aunt Rosemary was a very pretty woman, too," she said at last. "She was blond, though, and had blue eyes. But your features are like hers."

"In what way?"

"Well, uh, she was—she had large eyes and a slender, straight nose like you."

"That seems very little."

"What is the matter with you, child? Why are you asking me such odd questions?"

"Because it seems odd to me that there is no one among all my relatives who looks the slightest thing like me. Yet I saw the portrait today of a complete stranger who could have been my twin!"

Aunt Hortense stared. "What *are* you talking about?"

She explained about the Countess and how she had fainted when she met Alexandra the evening before, and how Thorpe had taken her to see the Countess. "She showed me a portrait of her daughter-in-law painted years and years ago, and she looked almost exactly like me!"

Aunt Hortense's eye widened. "But who—how..."

"Everyone says it's just coincidence. At least, that is what Thorpe and the Countess's daughter and I said. Only the Countess stubbornly held out the hope that I—"

"That you what? I don't understand."

"She thought I might be her granddaughter, whom she has thought dead for twenty-two years."

Her aunt blinked. "But that's absurd! How could you be related to some Countess in England?"

"I don't know! Neither does anyone else. The Countess theorized that her granddaughter could have escaped the mob, being so little at the time, or that some kind soul took pity on her and helped her escape."

"Escaped what mob?"

"In Paris, during the revolution. The same mob that Mother was so frightened of."

"Paris!" Aunt Hortense looked astounded.

"Yes. The Countess's son and his family were killed

by the revolutionaries in Paris. Their baby was named Alexandra.''

''Alexandra! What are you suggesting?'' Aunt Hortense's words were indignant, but there was an odd quality to her voice.

''I'm not sure. I only know that I look like a Frenchwoman who died twenty-two years ago.'' Alexandra began to pace the room, too agitated to sit down. ''Did Mother ever tell you any of the details of my birth? How much I weighed or how long I was or the name of the midwife who attended her? I asked her tonight, and she claimed she couldn't remember.''

''It has been a long time.''

''But it hadn't been a long time when she returned home from Paris. Did she tell you about any of it then?''

''Some things. She talked about how frightened she was and about how much you had helped her get through the ordeal. She talked about Hiram's passing, and how sad and lonely she had been.''

''But nothing about the birth itself.''

''You must remember, Alexandra.'' Her aunt blushed, amazing Alexandra. ''I never married. Your mother probably thought she needed to spare my sensibilities. There are some things married women simply do not discuss with spinsters.''

Alexandra knew that that was true. She had had enough experiences where, just when someone was about to get to the most interesting part of their story, one woman or the other would glance at her and say, ''No, you mustn't say that in front of Alexandra. She's not married, you know.''

Her aunt hesitated. ''There was one thing, though....''

''What?'' Alexandra turned on her eagerly.

Aunt Hortense sighed, holding back for a moment, then

went on. "Well, it always seemed odd that Rhea never sent home word about you. One day we got a letter from her, from England, saying she was sailing home, that Hiram had died of a fever, and she was returning with their baby. That was the first she ever wrote us about you."

Alexandra looked at her, dumbstruck. Finally she recovered her voice enough to ask, "Ever? She did not write you the news when I was born?"

Aunt Hortense shrugged. "I never received it. She said she sent me a letter at the time and that the mails must have lost it. Obviously, that can happen. But the odd thing is that even if that one letter had been lost, why wouldn't she have mentioned you in other letters? Baby's got two new teeth this week. That sort of thing. It seemed decidedly peculiar, considering the fact that she and Hiram had wanted a baby for so long and had never been able to have one. I would have thought that when she finally did conceive—ten years after they were married—she would have been so proud she was about to burst. She would have written us all your virtues." The words seemed to rush out of her aunt's mouth, as if she held them back all these years, and now, once the dam was broken, she could not stem the flood.

"Perhaps I had too few to mention," Alexandra teased.

"Not likely. Rhea had wanted that baby for so long, so hard. When she came home, that was all she talked about, Alexandra this and Alexandra that, until, if you hadn't been such a beautiful angel, I would have wanted to scream at her to shut up." She smiled, belying her words, then looked away. She bit her lip, then added, "Sometimes I wondered—I thought that there must have been something wrong."

"Like what? What did you think?"

Aunt Hortense glanced at her, embarrassed. At first Alexandra thought she would not answer, but at last she said, "I wondered if perhaps you were not Hiram's child, if you were a—a love child that she had conceived with another man. She loved Hiram—I know she did. But she wanted a child so badly I could imagine, if it was Hiram's fault they couldn't, that Rhea would have had an affair with someone else so that she could get with child. Or even that Hiram had perhaps had an affair. Men do, you know. And Rhea, wanting a child so badly, might have been willing to raise it as her own if he asked her to. But then I would reject the idea as soon as I thought of it. My brother would not have participated in a deception. He was always honest and straightforward."

"But he was dead by the time she came home," Alexandra pointed out. "So he wouldn't have been participating in it. Perhaps he would not have claimed the child as theirs."

"That's true." Aunt Hortense took her niece's hands and looked into her eyes. "I am sorry. You must remember that I don't know any of this. It is just something that I wondered about from time to time. I have no way of knowing. I could not tell you my speculations. Besides, what good would it accomplish? Rhea loved you, she was a good mother to you. Why cast doubt when there might not be any reason to doubt? Only my silly suspicions."

Alexandra sat back, aware of a curious sense of relief. Her aunt's guesses made sense. She supposed she should have been horrified at the thought that either her father or mother might have had an affair, that she might not be one or the other's daughter. But after the strange conversation with the Countess this afternoon, such an explanation seemed almost pleasant. It also made more sense than the idea that a two-year-old child had escaped the

mayhem that had killed the rest of her family and somehow wound up with Rhea Ward. It would explain her
mother's secrecy and deception. If her mother had happened on a little lost girl, orphaned by the revolution, she
could have openly said what happened and adopted her.
But if the child was a by-blow of her husband's or the
product of her own illicit affair, she could hardly have
admitted it. The strange resemblance to the Countess's
granddaughter could be because the man or woman in
question had been some relative of Simone's.

"Are you all right?" Aunt Hortense went to Alexandra
and took her hand. "Have I upset you? I don't know any
of it to be true. It is only guesswork. It may be that I am
a suspicious old biddy, and there was nothing odd about
your birth whatsoever. Whatever the truth, it makes no
difference—you are still my niece, and I love you
dearly."

"You are very kind. I love you, too. I don't think I am
upset...at least, not very upset. This whole day has been
so odd, I scarcely know what I think."

"Perhaps you ought to have a little lie down before
supper," Aunt Hortense suggested. "Put some lavender
on your temples and rest. Then you'll feel just the thing,
I'm sure."

"Perhaps you're right." Alexandra had to agree that
she was a trifle tired.

She allowed her aunt to shuffle her off to her bedroom
and put her to bed, then close all the curtains so that the
room was soothingly dark. Alexandra did not really intend
to sleep, but she thought that it would be restful to close
her eyes and drift for a few minutes. She did not realize
that she had fallen asleep until an hour later, when a loud
screech brought her fully awake. She sat bolt upright and
scrambled off the bed. Her first thought was that some-

thing had happened to her mother, and it was toward her room that she ran. The sound of a maid's frantic voice confirmed her fear.

Alexandra burst into her mother's bedroom. One of the maids was kneeling on the floor beside a prone body. Icy fear stabbed Alexandra before she realized that the brown head was not her mother's gray one.

"What happened?" she asked, hurrying forward and dropping down beside the girl.

The woman on the floor was Nancy. There was blood matting her hair. Alexandra drew a sharp breath and leaned closer. Good. At least she was breathing. She turned to the girl beside her and asked again, more sharply, "What happened here?"

"I don't know, miss!" The girl looked terrified. "I just came in to dust, and I found her like that. I let out a scream, it scared me that bad."

"I can imagine. Well, obviously something hit her on the head." Alexandra could hear steps pounding down the hall. No doubt Aunt Hortense and the other servants were running toward the scream, as well. She glanced around the room. "Where is my mother?" Panic began to rise in her. "Where is she?"

"I don't know, miss. She's gone."

"She can't just be gone," Alexandra snapped.

"I don't know, miss. But maybe she, well, ran away. I mean…" She looked at the still figure of Mrs. Ward's companion. "I reckon Mrs. Ward's the one who hit her, and now she's run away."

7

A few servants came running into the room, having heard the maid's screams. Alexandra sent them in search of her mother, then she had two footmen pick Nancy up and lay her on the bed so that she and Aunt Hortense could tend to her. The servants soon reported that they could find no trace of Rhea in the house or around it.

"Where could she have gone?" Alexandra asked, worried. "Why would she have left?"

Aunt Hortense, busy washing the blood from Nancy's head, did not answer. When she washed the blood away, they saw with relief that the wound was not as serious as it had first looked, only a small tear that had bled copiously. Beneath it a large knot was forming.

"Thank God. With luck she'll have nothing worse than a bad headache."

Nancy groaned and moved her head on the pillow, and a moment later her eyes fluttered open. She glanced around blankly, then closed them again. "Ow. My head."

"Nan? This is Hortense. Do you remember what happened?"

Nancy frowned, then her eyes flew open and she shot

to a sitting position. "Miz Rhea!" She let out a groan and sank back.

"It's all right. Don't try to sit up, you'll only make yourself feel worse," Aunt Hortense advised her.

Nan nodded weakly. It was obvious from the pallor of her face that she already felt worse.

"Just tell us what happened," Alexandra urged. "Where is Mother?"

"I don't know, miss. She was acting so strange. She kept wanting to leave, said she had somewhere to go, that she had to see 'them.' I kept asking who, but she wouldn't say, only 'them.' She was fair discombobbled. Ooh, I feel sick."

"Janey, fetch her a pan," Aunt Hortense ordered one of the maids who was hanging at the foot of the bed, watching. Aunt Hortense fixed them with a gimlet eye. "After that, you may leave."

Reluctantly the servants obeyed her. Alexandra held the pan for Nancy, but after a moment of hanging over it, Nancy shook her head and sank onto the pillow. "I'm all right now, miss. I'm sorry." Tears gathered in her eyes. "I didn't watch her close enough." Her voice rose in dismay. "I never thought she'd *hit* me."

Alexandra's stomach tightened. Even though it had been obvious that must have been what happened, it was horrible to hear it. "I'm sorry, Nan. I never would have thought so, either. Why did she do it?"

"Because I wouldn't let her go. She grew more and more agitated. I should have fetched you or Miss Hortense, but I was scared to leave her. I figured she'd slip away by herself if I left the room. And I didn't want to ring for one of the servants and have her see Miz Rhea that way. I should have."

"Did she say where she wanted to go?"

"No. I asked her, and she just looked at me as if I was trying to trick her or something. She acted like she didn't know me—at least, after she got all agitated like. At first she was just lying there on her bed, staring at the wall, and then she got out of bed and started going around the room, putting on her cloak and bonnet and gloves, muttering about things. I couldn't understand her, and it was that scary, I'll tell you. Then she headed toward the door, and I stopped her, and that's when she told me she had to see 'them.' She said something like, 'I have to put it right.'"

"Put what right?"

"I don't know, miss, she wouldn't say. She wasn't making sense. I stood in front of the door so she couldn't get out, and she got more and more frantic acting. I was worried she was going to start screaming or something, and then she picked up that bookend there and hit me with it."

Aunt Hortense eyed the carved marble bookend. "It's a fortunate thing for you that Rhea doesn't have much strength. It could have caved in your skull."

"She didn't want to hurt me. She just wanted me out of the way."

Alexandra hurried to the kitchen and sent all the servants out to comb the area for her mother. She was sick with worry. She could not imagine where her mother had gone or what she thought she was doing. Rhea knew nothing about London; she would soon be horribly lost. It was dark, and that made it even worse. London was a dangerous place, and her mother would have no idea whether she was wandering into a bad neighborhood. Alexandra remembered the man who had jumped out at her. Obviously, even a good neighborhood was not exempt from violent events.

Alexandra went out and walked for almost an hour, searching the streets for any sign of her mother. She passed one couple, a man and woman who looked at her askance when she questioned them about seeing a middle-aged American and merely shook their heads and hurried on, as if to distance themselves from her oddity. Finally, discouraged, she turned her steps toward her house. She had almost reached it when she saw one of the footmen running from the other direction. She stopped and waited for him, her hope rising.

"Miss!" The man skidded to a stop a few feet from her and paused to catch his breath.

"What is it? Did you find her?"

He shook his head and gasped. "No, but I found... someone...who did."

"Who? Where is she?"

He nodded toward a house down the street. "Footman...at the Andersons'. He was coming home from the park, walking their dog, he was, and I asked him. He said as he'd seen a woman what sounded like Mrs. Ward. She was confused like, and he asked her if he could help her, and she told him she wanted to go to Exmoor House. So he hailed a hackney and put her in it and told him to take her to Exmoor House."

"Exmoor House!" Alexandra stared at him, stunned. Exmoor was the Countess's name. Had her mother gone to see the Countess? She wracked her brain, trying to remember if she had said anything about the Countess when she was asking her mother questions. She did not think so; it had been Aunt Hortense whom she had told about the Countess. She had asked her mother only about her birth. How could her mother know about the Countess? Could she have been listening outside the door when Alexandra was talking to Aunt Hortense?

The thought made Alexandra's blood run cold. If her mother had heard her doubts about being her daughter, perhaps it had completely unhinged her. Why else would she have run off to see the Countess?

"Where can I get a hackney?" she asked the footman. "I have to go get her."

"Yes, miss. I'll hail you one." He took off, hurrying in the direction from which he had come, and Alexandra followed him.

By the time she had caught up with him at the cross street, he had hailed a hackney and was holding open the door for her. He helped her inside, saying, "I told the driver Exmoor House, miss."

"Thank you, Deavers." Alexandra reached into her pocket and brought out a coin, which she pressed into his palm. "I'm very grateful to you. Now go home and tell my aunt where I have gone. I will be home as soon as possible."

"Yes, miss."

He closed the door, and the carriage started forward. It moved at a dignified pace, and Alexandra felt like screaming at the man to go faster. She thought of her mother talking to the Countess, and her hands clenched. The Countess would think her mother quite mad. She could not bear to think of the expression that would come over the Countess's aristocratic face, a look of revulsion and even fear as she realized that Rhea was not right in the head. It did not matter that the Countess seemed like a nice woman; everyone was frightened by the insane. Alexandra burned with empathetic humiliation for her mother. Rhea felt it when people withdrew from her or looked at her with apprehension. She obviously knew that the servants were scared of her. That was why Alexandra was careful to keep strangers away from Rhea.

The hackney came to a stop after a time, and Alexandra started to get out. Then she saw that they were not in front of the Countess's house. The home where they had stopped was larger and more imposing, almost a full block long, with a black iron fence running down the length of it.

"This isn't right!" she said sharply.

"'Exmoor 'Ouse,'" the lad said. This is Exmoor 'Ouse."

Alexandra frowned, looking around. Then she saw the dark figure standing forlornly at the fence, looking in. The woman wore a shawl over her head and shoulders, but it had slipped back, revealing her face and part of her head. It was Rhea. Alexandra let out a sigh of relief.

"Yes. You're right. I'm sorry. Wait here. I won't be a minute."

The driver let out a gusty sigh but did as she told him. Alexandra ran along the street to where her mother stood, leaning against the fence, her hands clenched around the metal rails.

"Mother?" She called softly to Rhea from a few feet away; she didn't want to startle her.

Rhea barely glanced at her. "I don't understand! They won't let me in! I don't know what to do. I promised her. I promised. Oh, I've been wicked. So wicked."

"Mama." Alexandra's heart twisted within her at the sight of her mother's distress, and the old childhood name slipped out. "Come home with me. You cannot stand out here all night. We'll see what we can do in the morning."

She took her mother's arm gently. Rhea turned toward her. Alexandra saw that her mother's face was streaked with tears.

Rhea looked straight at her and said, "I'm so sorry. Please forgive me, Simone."

* * *

Lord Thorpe looked up, surprised, when his butler announced softly that Lady Castlereigh was here to see him. "Ursula?" he exclaimed in astonishment. "What the devil is she doing here?"

"I am here to ask for your help," Lady Ursula said, sweeping in past the butler. "And I must tell you, I don't expect to be told to cool my heels in the entry by one of your heathen servants."

"Punwati has his orders, Ursula," Thorpe said pointedly, rising to his feet. "And you might remember that, to Punwati, *you* are the heathen."

Lady Ursula sniffed to show her disdain for what Thorpe's butler might think of her. "Really, Thorpe, this is no time for any of your absurdities. I'd like some tea."

Thorpe nodded toward Punwati, who backed silently out of the room and closed the door. Thorpe watched as Ursula planted herself in the chair across from his desk, then, with a sigh, sat behind his desk.

"All right, Ursula. Now tell me what is so urgent that you must disturb me in my study when you saw me only hours ago."

"I came to see what you intend to do about that girl."

"What girl?"

"Don't act the innocent with me, Thorpe. It doesn't become you. You know exactly who I mean—that American adventuress you brought to see my mother."

Thorpe's features settled into a cold mask. "Lady Ursula, you are older than I, and a woman, and I would dislike to show you disrespect. But if you again misname Miss Ward, I am afraid that I shall have to ask you to leave."

Ursula snorted. "Men are such fools. How could you have taken her there?"

"I am sorry it upset the Countess. I took her to the

Countess's because the Countess asked me to. She wanted to apologize to her. But of course I would not have introduced her to the Countess to begin with if I had had any idea how it would upset her. I didn't know what Lady Chilton looked like. I had no idea that Miss Ward resembled her."

"I suppose you could not know," Ursula admitted grudgingly. "But now that you've done it, you must help me."

"Help you what?"

"Keep that girl from defrauding my mother, of course!" Lady Ursula looked amazed at his ignorance.

"What the devil are you talking about? Miss Ward is not trying to defraud the Countess. How could she?"

"Come, Thorpe. I would have thought that at least *you* are not so naïve. It's one thing for my mother or Penelope to think that Miss Ward is a sweet girl. But you have had some experience with the world. With women, too, I might add. I wouldn't have thought that you were so easily bamboozled."

"Indeed, I don't believe I am," he replied curtly. "Exactly what, pray, are you talking about? How is Miss Ward going to defraud the Countess?"

"By hoodwinking her into thinking that she is Chilton's daughter, of course! Why can no one see this but me?"

"I would guess that no one else's mind has the same bent," Thorpe responded dryly.

"I shall ignore your tone because Mother needs your help," Ursula told him magnanimously.

"The Countess is upset because Miss Ward looks like her dead daughter-in-law. It's understandable that she would like to believe that Alexandra is her long-lost granddaughter, but she will soon see that it's a false hope."

"Oh, really? Not with that girl pretending that she is. She's out to deceive Mother. She'll convince her that she is *our* Alexandra, and then Mother will lavish her with gifts and money. She'll take her in to live with her and treat her like—like—"

"A beloved granddaughter?" Thorpe suggested. "Now, Ursula, don't fire up at me."

"You act as if you don't care if someone pulls the wool over Mother's eyes! I always said you were a selfish, cynical man, but I wouldn't have thought that you would stand idly by and watch someone swindle Mother."

"Of course I wouldn't, but no one is swindling the Countess."

"She will. Why else would she pretend to be Alexandra?"

"She *is* Alexandra," Thorpe pointed out. "That doesn't mean she's the Alexandra the Countess wishes she were. And it certainly doesn't mean she is trying to convince the Countess that she is. Why, she denied it! She told the Countess that she was not her granddaughter."

"Yes, that was very clever of her," Ursula remarked acidly. "Pretending that she didn't know who Simone was, that she didn't know she's the exact image of her. That she didn't know who the Countess was, or Chilton."

"How could she?" Thorpe asked. "She's an American."

"Hmph. That's what she says."

Thorpe sighed. "You're saying that she is only pretending to be American? Why would she do that if she were trying to make us believe that she is Chilton's daughter? Wouldn't it make more sense to be English—or even French?"

"How should I know? I don't know the workings of the criminal mind," Ursula huffed.

"Ursula, you are not making any sense. Alexandra denied that she was the Countess's granddaughter."

"It makes her look good. It makes her appear innocent. You mark my words, she'll come back later with some other proof that will convince Mother."

"This is all supposition. You haven't any facts to support what you're saying. Alexandra made no effort to meet the Countess. I am the one who introduced Alexandra to her. It is mere happenstance that she even met her."

"Is it?" Ursula asked, arching a brow. "An American comes to London and just happens to meet a man who is very close to the Countess and who is likely to introduce her to the Countess? How did you meet her, anyway?"

Thorpe hesitated. "Well, um, she was interested in seeing the things I brought back from India."

Ursula gave him a significant look. "Of course she was. Men are so easily taken in by a pretty face. It's a wonder they aren't all robbed blind. So this American girl just shows up, wanting to see your Indian nonsense, and you think there's nothing havey-cavey about it?"

Thorpe could feel his face reddening. "Some people have an appreciation for other cultures and for art in many forms. And she did not just show up. My agent brought her to see me because she was interested in my collection." Thorpe chose not to add that Jones had brought her only because Alexandra had bullied him into it. "She owns a shipping company. They import our tea."

"Really. A woman who owns a shipping company." Ursula's words dripped scorn.

"I presume she inherited it from her father. Or it may be her mother's, for all I know, and she runs it for her." He caught Ursula's look and added defensively, "Americans are different."

"Not *that* different. Men own businesses."

"Women inherit property, including businesses."

"Of course they do, but they have someone else run things for them. They don't do the buying and selling themselves. Oh, Thorpe, can't you see? She engineered meeting you so that she could meet Mother. She had obviously researched all of us and knew exactly what to do."

"I think you have an excessively devious mind."

"I'm just not a man and therefore not led astray by a curving figure and a fine set of eyes. I can see what's really happening."

"You're being absurd," Thorpe told her positively. "Alexandra is not capable of playing such a game. She is the most straightforward, honest woman I have ever met. She is downright blunt, in fact. She is not someone who plays games."

"I did not say she was playing at anything. She's deadly serious. She is trying to bilk my mother out of lots and lots of money. She obviously planned it out very carefully. She would be far less believable if she came up to my mother's door and said, 'Here I am—your granddaughter Alexandra.' She would also have to come up with some sort of story as to what had happened to her, why she hadn't been killed with the others, how she had found out who she was and so on. This way, she simply appears, lets the Countess see her and then artfully protests that she is not the Countess's granddaughter while she slips in the fact that her name is Alexandra. Don't you see? She made Mother trust her by pretending not to be Alexandra, all the while ensuring that Mother thinks she is."

"How could she be sure that I would introduce her to the Countess?" Thorpe countered. "I might not have taken her with me to that ball. Or your mother might not have come to it."

"She was counting on her appeal to get you interested in her. If you hadn't taken her to the Duchess's ball, it is quite likely you would have taken her some other place— the opera or a play, perhaps. She plays a genteel woman well enough. You wouldn't have just given her a tumble as if she were a doxie."

"You have a certain inelegance of expression, my lady."

"Nonsense. I am speaking the truth, and you know it. And Mother didn't have to see her at the ball. If anyone who knew Chilton and Simone had seen her, they would comment on it. It would have eventually gotten back to Mother, and she would have demanded to meet her. If you weren't interested in her, the girl would have lost nothing. She would have found some other way to meet Mother."

"You haven't a shred of proof."

"Proof! This isn't a court of law. We are talking about saving Mother from being swindled by this imposter, not about sending the girl to jail."

"I see. So for vilifying someone's character, you need no proof at all."

"Anyone who hadn't had his head turned by the woman could see that it makes sense!" Ursula made an exasperated noise. "Honestly, Thorpe, I gave you credit for more wit. You've made a fool of yourself for a woman before. I would have thought you had learned your lesson."

Thorpe's eyes narrowed. "If you think that this is the way to convince me of what you say, you are dead wrong. Miss Ward has done nothing except deny that she was the

Countess's granddaughter. She has made no claims and has tried to get nothing from the Countess.''

"You intend to wait until she has cheated Mother, then? Worse than that, she will have broken her heart, as well!" Ursula surged to her feet. "Well, I can see that it is useless talking to you. I only hope that you don't live to regret refusing to help Mother."

"I am not refusing to help the Countess," Thorpe told her grimly, rising also. "However, I have no intention of accusing Miss Ward without any evidence that what you say is true." He hesitated, then went on, "I will, however, set someone to investigate the matter."

He had already charged his valet with finding out all he could about the attack upon Alexandra last night, as well as the rat incident this afternoon. He could easily expand that search to learn whatever he could about Alexandra.

"You will?"

"Don't look so astonished, my lady. I am sure my agent has already checked out her business credentials. If she is, indeed, the owner of a shipping business in the United States, will that satisfy you that she is innocent of any wrongdoing in the matter?"

Ursula's eyes turned shrewd. "So you're hoping to persuade me that I am wrong."

"It seems the easiest way to get to the truth of the matter. Then we can cease to argue over it."

"As long as you make a complete investigation, I suppose that will have to do."

"I promise you, my agent is a very thorough man."

Lady Ursula left, still looking a trifle uncertain, and Thorpe turned to his study with a sigh. Trust Lady Ursula to stir up a controversy—as if the thing weren't enough of a mess. She had a way of making everyone's actions seem suspicious.

He sat behind his desk but found himself unable to work or read or do much of anything. Lady Ursula's accusations nagged at him. He could not stop remembering the way Alexandra had managed to meet him. She had written to him, and when he had turned down her proposal, she had found another way to meet him. Her eagerness to look at his Indian treasures was unusual.

But then, he reminded himself, Alexandra was unusual. The fact that she had been as bold and decisive as she had been was proof of nothing except that that was the sort of nature she had. And that nature intrigued him, even while it irritated him. Could she possibly have known that he would react that way to such a woman?

Grinding his teeth, he jumped from his chair and started to pace. It was absurd to think that Alexandra was anything other than exactly what she appeared to be. He had never met a woman of less artifice.

On the other hand, he remembered bitterly, he had been easily taken in before. His heart had played him false with Barbara, blinding him to her faults, deceiving him into thinking that she loved him as he loved her, when all the time she had merely been bored. Still, he argued, he was not the boy he had been then. He was far wiser—more cynical, the Countess would have it. No woman since Barbara had been able to play him for a fool. If there had been any falsity to Alexandra, he would have realized it. Yet he had to admit that no other woman had stirred such passion within him since Barbara. Perhaps it had not been that he was so wise, but that there had not been a woman desirable enough.

He cursed Lady Ursula for coming here and sowing doubt within him. It occurred to him that if he went to see Alexandra, it would resolve his doubts. A few minutes with her, he was sure, and he would once again be certain of her. He would see her bluntness, her honesty, and Ursula's accusations would crumble.

He glanced at the clock. It was growing a trifle late to call, perhaps. However, he could not convince himself to wait until the next day. He rang for his carriage and ran up to dress in proper evening attire. Thirty minutes later he was in his carriage, rumbling toward the Wards' house, anticipation rising in him.

As they neared the house, he caught sight of a figure of a woman walking briskly toward it. To his astonishment, he realized that it was Alexandra. Irritation flooded him. Hadn't the woman learned her lesson the other night? What was she doing out walking along the street alone in the dark? He tapped his cane once on the ceiling of the carriage, his command to stop, and started to open the door and climb out so that he could give this stubborn woman a piece of his mind.

But then he noticed a man in livery hurrying toward her. The two of them conferred for a moment, then the man scurried off, and Alexandra followed him at a rapid pace. Thorpe frowned, watching her stride away down the street. She was hatless and cloakless and still dressed in the gown she had worn earlier, not at all the sort of way a woman went abroad in London at night. His curiosity aroused, he leaned out of the window and instructed his driver to follow her—at a discreet pace.

He saw that the footman had hailed her a hackney. She climbed into it, and the conveyance pulled away, Thorpe's carriage following. After only a few moments, his carriage came to a halt, and Thorpe flipped aside the curtain to look out. The hackney had stopped halfway down the block in front of them, and Alexandra was climbing out.

She glanced up and down the street, focusing on the large house across the way. Thorpe followed her gaze.

They had stopped in front of Exmoor House.

Something cold and hard formed in Thorpe's stomach. Why had Alexandra come to the house of the Earl of Exmoor—she who had seemed not to know either the Countess or Richard, the present Earl? He waited, his fingers clenched around the carriage curtain, watching as she started across the street toward the house, her steps quick and determined.

He saw then that she was headed toward the figure of a woman, darkly dressed and head shrouded with a shawl. The two of them talked, and Alexandra turned, taking the other woman by the elbow and leading her toward the waiting hackney.

Something fierce and hot stabbed Thorpe through the chest. It was suddenly difficult to breathe. He could think of no reason this American, this girl who seemed so unknowledgeable about the Countess, would be meeting anyone secretively outside the home of the Earl of Exmoor. No reason—except, of course, that she was gathering information from some maid or other who worked at Exmoor House, someone who could tell her all about the family and its history.

Dear God! Could Ursula be right? Had Alexandra deceived him? Had he played the fool again, stumbling like a naïve boy into Alexandra's web—and pulling the Countess into it, too?

8

Alexandra helped her mother from the hackney and into the house. She felt bone weary. All the way home she had tried to get her mother to tell her why she had called her Simone, but Rhea had refused to say anything, just shaking her head and looking pitiful, until Alexandra had ground her teeth in frustration, wanting to shake her. Finally her mother had ended the interrogation by bursting into tears, crying, "I don't know what you're talking about! Why are you badgering me?"

When they stepped in the front door, they found Aunt Hortense waiting for them anxiously. "Oh, thank God!" She gave Alexandra a significant look. "I sent the servants to bed."

"Good." She knew that Aunt Hortense had wanted to avoid the servants seeing Rhea return, not knowing what she might do or say or what condition she would be in. It was better not to give them any extra fuel for gossip. As it was, their servants were probably the most popular guests in the servants' quarters for blocks around for the stories they could tell about the crazy Americans.

"Hortense!" Rhea threw herself into the other woman's arms. "I'm so glad to see you! She's been asking me all these questions, and I don't know what she's talking about."

Aunt Hortense glanced at Alexandra, who grimaced. "I'm sorry, Mother. I was...upset."

Rhea drew herself to her full height, such as it was, and said with a great deal of dignity, "Young lady, I cannot imagine why you keep calling me that. I am childless."

Aunt Hortense and Alexandra stared at her, rendered speechless by her pronouncement. Rhea turned and started toward the stairs, saying, "Come, Hortense. It's time we went to bed."

"Yes. I'll be right there." Hortense looked at Alexandra. "Sweetheart, I'm sorry."

Alexandra shook her head. "Don't worry. I realize she's not herself. She's been drinking. I could smell it. How did she get hold of liquor again?"

"I don't know. I will question the servants tomorrow." Hortense sighed. "I better follow her and make sure she goes to her room and stays there." Her face clouded. "I'm afraid that we may have to start locking her room. We cannot have her running all over London like this. Something's bound to happen to her."

Aunt Hortense turned to go up the stairs just as there was a heavy pounding on the door. Alexandra jumped and whirled, and Aunt Hortense stopped. Since the footmen were all in bed, Alexandra went to answer the door herself, opening it narrowly and looking out the crack.

"Lord Thorpe!" Alexandra opened the door wide, joy surging through her at the sight of him. Swift on its heels came the realization that Thorpe's face was set in cold, hard lines, and that his gray eyes were like granite. She took a step backward.

"What were you doing at Exmoor House?" he asked

abruptly, stepping into the entry without waiting for an invitation.

Alexandra gaped at him. "How did you—"

"Lord Thorpe," Aunt Hortense interrupted crisply, "I believe that even in London it is considered a trifle late to be calling on a lady."

He cast a glance at Aunt Hortense. "I am sorry, Miss Ward. However, I believe my business here is sufficiently important to warrant the late hour."

"Indeed?" Aunt Hortense came down the few steps she had climbed and started across the hall. "Perhaps I had better hear this business."

"It's all right, Aunt Hortense," Alexandra told her, her gaze not wavering from Thorpe's face, her own face polite and impersonal. A cold, hard knot was growing in her stomach, but she wasn't about to let Thorpe get a glimpse of her emotions—not the way he looked right now. "You go see about Mother. I can take care of Lord Thorpe's problem."

"It's hardly proper," the older woman began, scowling at Thorpe.

"It's all right. Really."

Grumbling, Aunt Hortense turned and went up the stairs. Alexandra gestured toward the drawing room.

"Would you care to sit down?" She crossed the hall into the room without waiting for an answer from him.

She sat on a chair, indicating the sofa across from her, but Thorpe remained standing.

"I asked you a question," he reminded her bluntly.

"Yes, and very rudely, too," Alexandra replied. "I am unaware of any reason I have to answer to you, Lord Thorpe."

"Do you have something to hide, Miss Ward?"

Alexandra hesitated. The truth was, of course, that she

did have something to hide. She certainly wasn't going to tell Thorpe that she had chased her mother to Exmoor House, where the woman had fled after knocking her companion in the head. But offhand, Alexandra could think of no plausible excuse for her to have been there.

Thorpe saw her hesitation, and his face grew grimmer. "Obviously you do."

"Tell me, Lord Thorpe, do you feel that you have to answer every insolent question a stranger asks you about your whereabouts or your business?"

If possible, his gray eyes turned even colder. She wondered why she had ever thought them warm; they reminded her of nothing so much as a cold, storm-tossed sea. "I am a stranger to you?"

"I think you are more a stranger every moment," Alexandra retorted. "I would have called you a friend earlier today, despite our short acquaintance, but friends do not spy on one another."

"I was not spying on you!"

"Then perhaps you would care to explain how you knew where I went just now."

"I had come over here to see you, to talk about...something. As my carriage pulled up, I saw you leaving in a hurried way. So I followed you."

"In what way does that differ from spying on me?"

He hesitated. "I was concerned."

"About me? Why did you not call out to me, then, when you saw me? Why did you hide in your carriage and furtively follow me?"

"I was concerned for the Countess."

"The Countess! How does spying on me help the Countess?"

"I must protect her from those who would take advantage of her," Thorpe replied stiffly, irritated that she was turning the tables on him and implying that he had been in the wrong.

It took a moment for the meaning of his words to register on Alexandra. When they did, fury flashed through her, flooding her cheeks with color. She jumped to her feet, her arms stiff at her sides. "You are saying that I would take advantage of the Countess?"

She looked beautiful in her rage, Thorpe thought, her skin luminous, her eyes sparkling. He was aware of an intense urge to pull her into his arms and kiss her. The fact that he could want to do so even when he felt so angry and betrayed made him furious.

"It is a possibility I have to consider," he said in a clipped voice. "You acted as though you had never heard of Exmoor before now. As if you did not know the Countess or anything about her family."

"I don't—or, at least, I did not until she told me!"

"Then what were you doing going to Exmoor House?"

"I don't even know what Exmoor House is! Who lives there? It isn't the Countess's house."

Thorpe grimaced. "You know very well that it belongs to the Earl of Exmoor."

"Do you mean that man I met last night? The one Nicola disliked? What does that have to do with the Countess?"

"It is the seat of the family. It is where the Countess lived before the death of her husband, who was then Earl—and exactly where you could find a servant who would remember details about the family, about Chilton and his wife and their children. The very sort of facts you need to convince the Countess that you are her granddaughter."

"What!" Hurt mingled with anger, and Alexandra trembled under the force of her emotions. "You dare to accuse me of—of pretending to be the Countess's dead granddaughter? To what purpose? Why?"

"For money. Isn't that always the reason?" Thorpe's mouth twisted.

"Money!"

"Yes. The Countess is a wealthy woman. Even though the title and the estates passed to Richard when the Earl and his son both died, her husband left her a great deal of money. A woman who was the granddaughter she had long believed dead would likely get things showered on her by her wealthy grandmother—and a good portion of her estate when she died."

"But I don't need money from the Countess, or anyone. I have plenty of money of my own."

"So you say."

"Oh. Of course. Nothing I say can be held as truth. Exactly why is that? Because I am not British? Or because by some strange quirk of fate I resemble the Countess's daughter-in-law? I suppose you think that somehow I managed to make myself a replica of this Simone person, too."

"Hair has been known to change color and can be curled. The likeness could be emphasized."

"Her portrait was enough like me to be my twin!" Alexandra cried. "You can't explain that away with talk of dyeing and curling."

Thorpe was silent for a moment, looking at her. "So now you are claiming a connection with Simone?" His mouth twisted. "And to think that I was fool enough to believe you, to think that you were interested in my collection or in me, when all you really wanted was entrée to the Countess."

"I didn't even know the Countess. What did I care about meeting her?" Alexandra cried. "*You* were the one who introduced me to her. *You* were the one who invited me to that ball.''

''Ah, but that was part of your scheme, wasn't it?''

Alexandra looked at him for a long moment, almost breathless from the pain of his words. She would never have guessed that it could hurt so much to have a man look at her the way Thorpe was looking at her, as if she were dirt beneath his feet.

''I would hate to be you,'' she said finally. ''To see the world the way you see it. You know me, you talked to me, you even acted as though you were attracted to me.''

''I *was* attracted to you, dammit! My folly, obviously!''

''It makes me ill to think that I kissed you, that I let you put your arms around me—''

''You did much more than that!'' Thorpe retorted hotly, surprised at the knife that twisted through his gut at her words.

''Get out of my house,'' Alexandra said, her voice level and cold, each word dropping like a stone.

''If you are innocent, tell me why you went to Exmoor House this evening. Tell me who that woman was!''

''I do not have to prove myself to you or anyone.'' Alexandra refused to tell him for any reason. Bile rose in her. She was afraid that she might burst into tears at any moment. ''Please leave my house, or I will have to call one of the footmen.''

''Gladly.'' The word sounded ripped from him.

Thorpe strode out of the room. He stopped just outside the doorway and turned, saying coldly, ''Stay away from the Countess. I'll do whatever I have to to keep you from hurting her.''

He turned and left, closing the front door behind him with a quiet, final click. Alexandra remained staring at the empty doorway for a moment. Then she reached down and grabbed the closest thing to her—a book, it turned out—and threw it after him. It hit the side of the doorway with a satisfying crash and fell to the floor. Alexandra liked the sound of it so much that she followed it with a vase of roses, and after that a couple of cushions that decorated the couch, a small statue, a paperweight and a set of bookends.

How dare he? How dare he imply that she was a criminal? A swindler! An adventuress out to get money from a sad old woman! How could he have kissed her the way he had and then think such a thing of her?

Rage and hurt churned in her. She realized how foolish she had been, how she had allowed her passion to take control of her usually level head. "I hate him!"

"Child, what is going on?"

Alexandra looked up at the sound of her aunt's voice. Aunt Hortense was standing in the hall outside the drawing room, looking in amazement at the variety of objects strewn over the floor, some intact, many broken.

Alexandra sighed. "A fit of temper. I'm sorry, Aunt. Did I disturb you?"

"Somewhat. I decided I should leave Rhea in Nan's care and come down here to see about you."

"I'm all right."

"Really?"

Alexandra shrugged. "I have been a fool."

"Mm. About the Englishman?"

Alexandra nodded. "I thought he—"

"Cared for you?" Aunt Hortense asked gently.

"Yes. But he had no real interest in me. He *desired* me, but he had no liking for me, no understanding of me." She raised her eyes to her aunt's with a sigh. "He accused me tonight of being an imposter."

"An imposter? Whatever do you mean?"

"He said that I had pretended to be interested in his Indian collection in order to wangle a way to meet the Countess. He said that I was after her money."

"Good Lord." Aunt Hortense goggled at the thought. "Whatever made him think that?"

"He saw me follow Mother to Exmoor House. Apparently that is where the Countess used to live with her family. He saw me with Mother outside the house, and he assumed that I was bribing a servant to tell me all sorts of things I could use to convince the Countess that I am her granddaughter."

"Why didn't you tell him that it was Rhea?"

Alexandra cast her a look. "And have to explain what Mother was doing there? What could I say? Should I have had him meet Mother and realize that she is…" Alexandra sighed. "I didn't want him to think that of Mother. I didn't want to see the way he would look at her…at me. And then—when I realized what he thought of me—there was nothing on earth that would have convinced me to tell him what I was doing there. He is nothing to me, and there is no reason I should tell him anything."

"Of course not, dear."

"Don't look at me in that sympathetic way. Perhaps my heart has been bruised a little, but I'll get over it quickly enough." Unexpected tears pricked her eyelids, but Alexandra blinked them away. "I think that I will settle my business here as quickly as possible. And then we should go back to Massachusetts. Let Thorpe have his precious Countess to himself. I have no interest in the woman."

Alexandra sighed, then went on. "That's not true. I like the Countess. She seemed to me to be someone I would enjoy knowing. I had wanted to go back to her and tell her about what you and I talked about this afternoon, only now he's spoiled it. I can't even talk to her without his claiming I'm shamming her.''

"What does it matter what he thinks?" Aunt Hortense asked. "As long as you know the truth."

"It shouldn't, I know, but..." Alexandra frowned. "Aunt Hortense, Mother said something to me this evening. I didn't have a chance to tell you, but when I found her this evening, she looked at me and started to cry. Then she said, 'I'm sorry, Simone.'"

"What?" Aunt Hortense gaped at her.

Alexandra nodded. "Just like the Countess did. It cannot be coincidence."

"No. I suppose not," Aunt Hortense agreed unhappily.

"Could Mother have known the woman? They were in Paris at the same time. Could it be that Father and this woman—"

"No! I don't know." Her aunt's frown deepened. "I have an awful feeling about all this. I wish we had never come to London."

"So do I." Alexandra shrugged. "Well, we will be leaving soon."

There was a pause, then she burst out, "Damn that man! I hate to run off and let him think that he scared me away. That I left because he had exposed my scheme and warned me away from the Countess!"

"I don't know what you can do," Aunt Hortense pointed out reasonably. "Unless you want to pretend to be the granddaughter in order to spite him."

Alexandra made a face at her aunt. "No, of course not. I would never do that to the Countess. Poor woman." She tilted her head, considering. "Though I might just go and see her before I leave, to say goodbye and wish her well." Her dark eyes flashed. "And make *him* worry a little."

* * *

Alexandra spent the next few days working on her business affairs, trying to get all the loose ends tied up so that they could return to the United States. She had found that there was a ship sailing for Boston in a little over a week, and she was determined to be on it. All too often, however, her mind wandered from the subject at hand, and she found herself rehashing her bitter confrontation with Lord Thorpe or remembering the look in her mother's eyes when she had called Alexandra Simone.

What had happened in Paris? Had her mother known Simone? Could she have rescued the baby, then adopted her? But if she had, why had she kept Alexandra's origins secret all these years? Alexandra could see nothing shameful in taking in an orphaned child.

Alexandra wished intensely that she could get her mother to talk to her. But though she had gone into her mother's bedroom several times, she had not managed to get the woman to say a word to her. Rhea had lain on her bed, sunk into silence, her eyes closed or staring off into space. Alexandra had seen her mother like this a few times before, and she did not understand it any more than she understood why Rhea secreted bottles of liquor about the house and drank from them furtively.

Three days after her confrontation with Lord Thorpe, she took a hackney to the office of her London agent, with whom her company had worked for years. Mr. Merriman greeted her with his usual politeness, but as they talked, Alexandra could see that there was something troubling him. Finally, he stopped in the middle of a discussion about a shipping contract, and said, "Miss Ward..."

He stopped and shifted uncomfortably in his chair.

Alexandra waited, and when he did not continue, she prompted, "Yes?"

"I—well, an odd thing happened two days ago. I don't know what it means, but I feel it incumbent upon me to tell you."

Alexandra stiffened. "Please do."

"Mr. Jones came to visit me. Lyman Jones, the businessman for Lord Thorpe. I don't know if you remember him—"

"Oh, yes, very well." Alexandra's face hardened. "Do go on."

"He asked me a number of questions about you—how long I had been your agent and how much business I had done with you over the years, things like that."

"What did you tell him?"

"Well, I said I had done business with you for many years, and our exact dealings were none of his business. As if I would tell him the details of one of my client's business transactions!" Merriman's eyes lit with remembered indignation. "I told him he was a presumptuous upstart and sent him on his way. I also reminded him that we had a signed contract with Burchings Tea, and if he tried to weasel out of it now, I would have him in court faster than he could blink. He was all apologies, of course." The agent looked a little smug. "Said he wasn't interested in backing out of anything, but his client, Lord Thorpe, had told him to find out all he could about you and your company."

"I am sure he did," Alexandra replied grimly, wishing that she had Lord Thorpe before her right now so she could tell him exactly what she thought of him.

"Then you know about it?" he asked, relieved.

"I did not know that Lord Thorpe sent Mr. Jones to question you. However, I am aware that he has taken some rather peculiar notions into his head."

"The oddest thing he asked was if I was sure that you were you."

Alexandra ground her teeth. "That blackguard."

"I told him that of course I had never met you personally before, but I had no reason to doubt that you were Alexandra Ward. Your credentials and letters of credit all were in order." He frowned, and Alexandra could see the faint touch of uncertainty on his face.

"I am so sorry." Alexandra was seething inside, but she forced herself to put on a pleasant face. "I can see that Mr. Jones's questions have upset you. There is nothing to worry about, I assure you. As you said, my credentials are in order. I am most definitely Alexandra Ward. Lord Thorpe seems to have become somewhat...disturbed."

Mr. Merriman's mouth formed an *O* of amazement, and he leaned forward confidentially, saying, "You mean he's touched in the upper works? I've heard some of those noblemen are mad as hatters."

For one gleeful instant Alexandra was tempted to let loose the rumor that Thorpe was indeed mad, but she did not. She was far too sensitive to the charge of madness to put it on anyone, even someone she disliked as thoroughly as she did Lord Thorpe at the moment.

"No," she said reluctantly. "He is not insane. He has an odd suspicion that I am an imposter."

Her agent looked at her expectantly, and Alexandra knew that he would like a full explanation. However, she was not about to plunge into the long, confused and highly personal story.

"It is far too silly to give credence to," she told the man. "I am sure you can tell that I am far too knowledgeable about every aspect of Ward Shipping to be anything but the woman you have dealt with in the past. As you mentioned, my company has done business with you for several years. I would certainly hate for this matter to end our business relationship.''

Merriman blanched at the thought of losing his lucrative share of the Ward business dealings. "No, Miss Ward, of course not. I have every confidence in you, of course. I trust that we will continue to do business for a good many years.''

"Good. Now, if you will excuse me, I should like to put off discussions of these other matters until another time. I think that I had better visit Lord Thorpe and put an end to this.''

She went first to Lyman Jones's office, which was just down the street from Merriman's, and rang a peal over his head that left him pale and shaken and babbling incoherent apologies. Next, she hailed a hackney to Thorpe's house. Thorpe's Indian servant opened the door, but before he could begin to speak, Alexandra sailed past him.

"No, Mr. Punwati, don't even bother to lie that he is not here. I intend to see Lord Thorpe, even if I have to wait on the doorstep until he comes home.''

Punwati looked distressed at the thought. "Oh, no, Miss Ward, he is here. He is in his study. Let me—''

"Never mind.'' Alexandra strode past him. "I know where it is.''

"Miss Ward!'' He came after her agitatedly. "You must let me announce you.''

But at that moment Lord Thorpe himself walked out of the study, his face set in lines of aristocratic disdain. "Miss Ward. I thought I heard your dulcet tones.''

Alexandra ignored the skip her heart took when she saw him. She strode forward, letting her anger sweep through her. "How dare you? How dare you send Mr. Jones to my business agent and plant doubts in his mind about me?''

''I think I have a right to ask questions about someone with whom I am doing business.''

''You implied to him that I was not Alexandra Ward. You shook his faith in me and damaged our relationship.'' Her dark eyes flashed, and her cheeks were high with color. She was aware of an intense desire to fly at him, claws out.

''If you are who you say you are, it should be no problem.''

''Please! Don't pretend to be any more foolish than you are! We both know that confidence is at the basis of business dealings, especially when an ocean separates you. Since I am sure that an appeal to your human decency would fall on deaf ears, I will address your pocketbook. If I hear of your spreading another word of slander or innuendo about me, I will go straight to a solicitor. Do I make myself clear?''

''Perfectly.''

''Good.'' Alexandra whirled and started to walk away, then turned abruptly. Tears glimmered in her eyes. ''And to think that I actually *liked* you! How could you turn out to be such a...such a snake?''

She left, Punwati scurrying to open the door for her. Lord Thorpe stood looking after her, his face bleak.

To Alexandra's surprise, she burst into tears in the hackney on the way home, and it took her a good two hours alone in her room to return to some semblance of normalcy. Finally, when she judged herself calm enough, she went down the hallway to her mother's bedroom to see how she was doing.

Nancy drew Alexandra into the hallway. ''If you could

sit with her a spell, Miss Alexandra, I could get a bite to eat.'' She glanced at Rhea's sleeping form on the bed. ''She shouldn't be any trouble.'' She touched the bandage on her head unconsciously.

''I know.'' Rhea was never any trouble when she was sunk in one of her glooms, though Alexandra found them almost more painful to watch than some of her other odd starts.

''She's just been holding on to that box,'' Nancy went on, shaking her head. ''And looking inside it and crying, all silent like.''

Alexandra nodded. ''I will sit with her. Take your time.''

Nancy left, and Alexandra went into the room. She stood beside her mother's bed and gazed down on her. Rhea was sleeping as peacefully as a baby, curled on her side. Alexandra's gaze went to the box beside her on the bed.

She had always wondered what was in that box. Her thoughts went to the time when she was nine or ten years old and had tried to look inside it. Rhea had come into the room and seen her. Rhea had grabbed the box from her and started shrieking like a virago. For the first time Alexandra had seen a glimpse in her mother's eyes of something mad, and it had frightened her to the very core of her being. She had never tried to get into the box again.

She looked at it, inches away from her mother's grasp. The key lay on its ribbon on the bedspread beside it. Nancy had said Rhea had been opening it and looking inside. What was in there? What had her mother been hiding all these years? Alexandra looked at her mother. It would be a violation of her privacy, she knew, to look inside the box. Normally she would not have considered opening it.

But the past few days had been so strange, her mother's actions so bizarre. Why did her mother refuse to answer her questions? Alexandra could not help but wonder if the secret to her past lay in that small box. She couldn't imagine what could be inside it. It was too small to hold much. Perhaps a very small book, a diary—or the letters of a lover, the father of her child? Or—or what? Surely she had the right to know about her own life.

Stealthily, Alexandra walked to the other side of the bed. She stood over the box for a moment, then reached down cautiously, her eyes glancing to her mother, and closed her hand around the box. She raised it from the bed and pulled at the lid. It opened easily.

Inside, on a bed of padded purple satin, lay a gold locket on a chain. It was beautifully engraved with swirls and some ornate letter in the center, though Alexandra was not sure what at first, for all the curlicues and twists around it. Then she saw, her heart thumping, that it was an *A*. Her stomach turned cold, and the freeze crept into her chest until she could hardly breathe.

She picked up the locket. It lay coolly on her fingers. She inserted her thumbnail in the thin line that lay between the two halves and gently pried the thing open. She stood for a moment, staring at what lay in her hand.

On either side of the locket was a miniature portrait, drawn with infinite care and infinitesimal detail. She had seen other tiny portraits like it. This one had been done by a master. On one side of the locket a man's face looked at her as solemnly as it had looked out of the portrait yesterday in the Countess's bedroom. On the other side was a smiling dark-haired woman who looked just like the woman staring down at her.

Alexandra backed up a step. She felt suddenly light-headed. Her stomach churned. *Chilton and Simone.*

She turned and walked numbly out of the room. Her aunt, who was leaving her room, saw her and said sharply, "Alexandra? What is the matter?"

Aunt Hortense hurried toward her. Alexandra looked at her blankly.

"I have to leave. Watch Mother for me." She gestured toward the bedroom, then turned and went down the stairs. Moments later she was in a hackney, rolling across the cobblestoned streets toward the home of the Countess of Exmoor.

The butler announced her to the Countess, then ushered her into the drawing room. The Countess looked up from her chair and smiled. "Miss Ward. How pleasant to see you again." The smile dropped from her face. "My dear, are you feeling quite well?"

"What? Oh. Yes, I'm fine." Alexandra glanced around the room, a trifle nonplussed to find that there were several other people in the room. Penelope was smiling at her, while Lady Ursula looked daggers straight through her. The Countess's companion, Miss Everhart, offered her a quick, timid smile before she glanced at Lady Ursula's stony face and immediately dropped the smile. Worst of all, Lord Thorpe was sitting not a foot away from the Countess, staring at Alexandra icily.

He rose, saying in a cold voice, "Miss Ward. I am surprised to see you here."

"Are you? And why is that?" Alexandra asked, recovering some of her aplomb. Let him explain his warning to her to stay away from the Countess in front of the woman herself.

His lips tightened, but he said nothing. The Countess glanced at him oddly.

"Come and sit beside me," the Countess told Alexandra, covering the awkward pause. She gestured gracefully toward the chair on the other side of her.

"I have something I wanted to show you, my lady," Alexandra said, clutching the locket tightly in one hand as she walked toward the Countess. "I found this in my mother's things, and I thought—I did not know where else to turn. Can you tell me what it is? What it means?"

Alexandra looked into the older woman's eyes, blocking out everyone else in the room, as she held out her hand to the Countess, the locket in the palm of her hand. The Countess, her face mildly curious, glanced from Alexandra's intense face to her hand. She stiffened, one hand rising slowly to her breast. Her face turned as white as a sheet of paper.

"My God." She reached out a trembling hand and touched the locket reverently, almost as if she was afraid it might disappear. "The locket." She took the necklace in her hand, bringing it closer to her eyes. She gazed at the engraving on the front, her forefinger tracing the looping letter. Tears glimmered in her eyes. "It is Alexandra's locket."

The Countess looked at Alexandra, tears spilling out of her eyes, and held out her hands to her. "My love. Welcome home. Oh, thank God. Welcome home."

9

"Mother! What are you talking about?" Lady Ursula exclaimed in horrified tones. "Thorpe! Don't just stand there, do something."

"And what, pray, would you have me do?" he asked dryly, but his face was tight, his lips bloodless with fury. "It would seem that Miss Ward is cleverer than either of us gave her credit for."

Alexandra ignored both of them, taking the Countess's hands. The Countess stood up, squeezing Alexandra's hands tightly, and looked into her face, her eyes lingering lovingly over each of Alexandra's features. "I knew it the other day, and I let them talk me out of it." She stepped forward, her arms going around Alexandra, and hugged her tightly. "I can scarcely credit it."

"Neither can I," Ursula interrupted acidly. "What are you talking about? What is that thing?"

"It's the baby's locket." The Countess released Alexandra and turned toward her daughter and Thorpe, dangling the gold locket in her hand. "Don't you remember? I gave them to the girls the Christmas before they went to France, matching lockets with miniature portraits of Emerson and Simone inside. A keepsake. Each of them was inscribed with her initial on the front, *M* for Marie, *A* for Alexandra.'' She smiled at Alexandra, her face shining. ''It was obvious to anyone who looked at you that you were Simone's daughter, but this clinches it. She is your niece, Ursula. My granddaughter.''

Thorpe took the necklace from the older woman's hand and studied it, flipping open the locket and looking at the little portraits inside. ''This proves nothing,'' he said gruffly. ''She could have found this anywhere—in a shop, on the street. After all, the men who killed your family doubtless took their jewelry and sold it. The locket is probably what gave her the idea in the first place. She happened upon this piece of jewelry, saw that the picture resembled her and set out to find out what the story was behind it. Doubtless she did whatever she could to make herself look even more like your daughter-in-law. All this proves is that she knew what Simone looked like before she saw that portrait in your bedroom.''

Alexandra forced herself to turn and face Thorpe's glacial gaze. Her rage at him had seeped away, and she felt only pain at his obvious hatred for her. ''I have never seen that locket before today, my lord.''

Ursula let out a snort of disbelief.

The Countess turned to her daughter and Lord Thorpe. ''Well, this is certainly a first. I doubt I've ever seen you two present a united front.'' She let out a sigh. ''I would have thought you would be happy for me, Sebastian.''

Thorpe looked stricken. ''I cannot be happy to see someone take advantage of you. You know I want you to be happy, but that doesn't mean I want you to be taken in by an imposter.''

The Countess looked puzzled. ''I don't understand. I thought you and Miss Ward—I mean, you introduced her to me.''

"Yes, much to my regret. I didn't know. I had never seen Simone. It never occurred to me that any of this would happen. I took Miss Ward for what she appeared to be. Foolishly, I was the one responsible for introducing her into your life. For making it possible for her to swindle you and break your heart. For that, I will never forgive myself. Countess, don't you understand? This is all far too fortuitous."

"Have you no belief in Divine Providence? Sometimes things are meant to happen a certain way. You lose something and then, one day, years and years later, you get it back. Only it is even more special because you know what you have missed."

"I only want you to be happy," Thorpe said in a tight voice, not looking at Alexandra.

"Then you have your wish." The Countess smiled at Alexandra. "I have my granddaughter back."

"Mother, that locket is not proof that she is Alexandra."

"I am Alexandra," Alexandra told Ursula firmly, then looked toward the Countess, her expression softening. "However, my lady, I am not sure that I am *your* Alexandra. Lady Ursula is right. That locket does not prove that I am your granddaughter. I cannot help but think that I must be related to your Simone in some way, but that doesn't necessarily mean that I am her daughter." She told the Countess of her aunt's suspicions about her birth, adding, "But I could just as easily be the result of a—a liaison between my mother and some relative of Simone's, a brother or uncle. Or, if I am not my mother's child, just one she rescued, then I could still be a niece or cousin to your son's wife, or even someone of low birth, a de Vipont by blood, but born on the wrong side of the blanket."

The Countess frowned. "I don't understand. Didn't your mother tell you anything when she gave you the locket?"

"She did not give it to me. I found it. I tried to speak to her about the matter after you and I talked, but she...could not answer. She is ill."

"Very convenient, I must say," Lady Ursula said. "Saves you from having to commit to a story that could be researched and disproved."

Alexandra looked at the other woman. "My mother's illness is scarcely a matter of convenience, especially to her. My lady, I harbor no dislike for you. Nor have I any plan to unseat you in the Countess's affections. Indeed, I am sure that I could not. You are her daughter, I am merely someone she just met. I see no reason we should be at such odds."

"I'm not so easily gammoned. You are able to speak very prettily, I see that. But that is not enough to convince me."

"I have no desire to convince you of anything. I don't want to convince anyone. I only want to find out the truth."

"I am sure we all do," the Countess agreed. "My heart already knows it, but it would be better if we could find something the rest of the world will accept. I think the best course would be to talk to Bertie Chesterfield."

"The man who informed you that your son's family was killed?"

"Yes. Perhaps he can shed some light on this matter."

Thorpe made a derisive noise. "Bertie Chesterfield never shed light on anything, including his own mind."

"He is a shallow and stupid person," the Countess agreed. "However, he is the only eyewitness we have. I did not ask him any questions at the time. I was capable of little but grieving then. And later, well, I did not really want to know the details of the destruction of my loved ones. But perhaps, if we learned some of the details, we might be able to find out how we got to this point. Sebastian..." The Countess gave Thorpe a look of appeal. "Will you go with Alexandra to visit Bertie? Find out everything you can?"

"You know that I would endure far worse than Chesterfield's inane chatter for your sake. I am happy to question him. But I see no reason for Miss Ward to accompany me. I am sure I will do much better by myself."

"Nevertheless," the Countess said firmly, "I think Alexandra needs to be in attendance."

"Very well, then." Thorpe bowed stiffly, shooting a look at Alexandra that would have dropped a person of lesser fortitude. "I shall take Miss Ward with me to Chesterfield's. I will call on you later to set the date and time, if I may, Miss Ward. In the meantime, Countess, I regretfully must leave you. Several matters need my urgent attention."

"Of course, my dear." The Countess nodded to him graciously. She turned to Alexandra, holding out her hand. "Now, come, sit beside me and tell me about yourself. I want to hear all about your life, your home, what you were like as a little girl...oh, everything I've missed."

"Mother, I must protest this folly."

"Ursula, you are my daughter, and I love you dearly, but if you intend to persist in this tone, I think it would be better if you left the room." The Countess's voice was pleasant, but the set of her mouth was firm.

Ursula drew in a breath, her eyes widening. Alexandra thought she was going to explode in a fit of anger, but then she swallowed her rage and folded her hands in her lap. Shooting a venomous look toward Alexandra, she said, "All right, Mother. If that is how you feel."

She did not leave, but she did sit back, lips pressed together, and watched.

Alexandra turned to the Countess. "But, my lady, what if I am not your granddaughter?"

The Countess smiled. "Then I will have spent a very pleasant hour getting acquainted with an interesting woman."

Alexandra sat down beside her with a smile, and they began to talk.

It was more than an hour later when Alexandra finally left the house, so she was surprised to find Lord Thorpe standing beside his carriage, arms folded across his chest, looking thunderous. It irritated her that she could not suppress a little thrill at the sight of him. Whatever was the matter with her? The man was a toad, and by rights she ought to be disgusted by the sight of him.

"My lord." She gave him the barest of nods and started along the sidewalk away from him.

He was beside her in an instant, however, his hand locking around her wrist. "I have been waiting for you. You and I are going to have a little talk."

"I think that you and I have already said more than enough to each other." Sebastian said nothing, just pulled her toward his carriage. Alexandra tried to jerk her wrist away. "Are you planning to abduct me now?"

"No. I have no intention of keeping you." Accurately judging the scowl that was gathering on Alexandra's face, he added, "It's no use kicking up a fuss. I don't embarrass easily, and no one will challenge me."

Given the look on his face, Alexandra suspected that was true. Since she had no real belief that he would harm her, she shrugged and climbed into his carriage. He followed, slamming the door after him, and the carriage rocked off.

Thorpe studied her for a moment, his eyes dark. Alexandra gazed at him, aware of a sense of anticipation at the storm that she was sure was about to break. There was, she realized with a start, something exhilarating about arguing with Lord Thorpe.

"How can you live with yourself?" he asked finally.

"Very easily, my lord."

"How can you deceive that kind, fragile woman? Do you have any idea how sad she has been for more than twenty years over the death of her son and his family?"

"No. I can only guess," Alexandra answered honestly. "I am very sorry for her."

He made a noise of disgust. "I doubt you are capable of feeling anything for anyone but yourself."

"Oh, no, that's not true. I feel a great deal of dislike for you."

His eyes flashed. "I still had some hope. Despite the fact that you hid your reasons for going to Exmoor House, despite the fact that you looked like the adventuress Ursula thinks you are, I had a faint, lingering hope that you would prove Ursula wrong. That you would stay away from the Countess, that you would not press your claim with her. I clung to the fact that you had told the Countess you could not be her granddaughter. This morning at my house, your indignation seemed real. But then you walked into that room today, and I knew that I had been a fool to even hope. It was just as Ursula predicted. You found something to make the Countess believe you, and you brought it to her with an air of innocence. 'What does this mean, Countess?' As if you didn't know! As if you hadn't intended to use it all along."

"I didn't know about it before today," Alexandra protested. "Not, of course, that I expect *you* to believe the truth. You are far too interested in the story you have made up to even consider the facts."

"There are no facts to consider." He leaned across the carriage, his eyes burning into hers. "There is nothing but what you have concocted. You are a cheat, a swindler, and you have had nothing on your mind since you got here except to worm your way into the Countess's confidence. You manufactured an excuse to see me. You flirted and—"

"Is it really the Countess you are so upset about my deceiving?" Alexandra asked astutely. "Or is what really galls you the fact that I supposedly deceived *you?*"

Thorpe's eyes flared with anger, and his mouth tightened. Suddenly his hand lashed out and grabbed her arm, and he jerked her across the carriage and onto his lap. Alexandra half fell across him, her bonnet knocked off her head and dangling by its ribbons. His other arm fastened around her, and his lips came down to take hers. Alexandra put her hands against his chest and shoved, trying to wriggle out of his grasp, but it was of little use. He held her easily while his predatory mouth claimed hers. Alexandra was infuriated. It was just like a man, she thought, to try to settle an argument by asserting his physical dominance. She went rigid, knowing it was useless to struggle against him. She would make him sorry, she thought, though she was not sure how.

Surrounded by his scent, his warmth, his strength, she began to soften. His mouth was hot and urgent on hers, searing her, and despite her irritation, her stomach quivered, her loins loosening and blossoming with heat. She heard the rasp of his breath in his throat, felt his heart thudding against the wall of his chest, and heat began to rise within her. Letting out a sigh, she relaxed against him. Sebastian felt her surrender, the flush of heat through her body, and triumph flashed through him, mingling with desire and rage. His hold on her loosened, and his hand slid over the curves of her body, exploring her softness. He touched her breasts, feeling the pointing of her nipples through the cloth, and slipped over the plane of her stomach and onto the curve of her hip.

Alexandra leaned against his arm, stunned by the rush of desire through her at the touch of his hand. She could not think, only feel, as his hand moved ever downward. Her skirt and petticoats were rucked up almost to her knees, and his hand slid onto the calf of her leg, her flesh separated from him by only the sheer stocking. His fingers moved beneath the dress and petticoats, sliding up her leg.

The bold move startled Alexandra out of the haze of her desire. With a jolt, she realized what he was doing, the liberties she was allowing him to take without even a word of protest. It was no wonder he thought she was wicked, she told herself, given the brazen way she kept responding to him whenever he made advances no decent man would!

She jerked away, tumbling off his lap and onto the floor. For an instant they stared at each other. Thorpe realized, with a rush of shame, that he had forced a kiss—and more—upon her, a thing he could not remember ever before doing to a woman. He reached toward her inarticulately, apology and excuses tangling on his suddenly thick tongue.

Alexandra glared at him, scrambling away and flinging open the door to his carriage. He saw, with horror, that she meant to jump out of the moving vehicle, and he rapped frantically on the roof of the carriage. They slowed and stopped, and Alexandra was out of the door in an instant. He watched her hurry down the street, straightening her bonnet, and he was not sure which one of them he disliked more at the moment.

Alexandra's emotions were as confused as Thorpe's as she hurried along. She had walked for two blocks in the wrong direction before she realized it and turned to retrace her steps. No one, she thought, had ever managed to confuse her the way Lord Thorpe did. He had behaved perfectly despicably—so she could not understand how she could feel so warm and jangly inside just thinking about his kiss. Was she shallow? A creature ruled purely by physical needs? It had never seemed the case before. She had always been a practical person, the kind who thought before she acted, who made plans and had reasons for her actions.

Since she had met Lord Thorpe, she had become a stranger to herself. She was feeling things she had never felt, acting in ways she normally would not, pulled this way and that by her passions. Why, she was no longer even sure of her identity! Was she her mother's daughter, her aunt's niece, as she had always thought—or was she the granddaughter of a Countess?

As soon as Alexandra entered the house, she went upstairs to her mother's room. She found her mother in a frenzy of anxiety, with Nancy trying vainly to calm her down. Nancy turned to her with some relief.

"Oh, miss, I'm glad you're here. She's all upset because something's missing from that box."

"I want it back!" Rhea cried. "They took it—I know they took it. They're always wanting it."

"No. I took it, Mother." Alexandra held out the locket. Rhea let out a cry and pounced on the necklace, grabbing it out of Alexandra's hand. "*You* took it! You wicked, wicked girl!"

"Why don't you want anyone to see that locket, Mother?" Alexandra asked, hardening herself to her mother's obvious distress. "Why do you hide it?"

Rhea, who had turned away to put the locket in the little box, swung around, her face contorted with fury. Without warning, she reached out and slapped Alexandra. "How dare you? How dare you?"

Alexandra drew a sharp breath at the blow. Nancy let out a cry and rushed to Rhea, but Rhea was already turning away, cuddling the box.

"Miss Alexandra, I'm ever so sorry," Nancy said, worried. "I don't know what's gotten into her."

"I disturbed her. I—I hardly know what to do anymore."

"Alexandra!" Aunt Hortense bustled into the room. "Where have you been? Why did you go rushing off like that? Did you take something out of Rhea's box? She's been in a state ever since she woke up."

"Yes. I just gave it back to her," Alexandra admitted wearily. "She slapped me for it."

"*Slapped* you! Rhea?" Aunt Hortense goggled at her niece, then turned to look at her sister-in-law, huddled in a chair, the box clutched to her chest. "I've never known her to hurt a flea. What is going on?"

"There is a picture in the locket—two pictures, actually. They are the same people whose portraits I saw in the Countess's house."

"What?" Aunt Hortense turned pale. "Oh, my."

"Yes. Oh, my. There is a letter *A* on it, for Alexandra. I took it to the Countess to see if she could identify it. She said that she gave that locket and another just like it, with the letter *M,* to her granddaughters the year before they were killed.''

"Oh, my," Aunt Hortense repeated weakly and sank into the nearest chair.

"Mother, why do you have that locket?" Alexandra asked in the gentlest voice she could muster, going to her mother. "Who was she to you? Who was she to me?"

"Go away," Rhea spat, bending over the box protectively. "You stole it! Nan, make her go away. I don't want her here."

"Why won't you tell me!" Alexandra exclaimed, frustrated. "I just want to know who I am!"

"No! No!" Rhea shrieked and turned away from Alexandra.

"You won't get anything out of her like this," Aunt Hortense said sensibly. "Come with me, Alexandra. You can talk to her tomorrow when both of you are calmer. Nan, see if you can soothe Rhea."

Alexandra strode out of the room. "I don't mean to upset her!" she exclaimed as soon as the door shut behind her and her aunt. "But why won't she tell me?"

"I don't know, dear. Perhaps she no longer even knows why she can't tell you. It's aggravating. But you know she only gets worse if you get angry with her."

"I'm not angry with her," Alexandra protested. Then she sighed. "All right. I *am* angry with her. What has she kept hidden from me all this time? It's horrible to know that she holds the secret, the key to all this, and she won't tell me."

"I know, dear. You would need the patience of Job to deal with your mother the way she's been lately. I get terribly impatient with her, too, and she's not even withholding something from me." Aunt Hortense linked her arm with Alexandra's and walked with her to her room.

"I wish I could help you. I wish I knew what was going on. This must be horrible for you."

"I don't know if she's really my mother," Alexandra told her. "The Countess is convinced that I am her granddaughter, but...you are my family, you and Mother and Cousin Nathan and everyone at home. The Countess is a wonderful woman, but I scarcely know her!"

"Darling, no matter what, we will always be your family. You remember that. I don't care if you're the granddaughter of that crazy King himself, you will always be my beloved niece."

Tears sprang into Alexandra's eyes at her aunt's words, and she bent to give the other woman a hug. "Thank you, Aunt Hortense. I love you."

"Good. Then that's settled. Now I suggest you come along, and we'll get you a nice cup of tea. That's one thing I agree with the English on. Nothing fixes you up like a spot of tea."

Alexandra opened her eyes. It was dark, and she was in bed. It took her a moment to orient herself. She had eaten supper and passed the evening with Aunt Hortense in a boring round of cards, then had taken herself off to bed. What had awakened her?

Something hit the other side of her wall. Alexandra leaped out of bed and ran out of her room, not even pausing to put on a robe or slippers. That wall connected to her mother's room.

The key was in the lock. Her aunt had followed up on her intention to lock Rhea in. Alexandra turned the key and flung open the door. She stopped, frozen in shock. A huge, dark figure had his hands around her mother's throat, and she was flopping and jerking, clawing at his hands. Nancy lay on the floor.

Alexandra let out a scream, and the large man whirled, his hands loosening. Alexandra grabbed the closest thing at hand, a candlestick, and ran at the man, bringing it down as hard as she could on his right arm. He let out a bellow and released Rhea, who fell to the floor. The man lashed out, knocking the candlestick from Alexandra's hand. She leaped at him, kicking and swinging her fists. He planted a big hand in the middle of her chest and shoved.

She staggered backward and tripped over Nancy's inert form, falling to the floor. Her head cracked against the hard wood floor, and everything went black.

The intruder took a step toward Alexandra and looked at her. His eyes traveled over her face and down her form to the shapely legs revealed by her rucked-up nightgown. He cast a glance at Rhea and started toward her.

"Alexandra? What's the matter?" a woman's voice trumpeted from the hall.

The man turned and scooped Alexandra up. He flung her over his shoulder as if she weighed no more than a child and strode to the window. He swung his leg out and onto the ladder propped beneath the window. With one arm wrapped around Alexandra to steady her weight, he backed out of the window just as Aunt Hortense hurried into the room.

Aunt Hortense gasped, staring, as the man started down the ladder, Alexandra over his shoulder. She let out a scream and ran to the window.

"Help! Stop him!" Aunt Hortense leaned out of the window. The man was at the foot of the ladder. "Help!"

A footman, the butler and a maid came rushing into the room and stopped, goggling at the sight of the two bodies on the floor and Hortense leaning out the window.

Aunt Hortense whirled to face them. "Stop him, you fools! He's got Alexandra!"

She turned to the window just in time to see the man disappear around the house, Alexandra dangling over his shoulder.

10

The footman and butler stared for a moment longer at Aunt Hortense before the message sank in, then they turned and pelted down the stairs. Aunt Hortense hurried to Rhea and knelt beside her, lowering her head to Rhea's face.

"She's still breathing, thank God. Here, don't just stand there, girls, help me get her into her bed."

Her words jolted the maids from their trance, and they scurried to help Hortense lift Rhea and put her in the bed. She went to Nancy next and bent over her. It wasn't hard to see that she had been knocked unconscious. A bruise was already forming on the side of her face. She, too, was breathing, her pulse steady, and the three women carried her to the cot.

Aunt Hortense wet a cloth in the washbasin and went to Rhea, bidding the maids to take care of Nancy. She washed Rhea's face, hoping to revive her, but Rhea did not waken. If it had not been for the faint rise and fall of her chest, Aunt Hortense would have said she was dead.

"That brute must have choked her!" she exclaimed, leaning over to examine the red marks ringing her sister-in-law's throat. "This is a mad country! I've never seen the likes of it."

And what could have happened to Alexandra?

The footman entered the room on the run, followed by the rest of the servants. "He was gone, miss. We looked up and down the street and couldn't find anyone."

"Damn and blast!" Aunt Hortense shouted, using one of her brother's favorite oaths. "The world has gone mad!"

She looked at her servants, and they all stared unhelpfully at her. She had always been a strong woman, but at the moment, she felt close to panic. She was alone in a strange country, her sister-in-law and Nancy unconscious and her niece kidnapped.

"What am I to do?" she asked, raising a hand to her whirling head.

"Shall I fetch a magistrate?" the butler asked.

"Yes. Get a doctor, too. And..." She hesitated. Alexandra would not like it, but Aunt Hortense could think of only one person she knew who could help. "And fetch Lord Thorpe, too."

Sebastian followed the footman into Alexandra's house, a scowl on his face. He had not been able to make head nor tail of the man's story; he had come with him only because the man's obvious anxiety had raised his own. When he strode into the house, the first sight that met his eyes was Alexandra's aunt pacing up and down the entry hall. She whirled with relief at his entrance.

"Lord Thorpe! Thank God you're here. What took so long?"

"I was asleep," he replied acidly. "My valet was— rightfully—reluctant to awaken me because of the babbling of some footman. What the devil is going on? If this is some scheme of Alexandra's to—''

"Oh, hush," Aunt Hortense snapped, causing the footman's eyes to nearly start out of his head. Americans, he was convinced, had no sense of correct behavior. Either of the Misses Ward would tell the Prince Regent himself to shut up if they felt like it. "This is a far graver matter than your loss of sleep. Someone has taken Alexandra."

Thorpe felt as if a shard of ice had plunged into his chest. "What? I don't believe it. Who? Why?"

"I don't know that," Aunt Hortense replied testily. "If I did, I would have gone after her. I don't know where to turn, who to go to for help. You were the only one I could think of."

"What happened?"

"Come here. I'll show you." Aunt Hortense motioned for him to follow her and started up the stairs. She led him into Rhea's bedroom. Rhea, pale as a corpse, was stretched out on her bed, still unconscious. Nancy, looking little better, lay on her cot against the wall. Her eyes were open and she was moaning. A maid sat beside each bed.

Both maids bobbed curtseys when they walked in, and the one beside Nancy said, "She's awake now, miss. She sicked up something terrible, but at least she can talk."

"I found both of them on the floor, unconscious," Aunt Hortense explained to Thorpe, pointing to the carpet where they had lain. "And a man was climbing out the window." She swung her hand to point toward the open window. "He had Alexandra slung over his shoulder."

"What!" Thorpe rushed to the window and peered out, as if he could somehow still see the scene. "Where did this ladder come from?"

"I have no idea."

"It's the one from the back, miss," one of the maids

explained helpfully. ''The footmen use it for washing the outside of the windows.''

''It makes no sense!'' Thorpe exclaimed. ''Why would anyone abduct Alexandra?''

''Nothing has made sense the whole time we've been in this infernal country,'' Aunt Hortense snapped. ''I wish to God we had never come. First that man attacked Alexandra, then there was the rat, and now this....''

''Whose room is this?''

''Rhea's.'' Aunt Hortense nodded toward the woman in the large bed. ''Alexandra's mother. He obviously tried to kill her. Look at her throat.''

Thorpe stepped to the side of the bed and gazed down at Rhea's abused throat. ''Has she awakened?''

''No, my lord,'' the maid replied softly, ducking her head in awe at speaking to a lord.

''Why did he take Alexandra?'' Thorpe turned to Aunt Hortense.

''I don't know. This is the only room he entered. He must have been after Rhea. He struck Nancy, apparently, but he did not try to choke her. I can only assume that Alexandra must have heard the struggle and come running in here to help her mother. I heard her scream, and by the time I got here, he was dragging her out the window.''

Thorpe clamped down on the fear swelling in his chest and trying to push out his throat. ''Well, one thing's for certain, he won't find her an easy captive. Perhaps that will at least make it easier to track his movements. Who would want to harm Alexandra's mother?''

''No one! It makes no sense. She doesn't know anyone in London any more than I do. Less—she rarely leaves the house.''

Sebastian ran his hand over his face, trying to force his brain to work. ''It could be that he was after Alexandra all along, but came in the wrong window. How would he know which one was hers? Mrs. Ward and the maid woke up and struggled with him, and he subdued them. It could have been that he did not mean to kill Mrs. Ward, only to render her unconscious, as in fact he did. Then either Alexandra came into the room by luck, having heard the struggle, or he found her room and seized her, and came back through here and down his ladder.''

"But why? What could he want with her?"

Thorpe clamped his lips together. It was obvious to him what a criminal would be likely to do with a beautiful woman like Alexandra, but he could scarcely worry the girl's aunt with such news.

However, Aunt Hortense read the truth in his eyes and recoiled a step. "No...no.''

"I'll find her," Thorpe promised grimly, his hands knotting into fists. "I'll send my men out to ask questions immediately. If anyone can find word of her, it'll be Murdock.''

"But surely he wouldn't do all this just to—despoil Alexandra. He went to a great deal of trouble. It seems to me that there must be something more behind it.''

"Yes. I imagine there is.'' He paused, studying her. "What other schemes has your niece been involved in?''

"Schemes?'' Aunt Hortense looked at him blankly. "What are you talking about?'' Then her face cleared. "Oh—I had forgotten. Alexandra told me you had decided she was a swindler.''

"The most likely reason for her abduction would be a grudge that some former cohort has against her—or even perhaps the victim of one of her swindles.'' He faltered in the face of Aunt Hortense's basilisk glare.

"If *that* is what you're going to be looking for, it was obviously no use calling you. You won't find any connection like that with Alexandra because there is none. You will waste your time—and, unfortunately, Alexandra's.'' She turned and began pacing. ''There must be someone else who can help me.''

''Miss Ward,'' Thorpe said in his most freezingly aristocratic voice, ''I will help you far more than anyone else. However, it would make it much easier if you did not persist in keeping secrets from me. I am aware that you must to some extent be involved in Alexandra's activities and so you would not want to admit anything. But in this instance, I think that Alexandra's safety outweighs any other considerations.''

''Of course it does. But I can't tell you about any victims or cohorts because there haven't *been* any. Alexandra has never been involved in any sort of trouble—at least, not until she came here and met you lot. From the moment you walked in our door, there has been nothing but trouble.'' She crossed her arms and glowered at him.

Thorpe sighed. ''Obviously I am getting nothing accomplished here.'' He turned toward the door, saying, ''I will let you know as soon as I find out anything.''

He strode out of the room and out of the house. By the time he reached the street, he was moving almost at a run. He could not remember ever having felt quite so helpless or frightened. Murdock would have more success than most people in finding out if a young lady had been abducted. Unfortunately, the scope of the investigation was so large and vague that it seemed almost impossible. London was teeming with criminals—how could they find one among so many? Nor did he imagine that there would be many witnesses to a kidnapping in the middle of the night. Eventually, he hoped, they would ferret out where she was. But how long would it take? *And what would happen to Alexandra in the meantime?*

* * *

Alexandra was aware of a tremendous ache in her head. She had no thoughts at first, only a throbbing awareness of pain that ran up one side of her face and exploded in her brain. There were voices, too, and her first conscious thought was that she wished they would go away, for they only added to the pain in her head.

"Very, very nice, Peggoddy," a woman said in a flat, nasal voice. "I must say your taste has improved. How did you find her?"

A deep rumble answered her, but Alexandra could understand only a word or two of the thickly accented male tongue. "Don't know. Seemed…waste, like."

"Yes, it certainly would have been," the woman agreed, with a chuckle. "You did right to bring her to me. Now you'll get paid twice for doing one job."

"That's right!" The male voice brightened, as if he had only just realized that fact.

Alexandra stirred. She wished they would go away. She would like to tell them to, but she couldn't quite summon the words. She tried to roll over, but couldn't. Her hands seemed to be awkwardly stuck above her head.

"Looks as if she's waking up," the woman said. "You'd best hold her, Peggoddy."

There was a grunt of assent, and something clamped on Alexandra's ankles, pinning them down. There was the sound of scissors, and she felt her gown move a little. The sound came closer and closer, and as it did, she felt air touch her skin. Suddenly the two sides of her gown were pulled apart, exposing her entire body to the air. At this Alexandra's eyes popped open.

She found herself staring into the face of one of the oddest women she had ever seen. The woman's face was wrinkled and lined, like an old woman's, yet her hair was not white, but an impossibly fiery shade of red. The mass of hair was done in an intricate style, and on one side three bright, long feathers were pinned in adornment. Gold and diamonds winked at her neck and pulled down her earlobes. She wore an emerald dress, cut indecently low to expose her wrinkled breasts almost to the nipples. But it was her face that was the most peculiar. She had covered it with powder and paint in the fashion that had been popular twenty or thirty years earlier, the skin utterly white, her lips and cheeks rouged red. Heavy black pencil lined her eyes and brows, and a beauty patch had been stuck on her upper lip near the corner of her mouth.

The woman was looking at Alexandra's body, bared to her gaze. She nodded, smiling a little in satisfaction. "Ah, this is a ripe 'un." She cupped one of Alexandra's breasts and jiggled it, studying the way Alexandra's nipple tightened in response. "Oh, yes, I think we'll make quite a bit on her."

Alexandra gasped when the woman touched her breast, and the woman glanced at her. "Awake now, are you?" she asked pleasantly, as if there were nothing bizarre about the situation. "Pretty eyes, too." She frowned. "Too bad you hit her on her face, though, Peggoddy. That bruise'll mar her face—and I don't want to make her up. She's too fresh-looking for that." She sighed. "I guess we'll have to wait a day or two for that bruise to go away."

"What—" Alexandra's word came out as a croak, and she swallowed and tried again. "What are you talking about? Who are you? What do you think you're doing?" She looked at the large man, and suddenly memory came rushing back to her. "What did you do to my mother?"

"I'm Magdalena," the woman said. "Catchy, isn't it? There's them say I'm wicked for using a name from the

Bible, but I ask you—isn't it a name they always remember? Don't you worry, you're in good hands. Magdalena knows how to make use of a girl when she gets her. I'm not one what just throws them in there. I make sure I present her right when I get a fresh one like you.''

Alexandra stared at her, uncomprehending. She tried to sit up, but once again was thwarted by her hands. She craned to look behind her and saw, to her astonishment, that a short velvet rope bound her hands and tied them to a hook in the wall behind her.

''What—why—''

''Peggoddy brought you here.'' Magdalena nodded toward the huge man at the end of the bed, who was leaning forward, his hands braced on Alexandra's ankles, weighing her down. ''He knows I'm the best, don't you, Peggoddy? Spread her legs, Peggoddy, and let me see what's what.''

Alexandra let out a cry of outrage as Peggoddy obediently pulled her legs wide apart. ''Stop! What are you doing?''

The woman did not answer, but put her hand between Alexandra's legs and inserted a finger. Alexandra gasped, rendered speechless by the crude gesture.

''Ah, better and better.'' The woman smiled. ''A virgin. I'll fetch a good price for your first time.''

''I don't know what you're talking about,'' Alexandra snapped, rage shooting through her. ''But you had better let go of me this instant.''

Both Magdalena and the man Peggoddy seemed to find this statement highly amusing, for they began to laugh. Alexandra seethed and struggled against her bonds, which provided the strange pair even more mirth.

''Oh, she's a feisty one.''

Magdalena signaled to Peggoddy, and he released her

feet. He stepped back, but not quickly enough to avoid a kick on his arm from Alexandra. He scowled and raised his hand, but Magdalena motioned him away.

"You've already done enough damage. You're not to touch her again." She turned and looked at Alexandra, who was twisting and turning and pulling at her bonds. She watched until finally Alexandra gave it up as useless. Alexandra lay, panting, looking at the woman with hatred.

"Yes, I can see you're going to be a stubborn one. Well, there's nothing to be done about that. There's plenty as likes 'em reluctant, 'specially when they're virgins. I can think of several who will be quite interested in you. In fact, I believe I'll start a bidding war among them— that should drive the price right up."

A chill ran through Alexandra. She was helpless and at this woman's mercy. She closed her eyes and drew a breath, forcing herself to sound calm. She had to get out of here somehow. She had to find out if her mother was all right.

"Look," she began. "I don't know how I got here or why Peggoddy took me, but I can tell you that you have made some sort of mistake. I realize that money is your first consideration. And I am worth a great deal of money. I can pay you more than any of these men you're talking about, if you will only let me go."

"More than ten good years' worth? I don't think so, Miss High-and-Mighty. Even if you could, I'm not stupid enough to think that I could trust you to pay me after I let you go."

"Send a note to my aunt. She will pay."

The woman rolled her eyes. "There'll be those who will pay me plenty a few nights from now, and I don't need to be sticking my neck out sending relatives notes and such to get it."

"No! Please, listen to me. You have to believe me. We could arrange it. I will pay you."

There was a knock on the door, and it opened. A girl came in bearing a small tray. She barely glanced at Alexandra on the bed, accustomed, presumably, to such sights as a woman in a torn nightgown lying tied to the wall. She set the tray beside the bed.

"Sit up now," Magdalena ordered. "Here's food for you to eat."

"I don't want any. I won't eat it."

"Won't you? It's mighty tasty, and here it is past breakfast." She picked up a glass of water. "At least drink this."

"No!"

"Jenny," Magdalena said significantly, and the girl went over to a low brazier not far from the bed. A few small sticks and such were in the brazier, and the girl efficiently lit them, sending a trail of smoke in the air. Then she dipped several spoonfuls of what appeared to be herbs onto the fire. The fire began to smoke heavily.

Alexandra coughed. "You'll asphyxiate us," she protested.

"Not at all."

The smoke was heavy and pungent. Alexandra coughed again, but she could not keep from breathing in the thick, dark stuff, as the girl was busy with a fan directing the smoke toward Alexandra.

"Please. Stop that. I need to find out—my mother, is she all right?" Alexandra's words sounded strangely slow to her ears. A strange sort of lassitude was creeping through her. She realized how hungry she was—and even more thirsty. Her mouth felt as dry as the desert, and she wanted water desperately.

She looked at the glass the woman held. She knew she

should not drink it, but she was having trouble remembering why. She drew a deep breath. The smoke no longer bothered her. In fact, nothing was all that bad. What could it hurt to drink a little water? Or eat some food? She looked at the tray. She could imagine the crisp, juicy tang of the apple, the smooth taste of the golden cheese, the thick slab of bread slathered with creamy butter.

Magdalena picked up the plate from the tray and held it closer to Alexandra. It seemed to Alexandra that she could smell each individual piece of food, and they were all wonderful. Her stomach rumbled hungrily.

"Maybe a bite," she mumbled.

Magdalena smiled. "First drink a little water. Peggoddy, help her up."

He came to the side of the bed and lifted her under her arms to as near a sitting position as she could get with her hands tied as they were. Magdalena held the glass of water to her lips, and Alexandra sipped.

She screwed up her face. "Bitter."

"Take another sip. It won't be long."

She held the glass to her lips again, and when Alexandra opened her mouth, she tilted it up and poured in a whole mouthful. Surprised, Alexandra swallowed. This time it didn't taste as bad, and in a few more drinks she had drained the glass. With Peggoddy still propping her up, she ate the food that Magdalena held to her mouth. It tasted delicious, almost as good as she had imagined, and she ate greedily. By the time she finished, however, her lips felt strange and rubbery, and she noticed that there was a hazy look to everything. She glanced around the room, amazed at how good she felt, how warm and wonderful everything seemed.

"I'm sleepy," she mumbled.

"Of course you are. You have a nice long sleep ahead

of you." Magdalena motioned to Peggoddy to release her, and he did so. Alexandra closed her eyes, slipping immediately into sleep. Magdalena looked at her with satisfaction. "Well, that ought to take care of her for the rest of the day. We'll give her another dose with her meal this evening. And for heaven's sake, douse that fire before we all get stupid."

Never in his life had two days passed so slowly for Sebastian. As soon as he had gotten home from his talk with Aunt Hortense, he had summoned Murdock and told him what had happened. He had laid whatever servants or money he might need at the man's disposal with only one directive—find her. Next he had hired a Bow Street Runner and given him the same mission.

But he could not sit at home waiting for the net to catch some word on Alexandra's abduction. He had gone to the rough sort of places he had frequented in his wilder youth, taverns where one had to watch one's back, and gaming hells where one had to watch everyone else's hands. He had made some friendships long ago in those places, and he called on them now, explaining the information he wanted and the money he was eager to pass on to anyone who could give him that information. By the end of the day, he had exhausted his sources, and there was nothing left for him to do except wait.

He did it poorly, pacing his study and snapping at every hapless servant who was foolish enough to interrupt him without bringing word of Alexandra. He did not pause to consider why he felt as if his life hung in the balance because a woman whom he held in contempt was in danger. The only thought that occupied him was the worry that the longer she was missing, the more likely it was that she had been harmed. He thought of the man taking her off somewhere and raping her, and his fingers curled into fists, red-hot anger coursing through him. When he got hold of the man, he promised himself, he would make him sorry he had ever been born.

Murdock urged him to eat and sleep, pointing out how little use it was to make himself less alert and strong for when the time came for action. Sebastian understood the logic of his manservant's words, but he could not follow his advice, however reasonable. Food seemed to stick in his throat, and though he lay down on his bed, sleep kept its distance from him, coming only in fits and starts. During the brief periods when he did sleep, he dreamed crazy, frightening dreams and awakened from them with a start.

By late the next afternoon, he looked as if he had aged years, and he felt worse. There were blue circles beneath his eyes, and lines had sunk into the skin around his mouth. He had not bothered to shave or to tie a cravat. The lunch that Punwati had brought him was on a tray on his desk, largely untouched.

He sat slumped in a chair beside the desk, his eyes closed, but he was not asleep. When the door opened, his eyes flew open and he was out of his chair in an instant. Murdock stepped into the room, and though his face was set, there was an intensity to his eyes that gave Sebastian hope for the first time in two days.

"What is it? Do you have news?"

"We tracked down a man. He's known for doing jobs that require brawn, not brain, and today he's been spending money and boasting about getting paid two ways, saying once for the old lady and once for the girl."

Sebastian's heart picked up its beat. "Where is he?"

"In a tavern. I got men watching him. He won't get away. But I thought you'd want to talk to him yourself."

"You're right about that." Sebastian was pulling on his jacket. "Get my pistols."

"In the hall, my lord." Murdock's pistol was already tucked into the waistband of his trousers, hidden by his jacket. "I took the liberty of having the carriage brought round."

A faint smile touched Thorpe's face for the first time since he had heard of Alexandra's abduction. "You know me well."

"I should hope so, sir," Murdock said with an air of indignation as he followed Thorpe out of the room.

A few minutes later their carriage pulled up in front of a tavern in the East End of London, a seedy place that, from the looks of it, was unused to customers arriving in carriages. A drunk, staggering out the door of the tavern, stopped and goggled at the sight of Lord Thorpe stepping from the vehicle, followed by Murdock. The driver glanced around the narrow street uneasily and was glad that Murdock had ordered him to bring the burliest of his grooms with him.

Inside the tavern, Murdock looked around until he spotted one of his men. A nod from the man indicated the table in the corner, where a large man sat with two smaller cronies, downing a glass of ale. Murdock and Thorpe strode through the crowded tavern and stopped beside the table. All three men looked up, bleary-eyed.

Murdock directed a hard look at the two companions and jerked his head in an unmistakable directive to leave. They glanced uncertainly at their large companion, then melted away. Murdock and Thorpe sat down, one on each side of the large man.

"Wot d'you want?" the man asked, slurring his words.

"Just to have a chat, Mr...."

"Peggoddy." The man scowled. "'Oo wants to know?"

Thorpe ignored his question. "I understand you came into quite a bit of money today," Thorpe said pleasantly.

Peggoddy looked at him suspiciously. "So? Wot's it to you?"

Thorpe's lips moved in something resembling a smile, but so chilling that the man slid back a little in his seat. "You were paid a bit to kidnap a young woman."

"No. Never." Peggoddy looked pleased with himself. "'E only said to take care of the old biddy. I thought of the wench on me own. Soon as I saw 'er, I thought, 'Madam'd pay a bit to get one like that.' Quality an' all, you know, an' lookin' like she did."

Thorpe's fingers curled into his palms, but he kept his voice level.

"How did she look?"

"Wot?"

"Describe her."

Peggoddy looked at him oddly. "Wot you want to know for?"

"Never mind that. Just tell me." He reached in his waistcoat and pulled out a silver coin, which he slid across the table invitingly.

Peggoddy snatched up the coin, saying, "Black hair, curly like. Fair skin. A looker, that one."

Sebastian wanted to wrap his hands around the man's throat and squeeze the leer from his face, but he forced himself to keep still. "Did you hurt her?" he asked, his voice like rust.

"The girl? I never touched 'er." He sounded disappointed. "She were a ripe 'un, too. But I knew madam'd 'ave my 'ead if I damaged 'er. Why, she docked me 'cause o' that little bruise on 'er cheek—as if I could 'elp that! She come flyin' at me, and I 'ad to do somethin', didn' I?"

"I'm sure." Thorpe controlled his voice with an effort. "Were only a tap, anyway."

"Where did you take her? Who is this madam?"

Peggoddy grinned slyly. "Oh, no, I ain't tellin' you that." The large man shook his head and took another quaff of ale. "She wouldn't like it. Madam's particular like that."

"I am particular, too," Thorpe replied, sliding a gold coin across the table toward Peggoddy. He lifted his hand to reveal it, then laid his hand over it again. "Now tell me where you took her."

The man swallowed, staring greedily at Thorpe's hand. Finally, with reluctance, he shook his head. "No. Madam'd 'ave my 'ead if I ratted on 'er."

"You're scared of her?" Thorpe's voice dripped scorn.

The man looked abashed, but he said only, "You don't know madam. You cross 'er, and yer dead with 'er."

Thorpe leaned forward conversationally. "And you're dead, period, if you don't."

"Wot?" The man blinked at him.

"You may notice that one of my hands is not on the table," Thorpe went on coolly. "That is because I have a pistol in it."

"Wot!" The man glanced at the table as if he could see through it to Thorpe's concealed hand.

"Yes. And it is pointed at a rather vital part of your anatomy. Now, if you don't tell me who this madam is and where her brothel is located, I shall fire, and you, my friend, will die a slow and painful death. I've seen men with their privates blown off, and it's not a pleasant way to go."

Peggoddy paled, and he glanced from Thorpe to Murdock, who said, "I would do as he said."

"But...but you're a toff! You can't do that!"

"Can't I? I'm afraid you will find that I am not the sort of toff you know." He leaned closer, his eyes boring into the other man's. "The only reason you are alive right now is because I need you to tell me where you took Alexandra. If you don't tell me, I'll have no reason not to kill you, which, believe me, would bring me a great deal of pleasure."

"Th-then you'd never find out." Sweat beaded on the large man's forehead.

"Oh, I think I would." Thorpe offered him a wintry smile. "I'd find someone willing to tell me what madam you supplied girls for. It would just take a little longer— which is why I am willing to bargain your life for the information." He paused. "So which is it? I need to get on with it, one way or another. I haven't the time to waste."

Peggoddy licked his lips and cast a last desperate glance at Murdock, who stared at him stonily.

"All right. All right. I'll tell you."

"Better than that. You will show us."

"Wot?"

"You didn't imagine that I would leave you here to run away after you had given me a false address, did you? Not everyone is as witless as you are. You are coming with us, and Murdock here will watch over you while I get the girl out of madam's house. If she is not there, I'll use you for target practice, starting with your ankles and working up."

Peggoddy stared at him, his eyes huge. Sebastian rose, his coat pocket distorted by the obvious shape of a pistol. Peggoddy's eyes flickered to Thorpe's pocket. Then he swallowed hard and rose to his feet. Murdock linked arms with the big man and steered him around the table. Thorpe followed them out.

Peggoddy directed them to a slightly better part of town, glancing nervously from time to time to the pistol Thorpe kept trained on him and then to Murdock, who sat beside Thorpe and had pulled a pistol from his waist and held it, too, on Peggoddy.

"'Ere now," he said finally, "You're not goin' to shoot me now, are you? I didn't 'urt 'er none."

"Other than sell her to a brothel?" Thorpe asked in an icy voice. "Oh, and give her a little...tap, was it?"

"It weren't nothin'," he protested. "I 'ad to knock 'er out, see."

"If I were you, I'd keep my mouth shut," Murdock offered. "You're digging your grave deeper every time you open it."

Peggoddy settled into an aggrieved silence. Thorpe studied him.

Finally he said, "No, I shan't shoot you—as long as you're telling me the truth about where Alexandra is. If I get her back, you'll live."

"There it is," Peggoddy said in a hushed voice, looking out the window.

Thorpe signaled to the coachman to stop. "Where?"

"The buildin' in the middle, the one with the green door. There's an alleyway beside it, see, and you can go down it and go in the back door. Madam's got stairs up the back, that's where I go."

"What room is she in?"

The man shook his big head. "I dunno that. Where I took 'er's not where she keeps 'em. Put her in a fancy room for the toffs, I imagine."

A light flared in Thorpe's eyes, and the big man drew back a little. "I didn't know she were nothin' to you! 'Ow was I supposed to know?"

"I'm going in," Sebastian said to Murdock, turning to

his servant as he put his pistol into his pocket. "You stay here and make sure this one doesn't get away. If he's steered us wrong, I'm coming back to kill him bit by bit."

"Harrison could watch him, sir," Murdock protested. "You might need my help."

"If I do, then I need you on the outside to rescue us, not in there with me and caught. Besides, while I'm gone, I want you to question him about the job he was hired to do. Find out who hired him and why."

Thorpe turned, cast one last icy glance at Peggoddy and stepped out of the carriage.

11

Sebastian strode rapidly across the street to the alleyway. He paused at the end of the long, dark corridor and looked down it cautiously, aware that Peggoddy could easily have given him directions that would land him right in a nest of his henchmen. However, he could make out no variation, no shadow along the blank wall until the darker indentation of a doorway halfway down.

Drawing his pistol out of his pocket and holding it at the ready, he made his way along the narrow pathway to the door. He was just about to ease the door open a crack when it opened, throwing a line of yellow light out, and he stepped back hastily. A girl came out, carrying a pail far too large for her, and poured out some water. She turned to go into the building, and Thorpe, who had pocketed his pistol, stepped up quickly behind her, grabbing her around the waist and immobilizing her arms. His other hand he clamped over her mouth to prevent a scream.

"I won't harm you if you'll be quiet. I only want information," he whispered. "Do you understand?"

The girl nodded, her eyes wide with fright.

"If you will give me the information, I'll give you

money—more than you earn here in a month, I wager. Are you interested?''

Again the girl nodded, this time with less fear and more interest.

''All right. I'm going to take my hand away. You have to promise not to scream—because if you do, I will have to hurt you.''

At her firm nod, he released her mouth.

''Cor!'' the girl whispered. ''You scared a girl to death, you did.''

''Sorry.'' A faint smile touched his lips. ''Somehow I don't think you're one to scare easily. What's your name?''

''Janet, sir.'' Even in her fright, she recognized the tone of class and authority, and she responded to it.

''All right, Janet, I'm going to let you go, and we'll talk.''

''Yes, sir.'' He released her, and she turned to look at him. ''Were you lyin' about the ready?''

''No, indeed.'' He fished out a gold coin and held it between his fingers. Janet's eyes widened.

''Wot you want to know?''

''The whereabouts of a young lady. She was brought here by a man named Peggoddy in the last day or so. Beautiful.''

''Black 'air?'' the girl asked. ''Funny talkin'?''

Relief flooded Sebastian. He had been worried that perhaps they had taken a wrong turn with Peggoddy, and that he was not speaking of Alexandra. ''Yes. She is an American.''

''Aye, I seen 'er. Peggoddy brought 'er in t'other day. Stubborn sort.''

Sebastian couldn't quite suppress a smile. ''That would be her.''

"She's 'ere. Madam's 'olding 'er till tonight. She's got three lords wantin' to bid on 'er."

Ice settled in the pit of his stomach. "Tonight? When?"

"In a 'alf hour or so. She's in there, gettin' 'er ready. I was just carryin' down the water from 'er bath."

"Can you take me to her?"

"You goin' to steal 'er?" Janet asked, eyes great with curiosity.

Sebastian nodded. "She was stolen from me. Will you show me where she is?"

"It'll be worth me 'ide if old Mags finds out."

"The madam?" He tossed the girl the coin, and she caught it deftly. He plucked another from his pocket. "Perhaps you won't have to stay here with the madam. Take me to her, and I'll give you this coin, as well. You can go elsewhere and get a new job."

Janet looked intrigued. Suddenly she grinned, exposing crooked teeth. "Aw right, I will. Wait 'ere a sec."

She went into the house with the pail. Thorpe was about to decide he had made a terrible mistake by already giving her the coin when she popped her head out. "Aw right, come on."

She disappeared, and Sebastian stepped in after her. They were standing in a small entry. The door beside them led into the kitchen area, where several servants were at work. In front of them was a narrow corridor, lit by a few sputtering lamps.

"Old Mags don't believe in wastin' light on the likes of us servants," Janet whispered to him, then started down the hall, waving to him to follow her.

Sebastian did so quietly, tiptoeing up the stairs after her. The girl gestured to him to wait at the top. She stuck her head out and surveyed the area, then signalled to him. She moved noiselessly down a more elegantly decorated hall to a doorway, turned the knob and went inside. Sebastian was right on her heels. He was expecting to find Alexandra in the room, and he was disappointed to find that it was very narrow and small, more like a hall than a room, unfurnished, and containing no one but himself and Janet.

"Where is she?" he demanded.

"Shh." Janet lifted her finger to her lips and pointed to the wall in front of them. "They may still be with her," she whispered.

She took him by the arm and led him to the center of the wall, once again gesturing with her fingers to be quiet. A small knob stuck out from the wall, and she slid it to the side. Two eyeholes appeared, and Janet motioned to them. He bent and looked into the holes.

He almost gasped when he saw that they were only three or four feet from a bed. A man, a woman and a bizarre old harridan stood beside the bed, studying the young woman who was on it. The woman on the bed was dressed all in white, sitting up with her legs curled under her. Her head was turned away from him and toward the other people, so that all he could see was the cloud of thick black curling hair that tumbled around her shoulders. The sight of it hit him like a blow to the solar plexus. Alexandra!

Janet closed the eyeholes and whispered. "Soon as that lot leaves, you can go in through the hall door." She pointed to the hall from which they had come. "Don't let 'em catch you. I gotta go now."

"Thank you." Sebastian pressed the other coin into her palm.

The girl smiled, and her plain face was almost pretty. "She's lucky to 'ave you, she is."

"I'm not sure she would agree, but thank you."

Janet opened the door and peeked out, then exited quietly, closing the door behind her. Sebastian went to the peephole and opened it.

The woman pushed a lock of hair from Alexandra's face and tugged her dress so that it exposed the creamy curve of her shoulder. The harridan nodded.

"That should do it. A right picture you make, girlie." She let out a gleeful cackle. "When those gentlemen see you, I'll have 'em bidding high as the moon."

The woman on the bed moved restlessly and ran a hand down her chest and over her breast in a seductive gesture. Sebastian was aware of the sudden fluttering of desire deep in his loins. He was looking at her from the side, but he could see the curve of her breast through the thin material and the pointing of her nipple.

"I feel...funny," the woman said. Sebastian recognized the voice as Alexandra's, but it sounded odd, almost slurred.

"No, you don't, girl," the harridan said crisply. "No satisfaction till later. Ned, tie up her hands so she can't touch herself. We want you good and ready by the time the gentlemen come."

The man pulled Alexandra's hands behind her back, tying her to the bedpost by her upper arms, which pulled her into an awkward position, her breasts thrusting out sharply.

"A right picture," the woman in charge repeated, and the three of them left.

Sebastian went swiftly to the door, leaning against it to listen for the sound of their footsteps. When he could no longer hear anything, he eased the door open a crack and checked the hallway. No one was about, so he slipped out and hurried to the next door. He turned the knob, for a moment afraid that it might be locked. But it opened easily to his hand, and he slid inside.

He turned to the bed. "Alexandra!"

It was indeed her. Her vivid black hair tumbled around her face and onto her shoulders like a silken cloud. Her cheeks were flushed, her eyes huge and dark in her pale face. She looked beautiful...and utterly seductive. They had dressed her in a simple white dress of the cut and style worn by any well-to-do young woman, a maiden's dress, quite demure—except for the fact that it was made of the sheerest material, revealing the curves of her breasts, the well of her navel, even the shadow of hair between her legs. The pink-brown circles of her nipples were pressed against it, their centers pointing. Her dress was shoved to her knees, leaving her stockinged legs bare below it. One stocking had been artfully shoved down, exposing her knee and leaving her looking as if she were in the middle of undressing.

Desire flared in Sebastian, unbidden and as hot as fire, making him feel guilty and ashamed for feeling it even as it weakened his knees. He swallowed, his hands tightening into fists.

Alexandra looked at him for a long moment, blinking. Then a slow smile curved her lips, and her eyes shone. "Thorpe! Thank God."

He crossed the room to her, firmly pushing down his desire. "Are you all right?"

He started to work on the scarf the man had used to bind her to the bedpost. Alexandra shook her head, and her hair brushed against his knuckles, sending tendrils of heat sizzling through him.

"I feel...strange," she whispered, her voice husky and soft. "All hot and tingly."

"You've probably caught cold in that dress," Sebastian commented dryly. "There. Now you can stand up."

He tossed the scarf to the floor and put his hands on her arms, pulling her out of the bed. Her feet touched the floor, and she buckled against him. His arms went around her to hold her up.

"I'm all wobbly," Alexandra said with a little laugh, wrapping her arms around him.

Her breasts pressed into his chest, and her warm breath drifted over his skin at the open top of his shirt, sending a rush of heat slamming straight into his loins.

"Mm," Alexandra murmured and twisted a little against him.

He drew a sharp breath. "Bloody hell, Alexandra! What do you think you're doing?"

"I don't know," she murmured with a throaty laugh. "But doesn't it feel good?"

She leaned back and looked at him. She was smiling, her lips moist and inviting, curving upward seductively. Her eyes were huge and velvety, the color of night. She was softer than he had ever seen her, and—and there was something definitely wrong. For a moment he wasn't sure what it was, just a feeling, perhaps, but then he began to see the signs. There was a slackness to her face, particularly her mouth, a hazy, almost somnolent look to her eyes, and she swayed a little as she stood. The dark velvetiness of her eyes came from the fact that her pupils were huge, as if she were in Stygian darkness, not a lamp-lit room.

"My God!" he breathed in horror. "They've done something to you! They've drugged you!"

She nodded in that same slow, overly firm way she had before and said in a small voice, "I know. I've been sleeping and sleeping. But not so much now. The last few hours I've been awake. I just feel so...so languid.'' Tears welled in her eyes. "I'm sorry, Thorpe. I'm useless; I can hardly stand. And my brain isn't working very well.''

He set his mouth grimly. "Don't worry. I can carry you if I have to.''

"Mother!" She grasped the front of his shirt. "I for-got—is she all right?''

"She's fine. Don't worry about her. The main thing is to get you out of here. I'll take you home and pour some coffee down you. That ought to help.''

"I hope so. I feel so odd.'' She shivered and began to run her hands up and down her arms. "Hot one minute and cold the next. They gave me something else about—'' She frowned. "I don't know, a while ago. But it didn't make me feel sleepy. It's what makes me feel so odd, not numb, but tingly and—and itchy.''

A blush flooded her face, and she turned away, putting her hands up to her cheeks to cool them. She felt as if she were on fire. For the past while, a strange urgency had been growing in her, making her hot and stirring up all sorts of odd, vibrant sensations. The itch she felt was not the sort that one might have on an arm or leg, but an itching deep inside, a hunger and yearning that ached to be appeased.

When Thorpe had entered the room and she had rec-ognized him, she had been flooded with joy and relief. Whatever they had drugged her with had left her sleepy and languid, unable most of the time to move or talk co-herently, but still she had known, despite her enforced acquiescence, that she wanted very badly to be out of this situation. Otherwise, something terrible was going to hap-pen to her, and she was going to be powerless to stop it. When Sebastian walked in the door, her fears had fallen away. She had known deep within her that he would take her away from this evil place and that madwoman Magdalena.

However, the surge of joy she had felt on seeing him had only made this other feeling worse—this throbbing and burning that seemed to be centered between her legs. Even as she had uttered the words, she had known that what she wanted to feel was Thorpe's hand there, between her thighs, where she ached the most. It was, she knew, an utterly lewd and licentious desire.

Sebastian wasn't sure what had made Alexandra blush, but for some reason, his body responded with a surge of heat. He turned away abruptly.

"We better get you out of here." He walked to the door and eased it open, peering out the crack. "It's clear. Come on."

He turned to Alexandra and saw that she was standing beside the bed. She began to walk toward him in a slow, dreamy way, weaving as she came. He watched her, feeling his manhood respond to the sensual vision she created. It was impossible to see her lush body in the sheer material, breasts cupped by the high waist of the dress, nipples dark and straining against the cloth, hips swaying beneath the floating skirts, without thinking of slow, steaming sex. Of long, hot nights in tangled sheets, of endless kisses and the fragrant juices of lovemaking. Sebastian let out a little sigh. What was wrong with him that he could think of making love to a woman in a situation like this, with danger all around and no time to spare? Even worse, it seemed to him the mark of a roué, a libertine or worse, to want to take a woman who was drugged!

Gritting his teeth, he grabbed her by the wrist and pulled her to the door. Setting her behind him, he again looked into the corridor. To his amazement, he felt Alexandra plaster her body against his from behind, encircling his waist with her arms. He snapped the door shut.

"Alexandra! What are you doing?" Her hands were moving slowly up and down his chest, slipping beneath his jacket and burning through his shirt. "Stop it."

He turned, trying to ignore the myriad sensations that were awakened as their bodies rubbed against each other, and grabbed Alexandra's wrists. "We have to leave," he told her, enunciating each word as if he were speaking to a recalcitrant child. "All right?"

She nodded. "I know. I just...wanted to touch you."

"God." Her words almost undid him worse than her touch. He set her away from him, opened the door, took her by the wrist and led her into the hall. They had passed the next room when he heard voices from the far end of the hall, echoing in the stairwell. There was a murmur of male voices and a woman's high-pitched laugh.

Sebastian's first instinct was to run, but he knew they could not make it to the end of the hall without being seen, especially given Alexandra's wobbly state, and running would arouse suspicions more than anything else. It was better to playact, he decided, and so he dropped Alexandra's wrist and wrapped his arm around her shoulder, pulling her tightly against his side.

She looked at him wonderingly.

"Shh. Someone's coming. Pretend I'm a customer."

"A customer?"

"Uh-huh." He leaned his head against hers, nuzzling her ear.

A breathy gasp escaped Alexandra. She wasn't sure what he was talking about, but the touch of his lips against her sensitive skin, the hot brush of his breath, were almost more than she could bear. She shivered, moisture flooding between her legs. Her eyelids fluttered closed, and she stumbled.

"Keep walking," Sebastian murmured, the heat in his veins suppressed for the moment by his awareness of the sounds behind him. There were footsteps, and another laugh, this time a male rumble. It sounded almost like a crowd, he thought in irritation. His arm tightened around Alexandra's shoulders, almost dragging her. The stairs seemed a year away.

There was the sound of a door opening. They were almost to the stairs. Behind him there was a shriek, and an upraised female voice. Thorpe did not pause to glance back; he was certain they had been discovered. His arm dropped to Alexandra's waist, and he ran to the stairs, dragging her, stumbling, with him.

They raced down the stairs, Alexandra clasped tightly to his side, most of her weight borne by him. A harsh woman's voice screeched, "Stop them! He's taking her! Stop them."

They burst out of the stairs into the hallway, where two or three startled servants came out of the kitchen curiously. Thorpe barreled through the group, knocking them aside. Out of the corner of his eye he caught a glimpse of Janet standing just inside the door, and after he passed, he heard the clang of a bucket being upended, and dirty mop water flooded the floor. Janet began to wail, and the servants who were struggling to their feet began to curse, and the men who came bounding down the stairs ran full tilt into the mess. There was a tremendous amount of crashing and falling and cursing, but Thorpe laughed and didn't look back. He couldn't afford the time.

Alexandra couldn't keep up. She staggered and lurched against the wall of the building and would have fallen if the space had not been so narrow. Sebastian grabbed her and picked her up, threw her over his shoulder and began to run. He could hear running footsteps behind him as he burst out of the alleyway. Weighted as he was, it would not take their pursuers long to catch up. He raced toward the carriage just as the front door of the brothel opened and more men poured out.

Fortunately, most of the customers, though they obviously relished a good chase—there were even a few "View, halloos" and "Yoicks, aways" tossed out—were too drunk to make a good run of it, and their bumbling attempts hindered the others more than they helped.

Murdock opened the door of the carriage and hopped out. Peggoddy seized the opportunity to bolt out the other side of the carriage and take off. Murdock let out a curse and turned to look after him.

"Never mind him!" Thorpe reached the carriage and tossed Alexandra unceremoniously into it.

He climbed in after her just as the first brothel servant reached them. Murdock landed a good right to the man's chin, sending him sprawling. The coachman cracked his whip, and the carriage began to lumber off. Murdock leaped on the back of the vehicle. He kicked one man who jumped at the door of the carriage, and Harrison, the burly groom, leaned over and shoved another one off. Murdock pulled out his pistol and waved it threateningly, causing the others to stop. The carriage picked up speed, leaving them all behind.

Sebastian flopped against the seat, his chest heaving, as the carriage rattled away. Alexandra, who had made it no farther than the floor, slumped there, her head lolling against the bottom cushion across from Sebastian. Her skirt was shoved up around her, almost completely exposing her legs. She had no shoes, and the loose stocking had been lost altogether; the other was crumpled around her calf. Her eyes were closed, her mouth slightly open as she breathed deeply. Her face was dewy with moisture. Thorpe thought that he had never seen anyone look more desirable.

He shrugged out of his jacket and leaned down to wrap it around her shoulders. Alexandra looked into his eyes; it seemed as if her whole soul were in her gaze. He hesitated, hovering over her, and her hand curled around the back of his neck. She stretched and placed her lips against his.

Her mouth was moist and hot, her lips as soft as velvet, opening to him. Sebastian kissed her; he could not stop himself, even though he knew that it was wrong to kiss a woman not in full possession of her senses. Once he started, he could not stop. Her mouth was so sweet, so eager, her tongue darting in to play with his. He knelt on the floor, kissing her, unable to pull away as the carriage lumbered through the streets. His veins pulsed wildly; he could hear the roaring of blood in his ears.

Alexandra moaned, a primitive sound that jolted him with passion. He thought of being inside her, of feeling her close around him, hot and tight, moaning her passion as they rode to climax. He wrapped his arms around her more tightly, pulling her into him as if he could meld her to his skin.

The carriage turned a corner sharply, sending them sliding across the floor into the side of the vehicle. It startled Sebastian into some semblance of sanity. He took Alexandra by the shoulders and lifted her into the seat, then sat across from her. But Alexandra immediately left her seat, shrugged off the jacket and climbed onto his lap. She knelt with her legs on either side of him, the hot, damp heat of her desire flush against his legs.

"Don't stop," she murmured and began to kiss his face. "You smell so good. You taste like..." She paused, considering, and licked her lips, sending another spasm of hunger through him. "I don't know...something good." She smiled and bent to kiss his neck, saying, "I want to taste you all over."

"Alexandra," he began weakly. "They have done something to you. Made you..."

"I know. It was the dark drink. What they gave me right before you came. It tasted different from the other, not bitter, more like...herbs, I guess."

"It's that drink that's causing you to, uh..."

"Act like a tart?" Alexandra suggested.

"No. Of course not. I didn't mean that."

"Why not? You think I'm vermin anyway, don't you? Why not a doxie as well as a swindler?"

He could tell that the other drug was wearing off; her speech was becoming clearer and quicker, her thought processes obviously working at a higher speed. But this latter drug was just as obviously in full bloom. Her skin was hot, her color high, and there was an almost feverish glitter in her eyes. Sebastian could not keep his gaze from dropping to her bosom, clearly visible through the sheer gown. Her nipples were dark and engorged.

Alexandra swept her hands to her breasts and cupped them, emphasizing the nipples. "Help me," she whispered. "I want you to touch me."

"You don't know what you're saying," he told her, clenching his fists as though physically holding on to his resolve.

"Please..." She circled her nipples with her forefingers, making them harden even more. "I'm burning."

"You'll regret this in the morning—more than you can guess now," he told her in a strangled voice.

Alexandra let out a frustrated noise and slid backward on his legs. That movement created a delightful sensation in her, so she slid forward and back again, then moved onto only one leg. There was more pressure, and she rocked against his leg, seeking relief. She felt so swollen and hot, so frantic with sexual yearning that she was lost to all embarrassment. All she could think of was the heat searing her body, the hunger that clawed inside her.

"Alexandra, don't!" His voice was desperate, and he clamped his hands on her hips, holding her still. She was tempting him almost past bearing. He felt as though any moment he would lose control completely and slam deep inside her, taking her as no gentleman should take advantage of a woman driven slightly mad by drugs.

Alexandra pouted in a way that made him long to kiss her lips. "All right. Then I'll do it to you."

"What?"

Her hands were already busy at his shirt, unbuttoning it down the front. He reached up to take her hands, and she began to move her hips again, freed from his restraint.

"Dammit!" He grabbed her hips once more, and she was free to finish unbuttoning his shirt. She bent and began to kiss his skin, traveling down the tender flesh of his neck and onto his chest. She tasted and licked and kissed, exploring every inch of him, every texture and taste.

Thorpe cursed, vividly and at length, as her hands and mouth roamed his chest, arousing him until he was so hard he thought he must burst. Then she unbuttoned his trousers, her hand slipping inside.

"No!" He set her firmly on the other seat and buttoned his clothes. "Alexandra, stop it! You cannot do this."

She started to protest, but he held up his hand. "No. Just sit there."

But he found that even sitting and looking at her was

an erotic experience. With that flimsy excuse for a dress, she might as well have been naked. The dress, in fact, was perhaps even worse, for he could see the material lightly scraping over her engorged nipples, arousing them with every breath she took. And her face, the eyes luminous with passion, the lips swollen and damp from his kisses, her cheeks flushed—it took all the control he could muster not to lean across and kiss her.

It was a relief when the carriage rolled to a stop in front of his house and he was able to get out of the cramped quarters. He wrapped his jacket tightly around her shoulders, so that it decently covered most of her. Then he climbed out and reached in to lift her out.

"I can walk," Alexandra protested.

"Not very well," he retorted dryly. "Trust me. It will be much better this way."

He carried her into the house, saying over his shoulder, "Murdock, send a message to her aunt that she is well and I'll bring her home tomorrow morning. And tell Punwati I want coffee and a meal brought to my room."

He could not take Alexandra to her house in this condition, he thought. Her aunt would probably collapse when she saw the way Alexandra was dressed—let alone the way she was acting. He would have to do what he could to overcome the drugs in her body and take her home when she was more presentable.

Thorpe carried Alexandra up the stairs and into his bedroom. He set her on the floor. Alexandra let out a sigh of pleasure, turning to look at the room.

"Sebastian...it's beautiful."

Though Thorpe had many Indian things scattered throughout his house, it was in his bedroom that he had allowed his love of the country to run free. Thick Indian carpets covered the floor, soft and warm beneath one's feet, and there were large plush cushions in jewellike colors scattered around the room to sit on. The bed was low and made of teak, with intricate carvings and ivory inlays. The tall English ceiling had been lowered and warmed by swags of material in the same rich tones as the pillows, stretching from the edges of the room to the center, so that the ceiling resembled a rich, Oriental tent. It was a room of texture and color, deeply sensuous, and Alexandra responded to it instinctively.

She crossed to the bed and leaned down, rubbing her hands along the peacock-blue velvet covering. Then she stretched out on the bed, moving against it a little.

Thorpe, watching her, struggled to suppress his desire. He had thought about Alexandra in this room, on his bed, her black hair spread out against the vivid color of the spread, and seeing the reality shook him. It was hard to remember that she was not in full possession of her faculties.

"You need to get out of those clothes," he told her, striving for a matter-of-fact tone, but the implication of his words hovered in the air around them, charging it with passion.

Irritated, he strode to the large wardrobe against the far wall and pulled out a heavy brocade dressing gown. It was his and, of course, far too large for Alexandra, but it would more than cover her, and that was all that mattered at the moment. He turned to take it to her and stopped, his breath suddenly short in his throat.

Alexandra had disrobed and was standing beside his bed, utterly nude, the flimsy white dress lying in a frothy pool at her feet.

He tried to speak, but nothing came out. He cleared his throat and tried again. "I meant for you to go behind that screen."

Alexandra glanced toward the carved screen in one corner of the room. "Why?"

"Never mind. Just put this on," he said gruffly, tossing the dressing gown onto the bed.

"But it's so heavy." Alexandra picked it up, making a face. "I don't want to. I'm hot."

"Just do it!"

Shrugging, Alexandra put her arms into it. The sleeves hung ludicrously over her hands, and the hem fell in a sort of train behind her. She did not close and sash it. A wide swath of white skin was exposed down the front, which was, perhaps, even more provocative than her entirely nude state had been.

Clenching his teeth, Sebastian walked to her and wrapped the robe around her, tying the sash with quick, jerky movements. When he was finished, the robe was closed, but the lapels gaped, offering a shadowy glimpse of her breasts and leaving a line open all the way down to her waist. He wished he had something better to put over her—like a tent, perhaps.

There was a knock on the door, and Sebastian opened it to his butler. Punwati, his usual imperturbable expression unchanged, set the tray on a low table and bowed, then left the room, all without casting a glance in Alexandra's direction. Sebastian poured a cup of coffee and handed it to Alexandra.

She looked at it. "I don't want it."

"Drink it anyway. It will help you."

"I don't want to."

"I can see that those drugs certainly did nothing for your stubbornness. Drink it."

She set her jaw. "I'm hot, and I don't want to drink something hot. I don't like this thing I have on, either.

I'm stifling." She wriggled a little inside the large dressing gown.

Sebastian ground his teeth and muttered a few heartfelt curses.

"Oh, all right," Alexandra acceded grumpily. "I'll drink it." She took the cup from him and drank from it. "But you have to do something, too."

She set the cup aside and came to stand only inches from him. She looked into his face. Sebastian could feel the heat of her body; he could not get out of his mind the picture of her slim body, naked before she had slipped on his dressing gown. He imagined the satin lining of his robe against her skin, caressing her with each movement.

He took a step back, reminding himself that she would not be looking at him this way or standing so close if she were not drugged. "All right." He cleared his throat. "What do you want me to do?"

"Kiss me."

He stared. It felt as if all the air had been suddenly sucked out of his lungs. "Alexandra, no. You don't know what you're asking."

"Yes, I do. You want something. I want something."

"Alexandra, this is mad. You'll—we'll both regret it."

"Why?" She went up a little on her toes, lifting her face toward him.

"I—I forget."

Alexandra put her hands on his stomach, and his skin twitched beneath his shirt. He could remember with great clarity the way her hands had felt on his skin in the carriage. He knew he ought to pull back.

Instead, he kissed her.

12

Alexandra's lips melted against his, their breaths mingled, and with a shudder, Sebastian pulled her to him, his mouth grinding into hers. His hands slid down her back and cupped her buttocks, lifting her up and into him, moving her against the thick ridge of his desire. Alexandra groaned and dug her fingers into his hair, moving erotically against him. Sebastian made an inarticulate noise deep in his throat and squeezed his fingers into her full, firm flesh.

Her hands came between them, and she started on his buttons. Again his brain registered hazily that he should not allow this, but the thought did not spark any action. Sebastian was too consumed with kissing her. He reveled in the tastes and textures of her, in the scent of her skin and the silken softness of her hair against his cheek.

She opened his shirt and pushed it off his shoulders, and he paused long enough in his caresses to rip it the rest of the way off. Alexandra's busy fingers went next to the dressing gown and undid the sash; then she shrugged out of the heavy gown in a single smooth gesture. It crumpled to the floor, and then it was Alexandra's satiny skin beneath his hands, her heat searing his fingertips.

"Touch me," she murmured, pressing herself into him. "Please, touch me."

He could no more have resisted her plea than he could have walked away from her at that moment. His hands came around to her stomach and slid up to cup her breasts. Alexandra gasped and jerked, and her fingers dug into his hair.

"Yes. Please."

Alexandra felt as if she were on fire. Her breasts ached for his touch; her nipples pointed and thrust toward him. And between her legs was a fierce throbbing, an unmistakable, undeniable hunger that she knew only Sebastian could satisfy. She whimpered as his fingers found her nipples and caressed them, gently squeezing and rubbing until they were as hard as pebbles, aching for something more.

He lifted her and carried her to the bed, laying her gently upon it. Then he lay beside her, propping himself on one elbow, and bent to run his tongue in a lazy circle around one nipple. Alexandra let out a choked noise, and her fingers dug into the cover beneath her. The velvet was soft upon her bare skin, unbelievably erotic as she moved upon the bed. She could not stay still as his tongue worked its magic upon her. Lightly, it teased the bud of her nipple, licking and stroking and lashing until she was digging in her heels and arching off the bed, her breath ragged in her throat. Then his mouth came down around her nipple, enclosing it in wet heat, and she shuddered in response. He began to suckle her nipple, pulling in long, lazy movements, while his tongue continued to play with the hard button.

While his mouth was busy on one creamy breast, his hand slid to her other nipple and teased it. Then he moved, trailing kisses across her chest to the other breast and took that nipple into his mouth. Alexandra moaned, feeling the pull of his mouth all through her, as if some cord ran straight from her breast to the center of her loins. His hand roamed down her body, smoothing over her flat stomach and down the sides of her legs, then up, drawing ever closer to the hot seat of her desire, until finally his fingers tangled in the thatch of hair and slid into the slick, wet folds of flesh. Alexandra groaned and began to tremble as he found her most intimate, neediest spot. Slowly he began to stroke, separating and caressing the folds, pressing and rubbing and gently arousing her. Alexandra writhed, panting, consumed by a fire she had never imagined. This was what she had ached for; this was what she wanted.

She breathed his name, arching against his hand, and he tightened upon her, his finger flickering over the tiny, slick nub that was the center of her pleasure. His tongue moved on her nipple in unison with his finger, heightening the pleasure almost past bearing. Alexandra thought that she might faint, but instead she let out a quiet scream as, suddenly, she was catapulted over the edge of her hunger into a pleasure more intense than anything she had felt before. She jerked, letting out little sobs, and Sebastian covered her mouth with his, taking her whimpers into his mouth, while his finger gently soothed and stroked until Alexandra was spent.

Alexandra looked at him dazedly. Sebastian gazed at her. Need raged in him so fiercely he could scarcely think. He wanted nothing but to be inside Alexandra, encased by her warmth, to drive to the glorious end that he knew waited for them.

He struggled to remember all the reasons he disliked and mistrusted Alexandra Ward, but none of them seemed very clear. What was clear, what was real, was the hunger that burned in him. When she had been kidnapped, he had been consumed by deadly fear and rage. Once he got her back, those violent emotions had turned into an ache to possess her that was equally fierce, exacerbated by her sensual aggression. Her beauty beckoned him like a siren's call. Her desire made it almost irresistible. She wanted him; he wanted her. What was wrong with that?

She wasn't thinking clearly, he reminded himself. She had obviously been drugged, not only into thinking poorly but also into feeling desire. Her sexual teasing had come not from true desire but from a false yearning created by the herb drink they had given her to make her "cooperative."

Yet, as she put her hand on the flat of his stomach and ran it up to his chest, he wondered how he was supposed to remember that distinction. She had been playing havoc with his senses all evening, and he felt ready to explode. It wasn't as if she were a maiden, the hunger inside him argued. She was, after all, an adventuress, not the young woman of quality she had pretended to be. And the way she had touched him this evening, the way she had kissed him, trailing her mouth all over his chest, had not been the action of an innocent.

Still, a small voice replied, that did not change the fact that she was drugged.

Sebastian closed his eyes, struggling to steady his breathing and bring his raging blood under control. Lying on the bed beside him, Alexandra watched him. She felt spent and satisfied, yet there was still something niggling at her, a feeling of incompletion. There was more, she was sure, judging from what she had seen during her stay with Madam Magdalena. The woman had told her she was going to start her education before the gentlemen arrived and had proceeded to have two men and women show Alexandra an astonishing array of things. Even though

Alexandra had been hazy with drugs, she remembered them well enough.

She reached to Sebastian's trousers, running her finger down the hard bulge there. Sebastian barely stifled a groan. "Bloody hell, woman, are you trying to drive me mad?"

"There's more," she began tentatively. "Don't you want—"

"Of course I want!" he interrupted her savagely. "Do you think I'm made out of stone?"

"Then why did you pull away?" Alexandra asked, beginning to work on the buttons of his breeches.

"Because you are not competent to—to make the judgment that—" He broke off, his eyes glazing, as her fingers slipped inside his breeches and grazed along his flesh.

"What judgment?" Alexandra could feel the heat inside her that had been sated begin to stir again. Just the sight of Sebastian's face going slack with desire was enough to arouse her.

She teased her fingers up and down the iron rod of his manhood experimentally, watching his face tighten, a flush rising from his neck. With every indication of his desire, her own built, too.

"No," he whispered, his eyes closed, his entire being focused on the pleasurable sensations Alexandra's fingers were creating.

"No, what?" she asked softly. His earlobe looked terribly inviting to her, and she raised herself off the bed to take it gently between her teeth. A soft grunt broke from Sebastian.

"Don't do this...."

"Do what? This?" She snaked her tongue into his ear, and a tremor ran through him. "Or this?" She curled her fingers around him.

He sucked in a sharp breath. For a moment he hung on the brink, uncertain whether he could stop the course of the passion that was sweeping through him like an avalanche. Then, with a muttered curse, he jerked away from Alexandra and stood from the bed.

"No," he said harshly, his face as stony as if carved from granite. "This is wrong. I will not."

He bent and grabbed his shirt from the floor, shrugging it on as he strode to the door. Alexandra watched, too stunned to speak or move. He yanked open the door and half turned back, not looking at her. "I shall send one of the maids to help you."

"Don't bother," Alexandra retorted acidly. She would like to say a great deal more, but her brain, assaulted by drugs and recently washed with passion, would not work quickly enough to make sense of the hurt and fury that were pouring through her. He was out the door before she could say anything else.

So she had to content herself with throwing every pillow from the bed after him. Then she threw herself facedown on the velvet cover and gave way to tears.

Alexandra woke late the next morning. Her head ached fiercely, and her mouth tasted as if she had been eating ashes. Letting out a groan, she sat up slowly. She rubbed a hand over her face. It felt strangely disconnected from her.

There was a knock at the door, and she realized that that must have been what had awakened her. "Yes?" She croaked the word out, pulling the sheet up to cover her naked front.

A fresh-faced maid opened the door and stuck her head inside. "Good, you're up."

Alexandra wondered how she could have been anything

else with the woman banging on the door, but she managed to keep her sour mood to herself and nodded. The girl moved the rest of the way into the room, closing the door after her, and came to the bed. Her face was agog with curiosity, her eyes taking in every detail of Alexandra's appearance. Alexandra suspected that the girl would be the queen of the servants' hall at mealtime as she regaled them with her story of the strange woman in the master's bedroom. No doubt they would relegate her to the realm of fallen women. If only they knew!

The maid carried a dress across her arms, with a small pile of undergarments atop it. "His lordship said I was to bring you these clothes and to help you dress. I wouldn't have disturbed you, but he said that your aunt would be getting worried."

"Yes, of course." Alexandra experienced a stab of guilt at the realization that she had not even thought of her aunt and the poor woman's state of mind. She remembered vaguely that Thorpe had sent Aunt Hortense a message that she was all right, but that alone would not be enough to keep her from worrying. And what about her mother?

She flushed with shame. She had asked Thorpe about Rhea, and after that she had not given her a second thought. She had been too consumed in her passion for Thorpe to devote any time to anyone else. Alexandra groaned, burying her face in her hands. She had been such a fool last night! How would she ever be able to look Lord Thorpe in the face again? He must think her a veritable doxie now, she thought. His opinion of her was low enough, and now she had thrown herself at him, practically begged him to bed her, indulged in the most wanton behavior. What must he think of her?

"Are you all right, miss?" the maid asked in some concern.

Alexandra raised her head to meet the girl's gaze. "Yes. Well, I've felt better, but no doubt it will improve."

She let the maid help her dress—although she would have preferred to be alone, it was difficult to do up the buttons down the back without help—but then she sent her away, telling her that she would deal with her hair herself. She brushed her hair quickly, ignoring the pain that jerking through her tangled curls brought to her already beleaguered head. It seemed, somehow, just punishment for her foolish behavior the night before. She had thrown herself at a man who clearly did not return her passion—indeed, he thoroughly disliked her, thinking her a lying swindler.

It would have been nice, she thought, to have blamed her actions on the drug that Madam Magdalena had given her, but Alexandra was too honest for that. The drug had certainly taken away her inhibitions, allowing her to act in ways that pride and embarrassment would never have allowed her to normally. However, Alexandra knew that the desire upon which she had acted was very real, indeed. She had felt the passion and was sure she would have felt it without having taken the slightest thing. All the drug had done was make her act out what she really felt.

She remembered with a deep, burning shame the way Thorpe had left the room last night, turning her down flat. He had obviously not felt the sort of raging desire she did. No doubt it had been very embarrassing for him to have to deal with her advances.

She drew a shaky breath. Well, there was nothing she could do now except go on. She would thank Thorpe for his help and try to ignore what had happened.

Alexandra finished brushing her hair and pinned it up with hairpins brought by the efficient maid. It was not the best arrangement, she thought, but it would have to do. She looked in the mirror, her eyes going to the dress she wore. She smoothed down the rose pink skirt. It was slightly out of fashion, but the color was good on her, complementing her complexion. It was a woman's color, not the insipid white that made up almost the entire wardrobe of the young, unmarried British girls. In all likelihood it had belonged to someone in her twenties or older, probably a married woman—and someone shorter and smaller than Alexandra, given the length of the skirt and the tightness of the fit across the bust. Who could have left a dress in Thorpe's house?

She grimaced at her reflection, reminding herself that he could have sisters or other female relatives—and besides, it was really none of her business to whom the dress belonged or why it was there. She turned from the mirror.

Another knock sounded on the door, and she called to the visitor to enter, assuming it was the maid again, but the door opened this time to reveal Thorpe. Alexandra could feel a blush rising up her throat into her face, and she looked away quickly, feeling unbearably awkward.

"Good morning. I took the liberty of bringing you tea and toast," Thorpe said stiffly, setting down the small tray he carried.

"Thank you. That is very kind of you." Alexandra twisted her hands together, still not looking at him. "I am very aware, my lord, of how much I owe you my thanks for coming to my aid. I realize you have no obligation to me. It was generous of you to find me and bring me out of there."

"There is no need to speak of obligation. I could hardly

let you be kidnapped without making some effort to intervene."

Alexandra felt every cool, formal word falling like a rock into the heaviness that pervaded her chest. "Still, I must offer you my gratitude and—and my sincerest apologies for my behavior last night. It was inexcusable."

"No." Thorpe spoke sharply and quickly, raising his hand as though to stop her. "There is no need to apologize. You were not yourself. *I* am the one who should apologize for not handling it better."

Alexandra felt a spurt of anger at his talk of handling her, as if she were a difficult horse or a recalcitrant child. However, she was aware of how much she owed him for rescuing her. With the drugs they had given her, she knew she would have been able to do little to avoid the fate that Madam Magdalena had in mind for her.

Thorpe went on, "It was unpardonable of me to—" He paused and cleared his throat and went on. "To, uh, take the liberties I took. I regret it sincerely, and I promise you that it will never happen again."

Tears stung Alexandra's eyes at his words. Thorpe was obviously horrified at what they had done. No doubt he was glad he had managed to escape her clutches eventually. She swallowed her tears and forced herself to speak calmly.

"Please, there is no need. Let us not speak of it anymore. Tell me, how is my mother? We spoke of it last night, I think, but..."

"She is alive and does not seem to be in any pain," he said, his voice filled with relief. "But she is unconscious and has been since she was attacked the other night. I took the liberty of sending my doctor to see her, but he was able to give us little information. She is in a coma, and he has no idea when she will wake up."

"If ever," Alexandra added softly.

"You must not think that way. I have known of others who have recovered from a coma. One of my cousins was thrown from a horse and did not awake for two weeks, but after that he was all right—at least, as all right as he had ever been," he added, with a wry smile.

"Thank you. I hope you are right. I am sure that my aunt has been taking excellent care of her."

"She seems a very capable woman," he agreed dryly.

"I cannot fathom why anyone would try to harm my mother," she went on, frowning. "I would have said that it was merely a theft gone awry, but the idea of another attack upon someone in my family is too much of a coincidence for me to swallow."

"No, he meant to harm your mother."

Alexandra turned to him sharply. "How do you know?"

"I spoke with the man who kidnapped you. That is how I tracked you down. His name was Peggoddy, and my man Murdock managed to locate him."

"How did you persuade him to talk to you?"

"He had little choice."

Alexandra was somewhat taken aback by the steel in his voice. "Are you saying you threatened him?"

Thorpe cocked an eyebrow. "He wasn't the sort with whom to use gentle persuasion."

"I see. And what did he say—besides where I was, I mean."

"That he had been hired to take care of your mother."

Alexandra stared at him. "Hired! But who—"

Thorpe shrugged. "I don't know. At that point I was more interested in finding you than in digging any more information out of him."

"You mean you let him go?" Alexandra asked in dismay.

"Hardly. He accompanied us to the bordello. I could hardly trust that he was telling me the truth, after all. I left him with Murdock in the carriage while I went inside to get you. He was the man who ran away as we were going to the carriage."

"Oh." Alexandra vaguely remembered a large figure bolting from the carriage.

"I talked with Murdock last night. He questioned Peggoddy, but he got little information that's of any use. The man maintained that he had no idea why someone wanted your mother harmed, only that he was hired by an intermediary whom he called Red Bill."

"Who is this Red Bill? Perhaps we could find him and talk to him."

"Murdock is already searching for him. I've hired a Bow Street Runner, as well."

"And is he investigating me, as well?" Alexandra asked, brows raised, arms crossed.

"Why do you say that?" Sebastian hedged.

"Because I sincerely doubt that you stopped having your agent make inquiries of my man of business."

"You're right," Sebastian agreed coolly. "I have been investigating you."

"Tell me. Did you find out anything to support your accusations?" Alexandra waited, brows raised, arms still crossed. "I know you found out Ward Shipping has dealt with my agent for years and that I have the proper credentials and letters of credit. What about the rest of it? No doubt you've been looking for frauds and schemes, people who have swindled innocent victims out of their money."

The carefully blank look on Sebastian's face told Alexandra that she was right. She pressed on. "Have you found anyone I've cheated? Any scheme I put over on someone?"

He shook his head. "No," he admitted slowly.

"But obviously you still have your doubts," Alexandra said scornfully.

"You are a careful and intelligent woman. I am sure you would not have been obvious or easy to catch in any scheme."

"Ah. I see. The lack of evidence merely proves that I am good at swindling people, not that I am innocent. I am sure you have some ingenious explanation for this senseless attack on my mother, too. Some way that my wickedness caused it."

Thorpe hesitated, then said, "Perhaps it is someone who wants revenge on you. Someone who wants to get back at you for what you've done to him in the past. Something you've taken from him or—"

"Of course," Alexandra said with a kind of grim satisfaction. "I should have known. It should be obvious— except that I haven't the sort of narrow, closed mind you have. You decided that I was a villainess, and therefore, everything that happens, you twist to fit that story. Who cares about the facts? Why take into account the fact that during this whole time the only people who have been hurt are me and those close to me? Not the Countess. Not you. Just my mother and me. Ignore the truth—that nothing untoward has ever happened to me in my life until I met you and the Countess. Oh, yes, and ignore the obvious, too, that suddenly someone wants to kill my mother, the only person who could shed light on this whole matter of who I am! Why are you so determined that I am wicked? Why do you hate me so much?"

"I do not hate you!" Thorpe ground out the words. "I

simply am not naïve." He moved toward her, his words falling like stones, his cold silver eyes boring into hers. "I am not gullible and eager to believe any cock-and-bull story someone tells me in the hopes that I might get some member of my family back, as the Countess is. I am not sweet or gentle—"

Alexandra snorted inelegantly. "You hardly need to tell me that."

"I am well aware of the character of most people, and I look beyond the surface of things. So when a very attractive woman practically forces her way into my house and seizes my attention, I have to wonder why—especially when that woman uses my friendship with her to meet one of my dear friends and feed her a ludicrous story."

"I did not feed anyone a story, ludicrous or otherwise!" Alexandra protested. "She is the one who told me the story, not the other way around. I never heard of the Countess until I came here, and I certainly had never heard the story of her family tragedy."

"Then why did you engineer a meeting with me?"

"Lord knows, I wish I had not!" Alexandra retorted. "The truth is no doubt too simple for you. I happened to be in London, and I was interested in your collection."

"If you know so little about the Countess, why were you sneaking over to Exmoor House to meet someone in the middle of the night? Why won't you tell me what you were doing there? How could I possibly think you are innocent of wrongdoing when you had a midnight rendezvous at Exmoor House?"

"You want to know why I was there?" Alexandra cried, goaded beyond endurance by his attitude. "And why I was reluctant to reveal it to a virtual stranger? Well, I'll tell you. I went there because my mother knocked her keeper over the head and took a hackney to Exmoor House. There! Now you know. My mother is not right in the head. She drinks secretly, and she falls into strange moods, and she keeps a little box with her at all times, stroking it and clutching it—and in that box is the locket I showed the Countess. She will not answer my questions, merely retreats into her strange silence. That night, when she escaped the house and I pursued her to Exmoor House, she did not even know me. She called me Simone, just as the Countess did. I have not gotten a coherent word from her since. *That* is why I did not tell you my reason for going to Exmoor House. Foolishly, I wanted to keep you from thinking badly of my mother. I did not want you to realize that the blood of madness runs through my veins!''

Alexandra stopped, panting with fury, and for a long moment she and Thorpe stared at each other in shocked silence. Then she made a noise and turned away. ''I think it's time you took me home.''

13

The ride home was an awkward one. Neither Alexandra nor Thorpe spoke, except for the merest necessities. Alexandra felt only like crying, and she had no idea what Thorpe was feeling. He looked determinedly grim. She knew that whatever he might once have felt for her was dead. His distrust and contempt had been bad enough, but now that he knew the truth about her mother, Alexandra was sure he must be thoroughly repulsed. Mad people were locked away in wretched asylums, embarrassments to their families, or, if they were wealthy enough, kept guarded in some sturdy room. To have madness in one's family, with the possibility of it popping out in oneself or one's children, was terrifying.

It was a relief when they arrived at Alexandra's house. Thorpe walked her to her door, although she assured him that it was not necessary.

"I promised your aunt that I would bring you back, and I intend to do so," he replied shortly, and Alexandra dropped the subject.

They had scarcely stepped into the house before Aunt Hortense appeared on the staircase. She hurried down the stairs, arms outstretched. "Alexandra! Oh, my dear, are you all right? We have been so worried!"

Alexandra went gratefully into her aunt's arms. The truth was, she felt very much like crying on someone's shoulder, though she had to admit that it had little to do with her ordeal. "I know. I'm sorry. How is Mother?"

Aunt Hortense drew back, shaking her head. "Alive, but still in a coma. I—I'm afraid that she may be like that forever!"

"Don't say that. I am sure she will recover."

"And here's Nancy being hysterical now," Aunt Hortense went on agitatedly, "and saying that she wants to leave this heathen country—well, one can hardly blame her, I suppose, for that, but I had thought that I could at least count on *her* not to fall to pieces. The butler's threatening to tender his resignation. He says he has never worked in a household where such things happened—as if it were our fault! Now, I ask you... Needless to say, I told him that we were not used to such things happening in America, and I pointed out to him that at least in the United States people have a sense of loyalty to their employers. Then, the next thing I know, there's Nancy blubbering like one of the upstairs maids and saying that she wants to go back home."

"We can't go back yet, not with Mother like that. We have to wait until she recovers. I suppose if Nancy is set on going, I could give her passage home by herself."

Aunt Hortense sniffed. "I thought she was made of sterner stuff."

Alexandra shrugged. "I suppose being hit on the head twice would be enough to jolt someone."

Aunt Hortense turned to Thorpe. "I'm sorry, Lord Thorpe. You must think me rag mannered, indeed. I have not even thanked you for returning Alexandra to me. I am eternally indebted to you. You have done so much for us.'' She turned toward Alexandra. ''I hope you thanked him properly.''

''Of course.'' Alexandra kept her eyes turned resolutely away from him. She was afraid that if she looked at him, Aunt Hortense would see written on her face everything that had happened the night before.

''I am only glad that I could be of service,'' Thorpe replied stiffly.

''Come into the sitting room,'' Aunt Hortense went on. ''You must tell me everything that happened. How did you find Alexandra? Where was she?''

Alexandra and Thorpe cast a quick glance at each other and followed Aunt Hortense into the other room. When they sat down, Thorpe told her aunt a carefully expurgated account of how he had found Peggoddy and gotten Alexandra's location from him, then had taken her away from Magdalena's.

''But, my dear, how dreadful for you!'' Aunt Hortense exclaimed, taking Alexandra's hand and squeezing it. ''But I don't understand—where were you last night? After I got the message from Lord Thorpe's servant? He said you were all right, so you must have been rescued by then.'' She turned a puzzled face toward Thorpe.

Thorpe shifted uncomfortably in his chair. Alexandra could feel heat beginning to rise in her face.

Thorpe cleared his throat and said, ''It was, ah, a delicate situation.''

''I don't understand.''

''I, um, Miss Ward was not herself at the time, and I thought it would be better if you did not see her until she was fully recovered.''

Aunt Hortense looked at him steadily. ''I cannot understand what could have been so wrong with her that she would not have been better off under my care.''

"I was drugged, Aunt Hortense," Alexandra said flatly. "I suspect that they gave me opium."

"Opium!"

"Yes—and some sort of herbal concoction. I am sure Lord Thorpe felt that you would be terribly shocked to see me that way."

"No doubt I would have," Aunt Hortense agreed heartily. "But I'm sure I have seen worse things than that. I did, after all, live through a war." She fixed her stern gaze on Lord Thorpe. "This is a terrible situation. Surely you must see what damage it would do to Alexandra's reputation if it were known that she spent the night at your house without any sort of chaperone!"

Thorpe set his jaw. "I can assure you that none of my servants will talk, Miss Ward. They are chosen for their loyalty, as well as their competence."

"Aunt Hortense, please…it was for the best."

"But it's hardly the thing for you to be spending the night unprotected with a—an Englishman."

"It would be no better if it had been an American man, Aunt. And you can rest assured that nothing happened." Her last words were uttered with a heartfelt bitterness that made her aunt blink.

"But the appearances—what about your reputation?"

"What does it matter?" Alexandra retorted. "No one will know of it. We will be going home soon, and there will be no possibility of anyone there hearing of it." Alexandra realized, with some surprise, that the thought of returning to the United States made her want to cry.

"You are going home?" Thorpe asked, startled.

Aunt Hortense looked at him oddly, and Alexandra

said, "Yes, of course. We did not intend to live in England."

"No, of course not. I just presumed that your visit would extend several months. I— When do you plan to leave?"

"We were planning to sail next week."

"Next week!" Thorpe looked thunderstruck.

"Obviously, with Mother in this condition, that is very unlikely. I presume we will go as soon as she improves."

"I see. Why didn't you tell me?"

Alexandra stared. "Tell you! Whatever do you mean? It was you who suggested in no uncertain terms that I leave. I cannot see why it is any shock to you that we were going to do so."

Sebastian looked decidedly uncomfortable. "Well, of course…but, well, I suppose I thought you would stay to see this thing resolved."

"In what way?" Alexandra asked wearily. "I don't know how we can get at the truth of any of this. My mother is the only one who would have any information about my birth, and she is unable to talk. Even if she should awaken and be lucid, I have explained to you about her. I was not able to get her to answer any of my questions before. I see no reason she would tell me now."

"But what about the Countess?"

"What about her?" Alexandra retorted. "I like the woman. I shall be sorry not to have more of her company. But my family has always been Aunt Hortense and my mother and the cousins I have back in Boston. That is where my home is."

Thorpe said nothing for a moment, just looked at her. "Of course. I see. Well, before you leave, I think there is one thing that we could do to try to clear up this muddled situation. We have not visited Bertie Chesterfield, as we promised the Countess we would. I think we should."

"All right. Whenever you want, though it does not sound as if he knows very much."

"Only what he saw, which, considering Bertie, is not necessarily something one can count on."

They agreed that he would find the man at White's and arrange a meeting with him. Then, wishing a speedy recovery for her mother, he left. Alexandra watched him go, thinking that she could not remember ever having felt this lonely. Was this what it was like to be in love?

She pushed the thought away. One thing she was determined not to do was to spend her time pining after some man—especially an arrogant British nobleman whom she scarcely knew!

"Come," she said to her aunt, rising briskly from her chair. "I want to see Mother."

There was a tap on the door to her mother's bedroom, and one of the maids entered timidly. "Miss." She bobbed a little curtsey to Alexandra. "Miss Ward requests your presence downstairs. She said I should look after Mrs. Ward for you."

Alexandra was less than certain about the maid's ability to look after her mother. They were all scared of Rhea, despite the fact that she was lying helpless and asleep on the bed. Alexandra and her aunt had taken turns sitting with her mother for the past day, for Nancy was still in bed, her head bandaged, and complaining of a sick headache. The blow on her head seemed to have changed her to a different person—a sniveling, complaining one—and Alexandra had bought her passage on a ship sailing for America in two days. It would mean that she and Aunt Hortense would have to bear the burden of looking after her mother since the servants seemed too skittish to be of much use in the sickroom.

She went down the stairs and into the drawing room, where she found her aunt with two visitors: Nicola Falcourt and Penelope, the shy daughter of Lady Ursula. Alexandra stopped, surprised. Her first thought was that Lord Thorpe had immediately spread the word about Alexandra's kidnapping and that the two young women were here to satisfy their curiosity.

However, it took only a few moments of conversation with them to dispel that idea. Minutes after exchanging greetings, Penelope gave Alexandra a shy smile and said, "Grandmama sent us over with specific instructions to invite you to the opera with us tonight. Please say you will. It would be most delightful. Nicola and Lord Buckminster are accompanying us, too." The girl colored a little as she said this, but she went on, "It should be ever so much fun. My mother shan't be accompanying us."

She stopped, sucking in a little gasp. "Oh! I didn't mean that the way it sounded!"

Alexandra rather suspected that she had, at least deep down inside, but she would not embarrass the girl by pointing it out. "Of course not. I understand what you mean. It would be much more comfortable for me if Lady Ursula were not one of the party."

"Yes, that's it." Penelope cast Alexandra a grateful look.

"And for Bucky," Nicola added a little roguishly. "Lady Ursula has little liking for Bucky. She considers him frivolous...which, of course, he is."

"He is *not* frivolous," Penelope protested. "He is simply fun-loving and—and easy to be around."

Alexandra was beginning to suspect that the plain young woman had something of a tendre for Lord Buckminster. It seemed a trifle odd to Alexandra, for Lord Buckminster had indeed struck her as an eminently frivolous sort, whereas Lady Ursula's daughter seemed both serious and retiring. Alexandra wondered whether the easygoing Bucky had any idea of Penelope's regard for him. Alexandra suspected, from the sideways look Nicola sent Penelope, that she, at least, was aware of Penelope's feelings.

"Of course he is," Nicola said lightly. "I was simply teasing about him. Bucky is a dear, and we probably none of us appreciate him enough. After Papa died, Bucky and his mother took Mama and Deborah and me in with all the good grace in the world." She turned to Alexandra and added hastily, "It was not that Papa left us unprovided for. We were perfectly comfortable, but of course we had to leave Falcourt Place."

Alexandra must have looked lost, for Nicola added, "The estate passed to the nearest male relative, you see, Papa having no sons."

"You mean you had to leave your house?" It reminded her of what Thorpe had said about the Countess and Exmoor House—that it had been where she used to live, but that it now belonged to the Earl of Exmoor. It seemed a cruel system to Alexandra.

Nicola nodded. "Yes, it was rather painful, especially for Mama. Papa's cousin Herbert got the place, and his wife and Mama never got along. It would have been impossible for us to stay, although for courtesy's sake he offered." She smiled, a dimple popping into the smooth skin of her cheek. "With his fingers crossed behind his back all the while, I'm sure. It was a relief all around to separate Mama and Lady Herbert. So we went to stay with Mama's nephew—that's Lord Buckminster." She smiled, her eyes going a little misty. "It was a wonderful time. I loved Buckminster House.'' Her smile turned wistful, and for an instant her eyes were cold and lonely. Then she seemed to pull herself to the present, looking at Alexandra and saying, ''Lady Buckminster is wonderful, too.''

''Lord Buckminster is married?'' Alexandra was surprised. He had not seemed wedded. She glanced at Penelope.

The girl was laughing. ''No. She means Bucky's mother. She is almost exactly like Bucky, except even more horse mad. As long as you ride well, she'll like you, and if you don't, well, she'll just feel sorry for you and go off for a ride without you.''

''But we are getting far afield here,'' Nicola declared. ''Lady Exmoor will have our heads if we come back without your acceptance as one of our party tonight.''

Alexandra smiled. ''I would love to, but I am afraid I must stay here and help Aunt Hortense. My mother is rather ill, you see, and needs looking after.''

''Don't be silly, dear,'' Aunt Hortense told her. ''You go on to the opera. I am quite capable of looking after Rhea by myself.''

''Oh, but Grandmama invited you, as well, Miss Ward,'' Penelope assured her. ''But it is all right. Sebastian told Grandmama about your mother's indisposition, and—''

''Oh, he did, did he?'' So he had run to the Countess to gossip, after all. Alexandra supposed she should have known better than to hope that he would try to protect her reputation.

''Yes, but you mustn't blame him. We had already heard all sorts of wild tales about what happened,'' Penelope said. ''The servants' grapevine, you know, is the fastest transmission of news known to mankind. Mama had heard that Mrs. Ward was dead and that you had vanished. So of course Thorpe had to step in and set the record right. He told Grandmama that it was errant nonsense—you should have seen Mother's face!'' Penelope's plain, heart-shaped face lit up at the memory, turning her almost pretty. ''She was thoroughly put out.''

''What did he say?'' Alexandra asked.

''That you were not gone, that he had talked to you that very morning right here in the house. He said a thief had apparently entered the house, and that Mrs. Ward must have disturbed him, for he knocked her unconscious and fled.''

Alexandra nodded, relief—and a kind of warm pleasure—spreading through her at the thought that Thorpe had covered up the scandalous incident as well as anyone could expect. It would have helped him to separate the Countess from Alexandra if he had told her about Alexandra's night in a brothel, but he had refrained. He had protected her name. It was also obvious that he had said nothing to anyone about her mother's mental condition before the blow.

''Mama was not pleased. She asked Thorpe if he was calling her a liar, and he said, 'Of course not, merely illinformed.' That made her even madder, I think.''

''She was furious at Sebastian,'' Nicola agreed. ''That's when Lady Exmoor said she thought she would ask you and your aunt to the opera this evening. She thought it would help take your mind off the ordeal.''

''That is very kind of her. But it really is impossible for both of us to leave. Mother's servant was injured, too, and she is feeling too poorly to take care of Mother, so I'm afraid that—''

''But, no!'' Penelope assured her. ''Willa Everhart—you remember, the Countess's companion—offered to come stay with your mother.''

"That is too kind. She must not."

"She insists," Penelope told her. "Lady Exmoor said that you must not deprive Willa of the pleasure of feeling useful. Willa, you see, is deeply grateful to the Countess, for she would be virtually penniless if it weren't for the Countess's support. She is always looking for some way to pay the Countess back, except that, of course, Lady Exmoor doesn't have enough errands to occupy Willa's time. Lady Exmoor said that you would be doing Willa a favor, really."

"I would like to go," Alexandra admitted.

"Then go ahead, dear," Aunt Hortense urged her. "I will stay here and help Lady Exmoor's companion. You know I'm not very fond of all that singing, anyway. I'm sure she and I will manage just fine."

"There, you see?" Nicola told her triumphantly. "It's all arranged. You must come. Lord Thorpe will be there." She added this last statement with a roguish air, as if Sebastian's presence would be what convinced Alexandra.

Penelope nodded eagerly. "Yes. I heard him tell Grandmama that he would be attending tonight, and he would drop by her box."

Alexandra hesitated. It would be an awkward situation if both she and Sebastian were there. "Then perhaps I had better not. Lord Thorpe would not want—I mean, well, we are scarcely friends."

"No, I would not call it friendship," Nicola agreed, her blue eyes dancing. "Quite frankly, I've never seen Sebastian so smitten."

"Smitten?" Alexandra repeated in disbelief. "Oh, no, I am sure you are mistaken."

Nicola chuckled. "Not about this. Trust me, I have known Sebastian for years and years, and I have never known him to act like this about any woman."

"Truly?" Alexandra could not quite suppress the leap her heart gave at the woman's words.

"Yes. He's a tough nut to crack. Believe me, untold numbers of women have tried."

Penelope nodded. "Mother always said that Sebastian hasn't a heart, that's why no one's been able to capture it."

"It's because of Lady Pencross, of course," Nicola explained. "It's not that he's heartless, but that he cared too much. She broke his heart, and he's never allowed anyone to get close to him since."

Alexandra's interest was by now thoroughly piqued. She leaned toward Nicola, saying, "Lady Pencross?"

"You haven't heard about that?"

"I just met the man recently."

The name Pencross sounded vaguely familiar to her, though. Then, with a jolt, Alexandra remembered. That had been the name of the woman at the ball who had come up to her and made the peculiar comments about Sebastian. She remembered Sebastian's stiff manner and brief words with the woman. She had wondered at the time what had prompted him to act that way.

"He wouldn't be likely to talk about her," Nicola went on. "When Sebastian was young, only eighteen or so, he fell madly in love with Lord Pencross's wife, Barbara. She was about ten years older than he, but a beautiful woman. She still is, actually, although she must be in her forties by now. Anyway, Sebastian met her and fell in love with her. They had a wild, passionate affair. Everyone knew about it—it was quite the scandal of the Season. Sebastian even called a man out in defense of her honor."

"He fought a duel?"

Nicola nodded. "Yes. Bucky was his second, so I know it's true. Needless to say, Sebastian's family was terribly embarrassed by the whole thing. Bucky says that Sebastian's father called him home and told him he was a disgrace to the family, and he cut off his allowance until he came to his senses. Sebastian was furious and hurt. His family stopped speaking to him—including his mother and sisters. He still hasn't forgiven them for it. He provides for them, of course, but he hardly ever goes home.''

"What happened with Lady Pencross?" Alexandra asked, too enthralled to bother to hide her interest.

"Well, the rumor is that Sebastian wanted her to run away with him, to leave the country and the scandal, and go to India.''

"He made the mistake, you see," Penelope added, "of thinking that Lady Pencross loved him as much as he loved her. But she was merely entertaining herself with a younger man. I heard she laughed in his face when he suggested giving up her money and position as Lord Pencross's wife to go live in love and poverty in India with Sebastian.''

"She refused him?"

Nicola nodded. "He was terribly disillusioned. He went off to India by himself and made his fortune. I don't think he would have come back except that his father died, and he had to assume the title.''

"I see." Alexandra thought that she did indeed see. It made sense to her now that Thorpe had been so quick to believe the worst of her. The woman he had loved when he was young had proven faithless, her love false. It would be hard for him to trust any woman, easy to be suspicious and hard.

"He hasn't loved a woman since," Penelope added. "It's very romantic, but sad, don't you think?"

"Yes, I do." Alexandra paused, thinking. "What happened to Lady Pencross?"

"It was a scandal, of course, but eventually it subsided. She is accepted by most, though not the high sticklers, of course. I have seen her several times this Season. Her husband is much older than she, and he is in ill health. But she is not at his bedside. He is back on the family estate, and she is here, doing the social rounds."

"She sounds a heartless sort."

Nicola nodded. "I believe she is. But I have little connection to her. She travels in a different set, and I see her only at very large balls."

"Or at the opera or a play," Penelope added.

"Really?"

"Yes. I suppose we might even see her tonight."

Alexandra's interest was thoroughly kindled. She would like very much to see this woman again, now that she knew who she was. She had not been paying enough attention the first time.

"I'll point her out to you if I see her," Nicola told Alexandra shrewdly.

Their talk drifted away from the topic of Sebastian and his former love, but Alexandra's thoughts kept returning to it, and she paid only partial attention to what the others were saying. The conversation moved to various activities that were taking place in London. The Season was in full swing, and the June weather was glorious, prompting many an outing. Nicola and Penelope, it seemed, were going to a balloon ascension in a few days, and they urged Alexandra to come with them.

"They're terribly exciting, I hear," Penelope said. "I have never been to one before. Mother thinks that they are vulgar spectacles, but she finally relented this time. Please say you'll come."

"It's to be a race of some sort," Nicola added. "The

one who lands farthest away from London wins. It's quite something to see.''

"Bucky says balloons are the conveyances of the future,'' Penelope attested, her eyes alight.

"Is Lord Buckminster to be one of the party, too?'' Alexandra asked, thinking once again that Penelope seemed enamored of the man.

"No, but I am sure that we will meet him there. Bucky rarely misses these ascensions,'' Nicola said, glancing at Penelope significantly. The color in Penelope's cheeks rose.

"Well, I could hardly miss it, could I?'' Alexandra said. "I should love to accompany you.''

"Good. Then it's settled.''

They made a few arrangements for that evening, and Nicola and Penelope took their leave. Aunt Hortense rose from her chair.

"Well,'' she said, "they seem like nice girls.''

"Yes,'' Alexandra agreed absently. "I'm glad you like them.''

"Odd to think that Penelope might be your cousin.''

Alexandra turned toward her aunt, startled by her words. "Why, yes, I suppose you're right. I hadn't thought of it. But if the Countess is correct...'' Alexandra's voice trailed off. "Oh, Aunt Hortense! I feel so strange. I scarcely know who I am any longer! All my life I have been so sure of myself, so confident in the knowledge that I was a Ward, that you were my family. Now all that may be false.''

"But it hasn't changed the essentials,'' Aunt Hortense pointed out firmly. "Whether your last name is Ward or Exmoor—''

"Montford,'' Alexandra explained. "I think that Exmoor is a title.''

"Whatever it is." Aunt Hortense waved that aside. "You are still you. Exactly the same person. With the same strengths and weaknesses, the same beliefs."

"I know, Auntie, but still...I feel so unsettled. I wish I could learn the truth, one way or the other."

"Hopefully you will, dear. If Rhea comes to, she could clear it all up."

Alexandra did not respond. She had little faith in Rhea being able to tell them anything.

The Countess's carriage was a large, old-fashioned, elegant affair, a golden coat of arms painted on its gleaming black side. Lord Buckminster, who was riding a horse beside the carriage, dismounted, tossed his reins to a liveried groom and went to hand Alexandra into the carriage.

"Miss Ward," he said, grinning jovially. "Jolly good to see you again. I must say, you look a picture tonight."

Alexandra had taken some care with her looks, choosing a deep blue gown that she thought offset her coloring well and exposing as much of her white bosom as would be considered proper in polite society. Her hair was upswept in a mass of curls, pinned here and there with small white rosebuds. One long curl fell carelessly over her shoulder and trailed onto the creamy expanse of her chest, brushing against the top of her breast when she moved. Whatever Lord Thorpe might feel for her, she was determined that there be some desire intermingled with it.

Willa Everhart had arrived at their house an hour ago and, despite her constant flow of chatter, seemed to have Rhea's sickroom well in hand. Alexandra had left Willa sitting with her mother and Aunt Hortense in her room, ready to help should any crisis arise. So Alexandra was able to leave the house without worry and climb into the Countess's carriage.

The Countess leaned forward to take Alexandra's hand and patted the seat next to her, indicating that Alexandra should sit beside her. The Countess seemed in good spirits, her color high and her blue eyes shining. Her gleaming white hair contrasted elegantly with her gown of deep purple satin accented by black lace. Penelope, as usual, looked faintly dowdy in a white dress that was overly fussy. Lady Ursula—for Alexandra had no doubt that it was Penelope's mother who dictated her clothes—dressed the young woman in a girlish way that was entirely unsuitable for Penelope's looks, Alexandra thought. White with ruffles and pink bows might do for a cotton-candy sort of miss, but ruffles and bows looked silly on Penelope, and the white color merely washed out her already pale skin.

Nicola sat beside Penelope, looking, as she always did, both beautiful and elegant, with her blond hair and dark blue eyes. She was dressed in a deceptively simple sea-green gown that Alexandra could see at a glance must have come from one of the best modistes. She was a contrast of sophistication and beauty to Penelope, and Alexandra wondered why some of her elegant style had never rubbed off on Penelope.

They drove to the opera, making social chitchat along the way. None of the women referred to the recent trouble Alexandra had gone through, for which she was grateful. It would be grand, she thought, to forget all about it for a while.

Inside the opera house, they made their way toward the Countess's luxurious box. It was something like a royal procession, Alexandra thought, with the Countess nodding politely to acquaintances, giving some favored person a little wave or even, as she did with one dumpy, middle-aged woman, pausing to press her hand and murmur a pleasant greeting. Alexandra watched the older woman's tall, poised figure in admiration. The Countess, she thought, was exactly what a real lady should be.

They stopped along the way, and Nicola touched a finger to Alexandra's arm and leaned closer to murmur, "There is Lady Pencross. In the green, over by the potted plant."

Alexandra looked quickly in the direction of Nicola's gaze. It was, indeed, the small beauty who had approached Alexandra at the ball. She was smiling at the man standing in front of her, her lips curved in a subtle, mysterious way that hinted at delightful secrets. Alexandra felt a thrust of pure, bitter jealousy. This, then, was the one woman whom Sebastian had loved!

Lady Pencross's gaze slid to Alexandra and Nicola. She nodded faintly to Nicola, then gave Alexandra a second, measuring look. No expression marred her lovely features until she turned back to the gentleman in front of her.

"A completely vain woman,' Nicola said contemptuously. "She looks much younger than she is, I have to admit. They say it's because she rarely smiles or frowns. Emotions are too wrinkle-inducing, you see."

Alexandra smiled. "I take it you don't like the woman."

Nicola curled up one corner of her mouth. "Love is so rare. I cannot abide someone who could throw it away as she did."

A shadow touched Nicola's eyes, turning them a midnight-blue, then was gone. "Most women would give anything to have a man love them the way it is said that Sebastian did. And he is a good man, for all his determinedly misanthropic ways. I believe that he is cynical because he is a disillusioned romantic. That romantic nature will come out again." She cast a sideways glance at

Alexandra, a glance in which there was more than a little curiosity.

It was then that Alexandra saw Sebastian. He was standing some distance down the wide corridor, leaning negligently against the wall. His eyes had fallen on the Countess, and he was looking around searchingly. He saw Alexandra, and he straightened, levering himself away from the wall.

Alexandra stopped, her eyes locking with his. Heat spread through her as suddenly she recalled the feeling of his hard body against hers the other night, the insistent pulse of his desire. He began to walk toward her.

14

Alexandra blushed and glanced quickly away from Sebastian, only to meet Nicola's speculative gaze.

"You care for him, don't you?" Nicola asked.

"Don't be absurd," Alexandra replied gamely. "I think he is an odious creature, and he thinks even worse of me."

"I have never known Sebastian to introduce a woman to the Countess," Nicola said significantly. "And why did he go rushing over to your house when your mother was attacked?"

"My aunt sent for him," Alexandra replied. "She didn't know anyone else to turn to."

"That may be, but I have to point out that Sebastian is not known for flying to anyone's aid, whether they are strangers to London or not."

Alexandra shook her head, but she could not keep her gaze from returning to Sebastian, who had almost reached them. The Countess came up beside Nicola, and Sebastian politely bowed and spoke to her first. He turned to Alexandra and Nicola, greeting Nicola almost perfunctorily.

"Miss Ward." His gray eyes looked questioningly into Alexandra's. "I trust you are well."

"I am fine, thank you, my lord." Alexandra hoped he

did not see that her color was overly high or that her breathing came too quickly. Just the intent searching of his eyes was enough to turn her loins into hot wax.

"Come join us," the Countess said to Sebastian, her eyes twinkling. "If you are not otherwise engaged, that is."

"No." He glanced at her and allowed a rueful smile. "I am quite free."

"Excellent." The Countess smiled beatifically, and Thorpe walked with them to the Countess's box. It was, Alexandra saw, the door beside which Thorpe had been leaning when she saw him. Had he been waiting for them?

She told herself to stop thinking this way. Thorpe had made it abundantly clear that he was not interested in her—and now that he knew the truth about her mother, she had no doubt that he would shun her even more.

The Countess's box was luxuriously done in red velvet, with dainty cushioned chairs and red velvet curtains tied back to reveal the stage and the rest of the opera house. It was readily apparent to Alexandra that the majority of the people attending had come not to view the opera, but to see and be seen. Most of the occupants of the boxes were engaged in looking about the theater, lorgnettes raised to their eyes.

Nicola, on one side of her, busied herself pointing out people to Alexandra and supplying her with brief, often pungently funny, stories about each one. Alexandra listened with only partial attention. Most of her awareness was focused on Sebastian, who sat on the other side of her. He was dressed impeccably in black evening clothes, a snow-white fall of white at his throat. A single discreet ruby winked in the cuff of each sleeve. Alexandra stole a sideways glance at him. They had barely spoken to each other, yet it was he who occupied her thoughts—although she could scarcely call them thoughts, Alexandra told herself. What Thorpe seemed to occupy, quite successfully, was every nerve ending in her body. She was intensely aware of his bulk beside her, of his long fingers brushed with black hairs that rested casually on his legs. She could not keep from remembering the touch of those fingers on her skin, the pressure of his warm body against hers. Her brain might tell her to forget about him, but her senses refused to listen.

"You see now, Sebastian, that I was right," the Countess said, interrupting Alexandra's thoughts. "Alexandra must be my granddaughter. It is clear to me that Mrs. Ward knows the truth about her birth, and that is the reason someone tried to harm her."

"We don't know that, my lady," Alexandra reminded her softly. "It could have been a fluke, a coincidence."

"I don't believe in coincidence," the Countess stated flatly. "There is always a reason for what happens. The world moves according to a purpose, even though we may not always know what it is." She smiled at Alexandra. "Thank heaven you were not harmed. I was very frightened when Ursula told me that she had heard you had vanished. It was such a relief when Thorpe let me know that you were safe and sound at home."

"Thank you."

"I have been thinking," the Countess went on. "You are not out of danger; nor is Mrs. Ward. This person could come back to finish the job. I am afraid that Mrs. Ward is not safe until she awakens and tells us what happened in Paris twenty-two years ago. So I have come up with a plan. We shall all go to the Dower House—my home on the Exmoor estate. Your aunt, Mrs. Ward, all of us. We shall be perfectly safe there. Everyone knows us, and any stranger who came to harm you would stand out. All the villagers and tenants would help look out for us. We shall take several of my strongest footmen, and I shall make you, Sebastian, come with us, too, for protection.''

Sebastian sketched her a bow. ''At your service, my lady.''

The Countess smiled. ''There. It will be ever so much safer.''

''Thank you,'' Alexandra told her, ''but that really is quite unnecessary. We will be all right. I don't think it would be good for Mother to be moved, the condition she is in. Besides, I don't believe in running. I prefer to stand and fight.''

The Countess frowned worriedly. ''But, my dear...the danger! It's all very well to be brave, but three women alone...''

Alexandra grinned. ''I think you will find that my aunt and I are well able to take care of ourselves. We were not prepared before—we weren't expecting attack. But now that we know, we shall be on guard. We have armed ourselves.''

''Armed yourselves!'' Penelope exclaimed in astonishment.

''Why, yes. We have guns and know how to use them. I don't think anyone will get past us now.''

''You're not serious!'' This was from the Countess, her blue eyes rounded. ''You and your aunt have guns?''

Alexandra nodded. ''I have one with me right now.'' She reached into her reticule and pulled out a small pistol. ''I have a large pistol at home on the table beside my bed. Unfortunately, I didn't bring the rifle from America. I never thought that I might need it.''

Nicola smothered a giggle, and the Countess stared at Alexandra's gun in horror. ''My dear! I had no idea. I thought you lived where it was civilized!''

Alexandra chuckled. "We do. But you must remember that my aunt lived through a war, the only one there to guard the house while her father and brother went off to fight. She taught me how to load a gun and shoot. My mother had been terrified by the rioting she lived through in France, and she encouraged me to learn."

The Countess turned toward Sebastian in amazement. He shrugged, his eyes dancing, and said, "I have found Miss Ward to be a most unusual woman, my lady." He turned to Alexandra. "However, I do think, Miss Ward, that you don't need the pistol here at the opera."

"Oh." Alexandra looked at the gun in her hand and stuck it into her reticule. "Sorry." She turned toward the Countess. "I don't mean to displease you. But we really are capable of protecting ourselves. And if need be, I shall hire extra men for protection."

"I have a better idea," Thorpe suggested. "I shall lend you my valet, Murdock. He's worth five ordinary servants in a fight. He can stand guard outside your rooms."

Alexandra looked at him coolly. "It is quite unnecessary, my lord."

"But it will offer me peace of mind—as well as the Countess. Surely you cannot deny us that."

Alexandra would have liked to argue. She did not want any help of any kind from Lord Thorpe. If nothing else, it would probably mean that she would have to see him again, and that was much too unsettling for her peace of mind. However, she could not think of any way that she could refuse without sounding churlish, especially since he had come to her rescue when she so desperately needed it.

"All right." She gave in rather ungraciously.

Sebastian gave her an ironic little smile. "Thank you, Miss Ward."

Alexandra turned to look at the stage, grateful that the opera was finally about to begin, so that she would have something to divert her attention from Sebastian. However, she found that no matter how much she might concentrate on the spectacle onstage, she could not help but be aware of Sebastian's constant presence.

She thought about the Countess's suggestion. The idea of spending the next few days or weeks with Sebastian in the Countess's country home was dangerously appealing. It would be pure folly, of course, she reminded herself; the only good course was to turn it down, as she had done. And yet... She could not keep herself from indulging in a daydream about stolen kisses in the moonlight.

"Miss Ward?"

Alexandra started and turned, realizing that the intermission had arrived and the lights had come up. Lost in her daydream, she hadn't even noticed. It was obvious from his quizzical expression that this was not the first time Sebastian had said her name.

"What? Forgive me. I was...so lost in the story. What did you say?"

"I suggested that we take a stroll during the intermission, perhaps get some refreshment."

"Oh. Yes, thank you." She rose, tucking her hand into the crook of his arm, telling herself that in all politeness she could scarcely refuse to walk about the opera house with him. She could feel Nicola's speculative eye upon her, but she steadfastly refused to look at her, certain that she would blush if she met Nicola's knowing gaze.

They walked along the wide hallway for a moment without speaking, Thorpe nodding toward acquaintances, but not pausing to speak to anyone.

Finally he said, "I spoke with Bertie Chesterfield today. He said that he would be happy to talk with us about Lord

Chilton and his family and what happened in Paris. I suggested tomorrow afternoon, if that's amenable to you."

So he had gotten her alone only because he wanted to make practical arrangements about talking to Chesterfield! Alexandra tried to ignore the sinking feeling in her chest.

"Yes, of course, whenever you wish," she returned politely.

They lapsed into silence. Sebastian guided her into a somewhat secluded space beside a large potted palm and stopped. "Alexandra...about what you told me about Mrs. Ward..."

Alexandra straightened, her cheeks suddenly flaming with color. "About her madness? Really, I don't think there is anything to discuss."

He looked at her, his eyes dark with frustration. "I did not know—"

"Of course not. How could you? Please, I'd rather not—"

"Ah, Thorpe, there you are." A cultured male voice interrupted them, and Alexandra looked up to see the Earl of Exmoor standing only a few feet from them. "And Miss...Ward, is it not?"

Alexandra nodded, glad for any interruption to this talk. "Yes, that's right. Good evening, my lord."

"Exmoor." Sebastian made no effort to conceal his irritation. "What do you want?"

"Thorpe, dear fellow, even you are usually not so crude in your manners. Can't one stop to greet a...well, I guess one could not say friend...an acquaintance, then?"

"I've rarely seen you go out of your way to be friendly—unless you have some reason."

The other man smiled faintly. Alexandra, watching him, wondered what it was about him that made her instinctively dislike him. He was an attractive man—tall, with well-molded features and a slash of silver at each temple that gave him a rather dashing look. Perhaps it was the thinness of his mouth or the way his smile never reached his eyes. Whatever it was, he reminded her of a predatory animal, the sort that she would never do business with, no matter how attractive the offer might seem.

"You wound me," Exmoor said lightly. "But you are correct, of course. There was a matter I wished to broach with you. I have heard some rather, ah, alarming rumors about our mutual friend, the Countess."

Sebastian said nothing, merely raised his brows.

"I have heard—well, there is no other way to say it, I suppose, except baldly—I have heard that the Countess believes Miss Ward is her long-lost granddaughter, returned from the dead."

"I scarcely see how that is any of your business," Sebastian retorted tightly.

"Not my business that my cousin's child is said to have miraculously returned from the grave?" Exmoor asked in an amused tone.

"What the Countess thinks or does is not your concern."

"I am the head of the family. I think it concerns me deeply if the Countess is suffering from senile delusions. She is a lovely old woman, of course, but if she is no longer right in the head, I should—"

"There is nothing wrong with the Countess's mind," Thorpe retorted coldly, his eyes level on the other man's. "I would take it as a grievous insult if anyone were to suggest otherwise."

"My dear Thorpe, don't tell me you are hinting at calling me out?"

"I am hinting at nothing. I am telling you that no one says anything against the Countess in my presence. She has ample reason for suspecting that Miss Ward is Lord Chilton's daughter. I can assure you that the Countess has a great deal more wit than many who are younger than she.''

Exmoor looked at him shrewdly. "Don't tell me that you believe this fairy tale, as well.''

"I believe that the Countess is of perfectly sound mind,'' Thorpe replied. "And I would dispute anyone who tried to claim otherwise.''

"I would never dream of it,'' Exmoor said smoothly. He glanced from Sebastian to Alexandra, and Alexandra felt a little shiver run through her, as if a snake had slithered across her path. "However, as the head of the Montford family, I do have an interest in anything that touches on it, however true...or false. I will do whatever it takes to keep the family name from being tainted.''

"I am sure the Countess will be pleased that you are such a watchdog of the family honor,'' Thorpe said dryly. "Now, if you will excuse us, I believe the opera is about to begin again.''

He whisked Alexandra away from Exmoor and strode down the hall toward the Countess's box. Alexandra cast a glance at him. His face was taut and furious.

"The head of the Montford family!'' he spluttered. "It's a blow to the Countess every time she looks at him and knows that he occupies the place where her son should be.''

"I hope you don't expect me to believe that there is no bad blood between the two of you,'' Alexandra said.

"Nicola despises him,'' he said obliquely. "Bucky doesn't know the full story, only that Richard was responsible for breaking Nicola's heart.''

"What?'' Alexandra looked at him, astonished. "Nicola was in love with him?''

Sebastian shook his head. "No. Nicola and her mother were staying at the Buckminster estate in the country after her father's death. They are cousins, you know. Buckminster is not far from Tidings, the Exmoor estate where Richard lived. Richard, apparently, was quite enamored of Nicola. He is older than she, but still, it would have been considered a good match. But Nicola did not love him. The rumor is that she loved another."

"Who?"

Sebastian shrugged. "Bucky doesn't know, and Nicola won't talk about it. Apparently she didn't tell even her sister. I assume it must have been someone unsuitable, for her to have kept it secret. Most of what Bucky knows is surmise on his mother's part. Nicola seemed suspiciously happy, then, suddenly, she was grief-stricken. She wouldn't eat, wouldn't talk to anyone, went around looking like a wraith. And she refused to be around the Earl. If he came to call, she left. She would not accompany the family if they went to his house. After a week or two, she left to stay with her grandmother in London. Her mother and sister remained, and about a year later, Exmoor married her sister, Deborah. Nicola rarely sees her. She won't step foot inside Tidings, Bucky says."

"Poor Nicola." She paused and looked at Sebastian. "Is it because of her that there is ill will between you and the Earl?"

Sebastian looked at her, and a reluctant smile tugged at the corner of his mouth. "Persistent, aren't you? No, that is not the reason for it, though it certainly does not endear him to me. However, my dislike for the Earl goes back farther. He was—let us say that he was part of an episode that destroyed my naïve illusions in a particularly painful way." He grimaced. "Part of a past that I would as soon forget."

"I see." Alexandra thought she did. Somehow the Earl must have been tangled up in the scandal Nicola and Penelope had told her about, the affair that had driven Sebastian to leave the country when he was young. Impulsively she laid her other hand on Sebastian's arm. "I'm sorry."

He looked into her eyes, surprised, and smiled. "Don't be. It was long ago and is no longer painful."

"It's not?"

He chuckled. "No. Looking back on it now, it seems merely the indiscretions of a callow youth. Hardly the tragedy it appeared to me at the time."

Alexandra smiled, finding herself curiously pleased by his words.

Sebastian came to Alexandra's house the following afternoon to take her to call on the Honorable Bertram Chesterfield. Alexandra could not help but be a little on edge. She had not been alone with Sebastian since the morning he had brought her home. Of course, seeing him the night before at the opera had lessened some of the awkwardness inherent in the situation, but they had been surrounded by people there, even when they were walking together along the hall. Here she was enclosed in the small space of the carriage with him, an enforced intimacy. She could not help but think of the way she had acted the other night in this carriage, the passion she had felt and Sebastian's rebuffing of her. She supposed that his actions had been those of a gentleman, but, frankly, she would rather that they had been those of a man in the throes of desire.

She could not meet his eyes.

"Miss Ward...Alexandra..."

"Do you think that we will discover anything useful

today?'' she asked brightly to forestall whatever he was going to say. His voice had a deadly serious tone that she sensed boded ill. She did not want to hear any sympathy from Sebastian about her mother's mental state, nor any further rehashing of his reasons for rejecting her.

He paused, then sighed and followed her lead, ''I dare say not. I have never known Bertie Chesterfield to say anything useful before.''

They continued to talk of trivial commonplaces until the carriage pulled up in front of Mr. Chesterfield's narrow town house.

It was something of a shock to Alexandra to walk into Chesterfield's drawing room. Because he was a contemporary of her parents, she had expected a man who dressed and looked like most men his age—sober, perhaps a little old-fashioned, maybe even sporting a wig or formal knee britches. Instead, the ginger-haired man who rose and came toward them was on the cutting edge of fashion—beyond it, one might even say.

His waistcoat was puce, his collar points so high and starched that he could barely turn his head, and his snowy cravat was an intricate tangle of cloth that must have taken his valet half an hour to achieve. Though his form was rather short and squat, he wore skintight breeches designed to show the muscular leg of a man like Sebastian. Unfortunately, what they showed of Chesterfield was every bulge and roll of fat. A large flower decorated the buttonhole of his lapel. His hair, an improbable shade of orange, was combed carefully over the balding front of his head.

''Thorpe, dear chap,'' he said in a cheerful tone, reaching out to shake Sebastian's hand. ''It's been an age since I saw you last. That curricle race of Crimshaw's, wasn't it?''

"I don't think so. I am not a fan of curricle races."

"Indeed?" Chesterfield looked faintly surprised that such a man could exist. "You always were an odd sort. All those years in the Caribbean, I suppose."

"India."

"Was it? Are you sure? Well, now, isn't that amazing? I would have sworn it was one of those islands. Ah, well. Delighted to see you anyway." He glanced toward Alexandra, frowning.

Thorpe politely introduced her as a friend of the Countess of Exmoor. Chesterfield spent several minutes extolling the virtues of the Countess before he pressed them to sit down.

"We have come to ask you about those days in Paris during the revolution."

Chesterfield looked surprised. "I say. That was an eon ago." He chuckled. "Can't think what you young people would want to know about such an old event. World's completely changed since then. Yes, passing of an era." He nodded as if in agreement with his statement.

"It is really for the Countess that we are asking. You see, some question has arisen about her grandchildren."

"Grandchildren! What—you mean the ones who were killed then?"

"Exactly," Alexandra said. "There may be some question, you see, as to whether all of them actually died."

"Died! Well, of course they did," he responded bluffly. "Saw it with my own eyes."

"Could you tell us exactly what you saw happen to Chilton and his family that day—moment by moment?" Sebastian asked. "It's rather important."

Though he feigned reluctance, Bertie Chesterfield launched into his story easily enough. "It was evening, you see, just turning dark. The mob came pouring down the street. I was across the way, staying with Lord and Lady Brookstone. They'd rented a house there, you see—didn't know something like this would happen, of course.''

"Of course."

"Nice neighborhood, but mostly rented houses. That's why Chilton was there. They'd taken the house so she could be near her mother—Lady Chilton, I mean, the French gal—'' He paused, suddenly struck by something, and peered at Alexandra. "I say, you look a rather lot like Lady Chilton. I thought you seemed familiar."

"I may be related to her," Alexandra told him. "That is why it's so important that we find out exactly what happened that day."

"By Jove." He gazed at her for a moment in wonderment.

"You were saying that Lord Chilton had leased the house."

"Yes. Well, the mob came pouring down the street, carrying torches and shouting. They were after blood. They tried to beat down our door, but we had good English servants, and we barricaded ourselves in. Across the street it was a different story. Poor Chilton came out and tried to tell them that he was English, but then his in-laws said something in French, and they knew they were Frogs. They went wild, shouting about the aristocrats and how they must die. Pulled Chilton and his lady right out amongst them and killed them. Parents, too. Then they stormed into the house, and when they were done, they set it afire.''

"So you actually saw Lord and Lady Chilton killed?"

"My, yes—gruesome sight, I must say. Although I never held with his marrying a Frenchwoman."

"What about the children, though?" Alexandra asked. "Did you see them killed?"

"No. Only Chilton and his wife, but the crowd went inside. Bound to have murdered the children, too. Burned the house to the ground, anyway. No way they could have survived that."

"Did you see their bodies, perhaps? After the fire?"

"Good God, no!" Chesterfield looked shocked. "Not a ghoul, you know. Besides, we didn't dare venture out of the house. No telling what might happen—they could have come back."

"Then you cannot be absolutely sure that the children died, too," Thorpe persisted.

"What else could have happened to them?" Chesterfield asked reasonably. "Poor little devils. They didn't escape that house. It was surrounded. If they had by some chance done so, we'd have heard about it, wouldn't we? No, I'm afraid they all died." He looked at Alexandra, understanding beginning to dawn on his face. "Are you saying that you're one of the children?"

"No," Alexandra answered quickly. "It is just that we wondered what the possibilities were that one or more of them might have survived."

"Not good," he said, shaking his head. "Not good."

"Well, thank you, Chesterfield," Thorpe said, rising and shaking his hand again. Bidding him goodbye, they began to make their way to the door, even though Bertie continued to talk happily about his other memories of Paris.

As they reached the doorway, Alexandra turned, struck by a sudden thought. "Mr. Chesterfield, I wondered—did you know other people in Paris at the time?"

He looked at her oddly. "Yes. Knew lots of people there. Friendly sort, you know."

"Did you by any chance know Hiram and Rhea Ward?"

He frowned, pondering the question. "Do you mean the Americans?"

"Yes." Hope rose in Alexandra's chest, and she prodded eagerly, "You knew them?"

"Acquaintances, really. Didn't know many of the Americans. Not long after their war, you know. But, I say, now that I think of it, I believe Lady Chilton was quite chummy with Mrs. Ward. She used to complain of feeling like an outsider, you see, with all us Englishmen—silly, really. I mean, after all, she was married to an Englishman, now, wasn't she? But I suppose that's why she used to gad about with Mrs. Ward."

Alexandra cast an excited look toward Sebastian, but spoke with admirable calm. "Thank you, Mr. Chesterfield. You have been most helpful."

"Have I?" Chesterfield sounded surprised. "Glad to be of service, of course."

Alexandra managed to hold in her excitement until she and Sebastian had taken their leave of Chesterfield and walked out the front door of his town house. Then she whirled to face Sebastian.

"Did you hear that? Simone knew my mother!"

Thorpe looked a trifle pale. "I heard. I—it certainly throws a different light upon things."

"It could explain everything! It could—it could mean that I really *am* the Countess's grandchild."

"It would make the story much less coincidental," Sebastian agreed. "It is possible that perhaps Alexandra was with your—Mrs. Ward for some reason when the mob came, and so she was spared."

"Or that Mother went over there looking for her friend

after the mob had been there and found the baby wandering around.''

They looked at each other in silence for a moment. It was difficult for either of them to speak of Alexandra as the lost baby. It seemed removed from Alexandra, as if they must be talking about a third person.

''I—I don't know what to think,'' Sebastian said slowly.

Deep down, he knew that he did not want to face the possibility looming before him. For the past few days, ever since Alexandra's mother had been attacked, he had been struggling against the evidence that was piling up— the fact that his men had been unable to dig up any adverse information on Alexandra; the coincidence of the attacks on Mrs. Ward at the time she might reveal what had happened in Paris; Alexandra's explanation about following her mother to Exmoor house, which rang with the authority of truth. It was becoming increasingly difficult to hang on to the idea that Alexandra was an adventuress out to cheat the Countess.

But if he changed his mind, if he accepted the idea that Alexandra really was the Countess's granddaughter, then he had made a ruinous error. He had accused her of being a criminal and a liar. She must hate him, despise him for his lack of faith. He had said and done things that were unforgivable. Nor was Alexandra the sort of woman who would readily forgive. In short, he had ruined everything with the only woman he had loved since Barbara.

That thought brought Sebastian up short. Did he love Alexandra? It seemed absurd. She was willful, blunt and argumentative, not at all the way a woman was supposed to be. She was accustomed to doing exactly what she wanted and saying precisely what she thought. Most of the time he had known her, he had spent arguing with her or distrusting her. How could he possibly love her? Yet he knew that he did—now, at this moment, when he had completely wrecked any possibility of her returning his feelings, he knew that he was hopelessly in love with her.

"Dear God," he breathed, stunned.

Alexandra glanced at him oddly. Sebastian looked as if he had been knocked in the head. The realization that they had some proof she might be the Countess's granddaughter was surprising, but it seemed odd that Sebastian should be in such a state of shock. Perhaps he had realized that he might have to put up with Alexandra for a long time if she was the granddaughter of one of his dearest friends.

"You needn't worry," she told him crisply. "Even if I am the Countess's granddaughter, I don't plan to take up residence with her. I shall return to the United States. The family I know is there."

She walked down the steps and climbed into the carriage without waiting for Sebastian's help. Sebastian hurried after her.

"Then you plan still to return?" he asked as he sat in the seat across from her and the carriage moved away.

"As soon as my mother is able to. There is nothing for me here."

"I am sure that the Countess will want you to remain," Sebastian began carefully, wondering how he could persuade her to stay longer. He had to have time to figure out his emotions, to straighten out the mess he had made of his relationship with her. "Surely you cannot mean to break her heart by leaving her. She has lost so much already."

Alexandra cast him a wary look. "Now you want me to be with the Countess? I thought you couldn't wait for me to leave."

"I didn't know—" Sebastian began stiffly. "Dammit,

woman, I do not want the Countess to be hurt. If you are her granddaughter, it will crush her if you leave."

"I would visit her, of course, if she wanted me to."

"I am sure she would want more than that."

And you? Alexandra thought. *What would you want from me?* All he could seem to talk about were the Countess's feelings, when all *she* wanted to know was how Sebastian would feel if she left. But that was too bold a question, she realized, even for a blunt American.

So she said nothing, and they continued their journey in silence, each of them occupied with their own gloomy thoughts.

15

Alexandra tilted her parasol to block the sun and looked around at the rows of vehicles that lined the open field where the balloons lay. There were open curricles, landaus, barouches, heavy old-fashioned carriages, all full of ladies and gentlemen. Obviously the balloon ascension was quite a social event. There was as much visiting back and forth between the vehicles as there was interest in the balloons.

Alexandra looked at the field, littered by large baskets, or gondolas, each of them attached by ropes to huge, colorful balloons spread out limply on the grass. People scurried, performing various tasks around the inert balloons, ignoring those who had gathered to watch. Alexandra had not wished to come today, and she would have cried off if she had not thought it would be too rude at such late notice. She had spent the day before in a gloomy state, a condition not helped by the fact that she had heard nothing from Sebastian all day. She had told herself that it was absurd to expect to see or hear from him every day, as if there were some sort of agreement between them. But she could not keep from hoping that he might come to call this afternoon. It had been difficult to force herself to smile and go with Nicola and Penelope when they came. But now, she could not help but feel a stirring of interest as she watched the proceedings.

"Look!" Nicola's voice was low but charged with emotion.

"What?" Alexandra glanced around the field, expecting to see something happening among the balloons. She turned to her companion in the open landau and saw that Nicola was looking not at the field, but down the line of vehicles to an elegant, high-sprung curricle that had just arrived.

A well-built man was maneuvering the vehicle, not very expertly, into place. Beside him sat a woman in a rose-pink dress, a dashing straw hat, upturned on one side, on her head. In her dainty gloved hand she held a parasol, which she tilted to keep the sun from her face. She smiled languidly at her companion and leaned over, her hand on his arm, to murmur something to him.

"Lady Pencross!" Alexandra exclaimed softly.

"Mother says that she is a disgrace to her sex and her station." Penelope, on the other side of Alexandra, spoke. "Of course, Mother is apt to say that about a lot of people."

"She's right about Lady Pencross. One would never guess to look at her that her husband is dying in Yorkshire."

"Look!" Penelope gripped Alexandra's arm, her fingers digging in in her excitement. "There is Bucky." Alexandra turned to look at the girl. Her face was glowing. "Lord Buckminster, I mean. I knew he would come today. And Sebastian is with him. Oh, dear, I hope he does not see Lady Pencross."

Alexandra followed Penelope's gaze, her pulse quickening. Lord Buckminster had just arrived in his curricle,

and he and Sebastian were climbing from the high seat.
Sebastian took off his hat as he turned to say something
to Buckminster, and the sun glinted off his dark brown
hair, warming it with reddish highlights. He was dressed
simply, as always, but the elegant cut of his fawn trousers
and dark coat emphasized the muscular lines of his legs
and the breadth of his shoulders. He was, Alexandra
thought, with a little catch in her breath, a man to whom
few could compare. How had that Pencross woman been
able to give him up for the sake of her husband's wealth?

He turned and spotted Alexandra and her companions
in their landau, the flexible top pushed back, accordian-
like, to allow them to see and be seen. A smile spread
across his face, lighting his features, and Alexandra felt a
corresponding lightening in her chest. He said something
to his companion, and the two men started through the
rows of vehicles toward them.

"Nicola. Penelope." Sebastian bowed toward the
women, his eyes going past the others to Alexandra. "Alexandra." His eyes searched her face, and Alexandra felt
herself warming under his gaze. "It is a pleasure to see
you here."

Alexandra blushed. His words were commonplace
enough, and she wondered if she was foolish to feel that
they had special meaning.

The five of them chatted for a few moments, talking of
commonplaces such as the weather and the balloons and
a party that lay a few days ahead. After a time, Sebastian,
who had worked his way around to stand beside Alexandra, inclined his head toward her and murmured, "Perhaps you'd care to stroll along the balloons and watch
them being filled?"

He gestured toward the behemoth creatures, beginning

to swell as the fires were lit and hot air directed into them. Alexandra smiled and nodded. "That sounds very nice."

He offered her his arm, and they walked away from the others, moving down the line in front of the carriages where they could see better. Workers scurried around the balloons, busily filling them with air and getting them prepared. It was interesting enough, but Alexandra's attention was scarcely on the activity. She was too aware of Sebastian close beside her, of his arm beneath her hand. She glanced at him, looking at his smooth cheek and the fall of his hair against his temple, the firm line of his jaw and chin. Why did he have to be so damned appealing? She thought about returning to America, and her heart was heavy in her chest. All the things she enjoyed there seemed suddenly bland and unappealing—work, her hobbies, the much quieter social round of parties.

"Alexandra..." Sebastian's voice jerked her from her reverie.

"Yes?" She shifted her parasol to the other shoulder so that she could see his face better. He was frowning, looking in front of him rather than at her, and she realized, with a sinking sensation, that he had maneuvered her away from the others in order to talk to her, not because he had wanted to be alone with her. She braced herself for another argument.

"I must apologize to you."

"What?" Alexandra gaped at him. That was the last thing she had expected him to say.

A smile tugged at the corners of his mouth. "A rare event, I grant you, but you needn't look quite so astonished. I admit when I am wrong."

"Rare as that is?" Alexandra said lightly, and Sebastian's smile grew larger.

"Yes. Rare as that is. I would like to say that it was

only out of my concern for the Countess, but, to be truthful, I allowed certain mistakes in my past to color my thinking. I too easily believed Lady Ursula when she questioned your motives in being friendly to me. When I saw you meeting someone outside Exmoor's house, it fanned the flames of my suspicion. I did not give you the benefit of the doubt, and when you would not explain why you were there, I believed the worst. I can see now that I have wronged you. I cannot expect you to forgive me, for I have said some unforgivable things, but—''

Alexandra was not sure how she would have answered him, for her heart seemed suddenly to be in her throat and her thoughts were a scattered mess, but she was not to find out, for at that moment, a low, melodious woman's voice interrupted them.

''Hallo, Thorpe. Such a surprise to see you here.''

Sebastian stiffened and slowly turned. Alexandra, with some irritation, turned, too. Lady Pencross stood a few feet from them. Alexandra cast a sideways glance at Sebastian to see how he was taking this meeting with his former love.

His face betrayed nothing except a certain wariness. ''Lady Pencross. I must say, I am even more surprised to find you at such an event. I would have thought you had little interest in scientific advances.''

The woman shrugged and made a charming moue of distaste. ''Duncan assured me that it would be fascinating. I shall have to take him to task for that later.''

''I'm sure,'' Sebastian commented dryly. He sketched a small bow in her direction. ''If you will excuse us, we were on our way to—''

''That suits me perfectly,'' Lady Pencross interjected smoothly. ''I was about to take a stroll myself.'' She shifted her parasol to the other shoulder and drew closer to Sebastian.

Alexandra sighed inwardly. The woman had made it socially difficult to do anything except allow her to walk with them. Sebastian, however, seemed to have few qualms about committing social solecisms.

"I did not ask you to accompany us," he said bluntly.

Lady Pencross stiffened at the blatant insult, and her eyes flashed. But she quickly brought her expression under control and said in her silky voice, "Still mad at me, Sebastian?" She smiled in a slow, sensual way. "Fourteen years is a long time to keep a flame going."

"Madam," Sebastian began in a clipped voice, "the only feeling I have for you is profound indifference."

He turned and started away, but Lady Pencross grabbed Alexandra's arm and jerked her back. Her eyes blazed into Alexandra's. "Do you think that you can catch him? Don't be naïve. He's toying with you, as he has toyed with every woman he's been with since me. I am the only woman Sebastian ever loved—or ever will love. If I wanted him back, he'd come—just like that!" She snapped her fingers contemptuously.

Sebastian made an angry noise and started toward Lady Pencross, but Alexandra spoke quickly, forestalling him. "I should not brag if I were you, my lady, about the fact that you threw away a man who loved you because you preferred money. You made your choice long ago, and you can't get back what you despised. If you think that you could ever get a man like Lord Thorpe back after what you did to him, you obviously do not know him, no matter how many times you were in his bed. Now, good day, my lady, and I would suggest that you not humiliate yourself by following us any farther."

Alexandra glanced significantly at the people in the carriages around them, who had fallen silent and were avidly watching the scene before them. Sebastian, who had been looking thunderous, had to smile at the look on Lady Pencross's face as she realized that a large number of her acquaintances had witnessed Alexandra giving her a set down. Embarrassment quickly turned to rage, however, and she glared at Alexandra in a way that would have made a lesser woman quail.

"You will be sorry for this," she hissed and stalked to her carriage.

"I appear to have made an enemy," Alexandra said lightly as she turned to Sebastian. They resumed walking. "It seems to be a habit of mine."

"She is not a pleasant enemy to have."

"I suspected as much. However, I'm too occupied with my present enemy to worry overmuch about her."

They walked to the end of the line of balloons, where a blue-and-white-striped one lay. Two men worked busily at filling it, while a third man, with a wild shock of white hair and a beard, spent his time shouting directions. There were few spectators this far down.

"I presume someone must have informed you of my youthful infatuation with Barbara," Sebastian commented, looking at the balloon rather than at her.

"Something of it."

"Funny, how easy it is to fool oneself into believing that a person is one way or another just because you want them to be. I never saw her selfishness or her mean spirit until the end. I told her about my plan, that we would run away to India, escape her husband and my family and all of disapproving Society. We would live in blissful love." A smile twisted his lips. "She told me that blissful love would purchase no dresses or jewelry for her, and that she would rather die than leave the social rounds of London for the wilds of India. The only women there, she said, were the dowdy wives of soldiers and merchants. I could not believe it at first. I argued with her. I believed, foolishly, that she was simply nervous and scared at the prospect of breaking with her past life. So I assured her that our love would make up for whatever discomforts we might have.''

He paused. ''She told me that it had been no grand love that had made her cuckold her husband, as I had thought. It had been merely an affair with a boy who took her fancy—an affair in a string of others. I didn't believe it. I raged at her. That is when she told me that she was growing tired of me, even without the dreadful prospect of going to India. She had, it seemed, already found a lover to replace me.''

''Sebastian! Oh, no!''

He nodded and turned toward her, his mouth twisting into a cynical smile. ''The man who replaced me was the Earl of Exmoor.''

Alexandra drew in her breath sharply. ''That is why you dislike him so!''

''Yes. Although, God knows, it could have been any one of a dozen other men. Barbara does not like to be alone. It broke my heart—for a time, at least. But it wasn't really Barbara that I cried for—it was all my pitiful, broken illusions.''

''I'm sorry,'' Alexandra said inadequately. She wanted to put her arms around him and hold him close to her, to stroke his hair and assure him that she would banish all thoughts of Barbara and her betrayal. Of course, it was far too public a place to do something like that. However, she was not sure whether Sebastian would wish it, even if they were alone. He had apologized to her for what he had thought about her, but he had not said that he had any feelings for her, any desire. She could not help but remember the way he had rejected her that night at his house.

Sebastian shrugged. "It was a long time ago. It's all over now." He glanced toward their carriage. "I suppose we had better return. Else it will set tongues to wagging."

"I find that tongues wag easily here."

They returned to the carriage, where the servants had laid out the picnic luncheon they had brought. They ate while the slow process of filling the balloons continued. Gradually, all over the field, the balloons swelled and then began to lift from the ground.

Thorpe went off with Lord Buckminster to talk to a friend, and one of Lady Ursula's acquaintances came over to talk to Penelope. Alexandra soon grew bored with the inconsequential chatter about people she did not know, and she decided to take a closer look at the balloons, which were floating above their baskets.

Taking her leave from the women, she strolled toward the jaunty blue-and-white-striped balloon that she and Sebastian had been looking at earlier. The man with the full head of white hair and the equally flowing white beard was standing in the basket of the balloon, arguing at full volume with the two younger men outside the basket.

Intrigued, Alexandra moved closer. The balloon was almost completely full, buoyant and straining against the ropes that held it tied to the ground. She watched the gesticulating men, who seemed to be arguing about the small bags tied to the side of the balloon. She wondered what the bags had to do with the flight of the balloon. Were they weights? She wondered how the whole thing operated and if the balloonists ever took passengers up with them.

Intent on the men and their vehicle, she scarcely noticed

the rustle of footsteps behind her, until suddenly an arm shot around her waist and a hand clamped over her mouth. She was being lifted and pulled backward almost before she knew what was happening.

The balloonists, wrapped up in their contretemps, didn't even look her way. Alexandra twisted and struggled, lashing with her feet. One heel cracked hard into a man's shin, and he let out an oath. His grip on her mouth loosened a little, and Alexandra grabbed at the hand with both of hers, yanking it from her mouth. She let out a piercing scream.

"Sebastian!"

The man who was holding her began to curse in earnest, and he clapped his hand over her mouth again. But Alexandra had managed to draw attention to them.

"I say! What are you doing?" Voices rose around them. To Alexandra's profound relief, Sebastian turned and saw them. He started toward them on the run.

"Alexandra!"

Suddenly the man released her mouth, and an instant later he jabbed something small, round and hard against her temple—a pistol! Alexandra's screams died in her throat.

"Stop!" He jerked the gun against her temple so hard it made her eyes water. Sebastian came to a halt, his face taut and furious. "I'll shoot the witch if you come any closer!"

"Don't be stupid," Sebastian told him, his hard gray eyes fixed on the man intently. He edged forward as he spoke. "You cannot possibly hope to get away. You're surrounded." He gestured toward the spectators blocking the man's exit. "Let her go."

"Wot? You think I'm a bleedin' idiot?" Alexandra's captor replied. "Ain't none of you doin' anyfing to me while I got this pop shooter to 'er 'ead. Not unless you want a dead lady on yer 'ands. I said, stop right there!"

His voice rose hysterically, and Sebastian stopped, holding his hands up in a peaceful gesture. "Nobody wants to hurt you. Just let her go, and you are free to leave. But if you take her, you will have half of London on your trail. You cannot possibly escape."

"He's right, you know," Alexandra agreed.

"You shut up!" Alexandra could smell the fear in her captor, hear his rapid breathing, and she wisely closed her mouth.

He hesitated, then jerked her to the side, pulling her to the balloon. The three men who operated the balloon stared at them, openmouthed, their disagreement forgotten. Alexandra's captor shoved her into the basket and followed her in.

"Here! You can't do that!" The fellow with the flowing white hair started toward them indignantly.

Alexandra's companion directed the barrel of his pistol toward him. "The hell I can't! You stay back."

"But—but the balloon's ready to leave," the balloonist protested.

"Then that's right lucky, ain't it, 'cause so am I." He gestured at the man with his pistol. "Start undoin' them ropes."

The man stared at him, his jaw dropping. "You can't be serious! You know nothing—"

"Shut up!" Alexandra's abductor roared, his face reddening, and the hand holding the pistol shook dangerously.

Now that the pistol was no longer pointed at her head, Alexandra thought about lunging against the man, but he still held her arms effectively to her sides, and she was also afraid that in his agitated state he would shoot wildly and hit one of the men before her. She dared a sideways glance in Sebastian's direction and saw that, while her assailant's attention was on the others, Sebastian was inching his way closer to the basket.

"I said untie those ropes!" Her attacker brought the pistol to Alexandra's temple. "Are you goin' to do wot I said, or do I 'ave to show you I mean business?"

"Yes, yes, of course." The men hurried to work at the knot holding one of the ties to a stake in the ground. They managed to untie it and turned. Alexandra's captor gestured at another rope, shouting at them to go on. With obvious reluctance, the men began to work on the second rope.

There were only four ropes holding the balloon to the ground, and as the second one was pulled free, the balloon bounced up a little, knocking Alexandra and her attacker back. The man's arm left her waist as he grabbed at the side of the basket to steady himself. Alexandra seized the opportunity to throw herself at his gun arm and knocked it aside. The pistol went off, the ball slicing through the third rope, and the balloon tugged upward, yearning toward freedom.

At the same instant Sebastian ran the last few feet to the basket and jumped in, crashing into Alexandra's assailant. The three of them, tangled, tumbled around the basket. The last rope jerked free from its stake, and the balloon surged up. The three balloonists grabbed the end of the rope, holding on for dear life as Sebastian and the ruffian grappled with each other. The attacker had his hand around Sebastian's throat and was squeezing. Sebastian lashed out, punching him in the side of the head, but the man's grip did not loosen. Alexandra threw herself at the man's back, wrapping her arm around his neck and pulling with all her might, kicking at his legs and pulling his hair.

He let go of Sebastian with a howl and swatted behind him, knocking Alexandra to the side. But Sebastian was up and caught him with a solid right hook. The man staggered and fell through the open door of the basket. They were a few feet off the ground, and he fell straight into the group of men struggling to hold the balloon fast. They went down in a heap of arms and legs, letting go of the rope, and the balloon shot up.

Alexandra gasped at the sudden movement. She had fallen to the floor, and now crawled until her back was against the solid wall of the basket. Hands braced on the floor on either side of her, she stared across the basket in consternation at Sebastian, who was standing, one hand on the edge of the basket and the other grasping a rope leading to the balloon. He looked at her in equal amazement.

Finally he reached over, pulled the hanging door to and shoved the bolt home. Alexandra stood up, holding on to the side of the basket for support, and joined him. Below them the balloonists on the ground were rapidly receding. The man with the flowing white hair was shouting and waving his arms at them, but they could not understand what he said. The other two balloonists were struggling to hold on to Alexandra's attacker, and as they watched, Lord Buckminster and some other spectators ran up to help subdue the man. Nicola and Penelope were there, too, shading their eyes and gazing at the balloon in wonder.

"Oh, my," Alexandra said, drawing in a breath as she looked at the trees and land falling away beneath them.

All around them the other balloons were beginning to rise, too, huge bright balls soaring in the sunlight. "Isn't it beautiful!"

She had never felt anything like this before. There was an exquisite freedom in floating away, escaping the bonds of earth. It was like flying, she thought. And even though it was a scary proposition to be dangling up here at the mercy of a strange contraption she knew nothing about, it was also wildly exhilarating.

She waved at her friends, then turned to Sebastian. His hat was long gone, the wind tousling his dark hair. His gray eyes were alive with the same excitement Alexandra felt. She laughed aloud.

"Isn't this glorious?"

Sebastian let out a bark of laughter. "God! You are one in a million!"

He pulled her into his arms and kissed her. Alexandra clung to him dizzily, the excitement of the wild ride mingling with the delicious passion of Sebastian's lips. Heat rose in her, melting her loins and sizzling through her veins. All the desire that had been simmering between them since the night Sebastian had rescued her burst into full flame, filling and consuming them. His arms went around her tightly, and he pulled her into him, his legs braced apart on the moving floor. Alexandra wrapped her arms around his neck, kissing him back with all her fervor. Sebastian murmured her name as his mouth left hers and began to trail fevered kisses down the side of her neck.

Suddenly something thumped the bottom of their basket, jerking them back into reality. They broke their embrace and looked out. Their basket was grazing the tops of some trees and ahead of them stood more, and taller, trees.

"Oh, my God, we're going to crash!"

"How the devil do you get this thing to go up?" Sebastian growled, searching the balloon for some mechanism that would help them.

"The weights!" Alexandra cried, remembering the argument she had watched among the balloonists. She leaned over the side of the basket, pointing to the small bags of sand tied around the outside.

She began to wrestle with the knots, but Sebastian reached inside his sleeve and pulled out a small knife. Leaning over, he cut through the rope, and the small bag fell. He moved on to the next. Gradually, the balloon began to rise, but the trees were still looming dangerously close. Frantically, he sliced through the ropes, dropping the weights, but still it wasn't quite enough. Just as it looked as if the basket would crash into the treetops, a gust of wind lifted the balloon, and they sailed over the trees, branches scraping against the bottom of the gondola.

Alexandra let out a gusty sigh of relief and sagged against the side. She looked at Sebastian. He straightened and slid the knife up his sleeve into the small scabbard on his arm. Her eyes followed the knife.

"I would not have thought that a concealed knife was de rigueur for a London gentleman."

"It seems advisable not to go out unarmed when you're around," he explained wryly.

Alexandra raised an eyebrow. "It's not my fault."

"No. But someone certainly seems to want to do away with you. The question is, why?"

"I don't even care about why!" Alexandra exclaimed. "I would just like to find out who is behind it all."

"Yes, but I suspect that the why would lead us to the who, if only we could figure it out."

"Right now, I would like to know how we are going to get down from this thing," Alexandra commented. "It's lovely up here, but I would feel quite a bit better if

I had some idea how it operated. There must be some way to bring it down. Surely they don't just rely on chance."

Sebastian looked around them. "We seem to have lost ground with the others."

He pointed ahead and above them, where most of the other balloons floated, moving farther and farther away. Alexandra nodded. They were being carried along by a current of wind, it seemed, that was bearing them off the path the other balloons had taken. She also noticed that, with most of their weights gone, they were continuing to rise.

"How high will it go, do you think?" she asked, alarm stirring in her.

"I don't know," he replied grimly, looking at the ropes going up to a sort of ring above them and from there up to the balloon. "How do you steer this thing?"

"I don't think you can," Alexandra replied. "I believe that we must be more or less at the mercy of the wind. Obviously those other balloons must have gotten caught on a different current of wind because they were higher."

"I am sure that we can control the going up and coming down, though, at least to some extent," Sebastian said. "Look, they are hot air balloons, right? They fill the balloons with heated air, and that is what made them rise."

Alexandra nodded.

"It would stand to reason, then, that if the air cooled, they would start to come down." Sebastian looked pleased with his reasoning.

"I suppose. You know, I think that there is a valve that you can use to let off air, with a cord that comes down."

Sebastian looked skeptically at the multitude of ropes hanging from the balloon on all sides. Most of them connected the net over the balloon to the gondola. "I don't know that I'd want to risk pulling on cords to see what would happen."

"You're probably right."

Sebastian went to the brazier suspended above their heads in the center of the basket. "I don't see any way to put out this fire, but if we don't feed it coal, eventually it will burn down, the gas will cool, and we will come down."

"Hopefully not into a house."

"Yes. Or a hillside." He looked at the scenery beneath them. "I would say that we are heading southwest from London."

"It won't carry us as far as the ocean, will it?" Alexandra asked worriedly.

"Let us hope that the fire will go out long before then."

"It's getting colder."

"Yes. I think it's because we are still rising."

Sebastian shrugged out of his coat and wrapped it around Alexandra. She smiled a thank-you at him, and they turned to look at the scenery. Despite the uncertainty of their situation, there was a certain peace and serenity to their trip. It was as if they were alone in the world, free-floating, the majestic beauty of the sky and land above and below them. Unconsciously Sebastian's arm stole around Alexandra's waist, and she leaned against him.

They began to talk, not about this latest adventure or about the mystery of Alexandra's birth and the attacks upon her, but about all sorts of other things—their philosophies, their childhoods, the value of good friends, the land that lay beneath them—moving desultorily from topic to topic as ideas popped into their heads. It was like a moment torn from time, too special and important to dwell on momentary problems. Later, Alexandra would look back on it as one of the best days she spent in London.

Slowly they became aware that the balloon was dropping. The earth seemed nearer than before. Figures working in the field or walking down a road were much clearer.

"Are we going to land soon?" Alexandra asked.

"I hope so. Look at the horizon. It won't be long before the sun sets. We would be in a bad way if we are still in the air when it turns dark."

Alexandra nodded. "Perhaps we ought to consider trying the ropes to see if one's connected to the valve."

"All right—if it doesn't land before dark. I don't want to be coming down at night with no idea what's below us." He looked over the side of the basket. "Of course, I have no desire to come down into those trees, either."

"Do you know where we are?"

Sebastian frowned. "We've been traveling southwest. My guess is the North Wessex Downs—although, God knows, we may have traveled so far that it's Dartmoor. I have never seen the land from this angle before. What I hope is that we aren't farther south and those trees below us are the New Forest."

The balloon dipped. It seemed to Alexandra that they had fallen from the current of air on which they had been riding. They were moving more slowly. Before long, they heard the thunk of treetops against the bottom of the basket. Alexandra and Sebastian cast a worried look at each other.

"I don't see any sign of these trees ending," he said. "I don't relish the idea of the basket crashing into the tops of these trees and us tumbling out."

"Nor do I," Alexandra agreed wholeheartedly. "Shall we cut loose some more of the weights?"

"I think we'd better."

They got rid of the other sandbags one by one, and the balloon rose, but not nearly as much as it had before. Finally they were rid of sandbags, and the trees were looming closer and closer. Once again, they bumped and skipped across the tops, once almost tipping over as a particularly high branch hit the side of the gondola.

Then, abruptly, they were past the trees, with a wide expanse of green pastures below them. White sheep grazed on the grass, undisturbed by the passage of the vehicle over their heads.

"This looks like an excellent spot to land."

"Yes, if only it will." They waited a little breathlessly as they dropped lower and lower, skimming over a wide creek.

Straight ahead of them lay a stand of trees.

16

Sebastian looked at the trees, cleared his throat and said, "I think it might be time to try that valve."

Alexandra nodded, her heart in her throat. Though they were much closer to the ground, if they fell, it would still be very serious.

"You will be safer if you sit," Sebastian directed.

"What about you?"

"I have to find this bloody cord. But there's no reason for both of us to stand."

"But—"

"Please don't argue about equality right now. I refuse to let you stand here and try the cords."

At the look on his face, Alexandra subsided and sat on the floor of the gondola. She wished she were standing. It might be safer on the floor, but there was something more frightening about not being able to see where one was going, only feeling the sudden drop if it came.

Sebastian tugged fruitlessly at one cord, then another. Finally, after he pulled one, there was the hiss of escaping air. Alexandra looked at the balloon. It looked to be slowly deflating. She jumped to her feet.

"That's it!"

"Yes, if only we make it in time."

She looked where Sebastian's eyes were focused and saw the trees coming up on them at an alarming rate. Sebastian pulled her onto the floor with him, sitting down and wrapping his arms around her, bending over her protectively. They waited, scarcely breathing, for the crash.

When it came, it was not the impact they had expected. The balloon hit and caught on the higher branches and stopped, causing the gondola to swing forward and sharply back. They went tumbling across the basket, coming up tangled against the other side. They lay for a moment, waiting for something more, but nothing came.

It sank in on Alexandra that they were still alive and whole and no longer floating through the air. In the next instant she realized that she was lying on top of Sebastian, her legs tangled with his, her face against his chest and his arms around her. She could hear the rapid thump of his heart beneath her ear, feel his warmth surrounding her. Her breasts were pressed against him, and their bodies lay flush against each other all the way up and down.

Alexandra could feel the heat rising up her throat and into her face, and she was not sure whether it was embarrassment or the more carnal flush of desire. Hastily she scrambled off Sebastian, unable to look him in the face.

The dangling gondola swayed at her movements.

"Careful," Sebastian told her, sitting up slowly. "We don't want to send this thing crashing."

The basket was tilted away from the tree. A branch, the end snapped off raggedly, poked through the opposite side, and several branches stretched across the gondola above their heads.

Carefully, Sebastian and Alexandra stood, balancing on the slightly tilted floor and easing around the branches. Grasping a couple of the larger branches, they eased forward to the edge of the gondola. It rocked a little, and Alexandra was glad that she had hold of a thick branch. She peered over the side at the ground below.

They were surprisingly close, hanging no more than eight feet above the ground. Sebastian turned to Alexandra with a grin. "No broken bones?"

Alexandra shook her head. "Just a few bruises."

"Then I would say we've come out ahead." He edged to the door of the gondola, unbolted it and pushed it out. Then he lay on the floor of the basket and slid out backward, holding on to the bottom of the basket with his hands and finally dropping the rest of the way to the ground.

Alexandra crawled to the edge and peered down. Sebastian was scrambling onto his feet. He looked at her. "Come on. I'll catch you."

The ground suddenly looked much farther away when she thought about jumping down. But Alexandra took a firm grip on her courage and swung around, slowly lowering herself out of the basket. She thought about the view she must present to Sebastian below, her skirt twisting around her legs as she slid out. That thought gave her the impetus to shove herself the rest of the way out and drop.

She fell into his arms, and he set her on the ground. He bent over her, laying his cheek against her head, his arms tight around her. Alexandra wrapped her arms around his waist just as tightly. Suddenly, in the aftermath of their adventure, all the tension that had been humming inside her for the last few hours broke loose, and she started to tremble. Her knees felt like melted wax. She drew a ragged breath and commanded herself not to cry.

Sebastian rubbed his hand up and down her back, soothing her without a word. She felt his lips brush against her hair. Desire flashed through her, exploding in her abdomen. She wanted him to continue to stroke her, to run his hands through her hair and move them all over her body.

Instead she forced herself to move away. "Well," she said a little shakily, avoiding his eyes. "I, uh, guess we had better start walking."

"Alexandra..."

She raised her eyes to his, steeling herself against their appeal. "What?"

"Nothing. You're right. Let's go."

They made their way across the verdant pasture, watched by the indifferent sheep. Alexandra's green half kid boots were scarcely made for such a procedure, and she thought with an inward sigh that they would be entirely ruined by the time they reached any habitation. She gathered her muslin skirt and wrapped the excess around her arm so that it ended at the more practical level of her knee. Alexandra saw Sebastian glance at her legs and then quickly away, and she wondered with an inner sense of satisfaction whether the sight had affected him.

They trudged for some time. The area seemed to be deserted, with dark clusterings of trees on either side of the lush pasture. They followed the course of a stream until they spotted a stile. They made their way toward it, crossed a fence and found themselves on a sort of track, not quite well-traveled enough to be considered a path, but eventually it led to a better-marked path, and that, in turn, fed into a narrow country lane, hedged on either side with rhododendrons.

As they walked, they talked. Alexandra found it curious that once they returned to earth, their conversation turned to more mundane matters.

"It's obvious," Sebastian began, reaching out a hand

to steady her as she jumped across a little ditch, "that someone is out to harm you. This latest attack had nothing to do with your mother. It was only you."

"I know. I've been racking my brain trying to think of who it could possibly be. I know no one in England except you and the Countess."

"It has to be connected to...well, to the mystery of your birth—whether you are Chilton's daughter and how you wound up in America. It seems far too coincidental otherwise."

"But who could it harm if I am the Countess's grand-child? Lady Ursula and Penelope are the only ones I can think of, and it seems absurd to picture either of them as a killer, even by proxy."

"Yet someone tried to kill your mother and has attacked you twice and tried to kidnap you. I have given up my position that you have past swindling victims seeking revenge. But what does that leave?"

"Nothing. No one...unless...what about Lord Exmoor, the one who got the title?"

Sebastian chuckled. "Believe me, there is no one I can see better in the role of villain than Richard. I would love to discover that it was he. But to what purpose?"

"You said that he inherited the estate because the Countess's son and his children were all dead. If one of them isn't dead, then—"

Sebastian shook his head. "No. The entire estate and the title pass only to males. Your appearance on the scene would make no difference to him. He would still be entitled to everything he inherited. Now, if the boy, your brother, were the one who had shown up after all these years, I am sure that Richard would be homicidal. But a woman—the most you could inherit would be part of the Countess's fortune when she dies. It is not enormous, but it would be a comfortable living. The problem is that only Lady Ursula could be hurt by any rewriting of the will. The Countess dislikes Richard and wouldn't leave him a farthing of her own money, anyway. I am sure he knows that."

They walked in silence for a few minutes, then Sebastian said, "Perhaps we are looking at this wrong. What about the Ward family?"

Alexandra gave him a blank look. "My family? What are you talking about? What do they have to do with this?"

"If you are really the Countess's granddaughter, then you are not Mrs. Ward's child. I would think that there might be some people who would resent that, who would feel that a stranger should not inherit Mr. Ward's estate."

"Well, I haven't inherited it. I mean, not really. Mother inherited it, and I manage it for her."

"But it will be yours when she dies."

"Then why would they attack Mother?" she pointed out. "That would only cause me to get it sooner."

He frowned. "You're right. That would not be logical."

"Besides, my closest relative is Aunt Hortense. And I will not believe that she could ever try to do away with me. She raised me as much as my mother."

"Which brings us back to square one. There are no suspects."

"Yet it happened. Someone did it. Someone hired that ruffian to kill Mother, and I would imagine that someone hired that man today."

"There has to be something we're missing. We're looking at it wrong somehow."

"But how else can we look at it? We come to London, and the very night I meet the Countess, I am attacked and told to go back where I came from. When I don't leave and instead start talking to the Countess and she declares that I am her granddaughter, someone tries to murder my mother, the only person who could tell us the facts of my birth. Now they're trying to kidnap me.''

''There must be some other person, some motive we aren't seeing.''

Alexandra sighed. ''We're getting nowhere.''

''In our discussion or our journey?''

''Both. I haven't seen a house along this road yet.'' Alexandra cast a look around. It had been growing darker as they walked. The trees and hedges on either side of the road had made the lane shadowy, and she realized that the sun was almost gone, and there was an evening gloom in the lane. ''Oh, dear. It's almost evening.''

''Yes. It won't make walking any easier, particularly on this road. Hopefully we will come upon something soon.''

They were tired, but the closing twilight made them pick up their pace. Night came fast, and they trudged on, picking their way more carefully. The road gradually widened, and after a while they came upon a crossroad that was larger than their lane. Their spirits revived somewhat as they started along the road.

They were nearing a curve when Sebastian stopped suddenly and raised his hand. ''Listen.''

Alexandra came to a halt, too, and they stood still and silent for a long moment, their ears straining. A noise sounded softly, and it took Alexandra a moment to realize what it was—the jingle of a harness.

''A horse?'' she breathed.

There was a cough and then the faint sound of hooves on a dirt road. ''Thank heavens!'' Alexandra exclaimed, her face lighting up, and she darted down the road, waving her arms. "Hello! We need help!"

"No, wait!" Sebastian reached out for her, but he caught nothing but air. With a grimace he started after her. "Alexandra!"

He reached her and grabbed her arm. "Shh! We don't know who it might be."

"They're bound to help us," Alexandra replied confidently.

"Not everyone is a friend."

The horses rounded the curve toward them. It was a small group of men, four at the most, and they led with them a riderless horse. When they rounded the curve and saw Alexandra and Sebastian standing before them, they paused, then came forward slowly. It was difficult to see them. They seemed very dark, with no spot of white on their clothing, and their horses were all black, without any markings.

They stopped a few feet from Alexandra and Sebastian. Alexandra drew in a sharp gasp when she saw that the face of the man in front was dark from the nose up. The next instant she realized that he was wearing a half-mask over his eyes and nose. The effect was chilling.

"Bloody hell!" Sebastian breathed beside her. "A highwayman."

She felt him tense beside her, and he crossed his arms. Alexandra remembered the knife hidden in a scabbard up his sleeve. A shiver ran through her at the thought of Sebastian going up against these four men with only a knife, and she quickly ran through her mind what she could use as a weapon to help him. She wished desperately that she had not dropped her reticule in the struggle with her attacker. Her gun was in it, useless, where the balloon had taken off.

"Good Lord! What have we here?" the man in front said lightly. Despite his appearance, his speech was that of a gentleman. "Out for an evening stroll?"

"Hardly the place I would choose to take a stroll," Alexandra replied. "We are lost and in need of help."

"Alexandra..." Sebastian cast her a quelling look.

The stranger glanced at him and grinned, his even white teeth glinting in the darkness. "Ah, the husband, I think."

Alexandra opened her mouth to deny it, but before she could speak, Sebastian said loudly, "Yes. This is my wife. I am Sebastian, Lord Thorpe."

Alexandra looked at him oddly, but said nothing.

"A lord?" The rider laid a hand over his heart in an gesture of awe. His dark eyes danced, and his lips curved in mocking smile. "I am—overwhelmed."

"I doubt that," Sebastian retorted dryly.

"It is most tedious to be lost," the stranger went on, ignoring Sebastian's comment. "Perhaps we can be of assistance."

"Yes!" Alexandra agreed quickly. "That would be very nice."

"But forgive me." The man made a show of looking around. "How did you come to this place?"

"Balloon."

"I beg your pardon." The man looked at them blankly, and Sebastian felt a certain sense of satisfaction.

"We came by balloon," Sebastian explained. "You know—in the air."

"Yes, of course, I know. But where is the balloon? And is it not usual to have people on the ground? Followers?"

"It was an accident," Alexandra explained. "We didn't mean to take off in the balloon, but that man attacked me, and he made them untie the ropes. Of course Sebastian knocked him out of the basket—"

"But of course." The highwayman's grin broadened.

"But it was too late. We were already going up by then. So we had no one to follow us, and we were blown off course from the rest of the balloons. We didn't know how to operate it, you see."

"It's not a common skill," the other man agreed reasonably.

"Of course everyone will be most worried about us by now, so we have to get back to London as soon as possible. If you would be so good as to tell us how to get to a village where we could hire a coach or catch the stage—"

The man leaned over. "For you, my lady, anything." He cast a roguish look at Sebastian. "Do not look so black, my lord husband, I mean no harm. She is too beautiful to resist a little flirting."

"Thank you," Alexandra told him. "You are very kind."

The man swung down from his saddle. He was tall and slender, broad-shouldered in his dark, loose shirt. There was, Alexandra noted, a pistol stuck through his belt. He was, she suspected, dangerous. However, he had also a certain grace and charm of manner, as well as an infectious grin.

He swept her an elegant bow. "Jack Moore, at your service, my lady."

Alexandra couldn't help but smile and bob a little curtsey in return. "Alexandra—"

"Lady Thorpe," Sebastian interposed, moving between Alexandra and the man.

"Tomorrow I will take you to Evansford. The London stage comes through at ten. The stage tonight has already passed." Another expression flitted across the man's face, a kind of amusement, as if he knew a joke that no one else was in on.

Behind him one of the men made a low noise, and the horses shifted restlessly. Moore glanced at the men, then returned his gaze to Alexandra and Sebastian.

"Tonight you must be my guests. My house is not far, and you will be able to rest and refresh yourselves. And after a good's night sleep, I shall escort you to the village."

"We could not impose on you, sir," Sebastian said firmly. "If you will just tell us which way the village lies, we will go there tonight."

"No, I insist. It is far too long for a lovely lady such as your wife to walk. This part of the country is somewhat isolated. I have room in my house, and it will be most pleasant to have company."

"You are too kind," Sebastian began.

The man grinned. "There are many who would dispute that. But I cannot let a beautiful woman languish by the side of the road. You must come with us." He paused, giving Sebastian a long, serious look. "You will come to no harm, you know. I give you my word."

He held out his hand to Sebastian, and after a brief hesitation, Sebastian shook it.

"I think it sounds lovely," Alexandra said, moving beside Sebastian. "A meal and a good night's sleep will be just the ticket. You are very kind, Mr. Moore."

"Thank you, my lady." He smiled at her. "We are even so fortunate as to have an extra horse with us tonight. We, er, came upon it on the road."

"That is indeed fortunate," Sebastian commented wryly. He winced as Alexandra trod upon his foot.

"Isn't it?" she agreed. "I have always found that

things come along just when you need them the most.
Like tonight, when you arrived so fortuitously.''

"It was fortuitous, indeed," Moore replied. "It has
been a while since I have had good conversation at the
supper table. My lord, if you will mount our spare animal,
I can easily take my lady up before me." His eyes twin-
kled roguishly.

"Alexandra will ride with me," Sebastian said flatly,
his eyes narrowed, and he moved his feet a little farther
apart, bracing himself.

Moore's teeth flashed. "But of course your lady will
ride with you. Everything will be quite proper."

He walked with them to the spare mount, but before
Sebastian could climb on the saddleless animal, Moore
put a hand on his arm, stopping him. "But first, I regret,
we must cover your eyes. It would be—let us say—awkward, for you to see the way we take. It is dark, I know,
but still…" He shrugged expressively.

A little to Alexandra's surprise, Sebastian acquiesced
easily to the idea, allowing Moore to tie a black scarf
around his eyes. Moore then gave him a leg up onto the
horse. He tied another dark cloth around Alexandra's eyes
and lifted her onto the horse in front of Sebastian.

"There. Are you comfortable?"

"Fine."

"Good. We will lead the horse. Do not worry."

With those cheerful words, he returned to his horse, and
in another moment their horse started forward. Sebastian's
arms went around Alexandra, and he twined his hands in
the horse's mane for purchase.

"Well, my dear," Sebastian murmured in her ear, "you
do introduce me to some interesting people. A highwayman now."

"It's not my fault we ran into him," Alexandra protested in a whisper. "I was afraid you were going to offend him by refusing to go to his house."

"I didn't see a way out of it, frankly. We are in his power. At least he blindfolded us so we could not see the way. That is the most encouraging thing that's happened to us. It means he's not necessarily going to kill us."

"I think I trust him," Alexandra decided. "He seems a nice fellow."

"Mm. A nice fellow who liberated someone's horse tonight."

They lapsed into silence, like the men around them. It was an odd sensation, Alexandra thought, to be sitting in the quiet, unable to see, the only noises those of the horses and the night, the only sensation Sebastian's arms around her. She felt strangely safe and peaceful, almost content, yet at the same time there was in her a burgeoning heat, an intense awareness of Sebastian's body against hers that seemed to be intensified by the loss of sight, as though her tactile sense had grown even stronger. She leaned against his chest, and she knew that it wasn't all weariness that made her do so. She liked the feel of his hard bone and muscle, the scent of him, the stirring of his breath against her hair, the rhythmic movement of the horse beneath her. She sat flush against him, sideways on the horse, with her bottom wedged into the V of his legs, an intensely intimate position. And Alexandra did not think, from the way the heat of his body rose and the surge of flesh against her hip, that Sebastian was indifferent to her presence there, either.

Heat blossomed between her legs, and soon she was damp and aching and thinking about the night they had spent together. She wanted to do those things again, she knew, except that this time she wanted to take the wild ride to completion. It would be utterly scandalous to admit, but since that night, she had yearned to feel Sebastian inside her, to experience not only her pleasure but the completion of his, as well.

Alexandra turned her face into his chest as if she could still the flush she knew must be rising in her face. When she did, she found that all she could think about was his skin, his chest, and she wanted to see it bare, to feel it against her skin, her mouth. Her heart began to skitter, and her mouth was suddenly dry. It was dark. No one would see; no one would know. She hesitated, then threw caution to the winds. Her fingers crept up the front of his shirt to the button beneath her face. Sebastian stiffened at the movement. Stealthily, Alexandra unfastened the button, then moved to the one above it. Sebastian's arms were suddenly as hard as iron around her, and she could hear his breath rasp in his throat.

She slipped her fingers between the edges of his shirt, touching his bare skin. His skin jumped beneath her hand. She drew tiny circles with her fingernail, then pressed her lips against his chest. He went utterly rigid. She could feel the pounding of his heart. Her tongue stole out, tasting his salty skin, and Sebastian made a soft, strangled noise.

He bent his head, so that his mouth was right at her ear. "Stop it, you little minx."

But with his next breath he was kissing her ear, slipping the lobe into his mouth and worrying it with his teeth. He pulled away, burying his face in her hair.

"Do you know what you're doing to me?" he murmured.

In response, Alexandra wiggled her bottom fractionally closer to him. Sebastian stifled a groan. Alexandra was seized with the desire to rip his shirt off and trail kisses all over his chest. She knew that she could not, of course; it would be sheer madness.

She must be, she thought, a lewd and licentious person. How could she be thinking of such things when they were perhaps prisoners of a highwayman, unsure what would happen to them next? Yet she could not seem to help it.

With a sigh, Alexandra clasped her hands together in her lap and turned her face to the side. She could not bring herself to straighten and remove at least some of her body from contact with Sebastian's, but she resolved not to cause any further mischief. A few minutes later, when Sebastian's hand let go of the horse's mane and slipped over her hip caressingly, she almost forgot her good intentions. She wanted to feel his hand on her breasts, her buttocks, her stomach, sliding all over her bare skin. She wanted to turn to face him and wrap her legs around his back like a wanton. Just the thought of doing so sent moisture flooding between her legs and her blood racing through her veins.

She could not, of course; she was well aware of that. She and Sebastian could not do anything overt. While she and he were both drifting in a sensual darkness, the rest of their party was not, and she certainly did not want to put on a show for these men. So she forced herself to stay still, even though her desire made her tremble. She felt Sebastian's hand tighten into a fist against her thigh, and he ceased his sensual movements.

Alexandra had no clear idea of how long their trip took. It seemed somehow both interminable and terribly short. She would like to have stayed in Sebastian's arms forever, yet at the same time, every moment seemed an agony of denial.

At last the horses came to a halt. A few moments later, a man's hands were on her waist, lifting her from the mount. Then he was leading her forward, his hand firm around her upper arm. She stumbled once, but his strong grip kept her from falling. Then they were inside a house, their shoes clacking on the wooden floor. The door closed behind them, and someone removed her blindfold.

Alexandra blinked in the low light of the room, her eyes accustomed to total darkness. She looked for Sebastian and found him behind her. Moore was removing his blindfold, as well. His eyes opened and met hers, and she saw reflected in them the knowledge of what had happened between them on their ride. A flush rose in her cheeks, and she wondered if he considered her a low, lustful person.

Moore untied his mask, revealing a handsome face framed by thick black hair. His eyes were black, his features large and strong, dominated by a wide, sensual mouth. He smiled at his visitors, and he looked suddenly like a mischievous boy.

"Now, we must eat, and then I will show you to your room. I am sure you must be tired."

An old serving woman shuffled in and out of the room, carrying in plates and bowls of food. She said not a word, just laid on extra plates at Moore's request. They sat down to a surprisingly good meal, accompanied by an even better wine.

It was, strangely, an enjoyable meal. Their companion was clever and well-spoken, and as they talked, Alexandra began to think that he had been telling the truth when he had told them that he wanted the company. He asked about London and wanted to know the details of their adventure. He was full of curiosity about why Alexandra had been attacked, but when she started to talk about it, she realized that she could not tell him the facts without revealing that she was not married to Sebastian. It didn't seem a wise idea to admit that Sebastian had lied.

She stumbled to a halt, saying lamely, "I, uh, we're

not sure why they happened. It may have something to do with the Countess.''

"The Countess?''

"Of Exmoor. I am, perhaps, related to her.''

He looked at her for a long moment. "Exmoor? You are related to the Earl of Exmoor?''

"No—well, I mean, I guess I would be. Some sort of cousin, I guess.'' She looked at him closely. "Why? Do you know him?''

His eyebrows soared upward, and he grinned roguishly. "I might have met the gentleman,'' he admitted, his tone leaving little doubt that their meeting had ended with Moore in possession of the Earl's purse.

"He is not a pleasant man,'' Alexandra confided. She realized that the wine was loosening her tongue; she was not accustomed to drinking. She looked at Sebastian, who was watching the other man with a guarded expression. He did not seem to be at all affected by the drink.

Moore chuckled. "No, I did not find him to be so, either. But tell me, how came you, an American by your speech, to be related to Exmoor? Or to marry Lord Thorpe, for that matter.''

"The vagaries of fate,'' Sebastian suggested.

"Mm.'' Moore's dark eyes went from Sebastian to Alexandra consideringly, and Alexandra had the impression that he did not completely believe in their marriage.

After the last course, Alexandra gratefully retired to the bedroom that Moore had ordered prepared for them. She was tired, and the wine had made her a little groggy, but, more than that, it was getting to be a strain to conceal the desire that throbbed beneath the surface. Her nipples were full and aching, and there was a yearning emptiness between her legs.

She looked at the bed and wondered what was going

to happen tonight. They could not ask for separate rooms, not when Sebastian had assured the highwayman that they were married. But Alexandra could not imagine how she and Sebastian could spend the night in a bed together without touching. Just thinking about it, her nipples tightened.

Alexandra undressed and washed, but since she had no change of clothes, she had no choice but to slip on her chemise and an inner petticoat to sleep in. She looked at herself in the small mirror above the dresser. The pink-brown circles of her nipples showed through the material, the points thrusting against it. Lightly she touched them with her fingertips, remembering the way they had responded to Sebastian's touch.

She sat on the side of the bed, listening to the men's voices downstairs and wondering how long it would be before Sebastian came to bed. They were drinking, she supposed, and now and then she could hear a sudden bark of laughter. She wondered sourly if Sebastian planned to spend all night drinking with the man in order to avoid her. She curled up on the bed to wait.

It was there that Sebastian found her, sound asleep, two hours later when he came up to bed. He closed the door behind him and turned the lock, relieved to find that they had a key. He walked to the bed, swaying a little under the effects of the highwayman's brandy, and stood looking at her.

Alexandra was lying on her side, her breasts pushing out of the top of her chemise. The thin material did little to conceal their size and shape or the saucily pointing nipples in their center. Her petticoat had slid up in her sleep, revealing her legs from the middle of her thighs down. He stood for a moment, looking at the curve of her calves and the long, slender line of her thighs. Her legs were long. He supposed some men might have found her too tall, but all he could think about was those legs wrapped around him, locking him against her. The barely dormant desire that had been thrumming in him all evening rose to a pulsating level.

He ran his finger slowly up her leg, stopping at the hem of her petticoat. He knew that he wanted to move onward, to slide between her legs and seek the hot center of her femininity. He had drunk too much, trying to keep up with Moore, he told himself; he hadn't his usual control. But he suspected that even if he had been stone cold sober, he would have been aching for Alexandra. He had wanted her from the moment he met her, and the past few days, since the night she had slept in his bed, he had been driven by desire. He could not get her out of his mind, could not stop wanting her.

But it would be the act of a cad to take her, he knew. Losing her virginity without marriage was the ruin of a woman. He could not be the reason for her reputation being dragged through the mud. He knew Alexandra well enough to know that she would scoff at the idea that he must protect her; she would say that she made her own decisions. But he could not live with himself if he did not protect her in every way he could. She was too dear to him, too—

He paused, struck by a new thought. He wondered why it had not come to him before. Slowly a smile spread across his face. He sat on the bed beside her and gently circled one nipple with his forefinger, watching it harden temptingly. Then he bent to kiss her into wakefulness.

17

Alexandra came slowly, deliciously awake, awash in a sea of pleasure. Her flesh tingled, and there was a melting heat between her legs. Sebastian was kissing her, his lips warm and gentle on hers. Even as she came to a dazed awareness, she was yielding to him, her lips opening beneath his. Was this a dream? It seemed so unreal. Yet at the same time, the pleasure, the warmth, the velvet touch of his lips, were vividly real. Finally, his lips left hers, and he sat up. Alexandra's eyelashes fluttered open, and she gazed dazedly at him.

He was looking at her as his hand caressed her body, moving over her breasts and down to her stomach, coming at last to rest at the V between her legs. Alexandra drew a quick breath at the intimate touch.

"Sebastian," she murmured, unable to say anything else.

"You are so beautiful," he told her, and the sound of his voice, husky with passion, was enough to stir her.

His hand slid up her body to the top of her chemise and untied the drawstring there. He pushed the top down, exposing the creamy orbs of her breasts, his face slack with hunger. Alexandra's breasts ached for his touch, her nipples thrusting out. He brushed his fingertips over one nipple, teasing and arousing. Alexandra arched toward him, her breath rasping in her throat. With every touch, her desire burned hotter, wilder, more out of control.

Reaching up, she tangled her fingers in his hair and pulled his face to hers. Their lips brushed; their breath mingled. For a moment, they held off, anticipating the kiss, until they could stand the exquisite torture no longer. They kissed, their lips grinding into each other's, their tongues thrusting and twining in a passionate dance. His hands swept over her body, caressing her legs and buttocks and back, coming time and again to cup her breasts.

Sighs turned into moans. Bodies clung and twisted. Legs intertwined. They rolled across the bed, kissing as if they would consume each other, their suppressed hunger of the past days rising like a storm inside them.

With frantic hands, Sebastian pulled her chemise up and over her head. Alexandra worked at the buttons of his shirt, and finally, with a low oath, he ripped the thing off, popping a button and losing a stud in the process. She ran her hands over his bare skin as she had wanted to earlier this evening, then followed the path of her hands with her mouth, tasting his skin and laving it with her tongue, taking the flat masculine nipples into her mouth and bringing them to hardness. He gasped at the pleasure of her questing mouth, his hands knotting in the sheets, struggling to hold on to the control she threatened to destroy.

Finally he rolled over, putting Alexandra on her back, and began to work the same tingling magic on her. His tongue circled her nipple, caressing and lashing it, teasing until she was almost sobbing, then pulling it deep into his mouth and sucking. She groaned as the sensation ran through her, bursting in her loins like molten fire. She was past all thought, a being of pure feeling and desire. His fingers fumbled at the drawstring of her petticoat, and he pulled it from her. His hand delved between her legs, divided from her flesh only by the thin cotton of her undergarments. The cloth was damp from her passion, and he rubbed his fingers over it, delighting in the evidence of her need for him.

But soon he could not stand even that barrier between them, and he rolled them over her hips and off her legs. She lay naked before him, her hair a lush backdrop to the white, glimmering beauty of her body. He stood for a moment, looking at her. His manhood throbbed, hot and thick with desire, pressing against his breeches. He felt as if he might explode, and yet there was still so much he wanted to do, so much he wanted to feel and give to her.

Alexandra raised her arms to him, and Sebastian could wait no longer. He fumbled at the buttons of his trousers, peeling them down and kicking them aside, then climbed into bed with her. Alexandra caressed him, taking his turgid member into her hand and stroking it. He let out a muffled groan and buried his face in her neck.

"Come inside me," Alexandra murmured into his ear, and desire shot through him like lightning.

He could wait no longer. He moved between her welcoming legs and eased inside her, moving gently despite the need that raged in him. Alexandra gasped at the slash of pain as he entered her, and sank her teeth into his shoulder. Sebastian groaned and paused, then began to stroke slowly in and out. Alexandra moved in rhythm with him, the knot of pleasure deep within her growing and tightening until she felt as if she would scream. Then it burst in her like a tidal wave, and she did cry out. Sebastian groaned, thrusting into her in his own paroxysm of pleasure. Together they plunged into the deep, mindless realm of passion, their souls melded together as surely as their bodies, lost for the moment in a pleasure so fierce and so pure that nothing else existed.

Afterward, they lay clinging to each other like survivors of a storm, and just as Alexandra drifted off to sleep, Sebastian heard her breathe something that sounded to him like *love*.

Alexandra's eyes drifted open lazily, and she found herself looking at a strange ceiling. She felt sore and incredibly happy and a little strange.

Suddenly she shot upright, her memory returning in a rush. She and Sebastian had made love last night! She looked around the room. There was no evidence of Sebastian's presence; no remnant of clothing, no boots. It made her feel strangely empty, and she wondered for an instant if what she remembered had been only a dream. But, no, that could not have been something she imagined.

There was a rap at the door, and she jumped, startled.

"Alexandra? Are you up?" It was Sebastian's voice, and her pulse skittered at the sound of it.

"Yes. Come in." Alexandra grabbed the sheet that had fallen to her waist and pulled it up, tucking it under her arms.

Sebastian opened the door and stuck his head in cautiously. The look on his face was a trifle uncertain, an oddity that made Alexandra feel even more nervous. What did he feel for her? What had last night meant for him? Alexandra was as certain as she was of her name that she loved him. But what of him? Had last night been love or only a moment's pleasure?

He pushed the door wider and stepped inside, carrying a tray of food. "I brought your breakfast. Our highwayman is up and tucking into a substantial breakfast. He says we have to hurry to reach the village before the London mail coach arrives.''

Sebastian set the tray on Alexandra's lap and stepped back awkwardly. Alexandra looked at the food before her, suddenly unable to meet his gaze. Two people who were used to being in command, normally sure of themselves, were tangled in a web of uncertainty, strangely shy and uncomfortable.

The moment he had awakened this morning, Sebastian had been seized with the dread that Alexandra would regret what had happened last night. He had washed and dressed, riddled with the fear that she would reject his proposal of marriage. Last night, a little drunk and in the throes of his desire, it had seemed perfectly sensible to him. He loved her; they would get married; and the slight prematurity of their honeymoon night would not matter. In the cold light of dawn, he was not so certain. Alexandra was an unpredictable woman, opinionated and strong. What if she did not love him? What if she turned him down?

All the way up the stairs with the tray, he had been rehearsing his proposal speech. It had sounded stilted and stupidly formal, even in his mind. Now, looking at Alexandra sitting in the bed, enticingly bare-shouldered, the sheet pulled over her breasts but not quite concealing their thrust and the dark circles of her nipples, he was shaken by desire and an equally strong certainty that she would find his proposal idiotic.

It was the place, he thought. He could not relax in the highwayman's den, unsure whether the man would turn them loose or take them to the woods and shoot them, robbing their dead bodies. He needed to be alert for any sign of treachery on Moore's part. Later, when he and Alexandra were alone, free of Moore and his men—that was when he would tell her. The words would come naturally then; he would be able to speak freely, to talk Alexandra out of any doubts she might have.

He gave her a stiff smile and said, "I, uh, I'll just go downstairs, keep an eye on our friend."

"All right." Alexandra's heart sank. She could see Sebastian's nervousness; it fairly radiated from him. He regretted what they had done last night; she was certain of it. He was worried that she would expect something from him, some declaration of love or even a marriage proposal.

Tears sprang into her eyes, but she blinked them away and gave him a smile that matched his. "I will be down soon."

He turned and left with visible relief. Alexandra felt like throwing the tray of food at the door. Instead, she set it aside and got out of bed. She washed and dressed, giving herself a mental lecture all the while. She had not expected Sebastian to love her; she had wanted him and had been willing to assume the risk. She had gotten what she wanted, and now it was over. It was absurd to think that he loved her; she irritated him to death. They were like oil and water. And it was ludicrous to think that he might marry her; she was an American of dubious origin, no match for a British aristocrat. Everyone knew that British aristocrats married to suit their position, not for love.

By the time she was through, she still felt like crying, but at least she had managed to stuff it down where it would not show. That, she told herself, was what was important. She would show Sebastian that she did not expect anything from him, that last night had meant nothing more to her than it had to him.

The ride to the village was a quiet one, broken only now and then by Jack Moore's chatter. But his irrepressible spirits soon flagged under the leaden weight of Sebastian's and Alexandra's stiff silence. He blindfolded them again and led them, though this time they had their own horses. They plodded along for what seemed hours before Moore finally stopped and removed their blindfolds.

After that he no longer had to lead them, and they moved more quickly. Finally Moore pulled his horse to a stop and turned to face the others. "It is less than a mile into the village. I, ah, am not eager to be seen there, so I fear that I shall have to take your mounts away from you."

"Of course." Sebastian dismounted and turned to help Alexandra, but she had already scrambled down by herself and stood waiting like a statue. She did not look at him, and his stomach tightened. He was certain that she would scorn his proposal.

Moore looked at them curiously but made no comment about their odd manner this morning. He dismounted and took the reins of their horses.

"Walk in that direction." He pointed. "Before long you will come to the village. The mail coach will be here in less than an hour. I bid you farewell. I enjoyed your company very much. Perhaps we will meet again."

"Here." Sebastian reached into the pocket of his jacket. "Let me give you something for your trouble." His hand closed on emptiness.

A pearly grin split the highwayman's tanned face. "Do not worry, my lord." He turned and leaped lithely into the saddle, reaching into an inner pocket of his coat and pulling out a small leather bag, which he dangled for a moment. "It is already mine."

With that, he wheeled his horse and took off, the other two mounts clattering after him. Sebastian stared after him, openmouthed. Alexandra began to giggle, and Sebastian shot her a look.

"That blackguard!"

"Well, he never made much pretense that he was anything but a thief."

"Laugh away," Sebastian snapped irritably. "I'd like to know how we are going to make it to London now."

"My pin money." Alexandra felt a trifle better now that she had laughed. She turned up the hem of her skirt and bent to unpin a folded bill from her petticoat. "I always carry a little something in case of emergency."

She handed the note to Sebastian, who looked at it and said grimly, "At least we'll be able to get to London, though scarcely in style. I had planned to take the mail coach to a larger town where I could hire a post chaise. It looks now as if it will be the mail coach for us the whole way."

As it turned out, Alexandra was glad they were forced to take the mail coach. Though it was scarcely an easy or elegant ride, and they stopped at seemingly every hamlet they passed through, at least she and Sebastian were not condemned to sit together in strained silence the whole way. Crushed in among the other passengers, their lack of conversation was not noticeable, and the variety of passengers occupied her interest well enough that she did not have to sit sunk in her own gloom. Sebastian, who did not seem to share her interest in their fellow travelers, spent most of the journey gazing out the window or leaning back against the seat with his eyes closed. They did not have to deal with one another except for the times when they debarked at an inn to get a meat pie or a juicy apple to eat.

It amazed Alexandra that it took so long to travel the

same amount of distance that they had covered in the balloon in a few hours the day before. She was thoroughly weary when at last the coach pulled into London, and she had also grown rather tired of the constant presence of other people. There was nothing she wanted so much as to shut the door, climb into her own bed and sleep for at least a day.

Therefore, she was greatly disappointed when their hackney disgorged her and Sebastian in front of her house, and they entered to find that not only her aunt was waiting for them, but also the Countess, Penelope and even the redoubtable Lady Ursula. Alexandra let out a groan when she walked into the drawing room, followed by Sebastian, and saw the group sitting there.

"Alexandra!" Aunt Hortense jumped to her feet, a broad smile of joy spreading over her face. "My darling girl!"

She hurried to Alexandra, laughing and crying all at once, and pulled her against her substantial bosom for a long, hard hug. "I was frantic about you!"

"We all were," agreed the Countess, who had risen from her seat and followed Aunt Hortense at a slower pace. When at last Aunt Hortense released Alexandra from her embrace, the Countess took her hand and leaned in to press her cheek against Alexandra's. "It is such a relief to see you alive and well."

"Thank you. I am very glad to be here, I can tell you."

The Countess turned to Sebastian. "Thank God you were with her. That is the only thing that kept me from worrying myself into an early grave—or, perhaps, not such an early one, but not a place I wish to be, nevertheless," she added with a wry smile. "It is good to see you, Sebastian. It would appear that the two of you have had quite an adventure. You must sit and tell us all about it."

"Yes," Aunt Hortense agreed. "I've already rung for tea. I am sure you must be in need of refreshments."

Alexandra sat on a chair near Penelope, resigned to not being able to escape for another few minutes. "First I want to hear what happened to the fellow who attacked me."

"Oh, Bucky and the others took care of him," Penelope assured her, her eyes shining. "The balloonists tried to hold the man, but he tore away. Bucky—that is, Lord Buckminster—came up just at that minute, though, and he planted the fellow such a facer that he fell to the ground."

"Penelope, such language!" her mother remarked with a frown. "You know I hate it when you use pugilist cant. I lay it at your brother's door, but a girl should know better than to use such words in polite company."

"Yes, Mama." Penelope subsided, the excitement in her eyes dimming.

"It sounds to me as if Lord Buckminster was quite a hero," Alexandra said, hoping to revive Penelope, but she offered only a wan smile at Alexandra's remark.

"I've always thought those exhibitions were not the thing," Lady Ursula announced. "That's why I never allowed Penelope to attend one before." She fixed her daughter with a stern gaze and added ominously, "And never again, I must say."

"I really doubt that the balloons had anything to do with that ruffian attacking me," Alexandra retorted. "Doubtless he had been following me, waiting for an opportunity. It could have happened right outside the front door, I suppose."

Lady Ursula looked shocked. "I've never heard of such a thing. Why are these people attacking you, that's what

I wonder," she went on darkly, her tone implying that the attacks were somehow Alexandra's fault.

"If I knew that, Lady Ursula, I wouldn't be as worried."

"I, for one, am certain that it has something to do with who you are," the Countess said. "If I needed any further proof that you are my granddaughter, that is it."

"Now, Mother, that doesn't follow. Just because someone tries to steal her purse or something does not prove that she is *our* Alexandra."

"It was scarcely a purse snatching, Ursula," the Countess commented mildly. "Thieves do not try to kidnap you. And while they may climb in windows, they don't knock people over the head or try to strangle them and take absolutely nothing with them."

Lady Ursula, for once, looked slightly abashed and lapsed into silence. Aunt Hortense seized the opportunity to ask a question. "What happened to you two? I was afraid you'd been blown out to sea or some such thing. I presume you must have landed."

"Yes. Quite far from here," Sebastian replied dryly. "It took us all day to get back to London on the mail coach."

"The mail coach!" Lady Ursula looked shocked. "Are you serious?"

"Very much so. It was not an experience I care to repeat."

"We spent the night at a highwayman's hideout," Alexandra added, aware of an impish impulse to shock Lady Ursula again.

"What!" The woman's bulging eyes were ample reward.

Alexandra hid a smile. "A highwayman. He very

kindly gave us a meal and a bed—beds.'' Color rose in her cheeks at her mistake.

"Yes, and took my purse for his trouble," Sebastian added, but his words could not divert their attention from Alexandra's embarrassed face.

"Lord have mercy!" Aunt Hortense exclaimed.

"Indeed." Lady Ursula raised her brows. "I shouldn't spread the fact around if I were you. There is already quite enough scandal regarding your little trip."

"It's scandalous to be nearly abducted and escape?" Alexandra asked coolly, giving the older woman a level look.

"Probably," the Countess replied. "In the *ton*, everything is food for scandal. But the real problem, of course, is the fact that you and Sebastian spent two days and a night together, unchaperoned."

"It was scarcely something we could avoid," Alexandra protested.

"That doesn't change the fact of it," Lady Ursula said flatly. "I am afraid your reputation is in shreds, Miss Ward." Her voice expressed extreme satisfaction at the idea.

"Don't be absurd, Ursula," Sebastian told her, his voice hard. "Miss Ward and I will be married, of course."

Alexandra's jaw dropped, and she turned to Sebastian. Her stomach felt as if it had suddenly been tied into a thousand knots. "I beg your pardon?"

Sebastian gritted his teeth. Damn Ursula for bringing the subject up, anyway! He had been unable to say a word to Alexandra about marrying him on the ride home, for they never had a moment alone for private conversation. He cursed himself for not having broached the subject early this morning. Now, because of Ursula's heavy-handed glee at the scandal they were in, he had had to blurt it in front of everyone, without even asking Alexandra first.

"I said that we will be married," he replied, meeting Alexandra's gaze.

"I think you are getting a little ahead of yourself, Lord Thorpe," Alexandra told him acidly. "There is such a thing as asking for a woman's hand before one declares that one is marrying her. Or is that not a practice followed in England?"

"Of course it is. But, dammit, I haven't had a moment alone to talk to you about it. There was always someone there—that portly woman going to visit her daughter, or that couple with the screaming baby, or—"

"You needn't enumerate them. I am quite aware of our fellow passengers. That hardly excuses your taking it upon yourself to say that we are going to be married."

"But, Alexandra, dear, you must be," the Countess put in, her forehead creasing. "Ursula is right. So is Sebastian. You have to marry, or your name will be ruined."

"As I don't even live here, I hardly see how that matters."

"Think of poor Sebastian. He will be considered a cad and a roué if he doesn't wed you after this."

Alexandra shot Sebastian a flashing look. "I doubt it will ruin him. I'm *not* marrying him."

She rose to her feet, her arms rigid at her sides. Sebastian stood so abruptly he almost turned over his chair. He glared at Alexandra, his jaw set in as mulish an expression as hers. "Devil take it! You *will* marry me, my girl."

Alexandra faced him, her eyes blazing. She felt as if her heart was breaking. How could he tell her she was going to marry him, and only because of a stupid scandal? She was so furious that she had to clench her fists to keep her hands from trembling.

"I wouldn't marry you if it was the only thing that would save me from hanging!"

Alexandra whirled and strode out of the room, leaving the others staring after her in consternation.

Alexandra indulged in a good bout of tears that night and woke the next morning puffy-eyed and headachy. She thought dispiritedly that she had probably thrown her life away with both hands the night before. But what else could she do with Sebastian asking her to marry him for all the wrong reasons? No matter how much she wanted to be with him, she knew that it would be hellish, not heavenly, knowing all the time that he did not love her as she loved him, that he had married her only because it was the gentlemanly thing to do. Moreover, she thought, just to drive her spirits a little lower, he probably would not have done that if she had been just Alexandra Ward, not someone the Countess of Exmoor thought was her granddaughter.

She rang for the maid and dressed listlessly, then went down the hall to check on her mother. Willa Everhart was sitting beside Rhea, embroidering, and she looked up at Alexandra's entrance and smiled.

"Good day, Miss Ward."

"Good morning. But you must call me Alexandra."

Willa smiled again. "All right. Alexandra. And I am Willa."

"How has she been?" Alexandra walked to the bed and stood looking at her mother, who lay motionless, her eyes closed. Except for the slight rise and fall of her chest beneath the sheet, she might have been dead. A shiver ran through Alexandra at the thought.

"Physically, she is doing as well as can be expected," Willa said. "The maid and I prop her up and manage to spoon some gruel down her a few times every day. We get her to take a little water the same way. But she is losing weight, of course.''

''Doubtless.'' Alexandra leaned against the post of the bed and asked wistfully, ''Do you think that she will ever awaken? Will she live like this the rest of her life?''

''I don't know. The doctor doesn't seem to, either. He will only say he's known of some that have awakened and resumed normal lives after days, even weeks and years. But then he's known those who have died, too. He says to keep turning her to keep away the bedsores and try to feed her and just wait for what happens.''

''Not a very cheerful prognosis, is it?'' Alexandra pulled up a chair beside Willa and sat down. ''I don't know if I have thanked you for coming here to help. I am sure I haven't thanked you enough.''

Color rose in Willa's pale face. ''There's no need to thank me. I am happy to do it. It pleases the Countess, and that makes almost anything worthwhile.''

''You are very fond of the Countess, aren't you?''

''Yes, very much. She took me in when I had nowhere else to go. She didn't have to—I am only a distant cousin to her. But she is the kindest of women. She has fed and clothed and housed me for almost twenty-five years now, and never a word from her of my obligation to her, never an unkindness or a cut.'' Tears sparkled in her eyes. ''There's little I wouldn't do for her. But this is an easy task. I rather enjoy looking after people. I looked after my father for years before he died. He was an invalid. That was one reason I never married—that and my lack of a dowry.'' She gave a small self-deprecating smile.

It seemed to Alexandra that Willa's life had not been easy—penniless, spending her marriageable years taking care of an invalid parent. But she seemed quite content with her lot, even grateful that it had not been worse.

"You must have been quite young when you came to live with the Countess."

"Twenty-four. It was in 1789."

"You were with her, then, when her son and his family were killed."

Willa nodded. "It was a terrible time for her. First her husband died suddenly—it was his heart, they said. She sent for Lord Chilton, but Paris went mad with revolution. The whole family was killed, every one of them." She cast a quick, embarrassed glance at Alexandra. "I'm sorry. I mean, that is what we all thought then."

"It's all right." Alexandra smiled at her. "I am still not convinced that I am the Countess's granddaughter."

"Her ladyship was terribly distraught. Practically all her family lost in one fell swoop." Willa shook her head. "Of course, there was Lady Ursula. I am sure that the Countess loves her daughter, but, well—the truth be told, I suspect the Countess always loved Lord Chilton best. The Countess took to her bed for weeks when she heard the news, wouldn't see or talk to anyone. She was inconsolable. It was all I could do to get her to eat. Some nights she would walk the floor hour after hour. I would sit up with her, and she would talk about Chilton and his childhood and—oh, it was a terrible time. Thank God she eventually came out of it all right."

"I am sure that a good part of that was due to your care."

"It's good of you to say so."

"It's only the truth."

Alexandra insisted that Willa go down to eat breakfast and take a break from her duties while she sat with her mother. After Willa had left, Alexandra edged her chair closer to the bed and took her mother's hand. Rhea's hand lay flaccid in hers, limp and unresponsive. Alexandra talked to Rhea, telling her about their adventures in the balloon and with the highwayman, making it all sound like a great lark. She wondered if her mother could hear anything she said. The doctor seemed to doubt it, but Alexandra thought there was no harm in assuming that she could. She talked to Rhea as much as possible, hoping that some word would reach her mother deep in her sleep and bring her back.

When Willa returned thirty minutes later, Alexandra went down to breakfast. She walked into the dining room and stopped abruptly. There, sitting at the table with her aunt, calmly downing a plate of ham and eggs, was Sebastian.

"What are you doing here?" she asked ungraciously. "Do you plan to plague us from morning till night?"

He smiled in the manner of one who enjoyed delivering bad news. "More than that, my dear. I have moved in."

"What!" Alexandra stared at him. "Are you mad? You can't live here!" She could scarcely imagine anything worse than having to be around Sebastian every minute of the day, always seeing him, wanting him, her heart breaking all over again every day.

"I don't know why not. Your aunt invited me."

"Aunt Hortense!" Alexandra swung on that good woman, who was placidly eating her eggs, long since used to her niece's temper. "How could you?"

"Quite easily, my dear. The Countess and Sebastian and I talked about it at some length last night after you went up to bed. We decided it was the wisest course."

"Obviously Murdock's presence hasn't been enough protection. I have brought over two or three of my other servants, including Punwati."

"Punwati! Whatever for?"

"He is quite adept at the Eastern arts of hand-to-hand combat. A good man to have in a fight."

"Do you plan to turn our house into an armed camp?" Alexandra asked scathingly.

"If I have to, in order to keep you safe. When you go out now, one of us will accompany you—Punwati, Murdock or I."

"I am to be a prisoner in my own house, then?"

"Not a prisoner, dear," Aunt Hortense said, shaking her head. "It's for your protection."

"You will protect me into an early grave! I cannot bear to have Murdock and Punwati and God knows who else hanging about all the time!"

"You'll scarcely notice they're here," Sebastian assured her. "Murdock and my two servants will primarily patrol the outside of the house. Punwati will keep a watch on the inside. And, of course, it is I who will be with you most of the time."

"You are the one I want to have around least," Alexandra retorted bluntly. "Talk about a scandal! If it was such an awful thing for the two of us to be stuck together one night because of that silly balloon taking off, imagine how the tongues will wag at the idea of your living here!"

"Since I plan to marry you, the scandal will not last long."

"Then I would say you are pinning your hopes on shaky ground. I have no intention of marrying you."

"You'll see the advantages of it eventually," Sebastian replied imperturbably. "Anyway, there's no reason for scandal. We will be in a house with your aunt, your mother and Miss Everhart. We couldn't be more well chaperoned. The Countess approved of the idea, and she knows all the ins and outs of Society."

"I don't give a damn about Society," Alexandra snapped. "I just don't want you here!"

"Careful, my dear, you may wound my feelings."

"You have none," Alexandra replied scornfully, "or you wouldn't be doing this to me."

"Doing what?"

"I know what your scheme is. Don't think I'm not on to you."

"My only scheme is to keep you safe."

"You think that if you are around constantly, you can wear me down, convince me to marry you. Well, I won't."

"Then you need not worry about my being here." He met her gaze blandly.

"Oh! You are the most infuriating man I ever met!"

"Sit down, my dear, and eat your breakfast. It will improve your temper."

"Nothing will improve my temper except your leaving."

"I am sorry to hear that. I suppose we will have to endure your bad mood for a while, then."

Alexandra scowled at him and plopped down in her chair. She had thought that things could not be worse this morning when she woke up, but she was quickly learning that they could. How was she to endure having Sebastian around all the time? Even now, annoyed as she was by him, she kept thinking about how much she would like to run her fingers through his thick, dark hair. She had the awful feeling that she would soon make a fool of herself.

She was contemplating these dark thoughts and pushing food around on her plate with her fork when the butler walked into the room.

"Miss?"

Alexandra looked up inquiringly. Their usually calm, dignified butler looked distinctly uncomfortable. "Yes?"

"There is, ah, a person who wishes to speak with you, miss." Every line of the butler's face showed his opinion of this person.

Alexandra's curiosity was aroused. "All right. Show him in."

"It is a female person, miss, and I—well, I think you would rather not see her here."

"I wouldn't?"

"She is, er, a trifle, well, dirty, miss. I would not normally bother you. No doubt she is begging. I tried to turn her out, but she was extremely insistent that you would wish to hear what she had to say. She said that she had information. About the attack on you the other day."

"What the devil!" Sebastian jumped to his feet, and so did Alexandra.

"Take me to her," she said calmly.

18

Sebastian and Alexandra followed the butler to the kitchen, where they found several of the servants standing on one side of the room watching a woman who stood on the opposite side. She was returning their gaze equally warily.

She was short and quite thin, dressed in an odd assortment of layers of clothing, none of them particularly clean. On her feet were an outsize pair of men's brogans, caked with dried mud and muck. Her hair was tied in a scarf, and it looked as if it had been some time since her face had seen a washrag. She was completely out of place in the tidy, sparkling kitchen, but she faced the situation boldly, her chin thrust out and her eyes snapping, as if to dare any of the servants to complain about her presence.

"Hello," Alexandra said, forcing herself to speak calmly and pleasantly. "I am Miss Ward."

The woman turned to look at her, then her gaze slid beyond Alexandra to Sebastian.

When the woman said nothing, Alexandra went on, "I believe that you wanted to tell me something?"

"I got sumfing you'd like to 'ear," the woman responded.

It took Alexandra a moment to figure out what the woman had said. The thick London accents still confused her. But Sebastian understood immediately.

"Indeed? And what would we like to hear?" he asked in an indifferent, even bored voice.

The woman let out a snort. "You fink I'm tellin' ye, just like 'at?" she asked scornfully. "I has important information, I do, an' I figure it's worf sumfing to ye."

"I can hardly judge that, can I, until I hear what it is?" Sebastian responded.

"'Ere! I ain't talkin' to you, any'ow. I'm talkin' to the lady."

"That's true," Alexandra interjected, frowning at Sebastian. "And I am very much interested in hearing what you have to say. What does this information concern?"

"It concerns my man, that's wot—the one you've got up in Newgate."

"In jail?" Sebastian looked sharply at the woman. "Are you saying that your man is the fellow who attacked Miss Ward the other day?"

The woman gave a firm nod, pride evident on her face. "That's 'im. Red Bill Trimble."

"And you are going to give us evidence against him?" Alexandra asked doubtfully. The woman seemed too proud, even fond of the man to be giving evidence against him.

"No. Wot's wrong with you? I'd never do nuffing like 'at. But it ain't right 'im sittin' there rottin' and the one wot 'ired 'im runnin' about free, now, is it?"

"Hardly," Alexandra agreed, her pulse quickening. "Do you know who hired him?"

A crafty look crept over the woman's face. "Mebbe I do. Wot's it worf to you?"

"It's worth you not going to jail," Sebastian interjected

hotly. "If you know who hired your man to harm Miss Ward and don't tell, that makes you an accessory to the crime."

"'Ere!" The woman recoiled. "There's no cause to do that! I ain't done nuffing wrong! I just offered to help, like, an' you're tryin' to put me in jail!"

"Sebastian, do be quiet," Alexandra said crisply. "You are not helping matters any."

"I'm not going to let that woman extort money from you on top of everything else. She'll bloody well tell us what she knows—"

The woman backed up quickly, her face going pale beneath its layer of dirt. "'Ere now, you got no cause—I ain't askin' you for money!"

"Of course not," Alexandra assured her, shooting a speaking glance at Sebastian. She moved toward her, holding out a hand. "Here, why don't you sit down at the table and have a nice cup of tea, and we will talk about this like reasonable people."

"I can see you're a real lady," the woman said, raising her chin and casting a triumphant look at the servants massed across the kitchen from her. She sidled over to the table and sat, keeping a careful eye on Sebastian.

"Thank you. Mrs. Huffines, tea, if you please," Alexandra said to the cook. "The rest of you, I am sure, have work to do—somewhere else."

The cook sniffed and bustled off to brew a pot of tea, and the other servants took themselves off reluctantly. Alexandra sat at the large wooden table across from their visitor, and Sebastian, after a moment, sighed and sat beside her.

"Now, then, Miss—" Alexandra began.

"Maisy. Me name is Maisy Goodall."

"All right, Maisy." Alexandra said. "If you don't want money, what is it you do want?"

"You could get Bill out of jail, you could."

Sebastian made a noise of disgust, and Alexandra shot him a warning look.

"I doubt that I have the power to do that," Alexandra told her. "Of course, if he were to tell us who hired him, I am sure that the magistrate would go easier on him."

"Not 'im," Maisy replied honestly. "Red Bill ain't one to rat out 'is mates. 'Sides, 'e don't know 'oo it is."

"But I thought you said—"

"I *seen* 'er."

"Her!" Alexandra sat forward. "It was a woman?"

Maisy realized that she had let some of her precious information slip. "I din't say 'at."

"You said 'her,'" Sebastian reminded her. "Now, come clean. Tell us what you know about her."

"I'll do what I can to help Red Bill," Alexandra told her. "The person who hired him is the one I want to see behind bars." She slid her hand into her pocket and pulled out a coin, which she laid on the table between her and Maisy. "Here's a little something to help tide you over until your man's out of jail again."

Maisy looked indecisively from Alexandra's face to the coin, then to Sebastian's implacable countenance.

"I don't know 'er name. I only seen 'er. She come to our place a couple weeks ago, told Bill she wanted 'im to take care of the old lady."

"The old lady? My mother?"

Maisy nodded. "I guess. She told 'im where she was and all. So Bill 'ired someone to do it. Only that silly oaf Peggoddy made a mull of it!" Her voice dripped scorn. "So she come back to Bill. Spittin' mad, she was. Says 'e madc a mess of it and she refuses to pay 'im. Bill weren't 'aving none of that, though, and finally she says she'll pay 'im, but 'e's gotta finish the job, like. An', she says, 'e's got to get rid of that innerferin' American bitch, too.''

Sebastian made a choked noise, and Alexandra shot him a quelling look. "Indeed?''

"So Bill did it 'imself. 'E din't trust nobody else again." She sighed. "Worse luck for 'im.''

"How did she get hold of him? I mean, how did she know to come to Red Bill?''

Maisy shrugged. "Ever'body knows Red Bill. If she asked around, she'd 'a found out well enough.''

"You have no idea what her name is?" Alexandra asked.

Maisy shook her head. "She wouldn't tell us sumfing like 'at, now, would she?''

"What did she look like?" Sebastian asked.

Maisy looked thoughtful. "I din't see her real good like. She wore a cloak, see, and pulled the 'ood forward so 'er face was in shadow. She wore a half mask, too.''

"Could you tell anything about her?" Alexandra asked. "Was she young or old? Tall?''

"No. She weren't tall. Leastways, not tall as you. But not as short as me, either. I couldn't see if she was young.''

Alexandra sighed. Since Maisy was quite small and Alexandra was a very tall woman, most of the women of London would fit Maisy's description.

"What about her voice?" Sebastian asked. "You heard her speak, at least. What did she sound like?''

"I dunno." Maisy gazed at him blankly. "Like a toff, like you." She turned toward Alexandra, a thought dawning on her face. "But not like you, miss.''

"So she was English. Not American.''

Maisy nodded. However, she seemed to have come to the end of her knowledge. Not all the prodding or questioning that Alexandra and Sebastian could do could dislodge any further nugget of information from her. Finally, Alexandra slid the coin across the table to the woman and promised to speak to the authorities on Red Bill Trimble's behalf. Maisy was quick to take the coin and jump up from the table. Alexandra watched her hurry through the kitchen and out the back door, and she turned to Sebastian.

He was watching her, his face faintly questioning. "Well?"

"Well, what? Do you believe her?" Alexandra stood and started out of the kitchen.

Sebastian shrugged as he rose from his chair and joined her. "I don't know. She certainly didn't give us any real description of the person—not tall, not short, disguised by a hooded cloak as well as a mask. It certainly wouldn't be hard to make something like that up. She made a coin out of it, as well as whatever help we might be able to give her Mr. Trimble."

"It would be just as easy to tell the truth as a lie, I would think."

"Provided she knows it."

"You don't think she is who she says?"

"Oh, I presume she is probably the common-law wife of the man who attacked you. Obviously she knew enough about the matter to come to you with her 'information.' And she knew that Peggoddy was hired the other time. But whether she actually saw the transaction between Trimble and this other person—" He shrugged again, then added, a twinkle in his eyes, "Although, I must say that comment about getting rid of that interfering American bitch does have a certain ring of truth about it."

Alexandra made a face at him. "You would latch on to that, of course. Still, it does make it seem authentic. I'm not sure we can credit Maisy with enough imagination to think up such details. I am inclined to believe that she is telling the truth."

They walked down the hall to the drawing room, but neither of them sat down. Alexandra wandered to the window and stood looking at the street. Sebastian lounged in the doorway, watching her.

"Why do you think it's the truth?" he asked.

"Because she said it was a woman. That is too strange. If one were making it up, the natural thing to do would be to say it is a man. Isn't that what you were expecting? Weren't you surprised to hear her say 'she'?"

"Yes," Sebastian admitted. "Of course, I suppose she could have said it to throw us off the trail—if she wanted the money but was scared of the man coming after her if she betrayed him."

"Or if someone hired her to tell us the story so that we would be led astray."

"Do you honestly think that?"

"No," Alexandra admitted quickly. "That seems far too devious. The truth, I find, is usually simpler—and rarely clever."

"I agree. If she didn't tell the truth, I think it was because she didn't know it or was scared of the person who hired Trimble." He paused and looked at Alexandra. "It seems we are talking all around the real issue here."

Alexandra sighed and nodded. "Yes. Who is the woman?"

"It *can't* be Lady Ursula."

"Who else could it be?" Alexandra countered. "The woman we know it can't be is Aunt Hortense—or any other person in my family. Maisy was definite that the woman was not American.''

"Unless she disguised her accent in order to fool them.''

Alexandra grimaced. "An American who is able to sound so like a toff that an Englishwoman is fooled?''

"I agree. It sounds unlikely. But I don't think we can rule out your American family entirely. They could, after all, be operating through an English friend or distant relative.''

"Then they would be letting yet another party into the situation—it seems unlikely. The obvious answer is an Englishwoman who would stand to lose something if I am the Countess's granddaughter. And who else could that be except Lady Ursula?''

Sebastian shook his head. "I have known the woman all my life. She is overbearing, annoying and sanctimonious. But I cannot imagine her killing to keep her mother from claiming you as her granddaughter.''

"Then who else could it be? Penelope?''

"Don't be absurd.''

"Who, then?''

"There must be some other person who we don't know about. Some reason they want your mother silenced and you out of the way.''

"What other reason could there be?''

"I don't know. That's the problem. At least when I am engaged in a fight, I usually know who my opponent is.''

"Perhaps we should leave for the United States. It is just that I am scared to do so while Mother is still—''

"It's impossible. You cannot move her now. Besides, I—''

Alexandra turned toward him, her chest tightening. "You what?''

"I do not want you to."

"It is the only answer." Alexandra tried to keep her voice steady. "It will nip the scandal in the bud."

"So will marrying me."

"That is a rather large sacrifice on both our parts, don't you think, for being forced to spend the night together by a freak accident?"

He crossed the room to her, his eyes boring into hers. "It was more than that. What they are whispering is exactly true. You were in my bed. We made love."

Alexandra found it difficult to breathe. Her knees trembled, and she was afraid she might embarrass them both by slumping against him.

"It isn't as if I were a naïve maiden," she told him shakily. "I went into it with my eyes open."

Her eyes strayed to his lips. She remembered how they had felt against hers. The truth was that she wanted to feel them again. Brazenly, right here in the drawing room in the middle of the morning, she wanted him to pull her into his arms and kiss her.

"Dammit! You were a maiden, naïve or not. Why are you so stubborn? Why won't you marry me?"

Because you haven't said you love me, she wanted to cry, but she held back the words. Words of love were no good if they were forced.

"You are a British lord. You can scarcely marry an American nobody."

"I can do whatever I please. I usually do."

"I have told you about my mother," Alexandra reminded him stiffly.

"Yes. What does that matter?"

"You think your family would want you to marry someone with madness in her family?"

"She is probably no madder than a good number of

peers I've met. Every noble family has one or two skel-
etons in their closet. Mrs. Ward would probably be considered merely an eccentric."

"Don't be flip. She is…peculiar in her actions and her
words. People would be bound to notice, and they would
comment on it."

"I believe I have told you how little public opinion
means to me."

"But you have to think about the future—your heirs."

"I am thinking about the future." The expression in
his eyes sent heat spreading through Alexandra's loins.
"You are the woman I want to have heirs with. I know
you, Alexandra, and I see little chance that you could have
a child who was not quite sane."

Alexandra turned away, breaking the spell his eyes cast
on her. "No. Please stop."

"I won't," he replied. "Besides, your reason is most
likely invalid, anyway. The way things look right now,
Mrs. Ward probably isn't even your mother, so it doesn't
really matter whether she is wholly sane or not."

"But we don't know!"

"There are many things we don't know. We cannot
foretell the future. But we cannot live our lives in terror
that something bad might happen."

He started toward her again, but much to Alexandra's
relief, her aunt walked into the room at that point, and
Alexandra seized the opportunity to flee.

There were no untoward events over the next two days.
No one tried to break in; there were no fights; no more
ragamuffins came knocking on the door wanting to give
them information.

However, Alexandra found the atmosphere anything
but tranquil. It was extremely unsettling to have Sebastian

around all the time. It was not that he irritated her nerves, for she discovered that he was surprisingly companionable. Nor was it that he bored her, for he was ever an interesting conversationalist. But she could not be easy. His constant presence was a reminder to her of the night they had shared—and of the many more nights they could share, if only she gave up her scruples.

But she refused to go into a one-sided marriage, where she loved and he did not, and Sebastian was maddeningly silent on the matter of love. Sometimes he tried to persuade her with reasoned arguments about the ruination of her reputation. Other times he teased her, laughingly reminding her of what a catch he was on the marriage mart. Now and then he lapsed into a brooding silence, watching her. And, far too often for her peace of mind, he looked at her with hot, hungry eyes or slipped behind her in one of the corridors and planted a kiss upon her neck or ear or cheek, and asked her in a husky voice when she would give in to him.

But never once did he say that she was the love of his life, that he could not live without her. Alexandra supposed it was a foolish thing to expect, especially given the businesslike transactions that British noble marriages seemed to be. But she could not help it. She wanted a marriage of passion, not reason. She wanted a husband who loved her beyond all else, the way her father had loved her mother.

She spent an extra amount of time in her mother's room, relieving Willa and Aunt Hortense. At least Sebastian did not disturb her there. But sitting alone with her silent mother, she found that she could not escape her thoughts, and those invariably returned to the night of love she and Sebastian had shared.

One afternoon she was sitting beside her mother, her

hand clasping Rhea's, talking to her about her indecision regarding Sebastian, when she felt her mother's hand close around hers.

"Mother!" Alexandra was instantly on her feet, leaning toward Rhea. "Can you hear me? You squeezed my hand. Are you awake? Do you understand me?"

But Rhea's face was as blank as ever, and her hand was already slack again in Alexandra's.

"Willa! Aunt Hortense!" Alexandra rushed to the door of the room and called into the hall.

A moment later, both women came hurrying into the room, their faces anxious.

"She squeezed my hand!" Alexandra announced.

"What?" Willa looked dumbfounded. "Are you sure?"

"Yes. I am positive. I was talking to her, holding her hand, and suddenly she pressed my hand. I'm certain of it."

"The doctor said sometimes their muscles will involuntarily contract when they are in this state."

"It wasn't that. I am sure she heard me—on some level. She hasn't reached full wakefulness yet. But it will come. Surely this means that she is beginning to wake up."

Aunt Hortense grinned. "Yes. It must mean that. We must watch for more signs."

They stood around the bed, gazing at the still, silent woman. Rhea did not stir or twitch. But Alexandra was not discouraged. She resumed her vigil, not leaving Rhea's side until it was time for supper and one of the maids came to take her place.

Alexandra had thought to go back to her mother's side that evening, but supper seemed unusually long, and after that, they had to sit through a tedious piano recital from Willa. Hearing her play, Alexandra wondered if the

Countess was forced to sit through her piano pieces every evening. If so, she must have the patience of a saint, Alexandra thought. Whatever warm and wonderful qualities Willa had, she was not an accomplished pianist.

Alexandra began to feel quite sleepy. She yawned, trying to cover it so as not to hurt Willa's feelings, and more than once she jerked awake and realized that she had nodded off. She decided to go straight to bed, only stopping by her mother's room to say good-night to her unresponsive form.

She sighed and left the room, trying not to let Rhea's lack of response discourage her. It would happen; she would awaken. She must just have faith.

Alexandra stopped abruptly a few feet from her door when she saw that Sebastian was standing beside it, leaning negligently against the door frame.

"What are you doing here?" she asked irascibly, walking around him to open the door.

"Waiting for you," he replied, reaching out and catching her wrist with his hand.

He stepped closer, looming over her. "I have been having trouble sleeping, Alexandra."

"I hardly see how that is my concern." Alexandra replied lightly, although warmth was already stirring in her at the implication of his words.

"It is because of you. I used to be quite content with being by myself. I find that I am not any longer."

Sebastian bent his head and brushed his lips against her hair. "I want you in my bed again."

"If this is another ploy to try to convince me to marry you…"

"No, just the plea of a desperate man. I was watching you all through that execrable piano recital. I kept thinking about that night in the highwayman's lair…."

He raised her arm and kissed the tender inside of her wrist. "Come to my room tonight."

"Are you mad? Under the same roof with my aunt and mother? Not to mention Willa."

"Then marry me, and we shall be under our own roof."

Alexandra grimaced. "You are not getting around me that easily. Besides, I'm terribly sleepy. Didn't you see me yawning all evening?"

"I thought that was due to Willa's piano playing," Sebastian said, and Alexandra chuckled. He brushed his knuckles slowly down her cheek and leaned over her, saying in a low voice, "I'll lay you odds that I have a remedy for your sleepiness."

His husky voice stirred a longing in Alexandra's loins, but she wasn't about to admit that to him.

"Stop." Alexandra shook her head in mock exasperation and went on tiptoe to brush her lips lightly against his cheek. "Good night, Sebastian."

"You call that a good-night kiss?" His arm swooped around Alexandra, and he lifted her into him as his mouth came down to claim hers in a dizzying, lengthy kiss.

When at last he released her, Alexandra stood for a moment dazedly gazing into his face, her lips slightly parted. He let out a groan.

"If you continue to look at me like that, I can guarantee that I won't leave you." He bent and pressed his lips against Alexandra's forehead. "Dream of me tonight."

He turned and strode briskly down the hall toward his room. Alexandra let out a shuddering sigh and went into her room. One of the upstairs maids was waiting to help her out of her dress and into her nightgown.

Languidly, Alexandra let the girl brush her hair and tie it back with a pink ribbon. Usually she hadn't the patience for letting someone fuss over her hair like that; she wouldn't even have used the services of a maid if it had been possible for her to reach all the tiny buttons down the back of her dress. But tonight, she was too tired and lazy to protest. Indeed, her eyes drifted closed as she sat on the bench while the maid brushed her hair.

"Miss!"

Alexandra opened her eyes and blinked at the maid standing over her, her hands on Alexandra's shoulders.

"You drifted right off there," the maid told her. "You'd best get up and into bed."

Alexandra tried to smile. "Yes. Thank you. I can't imagine why I'm so tired. It must all be catching up with me. Good night, Rose."

She stood, and the maid bobbed a curtsey and lit a candle from the oil lamp on the dressing table. "Good night, miss."

Alexandra picked up the lamp and crossed to her bed, which the maid had already turned down for her. Yawning, she set the lamp on the narrow table beside the bed and bent to blow out the flame. She crawled between the sheets and was asleep as soon as her head hit the pillow.

She was dreaming that she was sitting before the fire. It was too warm, and she tried to move away from the heat but could not. The damper must have been closed, too, for smoke was billowing into the room, making her cough. Then the Countess was in the room with her, shaking her roughly and telling her that she had to get out of her chair.

She shook her head, saying, "No, I'm too tired."

But the Countess would not stop. She kept shaking her and saying her name. Then Alexandra realized that it was not the Countess at all, but her mother.

She opened her eyes. And there was her mother's face,

looming over her in the darkness. But it wasn't dark, exactly. Rather, the air was thick with smoke, and above, the smoke flames danced, racing along the tester above her bed and down the long fall of the open curtains at the four corners of the bed.

"Mother?" Alexandra began to cough as she sucked the smoke into her lungs.

Her mother was tugging at her, and Alexandra saw in dazed astonishment that tears were running down the woman's cheeks. Everything seemed so strange and unreal. Her lungs felt on fire, and the air was thick with smoke. She was surrounded by fire, yet she could not seem to make herself move.

Suddenly several large sparks fell on the bed beside Alexandra, and the sheets began to burn. Alexandra gasped, and Rhea batted them out.

"Alexandra! Get up! What is the matter with you?" Rhea grabbed Alexandra's shoulders, wincing with pain as her burned palms touched Alexandra.

She jerked again, and this time Alexandra managed to push herself out of bed. Rhea staggered back under her weight, and the two of them fell heavily to the floor. The fall stunned Alexandra for a moment. But the air was clearer here, and she was able to breathe in air that was not smoky. She coughed, clearing her lungs. Shakily, she rose to her feet, reaching to help Rhea. They started groggily toward the door. The smoke was so thick, she could barely see, and she fell into another paroxysm of coughing. Rhea stumbled and went down on her knees, and Alexandra leaned over her, trying to help her up.

It was hard to breathe, and the room started spinning around her. Coughing, she fell forward onto the floor beside Rhea.

19

Sebastian lay staring at the tester above his bed. He was having no luck going to sleep. Every time he closed his eyes, all he saw was Alexandra. All he could think about was kissing her, holding her, making love to her again. They were not images that were conducive to sleep.

Sighing, he sat and swung his legs off the side of the bed. He might as well get up and dress and go to the library to see if he could find something to read. With any luck, he thought, there would be something dull enough to make him nod off.

He had pulled on his trousers and was in the process of buttoning his shirt when he stopped and lifted his head. There was the oddest smell, he realized—a smell of smoke, as if a chimney weren't drawing properly. He glanced instinctively at the fireplace in his room, but even as he did so, his brain registered that it was a warm summer night and the fire had not even been lit.

Fear gripped his chest, and he hurried to his door and flung it open. He could see nothing unusual in the hall, but the smell of smoke was stronger. He started down the hall, not pausing to light a candle or lamp, navigating by the moonlight drifting in through the long windows at either end of the hallway. As he drew closer to Alexandra's room, he could see wispy tendrils of smoke curling from beneath her door.

"Alexandra!" he cried, and ran the rest of the way to her room.

He flung open the door, and a thick pall of smoke rushed into the hallway. He saw at a glance that Alexandra's bed was on fire, the tester above the bed and the heavy bedcurtains blazing merrily, and flames were already starting across her sheets and bedcovers.

But Alexandra was not in the bed; he could see that much. He glanced frantically around the room, and his gaze fell on the two bodies lying on the floor a few feet from the foot of the bed. He ran to Alexandra and picked her up, carrying her from the smoky room. He bellowed for help as he laid her gently on the floor, then went into the room for the other woman.

Coughing and fanning away the smoke, he bent over her, surprised to find that it was not a maid or Aunt Hortense, as he had assumed, but Alexandra's mother. He picked her up and ran into the hall, where Aunt Hortense and Willa were crouched beside Alexandra. Several servants came pounding up the stairs and stopped, gaping at the scene before them.

"Stop gawking, you idiots!" he roared. "Can't you see the room's on fire? Get some water—now!"

They jumped to do his bidding as Sebastian went to Alexandra, moving aside her aunt and the Countess's companion and pulling Alexandra down the hall, out of the doorway.

The servants pounded into the room with buckets of water, and Aunt Hortense and Willa went to Rhea to minister to her. Sebastian knelt beside Alexandra and lifted her into his arms, cradling her against his chest.

"Oh, God, don't die on me now, love," he whispered, feeling for the pulse in her throat. He could not hear her breathing, so he draped her limp form forward over his arm and thwacked his open palm against her back until she began to cough.

"Thank God. That's it. That's my girl." He cuddled her to him again, running his hand down her hair and back and raining kisses over her sooty face and hair. "Stay with me. I couldn't bear to lose you now."

Alexandra coughed, and her eyes fluttered open. She saw Sebastian's face looming over hers, streaked with soot and torn with anxiety. "Sebastian?"

As she said the word, she gave way to a fit of coughing. Sebastian held her as she coughed out the smoke that had overcome her. Finally, with a sigh, she settled in his arms. It felt deliciously warm and safe there.

"Thank God you're alive," he murmured against her hair. "I was afraid I had lost you, love. I don't know what I would have done."

"What did you say?" Alexandra asked, sitting up and turning to face Sebastian as the import of his words sank in.

He looked at her oddly. "I said I was afraid you were dead."

"No, the other part—did you call me 'love'?"

"Yes." He frowned in puzzlement. "Alexandra...are you all right? You seem a little muddled."

"Did you—did you mean it? Calling me your love?"

"Yes, of course. Surely you must realize that I love you."

"No. No, I don't. You never said a word about it."

"But, darling...why else would I want you to marry me? Do you think I would marry any woman who came along?"

"But that was because of the scandal. Because everyone knew we had been together that night after the balloon took off."

"I have weathered scandal before." He raised a quizzical eyebrow. "If I was willing to run off with a married woman and earn the polite world's contumely, do you honestly think that a little gossip would frighten me into marrying someone I didn't want to?"

"Not when you put it that way," Alexandra admitted. "But I thought, since I might be the Countess's granddaughter and you are fond of her, that you would feel you had to marry me. Besides," she argued, "you never spoke a word about love. Only about the scandal and my reputation."

"I was trying to persuade you," he retorted. "I didn't think my love would do so. You don't seem to reciprocate the feeling, so it seemed better to present the practicalities."

"Not reciprocate!" Alexandra stared at him in astonishment. "Can you honestly be that obtuse?"

He gazed at her for a long moment. "Are—are you saying that you do? That you—"

"Yes! Of course! I love you!"

"Alexandra..." He pulled her to him, his arms wrapping tightly about her, and kissed her. When at last he raised his head, he looked at her, his hand caressing her soot-smeared cheek. "Then you will marry me?"

Alexandra frowned, a chill coming over her happiness. "But there is still the problem of—oh!" She sat up straight, pulling away from him. "How could I have forgotten? Mother! She was with me in the bedroom. I saw her, leaning over my bed."

"Yes. I pulled her out, too." Sebastian nodded toward

where Rhea lay on the floor a few feet away, Hortense and Willa beside her.

Alexandra turned, pulling away from him, and crawled to her. "Mother?"

Sebastian followed, crouching beside the others. "How is she?"

Aunt Hortense shook her head. "She is breathing, but she's unconscious. Her hands are burned. I cannot imagine what she was doing in there."

"She was awake. She woke me up," Alexandra said. "She said my name, and she tried to pull me out of bed. She put out the sparks with her hands, that's why they're burned." Tears welled in her eyes.

"We need to get her back into bed," Sebastian said practically. "Let me carry her there, and Miss Ward can clean and bandage her burns."

"Yes. Yes, of course." The women stepped back as Sebastian bent and picked up Rhea.

Alexandra walked behind Sebastian as he carried her mother down the hall. Although she still felt groggy, her brain was beginning to work.

"What happened?" she asked as Sebastian laid her mother on her bed.

"What do you mean?" Aunt Hortense said as she poured water into the washbasin and carried it to the bed.

"I mean why was my bed on fire? Why was Mother in the room?"

"I don't know." Aunt Hortense dipped a cloth into the water and wrung it out, then began to wash Rhea's face and, very gently, her arms and hands. "All I can think is that for some reason Rhea finally came out of her coma. Perhaps she smelled the smoke and that was enough to snap her out of it."

"Remember how she squeezed my hand today when I was talking to her?"

"She must have been close to the surface," Aunt Hortense reasoned. "Tonight she woke up. Probably she smelled the smoke and followed it to your room."

"That's how I came to find you," Sebastian added. "I began to smell smoke, and when I went into the hall, I saw the smoke coming out around the door."

"But what happened? Why was it on fire?"

Sebastian shrugged. "I don't know. I presume you must have left a candle burning. You were very sleepy tonight, remember."

"I didn't have a candle burning. I had an oil lamp, and I distinctly remember blowing it out."

"Are you saying—you think this was another deliberate attack on you?" Sebastian's eyes flashed silver in the darkness, and he turned, and strode to the door and threw it open. "Murdock! Murdock! Dammit, man, where are you?"

Murdock appeared in the doorway a few moments later, coatless, his hair disheveled, breathing hard. "Fire's out, my lord," he reported. "Bed's ruined, and it damaged the room a bit, but no major harm." He cast a glance toward Alexandra. "Is Miss Ward all right?"

"I'm fine, Murdock," Alexandra assured him, going to the door. She had become rather fond of the square-set man over the days he had been guarding their house. He was intensely loyal to Sebastian, and thereby, she had found, intensely loyal to her. He was hardly what one would picture as a valet, but Alexandra felt sure that he was, as Sebastian had said, a good man to have on your side in a fight, and certainly that was more important than any refinement of manner. Even Aunt Hortense had approved of the man, saying that if she hadn't heard him speak, she would have sworn that he was an American, not a Britisher.

Murdock nodded toward her. "Glad to hear it, Miss."

"Murdock, could someone have gotten into the house tonight?" Sebastian asked. "Miss Ward is certain that she did not leave a light burning. That would mean that someone must have sneaked in and set the bed curtains on fire."

"No, sir. Couldn't nobody have got into this house tonight—or any other night since I've been here." He turned toward Alexandra somewhat apologetically. "I'm sorry, miss, I'm sure you're right about the lamp, but I don't see how anyone could have got past me and my men. I have a footman patrolling the outside of the house continuously, three shifts of them, three hours each, so they don't get sleepy. To keep things right and tight, I patrol, too, half a lap behind him, just to make sure and keep the footman on his toes. Halfway through the night, Punwati relieves me. Ain't nobody getting past us, miss." He patted his side, where a pistol was stuck through his belt. "We keep a watch during the day, too." He paused, frowning. "Not so tight, of course, but a footman makes the circuit every few minutes. And the house is full of servants. I don't see how anyone could sneak in during the day and hide till nightfall, either."

"No," Alexandra agreed. "It sounds very thorough. I am sure you and Mr. Punwati are doing a wonderful job." Alexandra frowned. "But I know I blew out the lamp."

She thought of her mother in her room. It seemed so odd that Rhea had awakened just at the moment that her bed curtains had caught on fire. She thought of tales she had heard of madmen setting things afire, their warped minds drawn by the crackling flames. They could not know, after all, what had been fermenting in her mother's confused mind during the long period of unconsciousness. And perhaps, she thought, Rhea had not been unconscious the whole time. She remembered her mother gripping her hand this morning.

But, no! What was she thinking? Her mother was a trifle off, perhaps, but she wasn't mad in that way. She would never try to hurt Alexandra, no matter how fevered her mind might turn. Besides, she reminded herself, Rhea had tried to save her from the fire. She had awakened Alexandra and pulled her from the bed, had beaten out the fire with her bare hands when it lit on Alexandra's sheets. Alexandra felt ashamed for thinking such a thing even for an instant.

"Perhaps Mrs. Ward woke up." Willa spoke, surprising everyone. They all turned to look at her, and she blushed but went on. "Of course she would want to see her daughter. So she lit a candle and went down to Alexandra's room. Maybe as she leaned over to look at her, her candle caught the bed curtains on fire. They would probably have been in flames in an instant. So she tried to awaken Alexandra."

Alexandra felt a wave of relief wash through her. "Of course! That makes sense. Much more so than that someone could have sneaked into the house past the guards."

It was also much more reasonable than the coincidence of Rhea awakening at the precise time that Alexandra's room caught on fire.

"Yes, that explains it." Alexandra could hear the relief in her aunt's voice, and she wondered if she had had the same doubts about Rhea that Alexandra had. "A simple accident."

"It was my fault," Willa went on, her voice laced with guilt. "I should have kept better watch over Mrs. Ward."

"You cannot possibly stay awake watching over her all

night," Alexandra pointed out reasonably. "You sleep in her room so you could hear if she needed something. No one could expect you to do any more."

"Yes, but I was so heavily asleep," Willa said. "I generally don't go to sleep that early. But tonight, my head was incredibly heavy. I could scarcely keep my eyes open. Then I slept so deeply that I did not even hear Mrs. Ward leave the room! I should have heard her. I should have awakened."

"Nonsense," Aunt Hortense said stoutly. "You had no way of knowing that Rhea would awaken tonight, or that she would take it into her head to go visit Alexandra. None of us did. After tonight, we shall make sure that someone is up with her all night. We shall take shifts."

"Yes," Alexandra agreed, but her mind was only half on her aunt's words. A chill had run through her at what Willa had said. Willa had been unusually sleepy tonight, just as she had been, and she had slept heavily, finding it hard to wake up. Alexandra remembered how groggy she had felt when her mother woke her. She had felt almost...drugged. What if she really had been drugged? And Willa, too? What if someone had made sure that both she and Willa would be sound asleep tonight?

She pushed the thought away. It was too terrible to contemplate. For if someone had drugged their food or drink with the intent to keep her and Willa asleep, then that meant that it had been done by someone inside the house, a bribed servant or... Her eyes went to Aunt Hortense, then to her mother, lying in her bed. But, no, she was thinking crazily, more crazily than her mother at her worst. They were her family, the people who loved her most in the world!

Aunt Hortense would never harm her. It didn't matter

whether Alexandra was a Ward or not. And her mother's oddness would never have risen to such extremes.

"There is no need to keep going over this," Sebastian said peremptorily. "Miss Ward, Miss Everhart, I suggest that you bring in another cot, and both of you spend the night here with Mrs. Ward. I shall post Murdock outside your door the rest of the night. That way you will be here to tend to Mrs. Ward if she needs you, and I can be assured that the three of you are well-protected. Alexandra, you are coming with me."

"Sebastian!" Alexandra protested as he put his hand under her elbow and more or less propelled her from the room. "What are you doing? Where are we going? I want to stay with my mother."

"Nonsense. You're dead on your feet. What you need to do is get some rest. Let Aunt Hortense, who has *not* almost been killed tonight—for, let me see, the fourth time, or is it the fifth?—let her take care of your mother. You may sit up with Mrs. Ward tomorrow."

"I shall. And whenever else I wish."

"Murdock!" Sebastian led Alexandra toward her room. Sebastian's valet stood in the doorway, surveying the damage.

Sebastian and Alexandra came up beside him and looked into the room. Two footmen were poking about, making sure every possible stray spark was extinguished. Alexandra drew in her breath sharply. "Oh, no!"

Her room was a wreck. The bed was blackened, the charred bed curtains trailing from the bedposts, and the tester had collapsed onto the mattress. There was a stinging scent of burned feathers hovering in the air. The chair on one side of the bed and the small table on the other had been singed, as had the drapes on the window. The wall behind the bed was blistered. All the burned mess, as well as the rest of the floor, was sodden with water.

"At least it didn't reach your wardrobe, miss, or the dresser," Murdock said encouragingly. "All your clothes should be all right, once they're washed and aired out, of course."

"Mm," Alexandra responded noncommittally. Looking at the wreckage, she found it a trifle hard to look on the bright side.

"I want you outside the door of Mrs. Ward's room tonight," Sebastian told Murdock. "I don't want anyone going in there."

The short, muscled man nodded his agreement. "Won't nobody get in, sir."

Grabbing a straight-backed chair from Alexandra's room, he carried it down the hall and planted it squarely in front of Rhea's door and sat in it, arms folded, obviously prepared to wait out the night.

Alexandra looked at her room. "Where am I going to sleep? Aunt Hortense's, I suppose, if she is going to be sleeping in Mother's room."

"You will be sleeping with me," Sebastian replied.

"What?" Alexandra looked at him in shock. "You can't be serious!"

"Can't I?" He hooked his hand under her elbow and steered her down the hall toward his room.

"Sebastian, no! We cannot—the servants—it would be scandalous."

"I've told you before—I am impervious to scandal. Anyway, if the servants are foolish enough to talk, it will be only a tempest in a teapot, since you and I are engaged to be married."

"We are not."

He stopped and looked at her sternly. "Do you intend to play fast and loose with my affections?"

"Sebastian! Don't be ridiculous."

"What else would you call it?" he asked, starting toward his room again. "Did you or did you not admit to me only a few minutes ago that you love me?"

A blush stained Alexandra's cheeks. "Well, yes, but..."

"No buts." He raised a finger to her lips for silence. "You say you love me yet refuse to marry me. What else can you call it except toying with me?"

Alexandra had to smile. "Don't be an idiot. You know why we cannot marry."

"I know the foolish reasons that you have put forth, and none of them are persuasive."

He opened the door of his room and ushered her inside. Alexandra could not seem to find the will to resist him. She let him guide her toward the bed and help her into it.

"Sebastian, we shouldn't...." She made one last weak protest.

But he ignored her and climbed into the bed beside her, pulling her back to him, so that they lay curled together like spoons in a drawer.

"Your sheets," she objected, yawning. "I'm filthy."

"Sheets can be cleaned." He kissed her on the cheek and curled his arm over her.

Alexandra closed her eyes, feeling blissfully safe and warm, and in an instant she was asleep.

When Alexandra awakened the next morning, it was late, and the sun was streaming in through a crack in the curtains. Sebastian was gone. She rang for a maid and ordered a bath drawn for her. After washing away all the soot from the night before and dressing in a day dress the maid had been airing all morning and which smelled only faintly of smoke, she made her way downstairs to the dining room.

Aunt Hortense was the only occupant of the room, obviously at the end of her meal, and she looked up with a smile at her niece. "Alexandra! You are looking much more the thing this morning, I must say."

"Thank you. I feel much more the thing." She sat down, and one of the servants brought her a cup of coffee. "Where is Sebastian?"

"Bustling about arranging things." Her aunt leaned closer, smiling warmly. "He says the sooner you are married, the safer you will be, but personally, I think the man is simply impatient."

"But I didn't—"

"I am so glad you finally agreed to marry him. Of course, there was little other choice, after all that's happened."

"I have not agreed to marry him," Alexandra stated flatly.

"He seems to be of the opinion that you have," Aunt Hortense remarked.

"That man takes entirely too much on himself," Alexandra said darkly, grabbing a piece of toast and beginning to butter it.

"If you ask me, dearest, you might as well stop fighting it."

"What? Are even you turning against me?"

"Not against *you*, my dear, just against your bullheadedness. Any fool can see you're head over heels in love with the man."

Alexandra drew a breath, about to flare up in denial,

but the wry look her aunt sent her made her break into laughter instead. "Oh, Auntie, am I that obvious?"

"Mm. 'Fraid so. 'Tis no crime, you know, to fall in love or to want to marry a man."

"I know. But I feel as if it would be wrong of me, not even knowing what my parentage is."

"If Lord Thorpe doesn't care, I don't see why you should bother *your* head about it." Aunt Hortense fixed her with a stern gaze. "Whether Rhea is your blood mother or not, you have never been the least like her, and I see no reason you should suddenly change now. It isn't as if Rhea is someone who has to be locked up in the attic. She has behaved a trifle oddly at times, I'll admit, but she isn't *mad*. I mean, look at the way she tried to save you last night."

Alexandra thought about her brief flash of fear last night as she had wondered if her mother had set the fire in her room purposely. Why, she had even for a moment thought that Aunt Hortense could have drugged her and Willa and set the fire! The notion seemed absurd in the light of day, especially looking at her aunt's plain, honest face, warm with caring.

"No, of course not. She is not mad," Alexandra agreed, and she felt suddenly lighter than she had in days. However strange all the things that were happening, she couldn't help but be happy. Sebastian loved her, and she loved him. He wanted to marry her. Why was she putting him off? Why was she denying herself exactly what she wanted the most?

There was a noise behind her, and Alexandra turned to see Willa standing in the doorway. She smiled in her timid way. "Hello. I hope I'm not intruding. One of the maids was kind enough to sit with Mrs. Ward so that I could come down to eat. It gets a trifle boring sometimes eating one's meals in the sickroom.''

"Of course. You must take off the morning, as well," Alexandra added, smiling. "I shall sit with Mother this morning. I'm sure that you have many things that you have neglected, spending so much time with us. It has been wonderfully kind of you.''

"I have enjoyed it. I have so little to do at the Countess's.'' The small woman came around the table and sat beside Alexandra.

Alexandra truly was grateful to Willa; she had greatly eased the burden of caring for Rhea. But Alexandra also could not deny that the woman's self-deprecating way of talking wore on her nerves, as did her rather dull chatter. Alexandra finished her breakfast as quickly as was reasonably polite and excused herself to check on her mother.

As she went up the stairs, she began to worry that Willa had left her mother in the care of one of the maids. If there had been no intruder last night, as seemed likely, and if the fire had been deliberately set, then the likeliest culprit would be a servant hired by the villain who had hired the other men to harm Alexandra and her mother. It would certainly fit his—or her, as Maisy had said the other day—method of operation. Alexandra's steps quickened, and she was close to running when she reached her mother's room and flung open the door.

Her mother was lying still in her bed, the maid Rose sitting in a chair a few feet from her, her eyes closed. At Alexandra's abrupt entrance, Rose's eyes flew open, and she shot out of her chair.

"Oh, miss! You gave me a fright!" She laid a hand over her heart.

"I'm sorry." Alexandra felt faintly foolish for her fears, given the peaceful scene she had come in on.

"Thank you for sitting with her. I take it she's been quiet."

"Yes, miss, not a sound." The girl looked at Mrs. Ward and sighed. "Poor thing. Seems 'orrible, don't it, to come out of it like that and get knocked right back in?"

"Yes. We can only hope that her unconsciousness will be briefer this time."

The maid bobbed a curtsey and went out, and Alexandra pulled the chair closer to the bed, where she could sit and look at her mother's face. She touched her mother's bandaged arm lightly, tears welling in her eyes as she thought of Rhea batting at the sparks on her bed. Rhea loved her and had done her utmost to save her. However much Alexandra might resent the fact that Rhea had kept the secrets of her past from her all these years, she knew that Rhea loved her.

The morning crept by slowly, and Alexandra picked up a piece of mending from her aunt's sewing bag and began to work on it, to give herself something to do. Suddenly Rhea moaned, startling Alexandra into jabbing her finger with the needle.

She looked at her mother. Rhea's eyes were still closed, but she was turning her head restlessly against the pillow. She raised one of her hands and moaned at the pain the movement caused.

"Mother?" Alexandra said, leaning forward and laying her hand lightly on Rhea's shoulder. "Mother? It is I, Alexandra. Can you hear me?"

"Allie," her mother breathed, using the name she had called Alexandra when she was a child.

Hope stirred in Alexandra's chest. "Yes. It's Allie. Can you wake up, Mother? Can you talk to me?"

Rhea let out another soft moan. Slowly her eyes fluttered open, and she looked at Alexandra. "Simone?"

Alexandra slumped, disappointment slicing through her.

"I'm sorry. I'm so sorry." Tears pooled in Rhea's eyes and spilled over. "I tried. It was so hard. I'm sorry."

"Oh, Mother." Alexandra felt her eyes well with tears. "Why don't you know me?"

She leaned against the bed, laying her head on the mattress, discouraged. "Won't you ever recognize me again?"

Something touched her hair, and she realized, surprised, that it was her mother's bandaged hand, clumsily stroking her.

"Of course I recognize you, Alexandra." Her mother's voice was hoarse from disuse.

Alexandra's head snapped up. Rhea was looking at her, her expression infinitely sad.

"Why wouldn't I know you?" she asked. "You are my daughter."

"Mother!" Alexandra beamed, taking her mother's bandaged hand gently in hers. "You've come back. I'm so happy to see you!"

"I'm happy to see you, too," Rhea responded, smiling weakly. "Oh, Alexandra, I've been such a terrible mother to you."

"Don't say things like that. You haven't."

"I have." Rhea shook her head, tears spilling out of her eyes and streaming down her cheeks. "I have been a terrible person."

"No."

"You just don't know," Rhea wailed softly. "I didn't mean to hurt anyone. I really didn't. But I know you would hate me if you knew the truth!"

Alexandra's heart began to pound. She swallowed, trying to remain calm. "I wouldn't. I swear. I could never hate you.'

"You don't know what I did." Rhea wiped at her tears with her other hand.

"It doesn't matter. I couldn't hate you. You are my mother. You raised me. You loved me all those years and took care of me."

"But I'm not!" Rhea broke into sobs. "I'm not really your mother! Oh, God! I didn't mean to hurt anyone! I was just so lonely."

"I know you didn't mean to hurt anybody," Alexandra said soothingly, leaning closer to Rhea. "And I swear I won't hate you. Please, just tell me. Tell me what happened in Paris."

Rhea sighed. "All right," she said. "I will."

20

"Simone came to me that night," Rhea said dully. "The mob was out." She shivered, remembering. "It was awful. I was so scared. They were like animals, wild and howling. We were leaving the next day. Hiram—Hiram had that cough, and he didn't really want to go. He said that they had nothing against Americans. They wouldn't harm us. But I was so frightened that he agreed to take me to England. Everyone was running around, packing. There was so much I couldn't take. But I had to get away."

"Of course you did. I am sure it was terrifying."

Rhea nodded, reaching for Alexandra's hand. "Simone came with the children. John must have been about seven. He was trying hard to be a little man about it. Marie Anne—she was a year or two younger than he, and she was clinging to Simone's hand, crying. She was scared at leaving her father. And there was the baby—Alexandra. You."

She smiled tremulously at Alexandra.

"You were so beautiful—that cloud of curly dark hair. I always coveted you. I knew it was a sin, but I couldn't help it. You were such a beautiful, happy baby. I couldn't have children. Hiram and I had tried, but it never worked. Simone thought it was funny that I always wanted to visit the nursery when I called on her.''

Rhea fell silent, and Alexandra prompted, ''Why did Simone and the children come to your house?''

''They were on foot,'' Rhea said, sighing. ''Simone was terrified. She wore a cloak with a hood pulled around her face, and she had the children dressed in plain clothes. She and John carried little bags for them. She said—'' Rhea drew a shuddering breath. ''She asked me if I would take the children with me. She was so afraid for them. She said that she and her husband were trying to persuade her parents to leave with them, to go back to England, but her parents were reluctant. They didn't want to leave their home and their possessions. They kept saying that the mob would quiet down and everything would go back to the way it had been. Silly, of course. They had stormed the Bastille. Nothing would ever be the same. Chilton, of course, had that English arrogance, that assurance that nothing would happen to them because he was British. But Simone was not so sure. She had a mother's fear, a terror that the mob would kill her children. So she asked me to take the children to England with us, just in case she and Chilton could not get away. She said to take them to the Earl and Countess of Exmoor, Chilton's parents. She gave me a letter she had written them, as well as a velvet bag of her jewelry, in case we needed extra money to get out—and, I think, as an inheritance. The two little girls had their lockets, and John had the Exmoor ring, a plain-looking thing, but Simone said it was very precious to Chilton's family. It was the ring of the Exmoor heir. She knew, you see, that she and Chilton were going to die. I could see it in her eyes.''

Tears welled in Alexandra's eyes and spilled over as

she envisioned her mother, frightened, doing what she could to protect her children. "Oh, Mother, how sad!"

Rhea nodded. "Yes. Simone kissed them and hugged them, and they clung to her, crying. Finally, she tore herself away and left, and I took the children upstairs and put them to bed. Then I went up to the top floor and looked down the street. We lived only a few houses from them. It was an area where several foreigners lived. I could see the mob moving up the street like a great angry sea. It was awful. I could hear screams, and they set the house on fire. I knew they were dead." Rhea began to cry, and it took her a moment to collect herself and go on in a calmer voice. "We barricaded ourselves inside the house. When the mob came, Hiram opened the window on the second floor and talked to them. When they realized that he was an American, they cheered and left us alone. The next morning our neighbors told us that everyone in the Chilton house had been killed—Chilton, Simone, her parents, the children. Of course, I knew that the children had not, but I wasn't about to let on where they were. We left that afternoon. I have never been so scared in my life. Scared of the mob, of someone stopping to search us, of one of the children speaking in French and making people suspicious."

Rhea shuddered, remembering. Alexandra patted her arm.

"It must have been a harrowing experience. You were very brave."

"No." Rhea smiled weakly. "I wish I could say that I was. Hiram was brave. He did all the talking, even though he was growing sicker and sicker by the day. I felt as if I were in a nightmare—trying to take care of him and the children and not give us away. I knew that it was my fault that he was sicker. I had insisted on leaving. If only we had stayed in Paris, he might have recovered. He would have had proper rest and care, but rocking along in that carriage, day after day, staying in whatever inn we came to—and then the crossing over the Channel! It was too much for him." She shook her head, sighing. "He was a wonderful man. He would have done anything for me. And I was responsible for his death."

"No!" Alexandra cried in protest. "You don't know that. The fever might have killed him anyway, even if you had stayed in Paris. Or you could all have been killed in the rioting. I am sure you were right to be afraid, and no doubt Hiram wanted you to be safe. I am sure he was determined to do whatever it took to make you safe. And to rescue the children. If you had stayed in Paris, what would have happened to them?"

Rhea smiled faintly. "You are very sweet to try to reassure me. Perhaps you are right. But I'll never know. Hiram died shortly after we reached England. We stayed in Dover for two weeks. Hiram had grown too sick to travel, and you children had caught the fever, too. Thank heavens you and Marie Anne did not have it badly. You got over it quickly. John was in a bad way. Hiram died finally, and I was lost without him! I didn't know what to do. You were the only thing that kept me going—you were such a bright, beautiful baby. You were two, and you could walk, of course, and talk a little, mostly just babble. But you were so precious and funny and sweet. Whenever I needed it the most, you would come and sit in my lap and hug my neck. You called me Ree-ree, and you'd say, 'Don't cry, Ree-ree, don't cry.' Somehow it always made me feel better. I loved you so—you have to understand."

Rhea looked at Alexandra with desperation in her eyes and sat up, clutching Alexandra's shoulders. "You have to understand. I didn't think it would hurt anyone, and I loved you so much! Your parents were dead, only your grandparents to take care of you, and they would have the other two children. I know it was wicked of me, but I— I was bitterly unhappy and lost. I didn't know how I was going to live without Hiram. But you made everything bearable. It seemed so unfair that I had never been able to have children. All I wanted was just one, just you—''

"Calm yourself, Mother. It's all right. You are not wicked. I am sure that whatever you did, you did with the best of intentions."

"No," Rhea said sadly, "only the most selfish. I had no right to take you. Legally you belonged to the Countess. But I—I simply could not let you go."

"Mother, I don't understand. What did you do?"

Rhea sank back against her pillow, resignation filling her face. "I told them you had died. I said the baby had taken sick with the fever and died. It was easy enough to believe. John was terribly sick with it. And I took you home with me. I raised you as my own. I lied to everyone, including you. I kept you from your true family." Tears coursed down her cheeks, and she turned her head away.

Alexandra had known what was coming, at least to some extent, but still it stunned her. She stood staring at her mother, her face pale.

"God forgive me. I stole you from them." Rhea pressed her fingers to her lips. "I know that you must hate me."

"No! No. I could never hate you!" Alexandra cried. "You are my mother. You raised me. You loved me. I have been your daughter all my life. How can I blame you for loving me so much?"

"Truly?" Rhea turned toward her, her face lighting with hope. "You don't despise me?"

"Of course not. I love you. You were in a terrible situation. What you did was wrong, but it is easy to understand why you did it. How you felt. I have had a wonderful life, a wonderful family. How could I despise you for what you gave me? And now—now you have given me back my other family. I have two."

"Oh, Alexandra!" Rhea threw her arms around Alexandra. "You were always the best child in the world."

They sat that way for a long moment, clinging to each other, tearful and happy at the same time. Finally Alexandra pulled away and looked her mother in the eye, taking Rhea's hands in hers.

"But, Mother," she began earnestly. "I don't understand. What happened to the other two children? What about my brother and sister?"

Rhea gazed at her in confusion. "What do you mean? Nothing happened to them. John was very sick, but—he lived, didn't he? Don't tell me he died."

"Mother, the Countess knows nothing about any of us. She thought that all three of the children died with their parents in Paris."

"What? But I took them to her. I brought Marie Anne and John here, to London. I turned them over to the Exmoors."

"You gave them to the Countess?" Alexandra had the sinking fear that Rhea had come completely unhinged.

"No, not directly. She had taken to her bed, they said, stricken by grief at what had happened to her family. I believe they said that her husband had died, too, poor thing. She refused to see anyone. When I told that woman who I was and who the children were, she said that the Countess could not come down and see me. So I gave the children to her."

"Who? Who is she?"

"Why, that young woman. She wasn't a servant. She was a cousin or something, a poor relative who lived with the Countess as her companion. That woman—that woman who's been here watching me!"

"What!" Alexandra exclaimed, jumping to her feet. "You mean Willa? You gave the children to Willa?"

"Yes, Miss Ward, that is exactly what she means," a woman's voice said.

Alexandra started and whirled around. There was Willa standing in the doorway, as composed and quiet as ever. She walked into the room, closing the door behind her, and came to the other side of the bed.

"I was afraid that you had recognized me," Willa told Rhea conversationally. "I had a suspicion that you were only pretending to be unconscious the last day or two. Did you follow me last night?"

Rhea's eyes skittered away from the woman, and she did not answer. Alexandra stared, hardly able to take it all in. "Follow you! You mean to my room? It was you who—" She stopped, too stunned to complete the thought.

"Yes, it was I. It was obvious that you were never going to give up. At first I thought it would be all right if I simply got rid of Mrs. Ward, but then you kept on asking questions and digging. You had even gotten Lord Thorpe on your side! I knew that if your mother died, you would still manage to dig out the truth somehow."

Willa grimaced, looking more exasperated than anything else.

"You were willing to kill me just to keep me from finding out that Mother had given my brother and sister to you?" Alexandra asked. "Why?"

Willa looked at her as if she were a dim student. "Are you mad? What would have happened to me if the Countess found out? She would have turned me out. After all these years, all the devotion I've given her, she would have cut me off without a farthing. What would I do if the Countess turned me out? I would have nothing! No one!"

"But why did you—what happened to John and Marie Anne? What did you do with them?" Anger rushed through Alexandra, sweeping away the shock, and she started around the bed toward Willa.

But Willa struck as quickly as a snake, pulling her hand from her pocket, a long, sharp knife gleaming in it. With her other hand, she grasped Rhea's hair and jerked her roughly, the knife coming to Rhea's throat. Alexandra stopped abruptly, her eyes on the deadly knife.

"Wait," Alexandra began shakily. "It doesn't have to be like this. Maybe if you told the Countess what happened... There must be an explanation."

Willa let out a short, harsh laugh, her face contorting and her eyes glittering. "Oh, yes, there is an explanation, all right. Its name is Richard! Not much chance the Countess will approve of that."

"Richard? You mean the Earl of Exmoor?"

"Yes, the Earl," Willa agreed bitterly. "I was mad to do it! Mad with love for him. I would have done anything he wanted. I risked my position, everything, just to be with him—the Countess would have thrown me out on my ear if she had known that I was sneaking out to lie in his bed. And when that American woman came that day with the two brats, I knew what it would mean to him. He was the Earl, or would be once John and his father were declared legally dead. Everyone was already treating him as the Earl. After all, Bertie Chesterfield had come home and told everyone that Chilton and the children were dead. With the old Earl dead, the title was his. The estate, too. I couldn't let that be taken away from him. I couldn't!''

"So when Mother came to you, you didn't tell the Countess about her visit. You never told her that her grandchildren had been spared." Alexandra's eyes flashed, and her fingers itched to grab for that knife. But she knew that it would be madness to do so. Willa could slice Rhea's throat before Alexandra's hand wrapped around hers.

"I wanted to help Richard. I thought—I thought I would keep his love forever if I gave him the children. I thought he would even marry me. Ha! I should have known the snake would cast me aside. He knew I could never tell the truth, never reveal what he had done, because it would have ruined me, too."

As the words spewed out of her, Willa let go of Rhea's hair, and the hand that held the knife trembled, falling a little from Willa's throat. Her gaze was fastened on Alexandra, and she did not notice Rhea's hand slide ever so slowly up. But Alexandra saw, and her stomach tightened.

To keep Willa's attention focused on her, she said quickly, "Then it was Richard who was the bad person, not you. It was Richard who took the Countess's grandchildren away from her. She will understand. She'll see that—''

Willa laughed, hysteria creeping in around the edges. "Understand? No one could understand that—or forgive it! Do you think I'm a fool?"

"No, of course not." Alexandra nervously eyed the knife that trembled in Willa's hand. "Normally perhaps one could not forgive that. But given the circumstances— I mean, the Countess will be so happy to know that I am really her granddaughter that she will be in a forgiving mood. Don't you see? And the other two children, John and Marie Anne—if you could tell her where they are, what happened to them…''

"That will get me no favors from her," Willa snapped, and Alexandra's heart sank. Did this mean that her sister and brother were dead?

"Why? What happened to them?" Alexandra asked, paling. "Where are they?"

"Why should I tell you?" Willa demanded scornfully, unconsciously swinging her arm forward.

Suddenly, moving faster than Alexandra would have thought possible, Rhea grabbed the other woman's wrist. Willa let out a shriek of outrage, jerking her hand. But the movement had given Alexandra enough time to race around the bed and throw herself at Willa just as Willa lashed out with her knife at Rhea. She aimed for her throat, but Alexandra knocked her arm aside, and the knife slashed down across Rhea's arm, laying open a long, red cut.

Alexandra's rush carried Willa backward, but she did not fall. She was preternaturally strong in her madness, and she fought back. They careened around the room, Alexandra holding Willa's knife arm up and back while Willa scratched and kicked and beat at her, trying to loosen her hold. They crashed into the wall and slid along it to the highboy, sending a porcelain dish of pins crashing to the floor, followed a moment later by a small box. As they fought, Rhea climbed out of bed, clasping the sheet to her upper arm. Blood poured forth, staining it red. She staggered toward the door, screaming for help.

Willa turned as she and Alexandra shuffled in a deadly dance, then shoved with all her might, throwing Alexandra against the wardrobe. Alexandra's head smacked against the tall cabinet, and she loosened her grip on Willa's arm enough that Willa was able to jerk it down.

Willa shoved her arm forward, aiming for Alexandra's stomach. Alexandra twisted and pulled away, and the knife sliced harmlessly through her dress and chemise. She turned, grabbing Willa's arm again with both her hands, and they grappled.

The door to the room was flung open, and Aunt Hortense let out a cry of horror. An instant later, she was unceremoniously shoved aside as Sebastian barreled into the room.

Willa, seeing the reinforcements arrive, let out a high animal scream of rage and pushed against Alexandra with all her might. Alexandra staggered backward, her hands still clenched around Willa's arm, and stumbled over a footstool. They went crashing to the floor, Willa landing on top of Alexandra.

Thorpe rushed forward, grabbed Willa by the shoulders and pulled her off Alexandra. All he saw at first was the blood staining the front of Alexandra's dress, and he went pale.

"Alexandra!" He let go of Willa to go down on his knees beside Alexandra, and when he did so, Willa crumpled to the floor. It was then that he realized the knife was deep in Willa's chest, not Alexandra's.

He gathered Alexandra in his arms, and she clung to him, crying. She pulled away suddenly. "Willa!"

"Don't worry. She is beyond hurting you any more."

"No! It's not that!" Alexandra scrabbled across the floor to where Willa lay.

The knife was sunk into Willa's chest, but she was still alive, her eyes open. Blood had soaked the front of her dress. Her breathing was labored, and there was an odd gurgling noise in her throat.

"Tell me what happened to them!" Alexandra begged,

bending over her. "Please…tell me what happened to my brother and sister!"

She heard Sebastian's astonished exclamation behind her, but she ignored him, leaning closer to Willa to catch her words.

Willa looked at her with hatred. "Why should I? You've ruined me."

"For your soul," Alexandra pleaded. "Do you want to go to your Maker with that on your soul, too? Tell me what happened to them. What did Richard do with them?"

"Boy had fever." Willa choked the words out, bloody bubbles seeping out of her mouth. "Died. Girl… orphanage…no name."

She began to cough, and blood poured out of her mouth. Then the light of hatred dimmed in her eyes and went out. She was dead.

Alexandra stared at her. A wordless moan of grief issued from her mouth.

"Alexandra, my darling." Sebastian pulled her into his arms and stood, taking her with him. Alexandra rested her head upon his chest and sobbed.

Finally she calmed down and raised her head. "Mother!" She pulled away and looked around the room. Her mother was seated in a chair, Aunt Hortense kneeling beside her, wrapping a strip of sheet firmly around her arm.

"Mother, are you all right?" Alexandra hurried across the room to Rhea.

Rhea smiled at her. "Yes, darling. I'm fine. Aunt Hortense is bandaging me. It was just a cut."

"Alexandra," Sebastian said, his voice taut with frustration. "What is going on here? *Willa* is the person who has been behind all these attacks?"

"Yes—or at least the hired ones. I don't think she could have been responsible for that man who attacked me when I walked home from the ball— Oh!'' Alexandra's eyes widened. "That must have been the Earl! He had just met me that night, and he must have realized who I was.''

"The Earl?'' Sebastian exclaimed. "You mean Richard? He really was involved in this? But why?''

"Willa?'' Aunt Hortense interrupted, amazed. "Oh, my God, and we have left her in the room alone with Rhea time after time!''

"I know. Apparently she wasn't going to hurt Mother unless she regained consciousness. Fortunately Mother sensed that and pretended to still be in a coma. You were awake the other day when you squeezed my hand, weren't you?''

"I was coming to, but I was very confused. I knew I had seen that woman before, and it scared me. I wasn't sure why, but I didn't want her to know.''

"But why?'' Sebastian asked, frustrated. "Why did Willa—or Richard, for that matter—want to get rid of you?''

Alexandra drew a deep breath. "My mother told me everything tonight. Simone gave her the children, and she brought them to the Countess. She kept me as her own. She pretended that I had died. But she gave the others to the Countess.''

"What?'' Sebastian stared at her, astounded.

"Well, not to the Countess. She gave them to Willa, actually, because the Countess was not receiving anyone. She was prostrate with grief. But Willa was having an affair with Richard, the new Earl, and she realized what it would mean to him if my brother suddenly showed up.''

"Of course. He wouldn't be Earl anymore.''

"Exactly. So she gave the others to Richard instead of the Countess, and she kept it a secret from everyone."

"But, then, what Willa just said...the little boy died?"

Alexandra nodded, tears welling in her eyes again at the thought of the brother she had never known and who had died so young. "Yes. He had a bad fever. Fa—Mr. Ward had died of it, too. And the girl, Marie Anne—that wicked, wicked man gave her to an orphanage. She grew up poor and alone—and we have no idea who she is now."

"Poor little John," Rhea said and began to cry. "Poor Marie Anne. I did so poorly by Simone! She entrusted them to me, and I failed her. If only I had known, I would never have turned them over to that woman!"

"Of course you wouldn't, Mother. But you couldn't have known what would happen. You did all that anyone could ask of you."

"Did I?" Rhea asked mournfully.

"Yes. Yes." Alexandra bent to hug her mother. "And this thing that you have suffered over all this time—taking me for your own? You saved me! Don't you see? You kept me from the same sad fate as my sister!"

"Oh, darling," Rhea began to cry, and so did Alexandra, and they clung to each other.

At last their tears dried, and Rhea gave a weary sigh, laying her head on Alexandra's shoulder. Aunt Hortense intervened, circling an arm around Rhea's waist and pulling the smaller woman onto her feet.

"I think it's time you were in bed. You've lost a fair amount of blood." She bundled Rhea into bed, fussing over her.

Alexandra turned to Sebastian, who took her hand in his. "So the attacks on your mother and you—Willa hired them done so that no one would find out what had happened to the children?''

Alexandra nodded. ''If Mother told the Countess the truth, the Countess would have realized that Willa and Richard had done away with her other grandchildren. It would have been a terrible scandal, at the least, for the Earl, and Willa knew that the Countess would never forgive her for what she had done. She would be ruined with the woman who was her whole life. I don't know if they acted together or separately, but I am sure that they are the ones who were behind the attacks.''

Sebastian put his arm around her, and she leaned her head against his shoulder. He led her into the hall, away from Aunt Hortense and Rhea and the gathering crowd of servants.

''I have sent for the doctor for Rhea and the magistrate for the rest of it.''

Alexandra nodded, then sighed. ''Oh, Sebastian, what a terrible thing! How are we going to tell the Countess? To find out after all this time that her grandchildren did not die in Paris twenty-two years ago—and at the same time to learn that they are still lost to her.''

''It's a hard thing,'' he agreed. ''But the Countess is a strong woman. And now she has you to help her through it.'' He squeezed her hand. ''We will find your sister. I shall put a Bow Street Runner on it right away. We'll search every orphanage in London if we have to.''

''Do you think we can actually locate her?'' Alexandra asked, hope beginning to stir in her. ''It seems a hopeless task.''

''Not as unlikely, I should think, as you being restored to your grandmother,'' he told her. ''At least we know that she grew up in this country.''

"That's true." Alexandra brightened. "Perhaps we can investigate it on our own."

"Oh, no." Sebastian shook his head, pulling her against his side. "I do not plan to engage in any more mysteries with you. We are going to be married, and you are going to be a good and proper wife, not one who gets kidnapped or stabbed or winds up in a brothel every few days."

Alexandra chuckled. "I promise I shan't get kidnapped anymore. But if you expect me to be a good and proper wife…"

"I know." Sebastian sighed. "I am doomed to disappointment."

"You needn't marry me," Alexandra replied.

"There you are wrong. I need very much to marry you."

He bent and kissed her lips tenderly. "If I don't marry you, you see, I shall be doomed to spend the rest of my life in boredom."

"That will never do," Alexandra responded, smiling. "I suppose I simply shall have to marry you."

"Thank God. I was beginning to think I would never get you to agree."

"And if I hadn't?"

He grinned wickedly and swept Alexandra up in his arms. "Then I would have had to kidnap you."

He turned and strode down the hall toward his bedroom, carrying her. Alexandra's delighted giggle floated after them. He halted at the door of his bedroom and bent to kiss her.

"I love you," Sebastian told her, all laughter gone from his face. "Promise me you will never leave."

"I will never leave," Alexandra agreed. "Why should I, when all I love is here?"

With a smile, he carried her into the bedroom.

Epilogue

The stone tower of the Norman church rose in the distance. It would not be long before the carriage reached it. Alexandra, who had had her head pressed against the window, leaned back against the luxurious squab. Across the carriage, the Countess smiled benignly at her.

"I am so glad you will be married in the family church," she said with satisfaction. "With all the tradition of the Earls of Exmoor. So much better than some impersonal pastor's study in London. Sebastian never did have much notion of what was proper."

Alexandra smiled. "So I have noticed. Perhaps we are well-suited that way."

Her hand went up to touch the delicate gold circlet around her neck from which several pendants of enameled gold dangled. Sebastian had offered her her choice of jewels to wear on their wedding day, and he had seemed quietly pleased when she had chosen the antique *satratana* instead of the heavy pendant of sapphires and diamonds. No doubt the sapphire and diamonds would have been more proper, but Alexandra preferred the history and oddity of the Indian necklace.

The Countess looked grim. "Richard will be there to-

day. I could scarcely leave him out with the wedding here
on his estate's doorstep.'' Her upper lip curled in scorn.
''The snake. I don't know how I will be able to look at
him, knowing what he did to my grandchildren.''

''I know.'' Alexandra felt the now familiar shadow that
settled in her heart whenever she thought about the fates
of the brother and sister she had never known. ''If only
we had some proof. But with Willa dead...'' She shook
her head. ''Perhaps if we could find those jewels in his
possession, the ones that Mother brought over from Simone.''

''I doubt that I would recognize any of them—except
the emerald pendant. That was a breathtaking piece. It was
Emerson's wedding present to Simone. But even if he has
it and your mother can identify it as what she brought
with the children, we cannot prove that Richard did anything wrong. He would lay the blame on Willa, say that
all she gave him were the jewels, that she told him the
children had died. She is not here to contest it. He would
say she was insane and point to the attempts she made on
your life and your mother's. Even if we could prove that
he knew about the children, what difference would it
make? It would be a scandal, a blot on the Montford
name, but nothing more. John died of a fever—and how
could we prove how much he neglected him? With John
dead, Richard is still the Earl of Exmoor.'' Her blue eyes
flashed. ''Sometimes I think that I could rip his heart out
with my bare hands.''

Alexandra nodded, then said, ''At least we may find
my sister someday.''

''Oh!'' The Countess sat up straighter, chagrin coming
over her features. ''How could I have forgotten? In the
bustle of getting dressed, I didn't tell you. I received a
letter from the Bow Street Runner today.''

"You did?" Alexandra leaned forward eagerly. "Did he have news?"

"Yes. He got little concrete news from any of the London orphanages, so he moved to the smaller towns outlying from the City. And he found one—the St. Anselm's Orphanage in Sevenoaks—where a small girl, perhaps five or six—was admitted late in the summer of 1789. She gave her name as Mary Chilton."

Alexandra drew in a sharp breath. "Chilton. You mean like—"

"Yes. Like my son's title. Just think. That is what he was called by everyone. If you asked a young girl what her father's name was, meaning his surname, she might very well have answered with the title by which he was called."

Alexandra nodded. "Yes, of course. It would make sense. And Mary, an anglicized form of Marie. It seems very possible."

"I thought so, too. I sent a note back to him immediately, telling him to pursue it." The Countess's eyes sparkled. "Oh, Alexandra, to think that I might someday have both of you back! I think I would die happy."

"Well, I wouldn't want that!" Alexandra protested with a chuckle. "You must promise me that you will live happily."

The Countess leaned across the carriage to pat her granddaughter's cheek. "All right. I can promise that easily—with you here. The Lord has given me a present in my old age." She settled back against the seat and flashed a wicked grin. "Now, if only you and Sebastian will provide me with great-grandchildren, I shall be a truly happy woman."

"Grandmama!" Alexandra exclaimed, feigning shock. "Surely talking about such things is not proper."

"Minx," the Countess said fondly. She leaned forward and patted Alexandra on the knee.

"I am sorry we missed all those years, but I cannot help but be grateful to Mrs. Ward for keeping you with her instead of giving you to Willa."

"I'm glad you feel that way. It has made Mother feel much better." Years of habit and love were too difficult to break. Alexandra knew that even though Simone had borne her, Rhea would always be Alexandra's mother in her heart.

"How is she doing? Is she still planning on returning to America?"

Alexandra nodded. "She and Aunt Hortense are leaving shortly after the wedding. She has been much better since she told me everything; I think it has relieved her mind a great deal to get rid of that burden of secrecy and guilt. But, still, she will be happier at home, among the people and things she knows. Sebastian has promised me that we will visit them next year."

The sound of the wheels changed beneath them, and the Countess said, "Ah, we must be there."

She lifted the curtain and peered out. The carriage had indeed reached the stone courtyard outside the church. They came to a stop, and a footman leaped to open the door and help the women down. They climbed the stone steps of the church and entered the narthex, where a maid waited to fuss over Alexandra's veil and train until they were exactly right. The Countess walked through the double doors of the sanctuary.

Moments later, Alexandra followed her. She walked slowly down the aisle, seeing the faces of her new life in Nicola, Penelope and the Countess. Even Lady Ursula was there. She had grudgingly admitted that Alexandra was her niece, although Alexandra was sure that theirs would never be a close relationship. There, too, were the faces of her old life: Aunt Hortense and her mother, both of them beaming at her. Rhea was crying unrestrainedly, and Aunt Hortense had her arm around her sister-in-law to comfort her. Aunt Hortense's eyes gleamed wetly.

Alexandra gave them a last smile and looked past them, down the aisle to the altar, where Sebastian waited. Alexandra's heart gave a little lurch, as it always did when she came upon him. Here was the foundation of her new life, the heart and soul of it. Whatever came, good or bad, she knew they would get through it together.

She smiled at Sebastian, love shining in her eyes, and stepped forward to give him her hand.

MIRA Books invites you to
turn the page for an exciting preview of

PROMISE ME TOMORROW
by
Candace Camp

In this passionate new historical romance,
discover what became of
Alexandra's younger sister, Marie Anne.

Available in paperback
August 2000

1

Marianne drew a deep breath as she surveyed the glittering crowd. She had never been to a party this large, nor one filled with so many titled people. She wondered what they would think if they knew she was plain Mary Chilton from St. Anselm's Orphanage, not the genteel widow Mrs. Marianne Cotterwood.

She smiled to herself. This might be a larger and more cosmopolitan set of people than she had deceived in the resorts of Bath and Brighton, but essentially they were the same. If one spoke as if one were genteel, and walked and sat and ate as if one had been trained to do so from birth, people assumed that one belonged. As long as she kept her lies small and plausible and was careful never to pretend to be someone more than the minor gentry, it was doubtful that anyone would sniff out her deceit. After all, most of the people here were too self-absorbed to spare much thought for anyone else, for good or ill. That was one of the traits that made them so easy to prey upon.

Marianne regarded all members of the ruling class as her natural enemies. She could still remember the days at the orphanage when the grand ladies would come on their "missions of mercy." Well-fed and warm, they would stand in their elegant dresses that cost more than would be spent on any of the orphans in a year and look at them with pitying contempt. Then they would go away, feeling vastly superior and quite holy for their charity.

"It's a lovely party," Marianne's companion said, and Marianne turned to her, firmly shoving aside her thoughts.

Mrs. Willoughby was a fluttery woman, so proud of her invitation to Lady Batterslee's rout that she had simply had to invite someone along with her to witness her glory.

A party at the elegant Batterslee House was an opportunity that did not come along every day, and Marianne had seized upon it, even though it meant suffering Mrs. Willoughby's stultifying conversation all evening.

Not, of course, that she meant to stay by Mrs. Willoughby's side. She would stay with her long enough not to appear obvious—and to meet as many people as Mrs. Willoughby could introduce her to, for the chance to mingle with this many people who might invite her to other parties was almost as important as examining the treasures of the house. But as soon as she reasonably could, she meant to slip away and spend the evening exploring.

They were almost at the front of the receiving line now, just beyond the doorway of the ballroom. It was the sight of the ballroom filled with people whose clothing and jewelry cost more than most people would earn in a lifetime that had given rise to Marianne's jitters. The room was enormous, all white and gilt and filled with mirrors. A small orchestra played on a raised platform at the far end, but the noise from the crush of people was so great that Marianne could barely make out a tune. The walls were lined with spindly-leg chairs, as white and gold as the room, except for the red velvet of their cushions. Tall candelabra were filled with white wax candles, and more such candles blazed in the chandeliers, setting off bright rainbows in the prisms that dangled beneath them.

Marianne glanced around, hoping to assure herself that she was not out of place here. She stopped as her gaze fell upon a man leaning against one of the slender columns of the ballroom only twenty feet away from her. He was watching her, and when she noticed him, he did not glance away embarrassedly, as most would have. He continued to gaze at her steadily in a way that was most rude.

He was tall and lean, with the broad shoulders and muscled thighs of a man who had spent much of his life on horseback. His hair, cut rather short and slightly tousled, was light brown, streaked golden here and there by the sun. His eyes, too, were gold, and hooded, reminding her of a hawk. His cheekbones were high, his nose straight and narrow; it was an aristocrat's face, handsome, proud and slightly bored, as if all the world did not hold enough to retain his jaded interest.

The man's gaze unsettled her. She felt unaccountably warm, and it was hard, somehow, to move her eyes away from him. He smiled at her, a slow, sensuous smile that set off a strange, tingling reaction somewhere in the area of her stomach. Marianne started to smile back, but she caught herself in time, remembering what he was and how she felt about his sort. Besides, a genteel widow did not stand about smiling at strangers. So she kept her face as cool and blank as she could and raised one eyebrow disdainfully, then turned pointedly away from him.

Their hostess was only two people away from her now, expertly greeting her guests and sliding them along. She greeted Mrs. Willoughby with no sign of recognition on her face, then nodded to Marianne with the same polite, measured warmth. It was such a huge party that Marianne was sure there were many people there whom Lady Batterslee barely knew, which made it the perfect opportunity.

It was difficult to work their way through the crowd but finally they reached the wall and were able to find two empty chairs. Mrs. Willoughby plopped down in one, fanning her flushed face, and looked around with all the enthusiasm of a career social climber.

"There's Lady Bulwen—I'm surprised she's here. They say she is only a step away from debtor's prison, you know." She shook her head, clucking her tongue in apparent sympathy.

"Indeed," Marianne murmured. It took little effort on her part to keep the conversation going, only an occasional nod or comment to assure her companion that she was listening. It was her great good fortune that Mrs. Willoughby was a perfect combination of social climber and inveterate gossip. Before this evening was through, she would know as much about the *ton* as if she had been a member for years.

After a few moments, however, her attention was distracted by the imperious tones of a woman sitting to her right. "Don't slouch, Penelope. And do try to look as if you're having a good time. It is a party, you know, not a death watch."

Curious, Marianne glanced to the side. The voice belonged to a large woman clad in an unfortunate shade of purple. Her bosom jutted forward like the prow of a ship, and her chin had a matching forward thrust. She, too, was watching the crowd like a predatory bird, interspersing comments about this or that eligible bachelor with commands to her young female companion. The girl in question sat between Marianne and the older woman, a plain slip of a thing in a white dress. White, Marianne knew, was considered the only appropriate color for an unmarried girl at a ball, but it was not a color that did anything for this particular young woman, merely emphasizing the lack of color of her face. Nor was her appearance enhanced by the glass spectacles that sat perched on her nose, hiding her best features, a pair of warm brown eyes.

"Yes, Mama," Penelope murmured in a toneless voice, her fingers clenched together in her lap. She reached up to adjust the spectacles that were on her nose, and her fan, lying in her lap, slid off and hit the floor, bouncing over and landing on Marianne's toe.

"Really, Penelope, do try not to be so clumsy. There's nothing so unattractive as a clumsy female."

"I'm sorry, Mama." Penelope flushed with embarrassment and bent toward her fan, but Marianne had already retrieved it.

She handed it to Penelope with a smile, sympathy for the girl rising inside her. It must be bad enough to be sitting here against the wall, not being asked to dance, without having her mother carping at her the whole time.

"Thank you," Penelope murmured softly, giving Marianne a shy smile.

"You're quite welcome. A dreadful crush, isn't it?"

Penelope nodded emphatically, causing the light to glint off her spectacles. "Yes. I hate it when there are so many people."

"I'm Mrs. Cotterwood. Marianne Cotterwood," Marianne told her. It was not proper to introduce oneself, Marianne knew, but she suspected that Penelope was not the sort to mind. Others, like Penelope's mother, would meet such boldness with a rebuff.

But Penelope smiled and said, "I am Penelope Castlereigh. It's very nice to meet you."

"The pleasure is all mine. You must think me bold to introduce myself, but in truth, I find it excessively silly to sit here not talking because there is no one around at the moment who knows both of us to introduce us."

"You're absolutely right," Penelope agreed. "I would have introduced myself if I had more nerve. I'm afraid I am the veriest coward."

At that moment, Penelope's mother, who had been droning away the past few minutes, finally realized that her daughter was not listening to her and turned to see what she was doing. At seeing the girl engaged in conversation with a strange woman, she scowled and brought her lorgnette up to her eyes to peer disapprovingly at Marianne.

"Penelope! What *are* you doing?"

Penelope jumped a little, and a guilty look flashed across her face. She turned back to the older woman, saying brightly, "I was just talking to Mrs. Cotterwood. I met her at Nicola's last week."

Quickly, before her mother could inquire more deeply into the matter, she introduced Marianne and her mother to each other. Her mother, Marianne learned, was Lady Ursula Castlereigh.

On the other side of Marianne, Mrs. Willoughby leaned forward, saying with delight, "Oh, do you know Lady Castlereigh, Mrs. Cotterwood? Mrs. Willoughby, Lady Castlereigh. If you remember, we met at Mrs. Blackwood's fete, oh, sometime last season."

"Indeed?" Lady Ursula replied in a voice that would have daunted a less determined woman than Mrs. Willoughby.

"Yes, indeed. I admired the dress you were wearing." Mrs. Willoughby launched into a detailed description of a gown, popping up and moving around the others to plant herself in the empty chair beside Lady Ursula.

Marianne seized the opportunity to escape both women.

"Shall we take a stroll around the room, Miss Castlereigh?"

Penelope brightened. "That would be lovely."

Penelope visibly relaxed as they moved away from Lady Ursula's vicinity. Marianne glanced around them as they walked, automatically checking the room. There were few of the valuable items she sought in the large, open room. The only access to the outdoors was a series of long windows, opened to alleviate the heated stuffiness created by the crowd of people. Marianne maneuvered Penelope in the direction of the windows.

"Ah," she said. "It's much more pleasant here."

"Oh, yes," Penelope agreed, following her. "The fresh air feels good."

Marianne casually looked out. They were on the second floor, looking down at the small garden in the back of the house. There were no convenient trees or trellises nearby. Still, Marianne cast a professional eye over the window and its lock before she guided Penelope away.

As they walked, Marianne felt an odd prickling at the base of her neck that told her she was being watched. She turned her head, scanning the room, and after a moment she saw him—the same man who had been watching her earlier. As she looked at him, he sketched a bow to her. Warmth flooded her, a sensation she was unused to. She told herself it was embarrassment.

"Penelope..." She took her companion's arm. "Who is that man?"

"What man?" Penelope stopped and looked around.

"Over there." Marianne indicated him with her head.

Penelope adjusted her glasses, looking in the direction of Marianne's gaze. "Oh. Do you mean Lord Lambeth?"

"The good-looking wretch with a superior smile on his face."

Penelope smiled faintly at the description. "Yes. That's Justin. He's the Marquess of Lambeth."

"He keeps looking at me. It's most disconcerting."

"I should think you would be used to men looking at you," Penelope responded, grinning, looking at her companion. With her red hair, vivid blue eyes and creamy white skin, Marianne Cotterwood was stunning. Penelope had noticed her almost as soon as she had entered the ballroom. Marianne's dress, though simpler than most here tonight, was the perfect setting for her beauty, showing off her tall, voluptuous figure; she had no need for the frills and bows that many women added to their clothes.

"Thank you for the compliment—I think." Marianne smiled back at her. "But that is the second time I've caught him staring at me in the rudest way. And he doesn't seem at all embarrassed by being caught doing it. He just stands there looking…"

"Arrogant?" Penelope supplied. "That's not surprising. Lambeth's quite arrogant. Of course, I suppose he has every reason to be. Everyone fawns over him, especially giddy young girls looking to marry."

"He's a catch?"

Penelope chuckled. "They say he's rich as Croesus, and his father is the Duke of Storbridge, so all the matchmaking mamas consider him fair game."

"I see." *No wonder the man felt no hesitation in staring so rudely. Probably most of the women at the party would be thrilled to have him notice them.* Marianne glanced back in his direction, but he had gone. She and Penelope started their perambulation again.

"But I imagine it's all useless," Penelope went on. "Mother says that there's an unspoken understanding between him and Cecilia Winborne that someday they will marry. It would be a perfect match. Her lineage is as good as his, and there has never been a scandal in her family—they're all terribly priggish," she added confidentially.

Marianne laughed.

Penelope looked a trifle abashed. "I'm sorry. I should not have said that. You must think me terrible. Mother says I am always letting my tongue run away with me."

"I say—Penelope!" A male voice sounded behind them, and the two women turned to see a man strolling toward them. He was tall and sandy-haired, with a pleasant face, and he was smiling as he looked at Penelope. "What good luck, to catch you without Lady Ursula around."

Color dotted Penelope's cheeks, and her soft brown eyes lit up. She held out her hand to him. "Bucky! I wasn't sure if you would be here tonight."

"Oh, yes. I left the opera early." He paused, indignation clear on his face. "There's only so much of that caterwauling a man can be expected to take!" He nodded toward Marianne, saying, "Sorry, frightfully rude of me—"

His words died as he looked into Marianne's face, and the color drained from his cheeks, then came back in a rush. "Oh, uh, I—I say."

"Mrs. Cotterwood, please allow me to introduce Lord Buckminster," Penelope introduced them.

"How do you do?" Marianne held out her hand politely.

"Oh. I say. Great pleasure," Buckminster managed to get out, stepping forward to take her hand. As he did so, he stumbled, but caught himself. He took Marianne's hand and bowed over it, then released her and stood grinning down at her foolishly.

Marianne sighed inwardly. It was obvious to her that Penelope had very fond feelings for Bucky, but the man seemed oblivious to them. It was just as obvious that he was entranced by Marianne. She knew that she had the sort of looks that attracted men, although she was not vain about it—most of her life her vibrant good looks had been the source of more trouble than good fortune.

"It is very nice to meet you," Marianne said pleasantly to Lord Buckminster, "but I am afraid I cannot stay and chat. I must get back to Mrs. Willoughby or she will wonder what has become of me."

"Allow me to escort you," Buckminster said eagerly, straightening his cuff and in the process somehow dislodging the gold cuff link. It dropped to the floor and rolled away. "Oh, I say…" The man looked with some dismay at the piece of jewelry and bent to retrieve it.

"Oh, no," Marianne protested quickly. "You must stay here and keep Penelope company. I am sure that you have a lot to talk about."

She slipped away immediately, while Buckminster's attention was still concentrated on his cuff link. Her departure was a trifle rude, she knew, but she felt sure Penelope would not mind.

Weaving her way through the throng of people, Marianne made her way to the door. Snapping open her fan and wafting it as though the heat of the crowd was what had impelled her to leave the ballroom, she strolled along the corridor past a pair of footmen. She glanced about her in a seemingly casual way, noting to herself the locations of doors, windows and stairs. She paused as if to admire a portrait, and as she did so looked out the window, checking its accessibility from the street. Then she wandered to her right until she was out of sight of the footmen.

She made a quick check to be sure that there were no other guests or servants around, then started down the hallway, looking into each room as she passed it. Every one, she saw, was filled with expensive items, from artwork to furniture, but she was concerned only with those things which were easy to transport and just as easy to sell, such as silver vases and ornamental pieces. She was primarily interested in finding the study, for she knew that it was the most likely place for the safe to be located. Finding the safe and the best entrances and exits was always the focus of her job.

She located two drawing rooms and a music room, but no study, so she turned and made her way back down the corridor. As she neared the wide hallway that crossed this one and led back to the ballroom, her steps slowed to a seemingly aimless walk, and she once again began to ply her fan and to look up at the row of portraits as if she were studying them. She crossed the corridor, glancing down it out of the corner of her eye. She could not see that anyone, either the footmen or the two men standing outside the ballroom door conversing, was paying any attention to her.

Once across the hallway and out of sight, she resumed her investigation, opening doors and peering inside. The second door she opened was obviously the masculine retreat of the house, though it appeared to be more a smoking room than a study. There was no desk, nor were there any books, but the chairs were large and comfortable, and there was a cabinet with glasses and several decanters of whiskey and brandy atop it, as well as a narrow table holding two humidors and a rack of pipes. The drawings on the walls were hunting scenes, full of dogs and horses.

With a smile of satisfaction, Marianne reached into the room, picked up the candlestick on the table beside the door and lit it from the wall sconce in the hall. Then she slipped into the room and closed the door after her. This was the most dangerous part of her mission, as well as the most exciting. There was no good reason for her to be in her host's smoking room, and if someone happened to come in on her, she would be hard-pressed to talk her way out of the situation. She could lock the door, of course, but if someone tried to get in, that would seem even more suspicious. The best thing to do was simply to work as quickly as possible and hope that, if she did get caught, a winning smile and a quick tongue would get her out of the situation.

Heart pounding, Marianne set the candle down on the table and began to go around the room, shifting each of the hunting prints aside to examine the wall behind it. The third picture yielded the prize: a safe set into the wall. She leaned forward, examining the lock, which opened with a key rather than a combination.

"I do apologize, but I really cannot allow you to break open my host's safe," a masculine voice said behind her.

Marianne jumped and whirled around, her heart in her throat. Leaning negligently against the doorjamb, one eyebrow raised quizzically, was Lord Lambeth.

One small spark ignites the entire city
of Chicago, but amid the chaos, a chance
encounter leads to an unexpected new love....

THE HOSTAGE

As Deborah Sinclair confronts her powerful
father, determined to refuse the society
marriage he has arranged for her, a stranger
with vengeance on his mind suddenly appears
and takes the fragile, sheltered heiress hostage.

Swept off to Isle Royale, Deborah finds herself
the pawn in Tom Silver's dangerous game of
revenge. Soon she begins to understand the
injustice that fuels his anger, an injustice
wrought by her own family. And as winter
imprisons the isolated land, she finds
herself a hostage of her own heart....

SUSAN WIGGS

"...draws readers in with delightful characters,
engaging dialogue, humor, emotion
and sizzling sensuality."
—*Costa Mesa Sunday Times* on *The Charm School*

On sale mid-April 2000 wherever paperbacks are sold!

Visit us at www.mirabooks.com   MSW592

INTERNATIONAL BESTSELLING AUTHOR

DIANA PALMER

FIT FOR A King

They were friends, neighbors and occasional
confidants. But now Kingston Roper needs a favor
from Elissa Dean—he needs her to get caught in his
bed. Elissa's glad to play the temptress in order to
help King out of an awkward situation—just to be
neighborly, of course. But she's not supposed to
want the make-believe to become a reality. And he's
not supposed to find such passion. Could they go
from neighbors to lovers without destroying their
friendship...or their hearts?

"The dialogue is charming, the characters likeable
and the sex is sizzling..."
—*Publishers Weekly* on *Once in Paris*

Available mid-March 2000 wherever paperbacks are sold!

MIRA

CANDACE CAMP

66508	SWEPT AWAY	___ $5.99 U.S./ ___ $6.99 CAN.
66450	IMPETUOUS	___ $5.99 U.S./ ___ $6.99 CAN.
66633	INDISCREET	___ $3.99 U.S./ ___ $4.50 CAN.
66634	IMPULSE	___ $3.99 U.S./ ___ $4.50 CAN.
66166	SCANDALOUS	___ $5.99 U.S./ ___ $6.99 CAN.
66035	SUDDENLY	___ $5.99 U.S./ ___ $6.50 CAN.

(limited quantities available)

TOTAL AMOUNT	$_____	
POSTAGE & HANDLING	$_____	
($1.00 for 1 book, 50¢ for each additional)		
APPLICABLE TAXES*	$_____	
TOTAL PAYABLE	$_____	

(check or money order—please do not send cash)

To order, complete this form and send it, along with a check or money order for the total above, payable to MIRA Books®, to: **In the U.S.:** 3010 Walden Avenue, P.O. Box 9077, Buffalo, NY 14269-9077; **In Canada:** P.O. Box 636, Fort Erie, Ontario, L2A 5X3.

Name:_____
Address:_____ City:_____
State/Prov.:_____ Zip/Postal Code:_____
Account Number (if applicable):_____
075 CSAS

*New York residents remit applicable sales taxes.
Canadian residents remit applicable
GST and provincial taxes.

MIRA

Look us up on-line at: http://www.mirabooks.com   MCC0400BL